I0726487

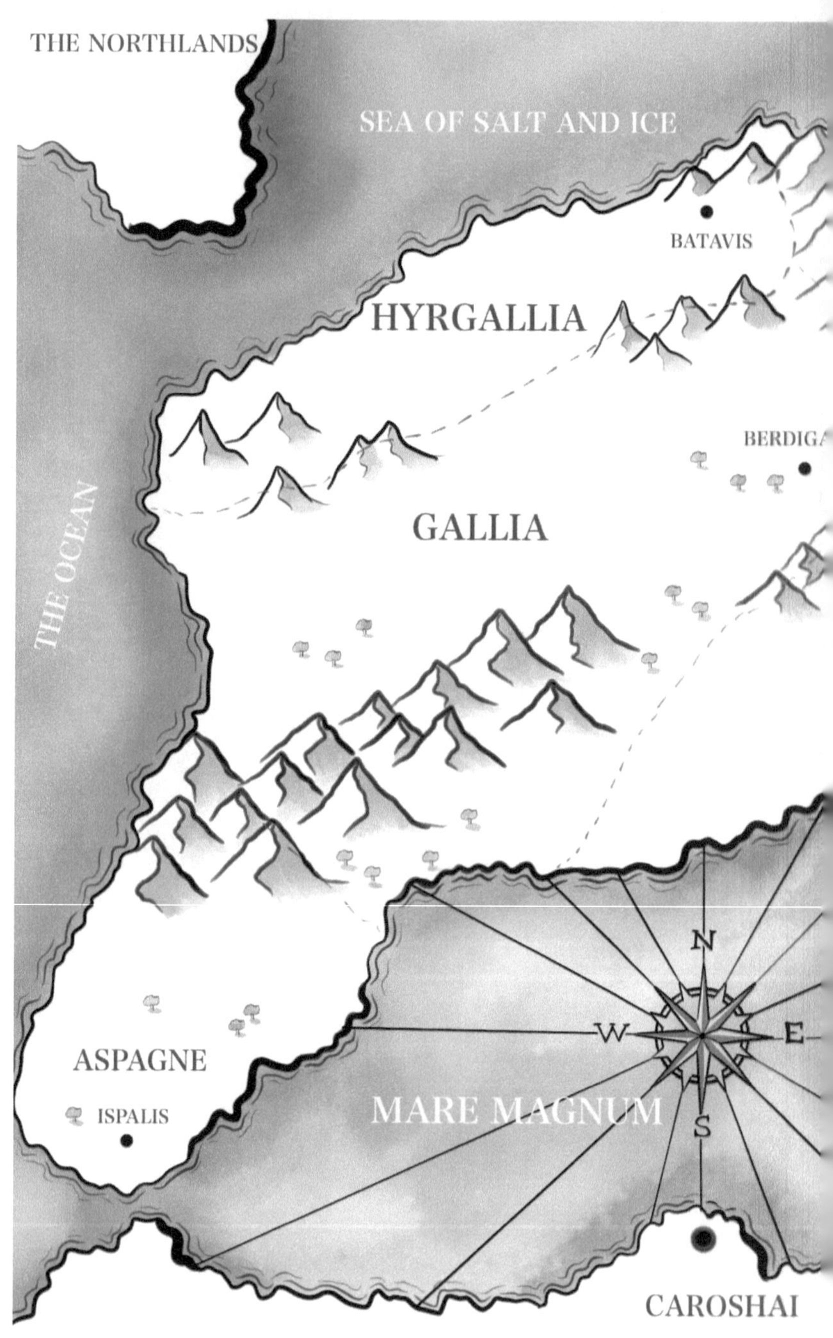

THE NORTHLANDS
SEA OF SALT AND ICE
BATAVIS
HYRGALLIA
BERDIGA
THE OCEAN
GALLIA
ASPAGNE
ISPALIS
MARE MAGNUM
N
W
E
S
CAROSHAI
THE SOUTHLANDS

THE GRAY WASTES
PARTHAVA
ZARUSH
CITY OF LIGHTS
IAN REACH
LAZARRA
BILDANI WOOD
TALYNIS
DAV-MAHR
SHUGRITH
RANOPOLIS
LLA
NEW MIZKHAR
THE SPINE OF THE WORLD
NINEGODS RIVER
ALARIA
MIZKHAR

Edited by Celestian Rince

Interior map illustrated by Meadow Holt

Cover designed by MiblArt

Paperback ISBN: 978-1-957611-02-0

nathantudor.com

ADEPT OF SHADOWS

NATHAN TUDOR

For those who would stay in the night.

CONTENTS

PART IV
THE FIRE BEHIND ALL THINGS

THE STORY SO FAR

The chronicle of *The Imperial Adept* records the lives and deeds of those individuals who played noteworthy roles in the events Lazarran historians variously dub the Imperial Crisis or the Diocletian Civil War. The anonymous Chronicler is distinct among his peers for taking Reiva the Lion as the orienting subject for the overall period.

While all historians of the Crisis recognize her importance, none had taken such close biographical interest in her. At first controversial, *The Imperial Adept* nevertheless became one of the most popular accounts of the period, though some of the Chronicler's critics maintain he veered away from historical fact in favor of thrilling narrative and unsubstantiated rumor.

The present text, *Adept of Shadows*, forms part of the Supplementary Corpus—that is, those documents traditionally attributed to the Chronicler but which deviate from the grand scope of the Main Corpus. The Main Corpus—referring of course to the three central volumes beginning with *The Empire's Lion*—stands without the Supplementary, but at times the Chronicler seems to assume the reader's familiarity with those events contained in the latter.

Adept of Shadows' narrative begins before *Adept Initiate*, the first text of the Supplementary Corpus, but ends around the conclusion of

The Empire's Lion. As such, the reader may find helpful the following summary of the events contained in those two works:

Adept Initiate records how Reiva the Lion (born Rebbaelah beyt'Avadh in her homeland of Talynis), was sold by her mother into slavery, taken to Lazarra where she was inducted into the Adept Corps, and then completed her training as the premier graduate of her Initiate Cohort. While enslaved, Reiva nearly attempted suicide but was stayed by a vision of the Talynisti god called the Wanderer. In the Sanctum, under the tutelage of Adept Alyat, Reiva honed her abilities in the Art of Fire and Lazarran martial doctrine.

Reiva's seven years of training concluded with an infamously lethal pirate-hunting mission that saw the demise of the overseeing Adept and two Initiates, one of whom was Initiate Tolm. While *Adept Initiate* records Tolm's survival (a fact of which Reiva was aware), the Adept Corps inquest ruled his disappearance a death. The text concludes with Reiva's preparation to serve the Empire in the northern land of Hyrgallia, while her dearest friend Adept Domi would sail with the Imperial Navy.

The Empire's Lion, first volume of the Main Corpus, tells how Reiva led a disastrous mission in Hyrgallia, as consequence of which she required major *Ars Viva* surgery to repair her maimed body, and for which she received a severe censure. Praetor Cassia Vantelle (superior of the Ninth and Tenth Legions) offered Reiva a chance to restore her honor and prove her devotion to the Empire: to assist in the conquest of her homeland Talynis. Alyat's old flame Adept Sharasthi approved Reiva for the campaign and instructed her in obscure magical practices.

In the Talynisti capital of Dav-maiir, Reiva joined Legate Flavia Iscator and the Ninth Legion's war effort against the Talynisti Loyalists, so named for their fidelity to King Malik in defiance of the Lazarran-backed usurper Prince Tamiq. At Reiva's side were the mercenary Yaros (otherwise known as Yradas Letiades, an exile from Karella and notorious Krypteian) and the Legion Scout Charas, a cavalry archer of Parthavan origin.

Disappointed with Legate Iscator's inability to crush the Loyalists,

Praetor Vantelle assumed control of the Imperial war effort. However, her ultimate aim was the destruction of the Talynisti Convergence, a place of great spiritual power located beneath Dav-maiir. It was Vantelle, with the Sanctum's cooperation, who conferred the title *Adepta Leona* on Reiva.

Meanwhile in Lazarra, Reiva's mentor Alyat was investigating the matter of Convergences, following tips from the Order of the Sleeping Dragon, an anti-Imperial conspiracy. On the verge of uncovering centuries of falsified history, Alyat caught the attention of a Carnifex and was murdered by the Art of Blood.

Though the Empire tried to cover up the nature of Alyat's death, Reiva discerned the truth, straining her loyalty. Around the same time, Adept Sharasthi revealed the Order of the Sleeping Dragon to Praetor Marcus Gallius (lord of the Third and Fourth Legions) in a bid to explain Alyat's shocking demise and turn him to the Order's cause.

Not long after, Reiva captured a leader of the Talynisti Loyalists, the *Nihilo* Blade-wielding assassin known as the Wolf—only to discover he was none other than her brother Aviqohl. In a moment of crisis, as the Loyalists mounted a desperate attempt to dislodge Tamiq the Usurper, Reiva chose to sacrifice herself and save her brother from Vantelle, betraying the Empire.

Though Reiva's doom seemed certain on account of grievous damage to her soul, the Wolf, Yaros, and Charas handed her over to the Talynisti Desert Sages who committed her to the Origin Spring, the site of Convergence between physical and immaterial realities. Healed by the waters, Reiva awakened to the true nature of magic: that is, the soulbond between an Adept and a spirit—in Reiva's case, the spirit of fire Rukhesh.

At the conclusion of *The Empire's Lion*, the kingdom of Talynis was once more under the rule of the rightful king Malik, and Aviqohl had been honored for his part, though the victory was a bittersweet one. His commander was dead and his closest comrades were departing Talynis; what's more, his secret love with the Talynisti princess Asrah posed an uncertain risk to their futures. Reiva was under the tutelage of the Desert Sages, and her bound spirit Rukhesh willed for her to bend her burgeoning power against the hegemony of Emperor Dioclete and the tyrant god Arkhon. The Lazarran Ninth Legion regrouped under Legate Flavia Iscator, herself a member of the Order of the Sleeping Dragon. Iscator was confident Reiva's defection would provide the spark needed for the Order to bring about its long-standing aim of restoring the Lazarran Republic.

The present text, *Adept of Shadows,* tells the story of Adept Sharasthi's life from her early childhood in Zarush through her legendary exploits in the Parthavan Campaign and ultimately her revelation to Praetor Marcus Gallius of the Order's aims. As with *Adept Initiate,* the Chronicler writes through the eyes of a single character throughout the narrative, with the exception of the epilogue.

PART I

SHROUDED TRUTHS

1

THE INNER TEACHING

THE CHILD IS BORN under the sign of Vahig, the Horned Goat of Winter. The hour is that which comes after sunset, the time of election to the war between the Light and the Dark. By the solar reckoning, the child is marked with *Fervor*. By the lunar reckoning, the child is marked with *Insight*. The primary planetary reckoning is *Tragedy*, the secondary is *Fortune* in the ambiguous mode, and the ternary is *Justice*. The summation produces the four hundred and ninth verse of Zaro's Sayings: "I do not declare famine a curse or prosperity a blessing." The child's parents have selected the name *Sharasthi*, bearing the major affinities of *Silence* and *Beauty*, and the minor affinity of *Holy Solitude.*

—Astrological chart drawn by Vohman the Priest on the occasion of his granddaughter's birth

SHARASTHI CROUCHED amid the towering stacks. The air in the temple archive hung heavy, filling her nostrils with the vanillin aroma of parchment, the dry scent of aged acacia wood.

She loved this alcove, tucked between census records and birth charts. She had loved it ever since she first found it, so young she could not remember, and so this little hiding spot had been constant in her consciousness as life itself.

Soon she would no longer be able to squeeze in here, and so she loved it all the more because soon she would lose it.

The door to the archive swung open, creaking at the spot it always did. A warm, orange glow flickered through the room—the light of an oil lamp. Relaxed yet purposeful footsteps sounded on the tiles.

"Sharasthi," called Vohman, "come give your dear grandfather some help, would you?"

Knees tucked up under her chin, she smiled, keeping her breathing soft as she could.

Vohman stopped walking about. Then he hummed, and there was the *tock* of the oil lamp set on a table. "Rascal must be somewhere else," he muttered.

Then much gentler, so gentle that only by straining her ears could she hear it, came the light pad of feet drawing nearer.

Sharasthi's smile widened, even as her heart twinged. How many more times would they get to perform this little play of theirs?

There was silence. She didn't dare breathe, her pulse fluttering in her chest and throat.

"Aha!" bellowed Vohman, his bearded face bursting into sight.

Sharasthi squealed, pushing herself further back into the nook, but her grandfather's strong, warm hands lashed out and closed around her ankles.

"I've caught a devil hiding in my temple!"

"I'm not a devil!" she giggled. "It's me!"

As Vohman tugged her out from the recess, he affected a frown. *"Me?* Who is me? My eyes aren't what they used to be, you know."

"Me Sharasthi!" she cried in mock outrage. "You should know my voice."

"Ah, I should, shouldn't I?" Vohman tapped a finger against the graying hairs covering his chin. "I think I can make it up to you."

Crossing her arms, she murmured, "Oh?" She imagined she looked quite aloof, but her grandfather seemed assured as ever.

"I need the help of a skilled reader. And since you have young eyes and such a good voice—a voice I will never forget, I assure you—I think *you* could be that help."

"Mmm..." After waiting what she imagined was an appropriately long time, she jumped up and said, "Okay! I'll help."

"Good girl," said Vohman, resting a hand on her shoulder. "Can you find me the Sayings?"

"The Sayings," she echoed before scampering off. The Sayings were one of the most important texts in the archive—one of the rare texts they had multiple copies of. She knew her grandfather wouldn't want the nicest one; he liked to use that only for public readings.

Instead, she found a worn scroll resting on a small desk tucked away in the corner. One of the other priests had been making another copy from this one. After making a mental note of where the scribe's work left off so she could return it open to the proper place, she ran back to her grandfather.

Vohman was seated, observing the flickering light of the lamp as he waited. Sharasthi put the scroll of the Sayings on the table, then delicately climbed onto the chair beside her grandfather's.

He nudged the lamp nearer the scroll, then, in his teaching voice, directed her to find a particular passage.

After searching her memory, she recalled the relevant scripture was right in the center of the scroll. Taking the handles, she began furling and unfurling. The scroll was written in Classical Zarushan, which used the same script as the contemporary, vulgar form of the language, but its grammar and syntax were more complicated.

Once the crackling of parchment stopped, Vohman said, "Begin with, 'There is Fire,' conclude with the gloss."

With a small nod to herself and a deep breath, Sharasthi found the line and began to read:

"There is Fire that burns true, and Fire that burns false.

There is Light that illuminates, and so it reveals; there is Light that blinds, and so it conceals.

There is Darkness where Light does not touch. When there is Darkness, true Fire drives it out with Light. But false Fires abide the Dark, and false Lights lead many astray.

Now Spirit is immortal. Flesh is transient. But Fire is in all things.

Fire is Truth. Fire tests Wisdom. Fire brings Life and Death."

Finally, she read the gloss after the passage: *"So said Zaro on the first day of winter in his fortieth year of life."*

Vohman never made a great deal of how she could read the classical form so well at so young an age—he only thanked her for doing so, as he did now. Then he sat in silence for a while, and so Sharasthi did too. She liked silence and stillness.

Then, as expected, he asked the question. "What is the outer teaching?"

"We should tell the truth. We should be careful about who we listen to. We should keep the Eternal Flame lit in the temple."

A gentle smile touched Vohman's lips. "I seem to recall saying as much in a homily last year. But you forgot the fourth point."

Sharasthi faltered. "We should..."

"We should neither dismiss nor accept people out of hand, but test them."

"That means give people a chance."

"Good. Now..." He touched a weathered finger to his lips, and in a low tone asked, "What is the inner teaching?"

Sharasthi touched a finger to her own lips. "It's..." She frowned. "Everything is made of Fire," she muttered.

Her grandfather chuckled. *"All is Fire* is the first of Zaro's teachings, so it is not particularly concealed, is it?"

Bunching up fistfuls of her garment in her hands, she looked down and scowled.

This was always the hard part of their lessons. Her grandfather never taught these things in his sermons. He said they were 'hidden mysteries.' She always needed them to be explained, but he always made her guess anyway. He said it was to keep her humble.

"Is it about the struggle?"

"It is, in fact. Go on."

Her eyebrows rose—she'd gotten a lucky start. "The struggle

between Truth and Falsehood," she said, letting remembered lessons flow through her lips, "is fought first in the realm of Spirit and second in the realm of Flesh. Zaro says, '*Spirit is immortal. Flesh is transient. But Fire is in all things.*'"

The dancing flame of the oil lamp caught her attention. Sharasthi looked at it, letting its wavering, wriggling form impress upon her vision.

"The struggle between Truth and Falsehood," she said at last, "happens in both realms...no, happens...when..."

She ground her palms against her eyes, the afterglow of the lamp still burning behind her lids.

Her grandfather patted her shoulder reassuringly. "That was good, Sharasthi." His tone bore no trace of condescension, but she still felt frustrated.

"I thought I was finally going to get it."

There was a smile in his voice as he said, in a rare moment of indulgence, "You're already far sharper than you should be at your age, child. Shall I tell you what it means?"

Sharasthi hugged herself, nodding.

"It means that the great struggle is not fought in two places, but one. There is Spirit, and there is Flesh—but see beyond this distinction and see that both make up what we call existence, this thing of burning Fire. Truth is where the authentic Fire burns, and that is where we find Wisdom and Life. Falsehood is where the imitation Fire burns, and that is where we find Foolishness and Death. Every day, this battle is fought."

Sharasthi huffed. "You always say we're fighting a battle, but all I do is chores."

Vohman chuckled. "Sometimes doing chores is how we fight the battle. Sometimes it's fought by armies. Sometimes it's fought between friends, sometimes between foes... Let me show you something."

Sharasthi perked up as her grandfather reached within his vestment. What he produced, she had never seen before. It was a bronze disc, stamped with a design of some strange beast.

"That," he whispered, "is called a *dragon*, and it is a very meaningful symbol."

He let her hold the disc, run her fingers along the relief pressed into the metal. She discovered writing engraved into the opposite side.

The writing was not Zarushan script, though. She frowned. "What does it say?"

Vohman patted her shoulder again. "Learn to read Lazarran and you'll discover for yourself."

"Lazarran?" Her frown deepened. "Isn't Lazarra far away?"

Vohman's smile tightened. "For now."

"So why is it here?"

"Ah, this seal is like a letter. One delivered many years ago, to some teacher in a long line of teachers that leads to me."

"In the City of Lights?" she breathed.

"Exactly so. But when the vision—no, now is not the time for that, but someday, child—sent me here, I brought it with me, because it is a hidden teaching, you see? It must be passed on." Vohman folded her fingers around it. "Pick a place to hide it, child. Somewhere no one will find it."

Immediately she hopped out of her chair. "Then I'll put it—"

"Ah! Somewhere no one will find it. Not even me."

Sharasthi cocked her head. "But it's your letter, isn't it?"

Vohman smiled. "It needs to be passed on, remember? And no one is as good at hiding as you, child."

"Then I'll put it somewhere so good even you can't find it, Grandfather."

"I'm sure you will. Because that seal is a secret so special that you are the only person I can trust to know of it. You must never tell a soul about it. Not that it exists. Not that you've even heard of it."

He pressed a finger to his lips.

Sharasthi mimicked the gesture. The lesson was over; the teaching sealed away.

After her grandfather left, telling her to hurry so she could make it to dinner, Sharasthi tucked away the bronze disc stamped with the dragon.

She hid it in her favorite hiding spot—behind a loose tile that not even Vohman knew of, which she had freed herself on one particularly rambunctious night when she had entertained designs of digging a tunnel out of the temple.

The tunnel, she had long given up on, but now it hid an even better secret.

2

A SENSITIVE CHILD

THE GIRL'S ailment has no bodily cause I can discern. Neither medicines administered regularly nor taken on the occasion of her fits bear any fruit. Perhaps it is a spiritual affliction.

—from the personal records of Meirco, physician of Ashmuz

SHARASTHI GRIPPED her grandfather's calloused hand and guided him to the altar.

Vohman, priest of the Eternal Flame, stared onward with webbed-over eyes. Sharasthi imagined her grandfather *could* see, but not those things the rest of humanity saw. She dreamed he had traded sight of sky and soil for visions of spirits, of soaring *ahura* bearing messages through the celestial sphere.

There was nothing mystical to it, he often assured her with an indulgent smile. Merely old age.

Old age, however, was no impediment to his vocation. Every day, he went about his duties. He performed sacrifices. He dispensed wisdom to those who sought it. He taught those who would hear. Always, Sharasthi was at his side, acting as his eyes.

Today was a day of sacrifice. A bull was to be offered to the Eternal Flame. The animal was already trussed and in place, prepared by the junior clergy. The town of Ashmuz was neither large nor small; its temple could afford a respectable retinue. But Sharasthi had heard from her grandfather how it had been in that most holy of places, the High Temple in the City of Lights, where once he had served and performed the liturgy.

It was there he had memorized the cuts, the maze of organs. Work he now did by touch alone.

As they approached the altar, Sharasthi checked her veil was secure. The laity were not to expose their faces to the Flame, lest it sear their souls.

The altar was a block of blackened stone, piled with crackling wood. The Flame burned in the heart of the temple, the smoke rising up and escaping heavenward through a vent cut in the ceiling. On rainy days, the priests hastily worked a mechanism that shut the vent. A thing of creaking metal and oiled gears, Sharasthi had been allowed to see it on her thirteenth birthday last year.

Today, the sky was clear. The sacrifice would burn in the Eternal Flame and rise unimpeded into the heavenly realm.

The bull lay before the blazing altar, its legs bound, its eyes dull. Some younger priests, Vohman once told her, slaughtered the beast without administering a pharmakon. They saw it as a display of devotion and piety. Vohman only saw it as a way to get gored.

After she brought her grandfather to the proper spot—engraved into her unconscious through innumerable repetitions—Sharasthi squeezed his hand and let go, stepping back.

Vohman took a half step, his free hand probing outward. His fingers quested through empty air, then seized on the bull's horn.

Sharasthi watched as the knuckles of his other hand tightened around the grip of the knife, a razor-edged, broad-bladed thing with a single ruby set in the hilt.

Vohman raised his head, looking into nothing, looking into heaven, and declared in a voice weathered by seven decades, "Here is offered to Truth, the flesh of life. To Wisdom, the blood of life. May the Eternal Flame, the Undying Fire, consume this gift and show it worthy, and so may it deem our spirits worthy at the end of all things."

The invocation complete, Vohman's younger colleagues stepped forward to hold the bull. He slashed the beast's throat—a laborious process, one that demanded several sawing cuts. The pain broke through the drug-haze upon the bull's mind, and it dimly struggled against the priests' holds, lowing in numb protest.

Sharasthi's heart twinged for the animal, but she had long grown callous to the sacrifice. It was necessary.

Her grandfather, hands scarlet, dragged the knife along the belly, and after opening its gut plunged his hand within. The creature had given up its ghost now; its blood flowed languidly.

In moments, Vohman cut free and withdrew the bull's still heart. This he raised high and threw upon the altar, shouting, "Test our offering, Fire Immortal!"

Sharasthi's head spun with secret teachings her grandfather had tucked away in her mind. Things she ought not have known. Things she was never to repeat.

At the fringes of her consciousness, she felt the *pull* of one of her fits. She took a slow breath. *Not today, please.* A sacrifice had not sparked one of her episodes in nearly a month—she had hoped this day, this *crucial* day, would be the same. Her spirit shuddered, tilting, nearly beginning the frightful whirling—then steadied.

She blinked away relieved, grateful tears, watching the holy Fire burn and crackle, and when her grandfather stepped back from the altar, she took his bloody hand. The other priests set upon the bull, hastily removing and feeding organs to the flame.

Ordinarily, certain organs would be set aside for divination—in his youth, Vohman had built a reputation as the most brilliant haruspex in Zarush—but that aspect of the ritual was dispensed with today on account of the guests attending the ceremony.

The Lazarrans.

Sharasthi's grasp tightened, the still-warm lifeblood of the offering making slick her fingers. Her grandfather gave her a reassuring yet weak squeeze. His body always tired after making a sacrifice. Or perhaps he was already weary, and the sacrifice filled him with strength for a moment.

After bringing him to a bronze basin where they both washed clean their hands, staining the water pink, Sharasthi led Vohman to the waiting Lazarrans, who stood at the edge of the space. Not quite within the sanctuary, but neither past the threshold.

Two of them were present, though they had more soldiers staying in the town.

First was a woman with close-cropped hair and a scar on her surprisingly youthful face. A silver eagle was pinned to her toga—a distinctive garment if ever there was one—and this signified that she was a general over a legion. They called this office the 'legate,' and so the woman was called Legate Cassia Vantelle.

At her side was a man wearing a red mantle fringed with gold around his shoulders. Unlike the legate, he wore armor. Yesterday he had introduced himself as Adept Rufus of the *Ars Vulcana*, and Vohman had later told Sharasthi this meant he was a magician of fire.

That had piqued her interest, and she could tell it had done the same to her grandfather—though she doubted anyone who had not spent so much time with him would have recognized it.

She had asked in a hush whether his magic came from the Eternal Flame. Vohman had told her she was not yet ready to learn that secret.

Now she squeezed his hand again, coming to a stop.

Vohman did not bow his head, though his tone was strong and cordial. "Thank you for giving your attention to the sacrifice."

Sharasthi translated this into Karellan. Her grandfather knew the language—he had taught Sharasthi—but in his age, he intended to spend the rest of his days speaking only the prophet's tongue, if he could help it.

The woman Vantelle nodded and replied smoothly, "Thank you for permitting us to observe. Are the intestines and liver generally burned as well?" Her tone was equally cordial, but not in any sense obeisant. Sharasthi thought she looked too young to talk like that, especially to a man as respected as her grandfather.

Vohman's smile was not without humor as the words reached him. "I am familiar with your beliefs; I thought not to scandalize."

The legate hummed. "How hospitable."

There was much hanging between the words, Sharasthi could tell. Some of it she could guess at, but she was glad her role for the conversation was just translating—that was a plenty fraught task on its own. She had no desire to stick her foot in her mouth and spark a war. That was how things were with the Lazarrans. At least, that was how everyone said they were.

Vohman tipped his free hand toward the antechamber. "Shall we eat?"

The legate assented, and so the lot of them moved into the fellowship hall, led by Vohman, led by Sharasthi.

The space had room for hundreds of people to dine. On high holy days, it was often packed to the brim or even overflowing. Today, a mere four people would eat in it—a realization that lanced ice down Sharasthi's spine.

What meat was not burned in the offering was shared by the worshippers who had sponsored the sacrifice. It was a time of fellowship and communion, not to mention a time of charity, as the poor and hungry were given a share as well. Today, the meat would be divided—a portion preserved for Vohman and the Imperials, the rest taken to the laity.

It was not that the people were *forbidden* from dining inside today; it was simply that no one wanted to. Ever since the Lazarrans had arrived, a delirious, anxious energy had infected the town.

Rumors of war flitted through Ashmuz. The Imperial delegation was small—small enough that, were it not for the presence of the Adept—they could perhaps be defeated; the fear of war was not an immediate one, but one for the future. No doubt the legate and her troops took note of the town's lackluster fortifications, the lay of the land, the number of able-bodied men.

All this Sharasthi had heard whispers of on her morning errands, as people had accosted her to ask what Vohman thought of it all.

All she had been able to say was that her grandfather looked forward to showing them the Light of the Eternal Flame.

Sharasthi removed her veil, the aroma of roasting meat curling into her nose, setting her mouth watering. Her stomach rumbled, and she clapped a hand over it. Her grandfather would worry if he thought her hungry, but she needed to help him eat first. That was one of the odd things about Vohman—his ability to perform rituals and sacrifices was unimpeded, but he needed assistance with more mundane, simple things.

Maybe that wasn't odd though, Sharasthi supposed. Maybe it was just that—for her grandfather—the religious rites were more simple, the sacred more his home than the mundane.

The walls of this room were engraved with vignettes from the life and teaching of Zaro, the great prophet of the Eternal Flame. Sharasthi could name and explain every one of them. They had been her bedtime stories growing up.

The clash between Truth and Falsehood.

The division of Spirit from Matter.

The all-pervasiveness of Fire.

Armies of righteous *ahura*-spirits waging war against corrupt *daeva*-spirits, their combat unseen in the midst of mortals.

Legate Vantelle observed that last scene with obvious interest. "What are the inscriptions? Names?"

Sharasthi whispered to her grandfather that she was asking about the Unseen Battle. Vohman cleared his throat. "Yes and no. The *ahura* are invoking the virtues of the Fire—truth, loyalty, wisdom, and so on. The *daeva* do the same for the vices of the Dark—deceit, treachery, passion. It is the teaching of Zaro that all these spirits have hidden names unknown to mortal tongues, and so we are left to call them by their professed natures."

Vantelle inclined her head. "And do *you* know these hidden names, priest?" A crooked grin touched her lips.

Vohman dipped his head. "What should a priest know of such profound enigmas? I am no mystic, Legate."

Sharasthi glanced at the *daeva* proclaiming 'Deceit,' then hurriedly turned her attention away.

Rufus crossed his arms. "Why call passion a vice of the Dark?"

Vohman smiled easily. "You disagree with the assessment, Adept?"

The man shrugged. "That unseen power grants virtues and vices—we know this in the Sanctum. But passion can be a virtue, don't you think?"

Vohman nodded. "To be sure. I think Zaro's teaching speaks of passion in the same manner as the Karellan sages—the disturbance and dominion of the soul by base emotions and desires. 'Mastered desire is a stallion who pulls the soul's chariot to glory; passion is a wild beast that hauls a man into the ditch,' so says the philosopher, yes?"

Rufus gave a noncommittal grunt, but Sharasthi thought there was a note of respect in it.

The legate, still turning about to admire the engravings, nodded with more obvious appreciation. "Well-cited, priest. Perhaps if I'd had you as a tutor in my youth, I would have paid better attention to my education."

Vohman's smile turned sly. "Call it an old man's intuition, legate, but I do not think much escapes your attention. But I *am* an old man, so shall we sit before my dear granddaughter is reduced to carrying me?"

Four cushions were arrayed like corners of a square. Sharasthi helped Vohman take a seat, then she tugged her cushion nearer to his so she could attend to him. She did not seat herself until the Lazarrans had taken theirs.

Temple aides brought a pitcher of chilled wine with four goblets. Sharasthi's was diluted with water. Muted though the taste was, she still enjoyed it. The deep violet color of wine had always delighted her. As a child she thought it would be perfect to swim in, diving and vanishing beneath the obscure surface. Vohman had only laughed and said it would be quite an expensive bath.

Sharasthi imagined the Lazarran Emperor could do something like that. A great Karellan emperor had once visited this town—many generations ago. He had accrued so much wealth from his conquests that rumor had it even now you could trace his travels by digging in the earth and following the trail of lost gemstones and gold.

Did this dinner herald a future when yet another emperor would come to Ashmuz?

There was a rhythm to dinner conversations, however. First, Vohman inquired after their travels, asking their route, any troubles they had encountered along the way. Naturally, they had come through Parthava, going along less-used trade routes. They had negotiated transit with urbanite Parthavan merchants rather than the nomadic Hunter tribes.

Hunters came to town once in a while, normally to barter for goods. They never visited the temple. Vohman said Hunters had their own religion, distinct from the settled Parthavans. In a sense, there were two Parthavan peoples, he had taught her. What did it say that the Lazarrans had chosen to travel with the merchants?

This led at last to their purpose for coming here. Sharasthi's ears perked up as she cut through a hunk of meat on her grandfather's plate, then nudged the slice into his waiting, wrinkled hand.

Cassia Vantelle took a sip from her goblet of wine. "We are seeking a route to the Spine. Old maps from the days of Alar the Great suggest he blazed such a trail."

The Spine—that awesome mountain range to the east, absolutely impenetrable save for a narrow pass between the southern kingdom of Talynis and the land of Endra.

Vohman chewed slowly, his expression impassive. "I'm sure," he said eventually, "that you know the risks of traversing the Gray Wastes."

Rufus leaned forward. "So there is a route?"

"There *once* was a route. Not one any sane Zarushan would try to navigate today."

Vantelle shrugged. "I am not afraid of madmen."

"The Wastes are inhabited by more than just madmen. It is the haunt of *daeva* who drive men mad. Sharasthi—recount the Possession of Marzud."

She swallowed, then raised a finger to an engraving along the northern wall. She hated this one; as a child, it had given her nightmares for months. Now, even at thirteen, she avoided looking at it as much as possible.

Vantelle and Rufus turned their heads. The scene depicted a bearded man, kneeling, his head thrown back and his arms spread wide. Over him was a winged spirit with the face of a man and the body of a vulture.

Sharasthi swallowed again, her mouth dry as desert. "The Possession of Marzud," she said, then stopped short and cleared her throat, suddenly finding it far more difficult to speak Karellan than when she practiced with the grandfather.

"The Possession of Marzud," she began anew, "happened near the end of the prophet Zaro's life. Marzud was Zaro's younger brother, and he thought the prophet's teachings incomplete. He thought that the Fire and the Darkness were not opposed, but complementary parts of some greater whole. And so he offered himself to a *daeva*. The words over his head are: 'Take me now, Ineffable Darkness, that I might know the truth of the lightless Abyss.'

"The *daeva* over him says, 'The reason of the Dark is madness; the truth of the Abyss is illusion.' After this, the spirit never departed from him. Marzud began to mutter to it at all times, and so what he had done was soon discovered, and his brother exiled him. Marzud went into the north, and a quarter of Zaro's followers went after him, seduced by the possibilities of the path he offered. These are the Marzudi, and they dwell among the Gray Wastes like scavengers among the charnel fields."

She had recited it just as it was told to her, and after the last word left her mouth, she took a breath in—and the breath was cold and obscure, circling in her lungs like smoke from a censer that burned without heat. Sharasthi shivered, suddenly feeling ill. She wanted nothing more than to crawl into some dark nook, perhaps her favored hiding spot in the archive, and sleep unseen and unknown in the gloom.

Vohman rubbed her back, and she was grateful for the warmth of his touch, though it was not enough to dispel the chill burrowing into her bones. "My granddaughter is a sensitive child," he said, slowly forming the Karellan words. Sharasthi felt guilty that she was failing her duty to him. Ever since the onset of these spells shortly after her sixth birthday, they rushed upon her in moments such as these. She had barely recovered during the sacrifice—it had been naïve to hope she would last the day.

"But now," Vohman continued, "you see how we view the Wastes. We do not fear the madmen, but that which drives them mad. You seek to follow Alar the Great's route? When he journeyed through the Gray Wastes, he irked a Marzudi. The fanatic laid a curse on him that he should lose what was most precious to him. Not one year passed from the day that his dearest horse broke his leg and needed to be put down—and so he lost the horse he loved most. Another year passed, and his dearest friend fell ill and begged for Alar to kill him, that he might die on a blade like a warrior as he had always dreamed —and so he lost the companion he loved most. And finally, the third year, Alar faced a mutiny by his own army, who swore they would kill him if he made them march another step—and so he lost his dream of conquering the world, the thing he loved most of all."

Vantelle received the story of Marzud and Vohman's tale of the Karellan conqueror with total equanimity. If Sharasthi had to stake a claim, she would wager the legate believed every word Vohman had just uttered, and she did not seem dissuaded in the slightest. "What I do, I do in the sight of Arkhon, high god over all the world. I do not fear wayward spirits, nor the men they hold sway over. Believe in your Eternal Fire, priest, but I need no faith to believe in the might of an Imperial Adept of the *Ars Vulcana*. Rufus, do you fear these Marzudi fanatics?"

The man did not even scoff; he merely flexed his fingers. The air trembled, and Sharasthi's soul whirled faster. "Not at all."

The legate nodded. "There you have it. If you cannot commend a guide, simply tell us the way and we will find our path. No terrain has ever defeated Legion Scouts."

Vohman shrugged. "I can give you what records we have, but it's been hundreds of years. Even if your Scouts are as skilled as you say —and I do not doubt it—you are risking much. The Marzudi destroy things as a matter of course; they adore the ephemeral and the ever-changing. Who can say if any landmarks remain, or if they have been moved..."

"Follow the gold," Sharasthi murmured, hugging herself.

The Lazarrans looked at her with narrowed eyes, and only then she realized she had spoken in Zarushan. "Follow the gold," she said again, this time in Karellan. "You know of the travels of Alar. They say riches fell from the baggage train wherever he went."

Rufus scratched his chin. "And these Marzudi, they care not to take such things?"

Vohman shook his head. "Wealth is meaningless to them."

"Then we may have a way to check our reading of the maps."

Vantelle eyed Sharasthi. "Your granddaughter is a curious thing, Vohman. How old are you, girl?"

Sharasthi fought the urge to shrink down. "Thirteen."

"Yet you speak better than some Lazarran aristocrats I have known. And they had orators as tutors. When Lazarra comes to Zarush—properly, that is—it will be a good thing for you, child. There are many opportunities for a sharp mind in the Empire. Woman or not."

Sharasthi wished she would stop talking. Her nausea was only worsening. Still, she managed to mutter a polite, "Thank you, your words are too generous for my ears." She hoped the expression translated well into Karellan.

Vohman rubbed her back again. "Sharasthi is a brilliant child indeed—the temple is a brighter place for her presence. But as I said, she is a sensitive one. Do you need to retire, child? You can send Atsan to attend me."

Seizing on the offer like an urchin offered bread, she murmured an apology and excused herself, bidding farewell to the Lazarrans with a polite bow.

The Adept inclined his head, but Vantelle spoke. "Remind me of your name, child."

She swallowed. "Sharasthi."

"Sharasthi. I will not forget that name again."

Sharasthi wished she would.

After leaving the fellowship hall and sending Priest Atsan to her grandfather, Sharasthi did not return to her room, nor did she go to the archive.

Instead, she stumbled out of the temple, hugging the shadows and avoiding the lights of torches and lamps. She even evaded the eyes of the Lazarran legionnaires outside awaiting their legate and the Adept.

That strange breath of air had not left her lungs—it just kept circling, a plume of vapor she could not cough out. No matter how she sucked down lungfuls of the cool night air, it still curled around inside her.

It was the engraving of the Possession of Marzudi—she could not abide being under the same roof as that terrible image. Not right now. She needed one of her other hiding spots. Thankfully, the streets were empty, people staying indoors to keep away from the Lazarrans, so no one accosted her as she sought her destination.

The town of Ashmuz had no grand ramparts, but it did have a wall of sorts. It came to a grown man's waist and had stood since the days Alar the Great came through, but was in disrepair in many places. Sharasthi slipped through one of the gaps, and like that she was outside the town.

To the west, south, and east, the town had sprawled past the wall —but not to the north. Zarushan cities never built past the northern wall, because to the north lay the Gray Wastes. Sharasthi could not explain why she was going this way since it was the story of Marzudi that had afflicted her with this terrible feeling, but she recalled an old proverb that the cause of a thing was also its end, and that the well of poison contained a drop of healing.

This hiding spot was one of her least-visited, and so it was precious to her. She had found it after her grandfather had given a homily on the virtue of courage. Testing herself, she had decided to go as far north of Ashmuz as she dared.

There was a thicket of reeds along a small lake—if it could even be called a lake. In the dark it was nigh invisible, but Sharasthi could have found the way with her eyes closed.

She dove into the thicket, burrowing down as close to the ground as she could get, and lay there.

Her imagination conjured up images of great, towering warriors marching across the land, giant Marzudi possessed by *daeva*-spirits, their eyes black and vacant. Sharasthi lay as still as she could, eyes shut, and saw them passing by the thicket, ignorant to her presence. Then she saw birds of prey soaring overhead, but the reeds screened her from their keen sight. She saw lions and wolves stalking the land, but the scent of the water masked her.

The wild night was her cloak, hiding her from all dangers. It was a heavy cloak, resting on her with a familiar and comforting weight.

With a start, Sharasthi awoke.

In an instant, she understood she had fallen asleep in the thicket, and that she had dreamed all of those terrible things. Ever since her fits had begun, she had found difficulty distinguishing dreams from reality. *Spirit and Matter...All is Fire.*

The stars had not moved much, but the grogginess of sleep had still taken up residence.

Crawling to the edge, she cupped her hands and washed out her mouth, then splashed her face and poured water over her neck. She realized she'd been sweating in her sleep—but now she felt much better, refreshed by the touch of the lake.

The nausea was gone too. The sense of being trapped and watched. She spent a while longer there, breathing in and out, relishing the feeling that her lungs were her own, full of pure night air.

When Sharasthi finally returned to the temple, on her way to her little room, she saw her grandfather sitting in the sanctuary, before the Eternal Flame. "Is that you, Sharasthi?"

Her grandfather was the only person who could hear her when she sneaked around. She affixed her veil and stepped into the sanctuary. "I am here, grandfather."

Vohman smiled, and Sharasthi realized just how weary he looked. She was not sure she had ever seen him truly look his age, but he did now. "I don't suppose you intend to tell me where you went?"

Sharasthi sat down beside him, taking his warm hand. "A secret place."

"Of course." Vohman sighed. "The Lazarrans are leaving in two days. I don't think you'll need to see them anymore."

"I was not rude, was I?"

"No, no. Not at all, child. And carry no guilt for what happened. I should not have pressed you to tell that story. I had hoped...well, never mind that."

Sharasthi rested her head against his arm. No one in the world was so kind as her grandfather. Given the pleasant moment, she was not sure whether she wanted to ask what was on her mind, but she forced herself anyway. "Is war coming? Now that they're here?"

Vohman shook his head. "War is always coming. When it will come *here*, who can say? But something has changed. Do you feel the Fire's warmth, child?"

Sharasthi tried to feel what he meant, but the Eternal Flame's heat seemed just as it always did to her. "I can't tell the difference."

Vohman smiled that weary smile again. "Perhaps it is but an old man's folly."

They sat a while longer in silence, allowing the Fire's glow and crackle to fill the space. Now and then, one of the priests or attendants on duty through the night would come to stoke and build it up, so that it would never die.

Sharasthi's renewed wakefulness from her nap began to drain away, and her head listed heavier against his arm.

"Go to sleep, Sharasthi. A growing girl needs her rest."

"Am I still growing?" she muttered, rubbing her eyes as she slowly stood.

"We all are, in some way or another. Now off with you."

Sharasthi departed for her bed, casting one more glance behind her as she slipped out of the room.

Vohman sat on the floor, staring with unseeing eyes into the Fire.

There was something sublime about the moment, and so Sharasthi fixed the memory in her mind, resolving never to forget it.

That night, she dreamed again of lying in the thicket by the water, and she dreamed of hands spreading a black cloak over her slumbering form.

When she awoke, she thought she felt those hands on her—but as soon as she did, the sensation fled, leaving only a vague impression, soft as a whisper.

3

THERE BURNS THE FIRE

FIRST IN MY travels beyond the lands blessed by the Four on High, I went north to Zarush. To my surprise, the people are not so wretched as we Talynisti oft-suppose. To be sure, the rusting and ruined remains of the Immortal Empire speak of a far more glorious time, but the Zarushans themselves are not so different from us. I think it is their ongoing devotion to the cult of Everlasting Fire that sustains them.

—*The Life and Wisdom of Simeon Binkhok As Told by Himself*

SHARASTHI DID GO to watch the Lazarrans depart, though she did so from one of her hiding places—a nook between a perfume stall and the wall of a tavern. Her nose itched with the mingling scents of floral musk and beer.

The Imperial Legions, she had heard, numbered in the thousands per army—even tens of thousands, some said—but this was not a full legion. Cassia Vantelle had mentioned Scouts during their dinner. Sharasthi guessed that was what most of these soldiers were. Lightly outfitted, on horseback. Rather than stiff and uniformed foot soldiers, many had the lean, wild look of survivalists, their skin tanned by long hours under the sun, their cheeks scruffed from days without the touch of razors.

There were the famed heavy infantry legionnaires as well, but their numbers were meager compared to the Scouts. These soldiers were thickly muscled, and they hung near the supply wagons in the center of the caravan.

Sharasthi could hardly imagine they were really going into the Gray Wastes—going to the *Spine*—like that, but then again, they had the Adept.

Rufus, wearing his red mantle as always, never went far from Legate Vantelle's side. He spoke little, though Vantelle was frequently giving orders to various aides or subordinates.

Something about that woman knotted Sharasthi's stomach. It was like she knew too much. The way she had taken in the story of Marzud still rankled Sharasthi. If she had mocked it, that would have been one thing, or even if she had believed it and shuddered—but no, she seemed to believe it, and she *did not care*. She intended to walk right into the haunt of *daeva* and the Marzudi who worshipped them.

Her faith in this high god Arkhon must have been great indeed. Having grown up serving in the temple, Sharasthi could appreciate that—but who had ever heard of Arkhon before scant centuries ago? Zaro had taught of the Eternal Flame nearly a *millennium* ago. Through the rise and fall of the Immortal Empire, then the conquest of the Karellans—the Fire had burned unquenched in the temples of Zarush.

The Lazarran Republic had fallen and been reborn as an Empire, reborn under the auspices of this so-called 'high god.' And to be sure, their expansion was great. Vohman said none of the old Zarushan writers ever speculated the Lazarrans would expand their reach so far—back in the days of their republic, that was.

And yet, somehow he had not seemed surprised when the Lazarrans did appear. If anything, he had seemed to greet the event as an inevitability.

Sharasthi desperately wanted to ask her grandfather about the bronze seal he had given her, the one still secreted away in the archive. She was supposed to keep it treasured and obscure, but... something about the Lazarran presence in the town dislodged something. The linear, angled script of their alphabet stamped in bronze —that image spun in her mind day and night. Eventually she could not bear it anymore and last night had gone to look at the seal in her hiding spot, to run her fingers over the impressions again.

What was this Lazarran artifact her grandfather had treated as so precious?

She had never been the sort to feel compelled to speak her secrets —that defeated the whole point, in her reckoning—and so she never found secrets burdensome, like others. Or, she never had. Now the secret of the dragon seal weighed on her heart, and she thought if she did not speak of it to someone she would fall ill.

So she resolved to talk to her grandfather about it. If he cut off her inquiry, that would be that, but she would not go another day without making the attempt.

As the Lazarran force marched out, Sharasthi turned to watch the townsfolk—those who were there, that was. Some peered out of windows, muttering to themselves with cynical faces. An old woman threw the evil eye after them. Children struggled to peer around fathers and mothers trying to shield them, as if the very sight of the Lazarrans might portend some future violence upon their offspring.

Only some of the merchants had a wistful look, as the Imperials had paid in ample coin to restock their supplies. Even so, they would need to find more if they were to make it all the way to the Spine. Sharasthi wondered if Vantelle would try to barter with the Marzudi, or if she would simply pillage them. One of the merchants, Darum, had gone with the Imperials to act as a translator; Sharasthi did not think any sum of coin in the world was worth such a thing.

It did not particularly matter to Sharasthi which path Vantelle chose—she cared not a whit for the fate of those fanatics, nor did she care for the Lazarrans. Maybe the best outcome of all would be some sort of mutual annihilation, out there in the Gray Wastes.

A twinge of guilt touched her heart. Compassion was a teaching of Zaro. The Fire burned within all things; one had an obligation to tend to it in all forms, not to quench it.

And yet, one also had to contend in the great struggle against the Dark. Did that not require one be willing to destroy, to kill? As she watched the Lazarrans depart into the dim horizon, she wondered.

Her questions rattled around in her mind long after they were gone, and she had resolved to ask her grandfather about all these things...but the day stretched on and faded away, and so did the next, and the day after that. Why, Sharasthi asked herself, did she shy away from this? That question disturbed her more than the initial ones—did she not trust her grandfather? Did she fear something?

Something deep within her was trembling, something she could not put a name to, but which warned her that if she asked her grandfather the questions on her heart, it would open doors that could never be shut again.

And so weeks became months, and Sharasthi's heart grew heavier with the dread of what was to come when she opened her mouth and asked.

ONE DAY, one of the Lazarran hawks flew into town, alighting on the temple.

It was the signal the Imperials were due to return in ten days. Sharasthi saw the bird as a horrible omen. A sign she had waited long enough, too long even.

But still, she waited. A day, a week. When the Lazarrans were two days out, she finally found the wherewithal to ask her grandfather. Feeling in the pit of her stomach that something irrevocable was about to happen, she girded herself.

In the evening, after she read from Zaro's Sayings to Vohman so he might prepare for his next homily, she presented the first of her questions. Thinking it wiser to begin with theology than the secret of the seal, she asked, "If the Fire is in all things, and we are to tend to the Fire, then how can we fight against that which is of the Dark?"

Vohman listened to her question, then sat in stillness. The dancing light of the oil lamp played across his bearded features, reflected in his pale, shuttered eyes.

"That is a question," he said at last, "that many a disciple of Zaro has pondered. In the City of Lights, men have nearly come to blows over the matter."

Sharasthi's eyes widened. "Not you, though?"

Whimsy touched his lips. "Your grandfather was once a young man too, child. It is a deeply important and—for some—deeply troubling question. In times past, whole sects formed and disputed over it, staking claim that their answer was the only possible interpretation of the prophet's teaching."

A presentiment of her grandfather's direction took root in Sharasthi's mind. "But what do *you* think?" Now that she knew how contested the matter was, she would be all the more disappointed if Vohman tried to leave her with some middle-of-the-road survey of common conclusions.

Hearing her barely withheld frustration, Vohman patted her knee. "How about I tell you of the Endric traditions?"

"Endra?" She was certain her grandfather could detect the frown in her voice. "What does Endra have to do with it? The Truth is the Eternal Flame."

"Indeed it is—but a keen mind can find mirrors reflecting the Truth in other places. Zaro said, 'As the Fire burns within all, so all feel its warmth, though they know not its essence.' You understand this?"

"I suppose that makes sense," she muttered.

"Good. Now, let me tell you a story. An Endric teacher had many disciples, but two were favored to succeed him. It was known to the school their teacher was growing old and soon would name his successor. And so, one day, the entire bunch of them split over who he would choose.

"The teacher discovered the argument and pulled the two disciples in front of the assembly. He asked them both a question: 'If I put a blade in your hand, could you kill me?'

"The first cried out, 'Never, my teacher! Your words are like flowing water to my soul, and I love you with all my heart. I would sooner die myself.'

"The second answered, 'Only say the word, master, and it shall be done.'

"The teacher smiled and said the second was worthy to inherit the school."

Vohman folded his hands. "Why?"

Sharasthi's forehead furrowed, her lips worked silently. Her gut told her it was ludicrous, but she knew her grandfather had told the story for a purpose. Somehow it must shed light on her question.

"The Endric," she said slowly, "believe in reincarnation."

Vohman tipped his hand forward, indicating she should go on.

"The soul is a truer self than the body. So if the second student was willing to kill his teacher, it showed that he believed the doctrine, that he believed he would not *actually* be killing his teacher. The first student did not understand that."

"Quite close to the mark," Vohman said. "The other piece you must know is that this school was of the belief that *all* souls are part of the same divine substance, which they call the Great One. Their fundamental axiom was, 'You are that, and that is you.' So what was the first student's other error?"

"It must be..." She pursed her lips. "'*You are that.*' It must be that he...because he said he would sooner die himself, it betrayed that he did not believe himself and his teacher to be part of the same whole. He saw them as different beings."

Vohman smiled wanly. "If only you had been born a boy, Sharasthi," he sighed. "They would profit greatly from one such as yourself in the City of Lights."

Sharasthi ducked her head, heat flushing her cheeks even as disappointment twisted her heart. "But we don't believe in reincarnation or some Great One," she muttered. "We believe in the body's resurrection in forever-burning glory. So what does it matter?"

"We believe in the Fire that pervades all things. The Fire that shall revive the faithful to eternal life. The Fire that burns away the

Dark—and will someday burn it away in entirety. The Fire is good, the Dark is evil. The Fire burns on its own, but the Dark can only exist where the Fire's Light is not.

"Sharasthi, sometimes there is a person who serves the Dark, and so they wish to quench the Fire within themselves and the Fire within all. That is evil in its most distilled form: a hatred of one's own existence so ferocious that it spills over and seeks the destruction of all others. Contempt for the Fire in oneself that begets contempt for the Fire in others. Pride and wrath and despair all writhing together in resentful strife.

"If such a person sought your harm, Sharasthi, I would fail in my duty to you—my duty as your grandfather, as your fellow man —if I allowed them to seek the destruction or corruption of the Fire within you. And I would fail in my duty to the Fire within *them*, because I would permit the life it fuels to act against the Fire itself.

"The *Kshara* warrior of Endra is among the most fearsome in all the world, and he goes into battle with a smile. Do you know why? Because he believes that he and his enemy are one, beyond the veil of flesh. Whoever lives and whoever dies—the Great One is unharmed.

"The Fire burns on. It is immortal. As I live, as I die, the Fire yet burns within this body. When a house is built, there burns the Fire. It falls, there burns the Fire.

"In the Lazarran legionnaire, in the Endric sage, in the grain of sand and the pool of water—there burns the Fire. We are taught not to quench the Fire, but the absolute truth is that we could not do so if we tried. The Fire is too bright, too brilliant. We do not perceive it with these weak eyes of ours—more than weak in my case—but we can perceive it with our hearts."

Vohman stroked his beard. "There I go again," he hummed, "pontificating."

Sharasthi felt like her head was stuffed with cotton. "I understood maybe half of that."

"Hm, making me waste my time, then." He punctuated the remark with a grin. "No, I shouldn't force such mysteries upon you at so young an age. Sometimes I forget that, for all your talent, you are still so young."

An unsettled roiling twisted Sharasthi's insides. "Grandfather... did you really mean it, when you said you wished I was a boy? So I could study at the High Temple and be a priest?"

Vohman started, then reached out an unsteady hand to set it on hers. "Forgive me, child, I did not mean it like that. I meant that it is a shame for Zarush that you cannot. If you had been born a lad, it would make no difference to me how I love you. You are of my own blood, Sharasthi."

She pulled her feet onto the chair, hugging her knees to her chest.

Vohman sighed. "You are thinking of your parents?"

"I know you wish Father had followed in your footsteps instead of running off."

"I wish my son had acted with more virtue, more wisdom—and more care for *you*, most of all. Now...who knows where he and your mother have gone."

"Do you regret coming here?" she blurted out. "Do you think if you had stayed in the City of Lights...?"

Vohman patted her head. "No, Sharasthi. I don't regret it. Of course I wish your parents had understood. But what was I to do?"

"So you still believe in your vision?" she asked, the words muffled against her knees.

Vohman sat in stillness. "Do you remember where you put that seal, child?"

A shock ran down her spine. "Of course."

"Go and bring it. It is time I told you what it signifies, and of the vision that brought us here."

4

ORDER OF THE SLEEPING DRAGON

SHARASTHI'S SUFFERING ONLY WORSENS as she matures. At first I thought this from the *daeva*-spirits, but now I dare hope it is a holy affliction. Perhaps it is my own folly, but I see signs she is born for the Unlit Path. Though it is forbidden, I continue to prepare her with the inner teachings. By her fifteenth birthday, she will be ready. If I am right, she will be healed. If I err, may the Fire's judgment fall on my head alone!

—from the private writings of Vohman the Priest

SHARASTHI HASTENED to retrieve the bronze seal from its hiding spot, stretching her arm into the place she could no longer fit. Her grandfather would glean from the sound where she had hidden it, so she needed to find another spot to honor her promise of keeping it a secret even from him—but that was a worry for later.

When she sat down at the table again, the oil lamp was burning low, its flame weak. Sharasthi pressed the seal into Vohman's hand. He ran his weathered thumbs over its face. "You have not learned any Lazarran since I first gave you this, have you?"

Sharasthi answered with some embarrassment that she had not.

"No need for shame, child. Tonight is your first lesson, then." He placed the seal on the table, then, feeling with his index finger, traced the inscription around the imprint of the dragon. "This reads, *Ordo Draconis Laevisomnis*, which is 'Order of the Sleeping Dragon.'"

Taking shallow breaths, Sharasthi whispered the words to herself, first in Lazarran, then Zarushan.

Vohman pushed the seal away. "Before I tell you what the other side says, I will tell you of the vision that brought our family here, away from the City of Lights."

Sharasthi clasped her sweaty hands. All her life she had known of 'the vision,' but never heard its contents.

What was this experience that had driven her grandfather to leave the prestigious office of a priest in the High Temple and come to this meager border town?

"It was the night of your parents' wedding. At the end of long celebration, I lay down to sleep at last, and found myself elsewhere. Not in a dream—I was *there*, my spirit having been taken from my body.

"I was walking beside a man with a hood pulled low over his face, such that I could see nothing but the barest edge of his profile. I thought it strange that his face was clean-shaven, and his manner of speech too was strange. Though he spoke flawless Zarushan, I could not place whether it was of a native dialect or whether his mother tongue was foreign.

"I did not know him, but he called me, 'Vohman,' and I answered, 'Yes, sir, I am he.'

"The stranger pointed ahead of us, and I saw this place. 'Your granddaughter will be born in the town of Ashmuz, and you will initiate her into the secrets which have been handed down to you.'"

"I trembled, stumbling to keep up with him as he walked onward. 'A granddaughter, sir?' He affirmed this, and then raised his hand to the west. I turned to look, and saw a great eagle spreading its wings across the sky—so great that the tips of its feathers stretched beyond the horizon to the north and to the south. And the eagle's face was covered with eyes, and when it shrieked, the whole world was compelled to kneel.

"I too would have knelt, but the stranger caught my arm and kept me on my feet.

"'Sir,' I stammered, 'I see now that you are endowed with power. Tell me, if I may be so bold as to ask, is this what is yet to be?'

"'Some have knelt, some kneel now, and some have yet to kneel. You have seen the truth of things unveiled—or, you have glimpsed a piece of it.'

"'Is this then the great struggle?'

"Here the stranger tilted his head. 'Yes. No. The struggle of which Zaro spoke prefigures this, yet also prefigures far more. The truth is a pattern within a pattern within a pattern, and so on unto infinity— and of those layers humans see but one, two if they are wise, three if they are mad.'

"Now he pointed to my chest, and I became aware of a weight within my vestment. I reached within, and where I expected to find the medallion of the Fire, which all priests keep at their heart during their service, I instead found the bronze seal.

"'This,' he said, 'is foremost of the secrets you must pass on to her.'

"Then the vision ended, and I awoke in my bed, shaking in terror such as I have never known."

Sharasthi had put her hands on her grandfather as he told the story, for he had begun to tremble. Even his forehead beaded with sweat, glistening in the frail light of the oil lamp.

"Of course," he sighed, "I went to my superior—the high priest of the Eternal Fire—and told him of what I had seen and heard. He was greatly disturbed, first thinking it to be a deception from the Dark, but as I described the seal with its imprint of the dragon, he suddenly turned severe. To my astonishment, he went and procured the seal from among his own possessions, and after giving it to me, told me of what I will now tell you."

Vohman reached out and flipped the seal over to reveal the lengthier inscription. "Now, the reverse." He had told her, years ago, the seal was a sort of letter, sent generations ago and passed down. "The inscription is abbreviated, but I was taught the unabridged form by my superior."

He took a breath, shut tight his unseeing eyes. Vohman's memory had not dulled a whit as he aged. If anything, it had only grown sharper. Every time he had to give a homily, Sharasthi read the scripture passage to him the night before, and then he recited it with perfect accuracy the next day before giving the lesson. Once she had been sick though, unable to read it to him, and still he had recalled the passage *exactly*. That was the day Sharasthi realized he did not have her read for his sake, but her own.

And so she did not doubt she was about to hear it word-for-word as Vohman had last read it, however many years ago it was.

"The Republic of Lazarra is going to fall. Dark days are coming. My children, do not trust yourselves to the smooth words of the thousand-eyed spirit who makes himself out to be lord of all. Verily I tell you, his words are but vain seduction, and he will free you only to make you his slave.

"You must make for yourselves friends, allies. I have long seen this coming, and made preparations. You will find brothers to the cause wherever you go, if you know the proper signs.

"Secrecy shall be your blood, the darkness your cloak. We who would safeguard the light must do so now with covered lanterns—such is the nature of our all-seeing foe.

"If you have not the stomach for the task set before you, either build yourself into one who does, or forget you ever knew my name. We have need of stern stock, of souls willing to take up arms against brothers, to lie to loved ones, to hate one's very flesh and blood, one's own country, all for the sake of the truth.

"Only by this can we endure. Only by this can we free ourselves.

"Find my archives—those that have not yet been destroyed. There are copies hidden in all the great libraries of the world; I am sure at least one will survive.

"For now, our enemies drive us into the shadows, beneath the ground. For now, we lie dormant.

"But a day will come when the Dragon is roused from slumber, and the tyrant's reign is broken. I pray it comes soon, but if it does not, then do not give up hope. So long as these words are etched in metal, so long as they reside in the hearts of those who cherish truth —we have not lost.

"Ciell Aenan, Last of the Lazarran Consuls."

Vohman took another long breath, opened his eyes. "My superior told me the story of how this seal came into his possession. Perhaps a year after the ascension of the First Emperor of Lazarra, in the wake of what they call the Dark Days, a Lazarran man came to the City of Lights. He traveled under a false name, though he had a noble bearing that could not be concealed, and he brought with him this bronze seal.

"It was this man who confirmed what had long been suspected, that Ciell Aenan had died in the tumult of the Dark Days, that the Empire of Lazarra was under the dominion of a formidable spirit, the one they call their 'high god.' I will tell you now, Sharasthi, you must not name him, for it shall draw his attention. If you must, call him the Far-seer."

Sharasthi was clutching her sides. Her grandfather was saying this all so grimly, and yet so quick as well. "I'm sorry," she croaked, "perhaps I should not have asked. This is all too much for me. Who is Ciell Aenan? What did he mean by archives hidden in libraries? Is that what the man bearing the seal was looking for?"

Vohman pursed his lips. "You need not apologize, child. Indeed, *I* am sorry. When a secret is long-held, the eventual telling rushes out as through a sundered dam. I have held this knowledge so close and tight to my heart for so many years that I have forgotten how it was fed to me, piecemeal and gradual.

"In short, Ciell Aenan was the last ruler of the Lazarran Republic. He foresaw its collapse and reconstitution as an Empire under the Far-seer's spiritual tyranny. Aenan formed the Order of the Sleeping Dragon, a clandestine organization devoted to the restoration of the Republic and the freeing of the world."

"Wait," Sharasthi groaned, "what do you mean the freeing of the *world*? The Lazarran high god is—well—the *Lazarran* high god. Their Empire is mighty, to be sure, and its expansion...we have seen how far it reaches, but all empires fall. The Immortal Empire of our forebears! And how long has it been since the death of Alar and the end of *his* empire?" She rubbed her eyes. "Of course I don't want to live under Lazarran rule, but..."

Vohman sighed. "I understand your thoughts, child, and they are not without reason. Yet...there is something you must know. You asked of the archives Aenan mentioned. Yes, that was the purpose for the seal-bearer coming to the City of Lights. Aenan was a man devoted to history; almost fanatically so. As the stories go, he spent every waking moment in which he was not governing comparing the accounts of the great historians, searching for discrepancies, trying to tease out the truth.

"Some would say he was paranoid and obsessed; others that he was perceptive and careful. Whichever is right, his extreme methods bore fruit. He had copies upon copies made of what he deemed the most valuable texts of the past, and he had them disseminated throughout the world's libraries. His own commentaries on these texts came with them."

Sharasthi frowned. "You speak as if Ciell Aenan was some great and notable man, renowned throughout the world. Why then is he not still famed in Zarush?

"And there it is," Vohman muttered. "Sharasthi, what if I told you that when the Lazarran seal-bearer came to the City of Lights, those many years ago, he showed us records we did not even know we held?"

Sharasthi puzzled over that for a moment. "What do you mean? That Aenan's archives had been forgotten? That's not surprising given how..." She slowed, then started again. "But you said the seal-bearer came only a year or so after the rise of the Empire. Aenan's death wasn't even certain at the time. And yet his records had already been forgotten?"

Vohman nodded, his features severe. "Now you begin to see. And this is the great tyranny of the Far-seer, Sharasthi."

Her grandfather ran his fingers along the seal's impressions again. "Memory," he breathed. "Tyranny over the world's memory."

Sharasthi blinked. Then swallowed. She must have heard him wrong, that was it. Any moment now, her grandfather would clarify what he had meant, or say he had misspoken, or…

But no, the look on his face said it all.

Sharasthi stood up, knocking the chair off its legs and sending it clattering to the floor.

"Fire," she said through trembling lips, "is Truth. You taught me that."

Vohman grunted. "So I did. And so I still believe."

"Then how could all the world be deceived? This god of the Lazarrans, this emissary of the Dark…"

"Sharasthi, child, you must underst—"

"How can I believe in a Truth that can be obscured? How can I believe in a Light that does not burn away the Dark?"

"I have not yet—"

"I don't need to hear any more!" she cried, clutching at her hair, squeezing her skull as if she could force out the knowledge. "Because I already know what you're going to say. You're going to say this Lazarran reminded us of what we had forgotten, and now you are going to pass it on to me. Please, Grandfather, I want no part of it! Zaro taught us the Truth in far more ancient days. Anything we could forget is meaningless compared to his teaching."

Vohman inclined his head. The nearly dead light of the lamp cast a mournful glow across his lined features. "Do you think I lost my faith in Zaro's teaching because of what I know, Sharasthi?"

She didn't have an answer to that, so she just hugged herself and muttered, "Do you believe in Zaro's miracles?"

Vohman cocked his head. "Where is this coming from?"

"When Zaro was born, they say his laughter shook the world. They say when his first sermon ended, lightning from a clear sky struck a terebinth tree and first kindled the Eternal Flame that to this day burns in the City of Lights, from which our own altar was lit. You taught me all these things."

"I did."

"Do you believe they really happened?"

"Of course I do."

"And you believe Zaro's word that Truth can never be smothered?"

"Without hesitation."

The air was perfumed again with that vacant, unseen smoke, filling up her lungs. Sharasthi swallowed, then suddenly tasted something sour. "Forgive me, excuse me," she stammered, then ran out—out from the archive, out from the temple. Her legs carried her just fast enough, as she made it out of doors just in time to make it around a corner and heave out the contents of her stomach.

Spitting again and again to expel the taste of bile, she sank down against a wall. It was night. Her grandfather always gave her lessons at night. Remembering her dreams of the cloak spread over her, she started meandering toward her reeded hiding spot by the little lake. Time dragged as she walked.

She had to stop to retch again once she stepped beyond the town wall, but hardly anything came up. The thought of washing out her mouth with cool water spurred her on, preventing her from just lying down and curling up in a ball.

Her grandfather had told Legate Vantelle she was a 'sensitive child.' That was a kind way of putting it. Sensitive children cried when the bull was offered. They blubbered when someone raised their voice.

Sharasthi would have given anything to be like *that*. It would be far preferable to what she had instead.

As she walked, she looked up at the stars. Those were *ahura* spirits, ministering in their divinely appointed courses, crossing the sky. Astrologers read clues to the will of heaven in the ways the stars shifted and arrayed themselves. It was permissible, but there was always a cautionary attitude held toward the astrologers—the night was also the time when *daeva* spirits roamed more boldly across the earth, emboldened by the lack of the burning solar radiance. Men who loved too much the night were thought to be susceptible to their temptations—even to becoming possessed like Marzud.

Sharasthi liked the stars. She liked the moon. She liked the night.

She had always felt guilty for it. She hid it—hid herself.

In a faith devoted to the illumination of the Eternal Flame, she had been born with a heart that found ease and comfort in the dark. What was she to do? She had always thought the problem lay in her affections, that if she could just commit herself sufficiently to the practices and rites of the faith, she would change.

It was why the story of Marzud horrified her so thoroughly— because she saw in him a warning of what might happen to her if she dropped her guard.

When she came to her hiding place, she went and lay down on her stomach at the water's edge, her elbows sinking in the shallow mud.

The water's surface reflected the stars, and though she did not want to see it, her face.

Serving within the temple kept her out of the sunlight. When she did go out of doors, it was either early in the morning or under the moon's tranquil face. The pallor of her skin marked her as quite unlike the laboring townsfolk. That was supposedly beautiful, but it only made Sharasthi feel more alien.

The Lazarran legionnaires were all bronzed by the sun, their eyes in perpetual half-squints. Warriors' bodies, warriors' faces, warriors' souls.

Sharasthi let her head tip forward, so that her chin sank beneath the water, then her mouth, her nose, her eyes. Near total darkness, within the lake.

In her mind's eye, things lurked just within that darkness. The possessor-*daeva* of the Marzudi. The Far-seer Arkhon, who she was meant to believe had deceived all the world by dint of his spiritual might.

Lifting her head out of the water to take a breath, Sharasthi raised her eyes to the night sky again.

All her life, she had thought that loving the Fire's Light meant denying her penchant for darkness—lest she find herself enslaved by the Dark, as Marzud had been.

But was darkness the same as the Dark?

That was the heart of it. That was why she had needed to leave the archive, why her soul had stirred so violently she lost her stomach. She was horrified of what she longed for.

Marzud's story was an ever-present terror. In her waking life, in her dreams. She would *not* allow herself to be taken. More than that, she would not allow herself to become the sort of person who *asked* to be taken.

Even when she sought these little hiding spots, when she secreted herself away in dark and dim places—it had been an indulgence, something she allowed herself as a momentary relief.

Zaro said, 'The drunkard swears off strong wine, then in a month drowns himself in it. Do not clear your entryway if it will entice the thief.' Many people thought that was one of the prophet's harder sayings, but Sharasthi had clung to it like a rope thrown to one sinking beneath the waves. She had granted herself these little pleasures as a defense. If she had denied herself entirely, she might have snapped and hurtled headlong into the Gray Wastes.

But now, now her grandfather meant for her to embrace deceit. He wanted her to be of darkness—and she did not know if she could do that without becoming of the Dark.

All her life, she had carried this twisted penchant inside herself. What if doing what was right was too dangerous? What if it brought her too close to the way of Marzud?

Those questions spun around and around in her mind, with no good answers presenting themselves. She feared what those answers might be, but feared even more of taking the questions to her grandfather, because that meant she would have to bare this deep-buried side of her. She would have to reveal fully who she was. Confront that these little indulgences of hers weren't just eccentricities, but hazards.

What was she to do?

She rinsed out her mouth, washed the sweat off her face, and bedded down amongst the reeds.

She did not want to sleep under the temple's roof tonight.

Tomorrow, she would need to help prepare for the legate's return. A day of work would be welcome—it would give her more time to think on how best to speak to her grandfather.

Her mind did not settle for hours, spinning and spinning and spinning, until finally sleep sprang upon her like a mountain lion upon its prey. Even then, she drifted in and out of unconsciousness, attuning to the rustling of the reeds, the lapping of the lake. Dimly, she plunged again and again into oblivion, then stirred again and again, awaiting the warmth of dawn and the clamor of the town that would finally signal her to rise once and for all.

It was not the peaceful rousing of the town that woke her, but screams.

5

VARMAKIS

THE CAPITAL of Zarush was once called Ezhae, but after the prophet's day became known as the City of Lights. When one stands near the High Temple, even midnight seems as brightest day, so numerous are the torches and lanterns. According to tradition, the Everlasting Fire atop the High Temple's central altar was miraculously kindled by the prophet Zaro himself and has been kept burning ever since. Even as the Immortal Empire crumbled and blood ran through the streets, the priests guarded the altar.

—The Life and Wisdom of Simeon Binkhok As Told by Himself

THE PROPHET ZARO SAID, 'To speak the truth and draw the bow—this is virtue.' Archery stood as one of the great pillars of Zarushan culture. It predated the Immortal Empire, and it endured since. The sound of arrows whistling through the air was not an uncommon one —even in a quiet town like Ashmuz.

What pulled Sharasthi from sleep was not the arrows, but the screams punctuating their flight.

The sky was gray, the air cold. The sun was perhaps half an hour from rising.

Her stomach dropped, her breath came fast, her hands trembled.

Sharasthi stared at the reeds, torn between peeking out and staying tucked within.

The horrid sounds only intensified. Thundering hooves, frantic neighing.

The first thought to well up was an image of the Imperial Scouts, mounted on their hardy steeds, sweeping through the town like an iron storm. The Scouts created chaos and confusion, and they paved the way for the legionnaire troops, marching in lockstep, marching with Adept Rufus and his fire magic, under the harsh eye of Cassia Vantelle.

The picture was so terrible that Sharasthi nearly convinced herself of it—but then she caught something else on the wind. It could not be the Lazarrans, because there was shouting, vicious and stoic in counterpoint to the panicked screams of the townsfolk (screams she dared not pay too close attention to, lest she recognize the voices).

Those shouts were fervent, harsh, masculine—and speaking Parthavan.

Curiosity finally overwhelmed fear, and she crawled to the edge of the reed clump, easing them aside to peek through.

Men were running out from the town, carrying bows and rattling quivers, brandishing spears, clubs, even swords.

They dropped as they ran, black-feathered arrows protruding from necks, eyes, mouths.

Sharasthi clutched the reeds in white-knuckled fists as she spotted the attacker.

A horse bolted to and fro like a ribbon of red wind, guided only by its rider's knees. The rider's hair streamed behind him like a black banner of neat braids and matted clumps, like he had only dressed it halfway before setting out for murder. One arm held a bow, the other flew from quiver to string, drawing and loosing arrow after arrow. It looked almost thoughtless, the way he did it, yet every shot dropped a man. All the while, he called out in Parthavan speech stained with solemn and violent intent.

His bow pulled her gaze—it was a thing of startling beauty. The body was an elegant curve of gray wood, the string so faint she could hardly see it. Only as he turned his horse did she catch its thin, silver line.

Once in a while, one of the defenders managed to get off a shot at the Parthavan. But his horse was racing around so fast, the shots almost all went wide. Once Sharasthi saw the rider duck, and if she didn't know better, she would have thought he'd actually dodged an arrow—but that was impossible. No one could see an arrow in flight, not even if it had been in the light of day, let alone the present gloom.

Sharasthi burrowed down further, transfixed by what she was seeing, even as it horrified her.

She had seen Parthavan Hunters before, when they came to town to trade.

But she realized, watching the scene before her, she had never *really* seen a Hunter until now.

Why? she asked herself in desperation. *Why attack the town?!*

Bandits raided and pillaged. But Hunters had never turned to banditry, not here.

Was he mad? Her grandfather had said the Parthavan Hunters practiced an odd religion—had he been taken by a spirit like Marzud?

A cluster of men rushed from the town, moving together behind shields. The Hunter did not waste his arrows—instead, he looped his horse around and began riding further out from town.

Sharasthi gasped, hiding her face as he galloped past the reeds where she lay hidden, before coming back around a few moments later, splashing through the shallows of the lake. The cold water soaked her, and she bit down on her arm to keep from crying out.

Once he made another pass at the men with the shields, loosing a single arrow before riding around them in a circle. They spun around in place, always keeping their shields facing him. More fighting men of Ashmuz arrived, hustling to try and hem in the Hunter.

Yet as Sharasthi watched, she thought there was something bizarre about the way the Hunter wove in and away from the town's defenders. Almost like he was…

Over the western hill, two more Hunters appeared, charging in on horseback. Then another three crested the rise. Then more.

The lone Hunter who had been toying with the townsfolk nudged his horse and took off to join the others.

It was a full-scale raid, and so many men had been drawn to the northern edge.

At full gallop, the Hunters broke into smaller groups—twos and threes—and their horses leaped straight over the wall before vanishing into Ashmuz. One pair entered by the butcher's home. A trio went between the carpenter's and the weaver's workshops.

Sharasthi thought of her grandfather.

Her arms and legs shook, her teeth chattered.

Hiding. She was good at hiding. She had *already* been hiding, even before she knew there was any danger.

She could draw a persuasive argument that the protection of the noble *ahura* had placed her here, so she might be spared the turmoil and bloodshed of this morning.

Zaro said, 'The child's virtue is tested in the parent's day of weakness.'

She got up and started running.

If the militia men saw her, they would no doubt grab her and force her to flee, so she avoided them. She crouched low in the dried-up riverbed, she crawled through the ruined section of wall by the undertaker's house.

The air smelled of smoke—and not the smoke of the temple's Eternal Fire. Profane smoke. The raiders must have started burns.

What were they after? If she could figure that out, she could plan, she could react.

Sharasthi nearly took a step into the street, then pulled back into the shadows when a pair of Hunters rode past at breakneck speed, calling to one another in their strange tongue.

Sharasthi stayed crouched in the darkness, breathing through fingers clamped over her nose and mouth to smother the fog from her breath.

If only the Lazarrans had arrived a day sooner! They could have fought off the Parthavans.

Heart thundering, she peered out from the alley, then darted into the open. Clamor arose from every which way, always drawing nearer and fading farther. Was there any pattern to their scouring? Were they looking for something? The chaos of it defied her.

Townsfolk ran every which way—fleeing bowshot, running toward fires with sloshing buckets. Tearful mothers carried wailing infants under either arm. Desperation and terror reigned.

Sharasthi's throat closed as she neared the temple. Shouts and horse-cries echoed through the streets. A nightmare painted her imagination with every step, telling her that as soon as she turned the corner, she would see her home in flames, or her grandfather riddled with black-feathered arrows, or—

She turned the corner.

Bodies. Bodies stuck with arrows, bodies with throats slashed.

There lay Priest Atsan, the whites of his vestments forever stained crimson. His vacant eyes stared at the sky. A few steps away lay one of the novices. His lifeless fingers still held a ceremonial staff—the only thing it had ever struck was the temple floor, but he must have tried to use it as a weapon before a Hunter shot him through the eye.

And there, on the steps of the temple, was her grandfather. He was alive—but the enemy was upon him.

Two Hunters, one on horseback, the other on his feet. The rider was the man she had seen from the thicket, the one with the beautiful bow. The one standing had a birthmark like a claw on his cheek —and he was clutching Vohman's vestments, yelling at him in broken Zarushan.

Every bone and nerve in Sharasthi's body demanded she flee. She was a girl; these were men of death.

But that was her grandfather, and he was still alive.

"*Why?*" shouted Claw-face, striking Vohman's cheek and

knocking him to the temple steps. Blood trickled from his mouth as he groaned.

Sharasthi strangled the scream that tried to rip free from her lungs.

Or, she tried to. The slightest choked squeak emerged from her lips, and the Hunter on the horse whirled on her, already drawing. Sharasthi scrambled, though she knew she had no hope of evading. She had seen how he dropped man after man outside the town.

But he only frowned, then eased his draw. He shouted something in Parthavan to Claw-face. The latter shot a glance at Sharasthi. His eyebrows furrowed.

Sharasthi froze. Two Hunters were looking at her—looking more with befuddlement than anything else—and there was something haunting about their gaze, something *wrong*. Her grandfather couldn't even see it was her that had distracted them.

Run! Hide!

Her legs shook beneath her. She must have looked like a startled deer, and she remembered how often Hunters like this had brought deer to barter at the market. She was only alive because they had not chosen to kill her. She was prey, nothing more, and dared not try to fight them.

But maybe she could do something else.

"He's blind!" she cried, hoping they knew enough to understand even as her voice trembled.

Vohman started, making a cry more pained than when he'd been struck. "Run, Sharasthi!"

Claw-face backhanded him, then pointed at her. "Come."

Don't!

"Fast, or I kill him!"

She stumbled forward, tripping to hands and knees before finally making it to the steps. She threw herself onto the Hunter's feet. "He's my only family!" she pleaded. "Family!" she repeated, hoping some pity in the Hunter might stir.

Claw-face's rough, calloused fingers wrapped around Vohman's jaw, digging into the sagging flesh. "Old man. I kill you in front of this girl if you do not tell me."

Sharasthi screamed, her fingernails digging into his legs.

Vohman coughed, specks of blood dotting the Hunter's face. "I told you," he mumbled, "the Imperials arrive tomorrow. You were given false information."

"The seer is never false!" he snarled.

The Hunter on the horse loosed two shots. Sharasthi whirled, looking over her shoulder just in time to see Bazak the tanner drop dead, a hammer in his hands. The Hunter said something to Claw-face in a terse tone.

"No time," Claw-face grumbled. "The empire-spirit, old man. Why an allegiance?"

Vohman groaned. "I don't understand. We've never—"

"Girl," he snapped, grabbing Sharasthi by the hair. Her scalp burned as he hauled her up. "You want this old man to die? Make him tell me."

Sharasthi blubbered. Her breath was coming too fast; her head was spinning, screaming. She didn't understand what he wanted. "Grandfather, please! *Ah!* Just tell him anything!"

Vohman's face contorted. "Do not hurt my granddaughter."

Claw-face wrenched her hair, wringing another scream out of her. "I do not kill a *varmakis,* old man, but you want her hurting to stop, you tell me what you have done." He twisted her hair again. Tears blurred her vision.

Vohman shouted, his orator's voice booming like a trumpet. "She is but a child!"

Both Hunters winced, and the one on the horse rubbed at his ear. He spoke to Claw-face, repeating that word *varmakis* as he gestured to Sharasthi with his bow.

The two Hunters looked right at her again, and Sharasthi finally realized what had seemed so wrong about their gazes.

Their eyes were *gold.*

Claw-face scowled. The Hunters exchanged hasty words. His grip on her hair did not slack in the slightest, and Sharasthi couldn't help but let out a frail whimper. She didn't want to think about how much pain Vohman was in.

Her grandfather muttered—not in vulgar Zarushan, but in the classical form of the scriptures: "Sharasthi, keep all secrets. Trust no one. Honor the Flame."

Claw-face scowled, then took a step up, hauling her and her grandfather up into the temple. He called something out to the other Hunter as he took them.

"You know old story," said Claw-face, "about Marzud. Zarushan tell it wrong."

Sharasthi thrashed in his grip, though it only hurt more. He dragged them into the sanctuary, to where the altar of the Eternal Flame burned.

"Marzud did not die among followers." He threw Sharasthi against the altar. She yelped as her skull and shoulders struck the hot stones, and she crumpled into a heap. Her vision swam. When she tried to lift her head, it weighed like it had been strapped to a boulder.

With both arms, Claw-face lifted Vohman up over his head. Her grandfather groaned, his limbs hanging limp. His face turned toward the heat of the altar, his blank eyes not beholding the divine manifestation he had worshipped and served so many years.

Sharasthi screamed.

"We hunted Marzud."

Claw-face threw Vohman upon the Eternal Flame.

His agonized scream filled the sanctuary.

Sharasthi wailed, trying to grab hold of the edge to haul herself up, but the stones burned her hands and she fell back, looking up at a horror worse than any nightmare.

Tongues of holy fire lapped up and over Vohman, already devouring his vestments, his beard, his hair. Her grandfather raised one trembling arm, and Sharasthi stretched her hand out, wishing more than anything else she could at least reach him, a few yards that might as well have been miles.

Vohman's hand dropped down. Another groan wrenched from his lips—and then changed in pitch.

The agonized wail rising from Vohman's lips undulated, swirling like the voice of a raging storm. Sharasthi's lungs filled with that smoke-perfume, its sickening scent covering the stomach-turning reek of her grandfather's burning flesh.

Claw-face made a strangled sound, then took a step back. "Tobron!" he shouted.

A moment later, the other Hunter rode into the sanctuary on his horse, a second horse's reins in his free hand.

As the Hunter beheld the sight of the altar and Vohman's moaning form, his golden eyes widened.

The horses screamed, the one that must have been Claw-face's rearing up and tearing free of the Hunter's grasp. It began running around the altar, its hooves throwing up sparks as it wheeled about.

"Tobron!" shouted Claw-face again. He jabbed a finger toward Vohman's burning, trembling body and cried out in Parthavan. He sounded *frightened.*

Vohman's strange groaning rose in pitch, loud enough that it over-came the crackling of the Eternal Flame. Sharasthi's head spun as the fit worsened. Hands wrapped around her shoulders; no one was there.

The other Hunter shook his head, his knuckles white as he clutched his bow. He looked at Claw-face with horror, the whites of his eyes showing all around the gold.

Claw-face made a despairing sound and ran to intercept his horse in its mad circling. Grabbing the reins, he fought with the beast, yelling at it in his tongue, before finally managing to unhook his bow from its saddle. The horse ran off as soon as he let go of the reins, but Claw-face didn't even watch it go.

Instead, he pulled an arrow from the quiver on his hip, and with teeth bared in a rictus, loosed it into Vohman.

Sharasthi let out another scream as her grandfather's finally cut off.

The ethereal smoke left her lungs. Her head cleared. The

phantom touch vanished from her shoulders. She pitched to the side. Hard tile struck her hip, her shoulder, her head.

The Hunter on the horse cuffed Claw-face over the head, shouting at him in a fury, spittle flying from his lips.

Claw-face looked pale as death.

Sharasthi lay on her side, staring at the Eternal Flame, at the charring shape that she knew was her grandfather's corpse, but which she could not accept as such. She was not crying anymore—she was only hollow. Her eyes streamed a constant flow of tears. Her nose stung with the grotesquely real smoke from her grandfather's burning body.

6

SOMETHING MOURNFUL

During my time in the City of Lights, I was granted access to their archives. The Zarushan priests are surprisingly open—I suspect because they are more given to proselytizing than priests of the Four. The one matter about which they are exceptionally tight-lipped is anything to do with magic. Nevertheless, through my efforts, I uncovered two crucial things:

One, there is an ancient mystical tradition called the Unlit Path, stretching back allegedly to Zaro himself, but which certainly existed in the time of the Immortal Empire. The sources I was able to read speak of it in cryptic terms, so I can only offer as presumption that this Unlit Path is a sort of esoteric twin to the priestly office.

Two, during the Immortal Empire, likely during the reign of Ahura Darius the Second, a Zarushan magician bound a spirit to his ring and bent it to his will.

—The Life and Wisdom of Simeon Binkhok As Told by Himself

~

The Hunters disappeared. Sharasthi did not know when—they were there, then they were not.

Her grandfather was still there. Or, this thing that had once looked like him.

He had taught her that even in death, the All-Pervasive Fire would burn within him. All she could think of was the Endric initiate who refused to kill his teacher. Supposedly, it was the other student who had given the right answer.

Nothing about that seemed right.

She wished one of her fits would come upon her right now. Spin her halfway out of reality. Wrap her in ephemeral touch and fill her with ethereal tastes. Then she would drift into dreams—hopefully never to wake again.

The Eternal Flame was shrinking. Its lapping tongues faded to trembling fingernails, then frail embers. How long had she been watching?

Her grandfather was a charred heap on the smoldering embers. Sleeping the sleep of death atop the Undying Fire.

Sharasthi's hollow, aching chest seized up.

With languid movements, she forced herself to her knees, then to her feet. Step by step, she fought her way to the keep room, where the wood and oil were stored. It was the task of the priests and conse-crated novices to preserve the Flame, but she had seen it done her whole life.

Her hands were not shaking. She was too tired to tremble.

First she took a vessel of the oil. It was half full, but still heavy. Having not the strength to carry it all the way, she dragged it by the iron handle. The bottom raked the tiles with a teeth-shuddering screech, and a wretched pain scouring her hands reminded her she had burned them on the altar.

At the steps, she paused. This was forbidden territory. She remembered, in her grandfather's voice, the saying of Zaro: 'The fool puts a fence around his favored tree, and the fruit rots on the branches.'

She began to climb. One. Breathe. Two. Breathe. Clutching the vessel of oil to her chest, she kept her eyes on her feet. Her arms trembled, and seeing she was not strong enough even to carry it up after all, she committed a sacrilege and poured some out on the floor.

At the fifth and final step, she finally made herself look.

For a moment, her mind forced her to see something else. A morning when Vohman had fallen ill, and so lain in bed as Sharasthi tended to him. He had always smiled and told her what a praise-worthy child she was. When she brought him water. When she changed his bedsheets. When she told him the sacrifice had gone well and what the homily had been on.

She had always told him he didn't have to praise her so, that she remembered from the last time, but he always did. She knew why. He was trying to make up for her parents' absence. Their abandonment.

The truth was: she had cherished every word, storing it in her heart like wood and oil, to be burned when the cold crept in and the Fire quivered.

All this passed through her in a blink, and now her grandfather was a heap of charcoal arranged in the shape of a man. Zaro taught that on the final day, at last all the faithful would revive, their flaming flesh and burning spirit forever united in perfect harmony, never to know death or frailty or illness or any evil thing again.

But now, her grandfather was dead. Now was not the final day—now was *today*, and every day would be another today.

She threw the oil across the altar, watching and listening to the enervated Fire lapping it up.

"Why should you still live?" she asked the Fire. "Did it mean nothing to you that my grandfather served you his entire life? You could not have protected him for just a little longer? Enough that he could die the death of the righteous, at peace and in his bed?"

The Fire only crackled.

As she stepped back down the ladder and made her way back to the keep room for wood, she told herself she was not doing this for the Eternal Flame. She was doing this because her grandfather would have wanted it.

It would grieve him to know that in his absence, the Flame was not kept. This was piety to her grandfather, not to the Fire.

That was a profane thought, she knew. She did not care.

They found her while she was hauling a log—far too big for her —up the steps.

"Sharasthi!"

She stopped at the third step, looking over her shoulder.

People were running to her. Those faces—she knew those faces. Who were they?

"Sharasthi!" someone shouted again. Did they not realize she had heard them?

"Help me," she croaked. "The Fire must be preserved."

Instead, they tried to pull her away, to take the wood from her. She moaned, thrashing—or trying to thrash—against them. "No! Grandfather wants me to do this!"

"Someone find a priest, one of the novices—anyone. Sharasthi, come with us."

They were taking her away from the altar.

Away from her grandfather.

"He needs me!" Finally the tears burst out, and they did not stop. She could not see for their outpour, could not speak, could hardly hear. No one tried to speak to her anymore. They put her on a bedroll, they tried in vain to make her take food and water, they rubbed her back and patted her head as she wept, but they did not try to speak to her.

What was there to say?

When Sharasthi woke, a lead weight crushed her chest.

Grandfather is dead.

It all came pouring back, and she shut her eyes tight, forcing herself to breathe. That didn't make any of it more bearable; it just kept her alive.

When she opened her eyes, she discovered she had slept under a canopy stretched out across tentpoles, a sort of makeshift shelter without sides. She did not see the point in that—it obscured the stars, but let in the wind. The air was too dry for rain.

Maybe whoever put it up had thought the intimation of a roof would be a comfort. It did not seem to be working. All around were yet more people sleeping, their faces twitching fitfully. Here and there, the muffled sound of stifled crying. What could a swathe of fabric do to ward off the horrors of the day?

The ache in her chest would not allow her to fall back asleep, so she crawled out of her bedroll, careful not to bother anyone nearby.

Someone had applied an ointment and bandages to her burnt hands. Presumably the same person who had taken off her sandals, but now she couldn't find them, so she had to go barefoot. The dull worry of stepping on a discarded arrowhead or dropped knife rang at the base of her skull, but she decided to take her chances.

She needed to see the rest of the town.

The question of whether her grandfather still lay atop the altar occurred to her. She pushed it away. If she went back there, she might just sit there until morning and she was discovered again—and who knew what people would think then? They had always said she was a sensitive child—a strange child, when they thought she could not hear.

Maybe she could embrace that. Live the rest of her days as the madwoman of Ashmuz, forever shattered, forever pitiable. She could beg for food. Maybe the temple would let her still live in her little room as a charity to her and a courtesy to her grandfather.

Grandfather is dead.

Sharasthi realized she was staring at the earth, watching her own shuffling feet. She had wanted to see the destruction, had she not?

Instead, she raised her eyes to the heavens, to the stars.

Impassive, that was what they looked like. Vohman had taught her the predictability of the stars was a promise—an image of the reliability of the Eternal Flame, the transcendent Truth and Goodness and Beauty beyond. As the *ahura* spirits circled in their celestial patterns, they showed humans unchanging glory.

That was supposed to be a comfort, but now it just seemed to signify detachment. If the divine was unchanging, then did that mean it could not care for the tragedies that befell humans?

Last night the stars circled.

A monster murdered Sharasthi's grandfather.

Tonight the stars circled.

What of the planets, the wandering stars? Those most powerful of spirits, moving along their own paths, yet even those paths were known, reliable.

Her grandfather had taught her how the Talynisti—especially their nomadic tribes—worshipped among their Four Gods one called the Wanderer. He had dominion over death, they said. Did they too see their gods in the planets? Which one might he be—Varazmut, the Northern Guardian? Arud, the Red Messenger?

Grandfather is dead. Grandfather is dead and no god or star can change that.

She lowered her eyes, and as she walked, took in the ghoulish sights of a ravaged Ashmuz.

None of the fires had burned too badly, but there had been many. Sharasthi had a hunch all of the Hunters had escaped. The people had likely been too busy fighting the blazes to worry about fighting raiders blitzing by on horseback.

The charred remnants of buildings—the blackened, cracked pillar that had once borne up a roof; the scorched facade that no longer had a home behind it—put skeletons into Sharasthi's mind.

How many people would they bury in the coming days? Had entire families been wiped out?

Were any priests alive to perform the rites? That was a harrowing thought.

In front of the potter's house, she stumbled over the first body. She had not realized it was there until her foot struck cold flesh and she went careening over it, falling to stinging hands and knees on the opposite side. Part of her wanted to just keep going, but she also had to know.

It was Nidal, the farmer. His eyes were closed, but his mouth hung open. He only came into town once a week, otherwise preferring the solitude of his farmhouse. Of all the days...

From that point on, she encountered more dead. Men, for the most part, though she spotted a few women. Maybe the Hunters had only killed those who got in their way. At least she had not come across any children.

What had Claw-face meant when he said, 'I do not kill a *varmakis*'? Was that Parthavan for *child*?

Sharasthi felt one of her fits coming on. She sagged to the ground, letting out a slow, tremulous breath as burning incense ticked the inside of her throat.

She waited for the touch of unseen arms around her shoulders, but it never came. Even her little madness denied her its comfort now.

When the spell did not pass, she gingerly stood and picked her way to the temple. She did not want to go back to the bedroll, surrounded by people. She hardly looked where she was going, simply trusting old memory and habit to bring her there. She kicked something and hoped it was not a body but murmured an apology anyway.

Her head listed to the side, then back, and the temple stood in front of her.

It looked too ordinary. Why were the walls this pristine? Where were the ashen scorch marks? The toppled colonnades? The splashes of blood painting the walls, the heaps of mangled bodies strewn across the steps?

The temple rose above the waves of the here and now—untouched, unaffected. It did not care that its steward had died within mere hours ago. It did not care that its sacred space had been profaned. It stood outside of time, a temple, yesterday, today, forever—until someone tore it down brick by brick, or the final day dawned and the Fire consumed and consummated all existence.

Climbing the steps might have taken her an hour or a minute—Sharasthi too stood outside of time as her soul whirled.

A hollow image of Vohman and the Hunters flickered as she crested the steps. She would never forget a moment of it.

At the top of the steps, she reeled, stumbled forward and braced herself against the engraved post framing the entryway, her eyes on the floor. Her fingers brushed Zaro's words—'Here is the Ineffable Truth, here the Eternal Flame.'

But was it here?

She raised her head.

The antechamber was dark.

Sharasthi stared into the darkness.

All her life she had felt an affinity for the black gloom, for the places light did not reach—but now it terrified her. It terrified her that *this* place, this place meant to house the Light, now lacked it.

But no, there was something...

She peered into that darkness, and as her eyes adjusted, embracing the touch of this space vacant of moonlight and starlight —she finally saw it.

Deep within the dark, she saw the smoldering play of light, alive in the innermost sanctuary.

The Eternal Flame was preserved and tended.

Who was tending it? What was the state of her grandfather's remains?

She did not have the courage to know.

Instead, she sat down, her back to the light, her face to the dark— and to the deeper Light—and let spin her soul.

Arms wrapped around her shoulders. At some point, arms of flesh filled the phantoms, attached to a body that murmured words she ignored. They put a blanket over her and left, but the unseen arms remained.

The sun rose, warming her back and piercing the shadows of the antechamber. The man who had tended the Eternal Flame retired from his duty and was replaced by another. She did not look at their faces.

She was waiting, she realized. Waiting for what, she did not know

—but still she drifted above the ravages of time and space, of here and now.

The clamor of the town coming to life, spurring to action in the wake of their tragedy. Someone put water and food in front of her. She did not touch it, and eventually it was gone.

Words whispered—of reproach, of worry. She heeded them not.

The clamor increased in its fervor. Something was happening. Still, she did not turn her head.

Then, the arms gave her a squeeze.

Sharasthi started. They had never done that.

She heard another voice, an unfamiliar voice. Rough like gravel. A strange dialect of Zarushan. "Can she hear it?"

"What is he saying?" asked a voice she *had* heard, but not for months. Female, Lazarran, speaking Karellan. So the legion had returned at last—right on time, a day too late.

"He is asking, 'Can she hear it?'" That was the merchant Darum. He sounded frightened.

A pause.

"Rufus..." said Cassia Vantelle, her voice pregnant with suggestion.

The arms gave Sharasthi another squeeze, and there was something mournful in that gesture. How could she perceive that?

A strong hand touched Sharasthi's shoulder.

She turned her head at last.

The severe, dust-streaked face of the Adept filled her vision. His pendant swung from his neck.

Another just like it was in his hand. He pressed the cold metal to her forehead.

Sharasthi shuddered—and the unseen arms' touch disappeared like early morning mist under the sun's blazing face.

Her fit expired in an instant; her soul anchored into place.

Rufus grunted, turned to Vantelle, and nodded.

The legate's face was unreadable. "Perhaps this venture was worth something after all."

Sharasthi realized she was shaking. The sun was too hot. The noise of the town too loud. She was here. She was now.

Darum the merchant was looking at her with fear and pity.

Cassia Vantelle seemed pleased.

Adept Rufus was inscrutable.

And there was a fourth person—a wild-haired, wild-eyed man, his face tattooed with Zarushan calligraphy, just like the calligraphy of Zaro's words engraved around the temple entrance.

This man stood with a hunch, one gnarled finger pointing at Sharasthi, and he croaked again, "Can she hear it?"

The lettering on his forehead declared: *Marzud.*

Sharasthi clutched the wall of the temple and screamed.

The man smiled—all crooked teeth and scornful mirth—and cackled. *"She cannot."*

7

A SILENT VOW

ONE FINAL INSTRUCTION, from the mouth of our Emperor: bring back one of the fanatics that dwell among the Gray Wastes, and direct Adept Rufus to requisition a spare focus from the Sanctum's quartermaster. The reason will make itself evident. Do not fail in this, Vantelle.

—from Praetor Sevol Braigis' correspondence with Legate Cassia Vantelle

CASSIA VANTELLE ORDERED her troops to assist in the collection of dead bodies and the clearing of rubble. The townsfolk, despite their wariness of the Imperials, did not hesitate to accept aid. No doubt, their gratitude contained notes of guilt and fear—guilt because they knew well they were in no position to offer proper hospitality as the strictures of faith and culture ordained; fear because the Lazarrans could wipe them out in hours with hardly any losses, given the dearth of war-capable men.

The return of the legionnaires occupied the town's consciousness so thoroughly that Sharasthi imagined she and the merchant Darum were the only ones who knew or cared about the presence of the Marzudi, whose abominable name was Gormish.

After collecting remuneration from Vantelle's aide for his translation services, the merchant had frantically departed to join the town's labors—or so he said. Doubtless he simply wished to be anywhere but near the fiend. Perhaps anywhere but near Sharasthi as well. She loathed him for it even as she could not much fault him.

Now, in a granary repurposed into Vantelle's command center, Rufus sat between Sharasthi and the fanatic, which she was grateful for, but it did nothing to alleviate the terror burrowing through her insides.

The Hunter with the claw birthmark had shaken her grandfather and spat in his face, screaming about an allegiance, about 'the empire-spirit,' about the Imperials.

Now Vantelle and her troops had returned with a Marzudi in tow, a Marzudi who kept babbling about Sharasthi.

"Does she know what it did? How long has it been with her? Gormish wants to know."

He croaked these things right at her, but he never said *you*. Neither did he say *I*. He spoke about himself and the world around him as though he were merely an observer.

Sharasthi muttered to Rufus, "It's all nonsense."

The Adept grunted.

She could not bring herself to truly believe it though, and she suspected neither did Rufus and Vantelle. Gormish had known something, still knew something, about her. Something beyond the realm of the senses. What his warped mind perceived, she shuddered to think—and yet she had a wretched curiosity too.

Ever since the moment Rufus had touched her with the focus and terminated her fit, something had gone hollow inside her, a distinct hollowness from the grief for her grandfather. This was a second grief—a grief she could not name or articulate, but nonetheless just as real.

Something had been taken from her in that moment.

'The essence of magic is to exert one's will upon the world. A spiritual

lever that moves the material. And it was a Zarushan magician who first bound a spirit.'

So Vohman had taught her.

Why had he taught her that? He had said it was because of his vision. Was that true?

Or had he always thought something deeper lay behind her fits, behind her 'sensitive soul'?

Did he think—did he *know*—that she was...*this*?

Gormish slipped into one of his cackling spells. "Prisoners watching their captors' gloom—what do they think? *Hihihi!* Even still, they love their masters. But Gormish is free. Gormish's ears are not stopped up."

Rufus spared a glance for the Marzudi, then went back to eating his dinner—a simple gruel. Sharasthi had something more substantial in front of her—bread and olives—but she had not touched it. Gormish had nothing before him, and by his skeletal frame, scarcely concealed by his sackcloth rags, Sharasthi wondered if he ate much of anything at all.

"When will the legate be here?" she asked.

The Adept shrugged.

"Are you going to take me away?" She had intended to wait until Vantelle returned from her meeting with the town elders to ask, but she could not restrain herself any longer.

Rufus ate a spoonful of his gruel. "If Zarush was already an Imperial Province, yes. At the moment, we have no legal authority for that."

He spoke as if the eventual subjugation of this land to Lazarra was a foregone conclusion.

"Where are *you* from?"

"Aspagne."

That was at the distant Ocean's coast, as far to the west as one could go. When had an Aspagnian last set foot in Zarush?

"And it is one of those Provinces?"

"It is."

"So you didn't have a choice."

"Not the kind you are imagining, but neither do you have that choice."

Sharasthi raised her tired eyes to him.

Rufus' face seemed a perpetual scowl. "Every generation, a few are born head and shoulders above the rest. Cassia Vantelle is one such person. If she wants you to come with us, you will. If the Empire had legal authority over you, that would just make it simpler."

Sharasthi took that in. "So I should just go along with her will."

"I did not say that either. I said neither of us had the choice you were imagining, but that does not mean we have *no* choice. Every day, I choose whether to serve the Empire. Years ago I chose whether to go from Aspagne to Lazarra."

Sharasthi sniffed. "How so?"

"There was a Karellan philosopher, some centuries ago, who was born a slave but bought his freedom. He scandalized freeborn men—even aristocrats—with a certain teaching of his. He would go up to them and say, 'Even when I was in chains, I was free. You were born with a silver spoon in your mouth, yet still you are a slave.'

"And he went on to say, 'I am free because my mind and will are my own. No man alive—not my old owner, not the magistrate, not even a king or an emperor—can compel me to do anything, because I care not a whit for what happens to me. If I die, I have done what all men are destined to do—what does the timing matter to me? Such is the design of God.'"

Gormish laughed. "Is there one God? Are there many gods? Yes, yes—and yes to the third question, which only Gormish knows."

Sharasthi ignored the Marzudi, turning back to her untouched food. "So you are saying I can choose death if I don't want to go with Vantelle."

"You can."

"Would you kill me if I asked you to?"

"I would not."

"If I begged you?"

"No, but I could tell you where to find a knife if you wanted one."

Sharasthi considered this. She considered her grandfather. "I do not."

"Good. The young should not choose death."

She frowned, glancing at his stoic, gruff features. "That's an odd thing to say after what you told me."

"I only wanted you to be aware of the choice. Now you will always be free."

"That seems a terrible burden."

The Adept shrugged. "It is, but better to know than to feel trapped like an animal."

"Are all Adepts so inclined to philosophy?"

"All warriors are, if they live long enough."

"How long is that?"

"Past their first brush with death. The rest die in blissful ignorance." He finished his gruel and pushed aside the bowl. "Lucky bastards."

Gormish laughed.

Sharasthi wondered, if she asked Rufus to kill the Marzudi, whether he would.

When Vantelle returned, Sharasthi noted she was wearing her armor. She had never worn her armor before—not on her first arrival, not while staying in the town, not on the departure.

Now, however, the breastplate enfolded her like a shell.

"I am told," she began, "I may have been the target of yesterday's attack."

Rufus grunted. "We should cut down to New Mizkhar and sail back. I can't protect you if Hunters ambush us on their home turf."

The legate went rifling in a trunk, then produced a map, which she spread among them. "You are suggesting, Adept Rufus, that we trace the border of Talynis and Parthava down to the coast?"

Her finger inscribed the route.

Rufus nodded. "Or even that we slip inside Talynis. They are not as zealous in protecting the fringes of their land as others. They trust the desert to keep outsiders at bay. If we hop from town to town, perhaps hiring some nomads as a guide…"

Vantelle made an appreciative sound. "It would also give us some opportunity to scout the area."

Gormish laughed. "Plans beget plans."

Sharasthi peered at him out of the corner of her eye. He only ever spoke that odd Zarushan dialect, but he seemed to understand other tongues perfectly well. She murmured the simple translation to Rufus, who arched an eyebrow. "The enthusiast is perceptive."

Vantelle's finger drifted into the hatchmarked section of the map signifying the Talynisti desert. "It's inevitable at this point."

The legate finally turned her attention to Sharasthi. "Tell me, Sharasthi, what you think is happening. Your best analysis."

She shrank under the woman's heavy, appraising gaze. "I'm sure I don't know, Legate."

"You showed yourself too keen a mind at our dinner for that. I told you I would not forget you, did I not? If you wanted me to think you a fool, you should have put that act on from the start."

Heat crept into Sharasthi's face, and she stared at the map to escape those hard eyes.

Her grandfather had said the Lazarrans would fail to find the passage they so desperately craved. He had said war was inevitable.

Inevitable. That word seemed so common in matters relating to Cassia Vantelle and the Empire she so adored.

"You did not find a way through the Spine," Sharasthi said. "You will need to go through Talynis to use the Endric Pass, and the Talynisti are a stiff-necked people who hate subjugation. When the Immortal Empire made them a vassal, there was no end to the trouble they made. Lazarra will need to prepare carefully for a war with them. It would be useful for that war if you scouted out the borders, and this diversion from your initial plan for a return journey is doubly useful as it gets you away from the Parthavan Hunters. Do I have it right?"

Vantelle favored her with a smile. "As I said then, Sharasthi, so I say now—a rare mind in so young a body."

"All thanks to my grandfather's instruction," she whispered.

The legate's expression cooled. "Yes, your grandfather. My condolences again. I did ask after him in my meeting with the elders. His bones have been gathered for interment."

A small groan escaped Sharasthi's lips. She had known that would be how things went, but to actually hear it...

Outsiders often reacted with confusion at the Zarushan attitude toward cremation—that dreadfully common practice among the western lands. They did not understand that Fire—the True Fire— was meant to *revive* the body, not destroy it. A person's remains were preserved for that final day of resurrection, when the long-awaited perfection allowed flesh and flaming spirit to unite in harmony.

"Thank you for telling me," she managed. *You who are an outsider.* "Have they set a burial date?"

There were many rites to be performed for many lost. Vohman would have a place of honor, given his service and stature in the temple, but the remaining priests might very well choose to prioritize those deceased who had putrefying flesh. A matter of pragmatism.

"The day before we plan to leave, in fact."

Sharasthi hugged her knees. Gormish laughed.

"May I ask, legate, if they did so at your insistence?"

"Insistence," Vantelle said without hesitation, "is a strong word. I simply made them aware of certain factors."

That was enough. Vantelle had told the elders that Sharasthi would leave with her. Had any of the elders resisted? Who was the senior priest now—had he even offered a token protest at the suggestion of Vohman's granddaughter being taken away?

She thought of what Rufus had told her mere moments ago. That Vantelle's will *would* come to pass. That the only choice available to her was the ultimate one.

Sharasthi's mind moved slowly, deliberately.

Her grandfather's final words to her were simple: *'Keep all secrets. Trust no one. Honor the Eternal Flame.'*

His last lesson to her—the murky mission of the Order of the Sleeping Dragon, a dark war against the Lazarran Empire and the tyrant god over it.

Rufus had shown her the choice underlying all other choices. Life —or death.

She would not choose death, but for what reason could she choose life? There was nothing in herself. In fact, if it was solely up to her, she would choose obliteration.

But her grandfather had given her a burden, a responsibility—a *vision*. Something that had mattered to him. And he had mattered to her.

'The child's virtue is tested in the parent's day of weakness.'

"Legate Vantelle, I understand what you want of me. It seems everything has conspired that you will get it. But may I make a request of my own?"

The legate cocked her head, an amused smile playing on her features. She gestured for Sharasthi to go on.

"When these inevitable wars arrive, will one be waged against the men who murdered my grandfather?" Her voice hitched on *murdered*, but she did not feel ashamed of it.

Vantelle spread her hands. "Our wills are the same in this, Sharasthi. My enemy is the Emperor's enemy. Graft yourself to Lazarra, and the same will be true of you."

Sharasthi nodded slowly. *But you will remain my enemy, Cassia Vantelle. You and the Empire you serve.*

"I will go with you, Legate Vantelle. Only let me bury my grandfather."

"Of course, Sharasthi. I would never dream of depriving you of that."

Remembering the words of Ciell Aenan, she made a silent vow— a vow of those words that had lain etched in bronze and in her grandfather's heart. *Secrecy shall be my blood, the darkness my cloak. For now, my enemies drive me into the shadows, beneath the ground. For now, I lie dormant.*

Sharasthi folded it all into a vault deep inside her. She locked the secrets away, and put another lock over them, and another, and she resolved never to violate her grandfather's charge.

'Keep all secrets. Trust no one. Honor the Eternal Flame.'

She would. No matter how many years or how much blood and sweat it demanded of her, she would.

And then she would avenge her grandfather on the men who murdered him, and on this woman and her Empire, who set into motion the events of his death.

8

DARK AND SECRET THINGS

THE RESULTS of the Gray Wastes expedition are unfortunate, but not surprising. Zarush holds no immediate promise for Imperial expansion: let the ruins of the Immortal Empire continue to collect dust for now. I suggest we turn our attention to Talynis and the Endric Pass.

—from Legate Cassia Vantelle's correspondence with Praetor Sevol Braigis

SHARASTHI'S REMAINING days in Ashmuz passed in a haze. Two things dominated her mind: her grandfather's funeral and her desire to avenge him on both the Hunters and the Empire. When she tired of considering one, she turned to the other.

At night, she slept in the Lazarrans' quarters. Vantelle made her the responsibility of a female captain. The woman was incapable of pronouncing Sharasthi's name properly, and she was obsessive in monitoring her.

The captain lacked the hardness of a soldier—indeed, she seemed to have a curious contempt for the legionnaires under her command. Most of all, she despised a certain sergeant (something that bewildered Sharasthi, as this sergeant struck her as a man of good discipline, well-liked by those legionnaires under his charge). Because the captain had a propensity to talk about herself, Sharasthi soon understood the matter.

The Lazarrans adored power; it was their lifeblood. All their social order seemed oriented around how one might ascend the constituent hierarchies. The Empire, Sharasthi heard often, was a household, over which the Emperor was the great father, his subjects devoted children.

Yet the Imperial Domicile was unique from any Zarushan household Sharasthi knew in one startling manner—it was ruthlessly meritocratic. It was not uncommon for an Emperor to disinherit his blood children and adopt someone totally unrelated—even someone of ignoble birth—whom he believed a greater candidate for rule. By this principle, some Emperors had even selected women as their heirs.

That said, there endured among the Lazarrans a concern for ancestral pedigree. The captain would gush about the legacy of the Vantelle family, rambling on about how honored she was to serve under the legate. Along with this, she slipped in remarks about her own heritage. While she made sure to emphasize her family was nothing compared to the Vantelles, she did not shy from singing their praises as one of the Empire's premier textile producers. What's more, she boasted how their renown dated back to the days of the Lazarran Republic.

The captain seemed to think Sharasthi a simple girl (something Sharasthi did nothing to dissuade her from) as once or twice a day she probed her about whether she spoke to the legate about her performance as Sharasthi's guardian. A great anxiety pervaded her on this topic.

And that, Sharasthi realized, was the source of her distaste for the sergeant under her command.

One of the chief advantages of affecting simplicity around the captain was that she was able to ask rather blunt questions in great quantity, and as the captain was so eager to speak of herself and her family, Sharasthi learned quickly about the nature of the Empire.

The captain came from a line that was fundamentally mercantile. And while economic power was nothing to sneeze at, the military was the true soul of Lazarra. Merchants were still of the plebeian class, ultimately, but (here Sharasthi made some reasoned assumptions based on her grandfather's wisdom), they were desperate to distinguish themselves from the 'lower' plebeians and strive to ingratiate themselves with the patrician aristocracy. This woman's family had purchased her an officer's commission in the legions to this end. The legions sold commissions as a way of funding operations, and it was also seen as a way for aristocratic families—and well-to-do plebeian ones—to demonstrate their devotion to the Emperor.

Sharasthi suspected there was a touch of bribery in the woman's particular case, that she might serve under the rising star that was Cassia Vantelle.

The despised sergeant came from humbler origins. He had even —the captain said with curled lip—spent several years as a slave, and when he removed his tunic you could count the lashes he had earned.

The sergeant had risen to his standing through performance; his captain had gotten hers through coin. This sort of arrangement was apparently common—whether deliberately or simply as a result of the system. Captaincies were often bought commissions (the highest a plebeian could purchase), while non-commissioned officerships were populated according to conventional advancement.

But the captain weathered constantly under dread that the sergeant might subvert her. As such, she often spoke against him, muttered that she suspected him of attempting to besmirch her reputation with the troops, even that he would someday attempt to get her killed in a battle (perhaps dealing the lethal blow himself in the confusion of the melee).

Sharasthi noted the captain lacked combat scars while the sergeant had several, and so she doubted the woman was anywhere near the fighting if she could help it—indeed, when the woman undressed for bed, Sharasthi noted a physique unhardened by labor. The woman had a personal slave, whom Sharasthi suspected carried the woman's pack and kit when needed. More and more Sharasthi saw how the sergeant and other officers under the captain's command assumed actual responsibility for leading their company.

Something about the whole state of affairs disgusted Sharasthi. She surmised the woman must be of so little use to Vantelle that she was along just for the sake of maintaining what connections and resources she represented. If anything, perhaps Sharasthi was doing Vantelle a service by giving the captain something inconsequential to occupy herself with. It put Sharasthi in a mind that—if all the Empire was like this—it would not be so difficult a thing to obtain her vengeance.

But as soon as this thought came, she considered again Legate Vantelle and Adept Rufus. Rot always took hold, but Sharasthi could not afford to rely upon it. The Immortal Empire had decayed for decades before its tumultuous downfall. Who was to say how long Lazarra would resist the same fate, or whether the Lazarrans would fare better at burning out the deadwood? Overconfidence on her part would lead to carelessness. Mistakes led to death. It became her earnest hope to spend more time with Rufus, so she might under-stand the strongest points of the legions and the Empire.

For the most part, the Adept was at Vantelle's side. The danger of a Hunter attack hung day and night over the legionnaires, evident in narrow eyes and taut shoulders.

The townsfolk were eager for the Imperials to be on their way, but hospitality forbade them from making any direct suggestions to that effect. That did not stop them from nudging Sharasthi with inquiries as to whether the Lazarrans might depart ahead of schedule.

Sharasthi had nothing to say on the matter. To her disheartenment, she no longer felt a bond between herself and Ashmuz. When her grandfather had died and the elders so readily permitted her departure, she became a piece on a board. The town elders used her in a gambit to appease Vantelle; Vantelle used her for the Imperial cause; but Sharasthi, unbeknownst to them all, was playing for a third side—her own.

It would be fraught with danger, but as night after night rolled by, as she lay awake listening to the whispers of her unconscious, an increasing certainty built that it was for this she had been born as she was. A sensitive child, a child predisposed to dark and secret things.

The day before the Lazarrans took her away, Sharasthi attended her grandfather's burial. Her eyes were dry as she sang the hymns of interment, and this startled her. When the ossuary was lowered into the grave, she bowed her head and wondered why she could not bring herself to cry.

That night, with special permission from Vantelle (who had observed the funeral from a polite distance, as befitted her status as an outsider and unbeliever), Sharasthi holed up in the temple archive, where Vohman had given her so many lessons, where he had found her hiding so many times.

The captain ordered a pair of legionnaires to guard the temple through the night, perhaps afraid Sharasthi would pull some disappearing act at the last moment, but that made no difference to Sharasthi.

She had told Vantelle she wished to spend the night studying Zaro's teachings, as a way to honor her grandfather's vocation.

This was a lie.

Years of liturgy and ritual had burned the most important passages into her mind already, and what she did not remember in exact words, she could still recall in substance.

In the dark of night, by the flickering glow of an oil lamp, she retrieved the hidden bronze seal.

By the wavering light, she committed to memory the etching, what her grandfather had described as an abbreviated form of the Order of the Sleeping Dragon's charge.

Vohman had never taught her Lazarran, not even the alphabet. He had thought they would have more time. She could not distinguish one word from the next. In conrast to the Zarushan scribal practice of setting dots between words, Lazarran flowed in an uninterrupted stream, leaving it to the reader to recognize where one word ended and another began.

So she memorized the characters. She did not even know what to call them, so she resorted to shape associations. One letter looked like an *arrow*. Another was like a *horseshoe*. She imagined stories linking these images together. An *arrow* dislodged a *horseshoe*, which fell into a *well*...

Now and then, she closed her eyes and transcribed the message in her mind, then opened her eyes to check her progress.

It was slow going, but thankfully the etching was an abbreviation of the full message her grandfather had recited to her that final night of his life. Once she had reconstructed it without flaw ten times in a row, she returned the bronze seal to its hiding place. It struck her that it might never be removed from this spot again, unless the temple be torn down or the world renewed in Flame.

With that done, since she had the time, she got the copy of the Sayings she had read to her grandfather from. The passage she sought was indelible in her memory, but she wanted to read it aloud.

She sat at the table, found the place nearly at the end of the scroll. She looked at the empty chair beside her.

She read aloud:

"My friends, you call me a prophet, you call me venerable, but I too shall die. Prophet or thief—all die."

According to tradition, this was from Zaro's last sermon, given mere hours before he was murdered by a Marzudi brigand. Tradition differed as to whether the prophet had foreseen his death, but all agreed the teaching was inspired and providential, given what was to befall him that night.

"Nevertheless, the Fire is unquenched, and I shall live in it until the renewal of all things, and then you shall see me again."

It had been her grandfather's favorite doctrine. More than all the esoteric teachings, more than the sacred hymns—this had been his favorite.

"When I depart, mourn me if your hearts demand it, but rejoice and delight, for this body you bury shall rise again."

She imagined her grandfather seated beside her, his unseeing eyes somehow bright with insight as he listened to her reading.

Her lips quivered, her eyes blurred.

She forced herself to swallow.

"And do not lose what I have entrusted to you, but keep it burning in your hearts until the last day when the struggle is complete and won.

"When I am gone, you will mourn me and malign the time, but I tell you now, all happens exactly as it ought. This is the Truth of Fire."

A long, tremulous breath slipped out from her lungs as tears spilled down her cheeks.

She set aside the scriptures, dried her eyes and face, and went to the door, lamp in hand.

After giving the room one last look, she whispered farewell and blew out the light.

9

THE WILL TO RULE ONESELF

I TEACH STRENGTH IS A VIRTUE, and those you call righteous blink, for they have made a virtue of weakness. Soon they will venerate sickness and offer sacrifice to deformity!

—Zaro's Sayings, verse five hundred and forty-two

SHARASTHI HAD NEVER TRAVELED FAR from Ashmuz. Now, every day was a constant haze of movement. As a prospective Initiate of the Adept Corps, she had the privilege of sharing the saddle with those few Lazarrans on horseback. In the first stretch of the southward journey, most often she rode with the captain.

Then, about two weeks in, she began to ride with Adept Rufus. They were far enough now that he no longer had to hang about Vantelle all day in case the Hunters launched an attack. Even so, Sharasthi noted that Legion Scouts frequently left the company, some going on ahead, others going backward, only to return a few days later bringing reports to Rufus and the legate.

Sharasthi recalled the vitriol in Claw-face's visage and voice as he upbraided Vohman about the Lazarrans. Extra caution seemed prudent.

It occurred to her that—if fortune was particularly kind—a fatal encounter between Vantelle and the Hunters would solve half her vendetta, or the entirety of it, were she lucky enough. But in her heart she knew such a thing would not happen. And even if Vantelle took a black-feathered arrow through the eye, even if Claw-face burned alive in Rufus' arcane fire, it would not satisfy the higher purpose she had inherited from her grandfather.

Ordo Draconis Laevisomnis. The Order of the Sleeping Dragon. Every morning, every night, she recited to herself the etching she had memorized. Somehow she would find this Order in Lazarra—wherever they were hiding—and bind herself to their cause. In truth, she already had joined herself to it, it was the organization to which she needed to graft herself. She had no choice but to hope that if she could recite Ciell Aenan's abbreviated message, that would be sufficient proof.

Doubtless it would be difficult—if they could hide from the eyes of Arkhon and his subjects for centuries, discovering them would prove no mean feat—but she had years. And, she believed, she had the will of her grandfather with her. Some spark of the Fire within him now burned in her. All was Fire. Even now, she was connected to him.

While dawn and dusk she spent ruminating on these things, the time between she spoke with Rufus.

One morning, before they mounted his horse, the Adept asked her age, and when she answered fourteen, he scowled.

"Most Initiates begin at twelve or thirteen. By the time we return, it may be too late for you to begin."

That sent a lightning bolt through her heart. Before she could gather her thoughts however, he went on.

"Only a young mind can integrate the arcane revelations properly. There is a narrow space between the youthful manifestation of potential and the shackles of a mature mind."

He fixed her with a stern gaze. "So we will begin now."

To keep the principles of magic secret, Rufus kept his horse at a distance from anyone else. After years of learning from her grandfather in the candlelit gloom of the temple archive, the bright, open space struck her as stark contrast.

Even so, hidden knowledge was hidden knowledge.

"Aether," said Rufus, "is the unseen power that fuels magic, but not only magic. Great men—be they warriors, orators, artists—all possess a subtle awareness and connection to the aether. The talent of an Adept is to draw upon more aether than any other mortal—to draw it *in*—and to shape it as the potter does the vessel."

Aether, Sharasthi decided, was not so different from the Eternal Flame. Rufus had no issue with her thinking of it like so; indeed, he suggested the prophet Zaro may have spoken of aether when he articulated his doctrines. The designation did not matter so much as how well she grasped the essence of it.

One of the prophet's dicta came to mind: '*What is unnamed is less than what is named, but the unnameable is greatest of all.*'

The Adepts did not worship aether though, and Rufus took care that Sharasthi would not hold herself back from applying magic out of some religious scruples.

Sharasthi had no such hesitation; if anything, it spurred her on to think the Eternal Flame would give her the ability to accomplish her desires.

She *did* wonder about what had happened to her fits. Ever since the Adept had pressed his arcane focus to her, she had not experienced even the slightest touch of one. *Touch*—why had she felt those arms around her shoulders? Why had they squeezed her just before Rufus banished them?

Her grandfather had taught her old secrets about the world—about the realm of spirits, the *ahura* and the *daeva*—and he had told her how it was a Zarushan magician who first bound a spirit, and how this same power underlay the Lazarrans' arcane focus.

The only conclusion she could draw was that her soul-whirling episodes had been the work of some spirit, and that Rufus had bound it.

What was she to make of that? Vohman had said she must never speak of such magical principles to anyone. Was this to come eventually in her tutelage under Rufus? Would she have to act surprised if he told her as much?

She knew too little, the risks were too great, and so she trusted her grandfather and resolved to say nothing of the matter.

Even so, Rufus noted she possessed an 'unusually strong inclination' to the arcane. She always seemed to ask just the right questions and to grasp his points with haste.

One day, as he was cataloguing the various magical Arts known to the Adept Corps, she asked whether she would choose her path, or whether Rufus would induct her into his *Ars Vulcana*.

"Neither," said the Adept. "Your Art will manifest on its own at the proper time."

"And when is that?"

Rufus scratched his stubble. "In a conventional Initiate's tutelage, it typically happens in the second year. The first year is focused on physical training and lessons such as these."

Sharasthi quailed at the thought of a warrior's exercise regimen. Since so much of the day was given to traveling, she had so far escaped anything particularly rigorous, but more and more Rufus required her to do calisthenics early in the morning. He made her cease sharing the captain's tent (something for which she was duly grateful) and forced her to learn to pitch her own and break it down. He also forbade her from hiding her face and arms from the sun, calling it an affectation unsuited to warriors.

So her frail body, bit by bit, was strengthening and tanning, and she thought with some bemusement that if she returned to Ashmuz not a single person would recognize her as the daughter of a priestly family.

Even so, Sharasthi got the sense that Rufus held a certain contempt—or at least pity—for her. She still wearied and grew nauseous quickly, and even though her skin had ruddied, it still burned if exposed to the noonday sun. "Something in the blood," he murmured.

Sharasthi did not feel particularly offended—her ancestors were priests and scholars. Nothing in her bore out a particular love for the violence of a warrior's life; pursuing this path was a necessity to a greater desire, not a want in itself.

Still, it would be troublesome if she never got up to scratch, so she asked Rufus how important that was for her to be an Adept.

"Well," Rufus sighed, "in most cases it would be a problem, but with your bias to the arcane there's a chance you can lean on that, like a crutch. And that's your best hope, since time is short."

He paused a moment as something turned over behind his eyes, then declared, "I'll get you to where you can manifest your Art in your first six months at the Sanctum."

Sharasthi did some brief calculations. The rest of the return journey ought to take two months, perhaps three if something went awry. At the outside, that meant she would be performing magic in less than nine months.

The thought sent a shudder through her as she recalled the relief of Marzud's possession. Every passing day seemed like a step further into some dark, yawning cave. Only the faith that she would find deep within that darkness the burning Light she sought, only that steadied her soul.

SHARASTHI HAD NOT WEPT since departing home. Instead, some roiling storm sat deep inside her throat, sending bolts of lightning through her bones and organs. In her stomach, in her skull, in her hands and feet—always screaming, always straining to shred her to pieces.

Lying alone in the night, she would stuff her cloak in her mouth and try to cry. Only heavy breaths came out. Try as she might, she could not break the lock that penned in her grief.

Time and again, she had a dream. In her hand lay a jagged rock. Inside her chest, a worm was eating her heart. She needed to take the rock and cut out the parasite.

But in front of her crouched a wolf with the head of Gormish. And as soon as she tried to extirpate the worm, the wolf would devour her—and as soon as she died, she found herself in just the same situation as when the dream began. And so it went, on and on in unbroken cycle until she woke from the dream, her jaw aching from how tight she clenched her teeth—but her eyes were still dry.

The memory of those unseen arms wrapped around her shoulders as she sat at the temple threshold—she remembered that touch, craved it, came to an inchoate certainty that if she could be held like that again, she could finally release her strife.

As the dream came again and again, she began to look for someone to protect her from the wolf with the Marzudi's face, so that she might rid herself of the death crawling inside her.

But she was alone in the dream, and when she woke, that loneliness still hung on her.

As her sleep worsened, so too did her performance in Rufus' exercises. She threw up after just an hour of running. The next day she passed out on her feet, half-delirious from the sun. Rufus channeled aether to heal and strengthen her body, but he had to ration it. There could be undesirable consequences to living off aether, he said, without treating the underlying issue.

Rufus started giving her entire days off from exercise, instead spending the time instructing her in magic, teaching her mental regimens by which to prepare herself for attunement to aether and—eventually—manifesting her Art.

That worked for a week, but her dreams took another turn. The wolf's head began to change. Sometimes it was Gormish. Then it was the engraving of Marzud, a twisted visage of chiseled stone sewn to fur and flesh at the neck. Worst of all were the nights it took the face of her grandfather's murderer.

Soon she could not sleep at all, instead lying awake, her eyes searching out the darkness for any sign of threat, until at last exhaustion claimed her as the sky lightened to gray.

The night had been her refuge. Now it seemed a haunt of monsters.

She stole an hour, sometimes two, of sleep. Her body shook, always cold. Her fingers faltered in simple tasks.

Whispers—faint murmurs of her name in the distance. She whipped her head around, only to see nobody.

Or worse, she caught sight of Gormish.

The Marzudi traveled with the lowest-ranking slaves, those responsible for menial labor and the refuse-clearing detail. Sometimes they would throw water over him in a desperate bid to wash away his horrid stench, but it never seemed to work. The writing on his forehead, too, did not wash away. *Marzud.* It was etched in him to the bone.

Why Vantelle wanted to bring Gormish to Lazarra, Sharasthi did not know and did not ask.

When she heard sounds in the night, she always imagined it was Gormish coming for her, ready to grab hold of her and babble his wretched madness before biting out her throat.

Did Marzudi really do that, or was it just an old ghost story? She did not want to find out.

Rufus, of course, took note of her deterioration, and thinking it an illness, summoned a medic to evaluate her. The legionnaire in question examined her and gave her a root to be brewed into a tea and drunk in the evenings, saying it would help her fall asleep and ward off dreams.

The tea worked, in a way. Sharasthi's nights became void. She loathed the waking hours and dreaded the coming of night, because she knew her only relief would come and vanish, and then she would have to face another day.

And even though she slept through the night, she still had not shaken off fatigue. Apparently the root could only guarantee dreamless sleep, not rest.

When she ran out of the root, the physician gave her another, smaller measure of it, telling Rufus if she became reliant on it there would be more problems down the road. It was only meant as a stopgap. So Sharasthi cursed the man in her heart, and she cursed the root, and she cursed her dreams, and she cursed the whole damnable situation.

Worst of all, she knew he was right. Her spirit had dulled from the day she began to take the brew. The more she took, the more listless she felt. The mournful storm inside her did not depart or lessen; it only withdrew deeper inside her, and so she grew even more anxious, because it too became to her like one of the wolves lying in wait just beyond her consciousness, ready to pounce.

Rufus' lessons on aether became interrogations of Sharasthi's mind. He asked her to describe her dreams. Reluctantly, she shared them, feeling like she was exposing her throat to a marauder's blade.

The Adept asked why she feared Gormish so much. She struggled to explain, but did her best. Rufus made her stop taking the root. The nightmares returned and her sleep fled, but Rufus stayed up with her through the night and started over, making her describe her dreams and why Gormish and Marzud haunted them.

Once he had heard her account, he taught her certain meditations. She was to recall the dreams in as vivid detail as possible, right up to the moment of her greatest horror—then she was to envision a different outcome.

Instead of using the rock to cut out the worm infesting her heart, she saw the pure All-Pervasive Fire burn it out. Instead of the wolf tearing out her throat, she saw the darkness turn to her aid and swallow him forever.

Sharasthi struggled through these exercises. Nine times out of ten, her imagination would slip from her control, and the nightmare would play out according to the typical pattern. Rufus looked on her with a solemn countenance and said, "Do you know the difference between man and beast? The will to rule oneself. Which are you?"

She detested the Adept for it, but she went on struggling. When she slept, the nightmares tormented her. In the day, she gave every free moment to the meditations. Rufus had her ride in his saddle so she could spend travel time on this endeavor, and she strained her heart and mind so fervently she soaked through her clothes with sweat. At first this embarrassed her, but Rufus said it was no different from training the body, and required her go on—if she would prove herself a warrior.

Her hatred for Rufus and for her life grew, but she took a grim satisfaction in what meager victories she had. The practice became so ingrained that soon she managed to keep at the meditation while walking and eating. Still, she never managed to change her dreams. Every night, she died countless times to the worm and the wolf. What did change: she managed to sleep through the night. She bore the nocturnal afflictions like a stone bearing a storm's lashes.

Her body strengthened again. She walked for an hour, then rode the rest of the day. Then for two hours. Past five, her constitution could not be pushed to bear it and she collapsed, but even so she was more hale than she had been in years.

A month into the journey, in the afternoon, Rufus took her away from the main camp. He had her sit with her back to a tree and pressed something cold into her hand.

Sharasthi looked down at the arcane focus. Fear surged up into her throat, as though Rufus had brought her to stand at the edge of a precipice. His lessons had instilled the horror of aether sickness into her, the surety that if she tried to perform magic before she was ready —a day she had believed lay months in the future—madness and death awaited.

"Perform your usual meditations," he instructed. "If you feel anything from the focus, disregard it until I give the word."

She closed her eyes and obeyed. At first, things went as normal. Then her palm tickled, the focus seemed to tremble in her hand, though she knew not whether this was real or merely a trick of perception.

As soon as she felt this, she began to withdraw from the exercise, but Rufus told her to continue. Sharasthi realized he was observing her with his aetheric sense. This both disturbed and comforted her. She pressed on.

The more times she worked through the vision, the greater the focus loomed in her awareness. Drumbeats, or perhaps thunderclaps, sounded in some distant land and reverberated in her palm, a hypnotic, swelling rhythm whose heart was the end and beginning of the nightmare. Sharasthi dreamed—was she asleep now?—faster and faster, until the full vision lasted fractions and fractions of what it once had, until the beat of the focus in her hand matched the beat of the heart in her chest.

It was a frantic, manic dream—she felt the Eternal Flame purging her heart, and she felt the darkness fill the world, devouring the man-faced wolf and plunging the world into total night.

Night. The stars wheeled above; they blazed with the light of Fire piercing through the material veil. The stars wheeled and wheeled, but never did the sun rise—it was night, and it was night, and it was night still. The Fire was light enough, and the Fire burned inside and behind all things, and the Fire filled the night—and so deep inside the darkness was an unquenchable radiance.

"Sharasthi," said Rufus. "Open your eyes."

She did so, and saw the sun had risen, saw it was day, and saw—Gormish.

Smiling, mad, babbling Gormish. The face of the wolf.

The beat in her chest and the beat in her hand stopped, and the whole world was like a breath held in.

"Sharasthi," said Rufus. "Rule yourself."

She let the breath in her lungs go, and the world exhaled with her, and the night burst forth.

From her hands, from her heart—the secret burning power inside and behind all things rushed out from her as a whirling darkness.

The Marzudi cackled as the darkness broke over him, smothered him. From inside the black, he laughed and laughed, and as he did he spat out in euphoric cadence:

"Gormish is a bull upon an altar! Where is Marzud? Where are the gods? Gormish lies where all things tie together—ah, and he is breaking, breaking upon a wheel turned by unseen hands!"

Sharasthi's jaw ached, but she did not scream. Her eyes stung, but she did not blink. She peered into the darkness and let the darkness continue its onward rush from somewhere inside her and behind her.

She was an aperture through which power flowed, just as the stars with which blazed the Fire.

The delighted visage of Gormish twisted further and further in mad ecstasy.

"Seers are blind—*ha!*—tricks play the magician upon the audience—*ha! aha!*—Gormish knows! Gormish knows!"

His words and laughter melded into one another, becoming some horrid half-language, neither a tongue of men nor of beasts. Moment by moment, the cacophony deadened to a rasping, hoarse noise.

"Sharasthi," Rufus called—and she realized her teacher stood within the darkness. Like closing a fist, she shut herself to the power flowing through her. Under the rays of the sun, the fuliginous torrent she had unleashed burned away like mist, leaving Rufus clutching a trembling, rictus-grinned Gormish.

That was the last thing she saw before she slumped against the tree, consciousness fleeing.

10

SOMETHING EXCEPTIONAL

Vantelle spoke of Sharasthi on a few occasions. She took pride in having been the one to bring her to Lazarra, of course. What's more, she wanted Sharasthi assigned to serve under her, both during her time as an Initiate and later as a full-fledged Adept. It was Vantelle's conjecture, and I am inclined to agree, that Adept Rufus and Officer Hannil somehow interfered. I have no clue how they did so or what their reasons might have been, save that they had a fondness for her and a mistrust of what Vantelle would have demanded of her.

—*The Memoirs of Flavia Iscator*

The first thing Sharasthi sensed was a bedroll beneath her, a cloak stretched over her like a blanket.

Her immediate thought was that something was missing. Then it came to her: after weeks of fatigue and strain, she had finally *slept*. Even this sleep though, was a weary one, and she longed to drop back into unconsciousness right away.

She did not want to open her eyes. She did not want to raise her head.

She did not want to think about what had happened.

Happenstance conspired to give her an excuse to lie still and silent, because just then she heard voices drawing near.

Rufus and Cassia Vantelle.

Sharasthi, well-practiced at pretending to sleep from her years living in the temple, allowed her breathing to fall into a deep, even rhythm.

"Well done, Rufus. I'm sure this will earn you some acclaim in the Sanctum."

"We'll see."

The sound of tent flaps pulled aside. Sharasthi felt eyes on her. Slowly, the tent flap went back into place. A few footsteps away.

Sharasthi had to strain her ears to catch the hushed speech from outside.

"I expected you to be more impressed with your pupil."

"It's astounding," he grumbled. "And that's what worries me. You see some kids like her, maybe two or three in a generation. Ones born with too much natural inclination to aether. It imbalances them, makes them overly reliant on magic to make up for physical frailties. One day they push themselves a hair too far and hurl themselves into the depths of aether sickness. She'll be lucky to make it to graduation."

Sharasthi's stomach went into dreadful knots, but Vantelle took it in stride. "So what is the solution?"

"Two options. One, she learns to balance herself. Trains and strengthens her body. Learns to temper and restrain her aptitude for magic." After a brief silence, Rufus went on. "That's not going to work. I've suspected from day one, but it's only become more plain since. You can see it in how she walks and talks—too much priestly blood. Even the Sanctum can only do so much to make someone like her into a warrior. She'll wash out."

"And the second option?"

"Ever been on a ship in a storm, bailing out water as you sail deeper into it, banking on the hope you'll reach the eye before you sink?"

"Once or twice."

"Same principle. The bane of an Initiate like her is to rely too much on aether and end up overstepping her tolerance. And yet, if she builds her talent as quickly and thoroughly as possible, she might be able to stay afloat until she's strong enough to make it work."

"And this has been done?"

A pause. "Supposedly an Initiate managed it during Empress Viviana's reign, but records from her time are...suspect."

"The Carnifex debacle," Vantelle muttered.

"Mm. In theory it's straightforward, but in practice? Like learning to juggle knives with a blindfold. I'll have to build her a separate training regimen. Plus take an extended leave from field work to keep an eye on her."

Vantelle digested that. "So I'd be giving you up for a few years, with an uncertain payoff."

"If it works, she'll be more than a generational talent—she'll be a once-per-*century* Adept. We might even be able to develop new training methods off of her."

Vantelle did not respond right away, so Rufus spoke again, more insistent. "I'm not one to appeal to superstition, Legate, but you said it yourself when I tested her at the temple threshold. Maybe bringing her back to the Sanctum is what makes this expedition worth something."

"You're saying this was fate?"

"Or something like it."

"I did not tell you this before, but the Emperor said I would bring him something exceptional from this journey. And he is rarely mistaken. A blade in the hand of the Emperor—that is an Adept. We bring a unique implement to his armory. See that it does not break, Rufus."

"I will do my—" Rufus cut off.

As the hasty beat of footsteps reached her ears, Sharasthi only had time to jolt upright before Rufus pulled aside the tent flap and glowered at her. Vantelle's amused visage appeared behind him a moment later.

After a few moments of tense eye contact, Rufus said, "You've a subtle presence."

Sharasthi swallowed and said nothing, unsure if she was in trouble.

Vantelle asked, "How much did you hear, child?"

"Most everything," she muttered. "My apologies." At a severe look from Rufus, she realized she was still seated in the presence of her superiors and scrambled to her feet.

"Well that spares us repeating ourselves." The legate seemed to turn something over in her head. "Rufus, you said she will need a unique training curriculum. She's manifested the *Ars Tenebrae*, and besides her talent for magic, she seems to have one for eavesdropping as well."

"Aye," he said, expectant.

A cold, satisfied smile appeared on the legate's features. "What say we put her on track with Legion Intelligence from the start?"

His brows knit. "Not a bad idea."

"Legion...Intelligence," Sharasthi echoed.

"Spycraft," said Vantelle. "Skulking about. Telling lies. A thrilling and deadly business."

Sharasthi remembered the *daeva* named Deceit cut into the temple wall. She remembered also her oath. "If you think I would be good at that," she finally said, "then I'll do it. Just..." Her eyes lowered.

Rufus gestured for her to speak.

"Just teach me how to control the darkness." Despite her best efforts, she failed to keep the tremor out of her voice. "Please."

Vantelle made a sympathetic sound. "It can be a curse to be born so exceptional—and most will never forgive you for it—but have faith, Sharasthi. You're in good hands with Rufus."

Forcing a smile, she nodded. Charming words, but as she looked at the Adept, she saw something far more authentic than what Vantelle presented.

Rufus knew she had heard everything. He knew she had heard

them speculating whether she would be able to survive training, whether she could serve as a profitable experiment.

There was a hard glint in the Adept's eyes as he held hers, and an understanding passed between them. The same sort of understanding that had passed when he asked if she would rather choose suicide.

Vantelle, for all her force of personality and self-assurance, would never know what it was like to be an Adept. Sharasthi would live with an unseen edge hovering at her throat—and if she tripped but once, she would open her jugular on it. That was not even to mention her secret loathing of the Empire, her aim to repay Vohman's death. So long as she kept up the facade, it would never harm her, but the truth was and always would be that she was *not* Lazarran. She was of Zarushan blood, and all her words and deeds of fealty would only be in service to her lineage—to her grandfather.

She feared Rufus saw through her in that moment, saw the animating hatred inside her—but then she wondered if Rufus felt the same, if he was just a man abiding in a lie so long as it served him.

She wondered.

11

TO TOUCH THE DARKNESS

YOU ASK which people is noblest under heaven. Is it we who draw the bow and speak the truth? What of the horse-tamers who draw the bow from the womb? What of the ship-builders who love truth dearer than life itself? I care too much where I set my own feet to strain my eyes peering at another's path.

—Zaro's Sayings, verse one thousand and one

THE REST of the journey passed without much fanfare. The Hunters never attacked, though there was a brief run-in with a bandit clan that quickly dispersed when they realized they were up against genuine Lazarran legionnaires.

Rufus began training Sharasthi in the application of her Art of Shadows. It was a bit like learning to walk—not with regard to any struggle, but because Rufus moved things along at a snail's pace. He said an Adept's initial awakening to magic was unique in terms of what could be done. If she tried to unleash anything close to that level of power now, she would almost certainly suffer aether sickness, or worse.

As a result, she spent most of her time practicing meditations. What little magic she was permitted to practice was this: wreathing her hands with shadows, dismissing them, then calling them forth again. Even something so unimpressive tired her out quickly, so her days were mostly unchanged and boring, but Rufus insisted she needed to progress slowly.

A benefit of her being gifted with the *Ars Tenebrae* was that it was quite safe to practice compared to other Arts. She wasn't about to accidentally burn anything down (as Rufus admitted he had during his training). The Art of Shadows was almost impossible to kill someone with.

Almost. It was rumored that, at the highest levels of mastery, such a feat was possible.

Sharasthi, for her part, was not eager to ever try anything close to that.

In other words, she was not eager to replicate what she did to Gormish.

For days after Sharasthi manifested her Art, the Marzudi fanatic was catatonic. He spent his days strapped to a stretcher in the baggage train, staring off into nothingness, occasionally flashing that rictus grin of his. He did not speak anymore, unless one considered a rare incoherent muttering to be speech.

So it went, until one cold morning when Gormish was found dead, blood overflowing from his mouth and pooling under his head. He had bitten off his tongue.

His eyes were still open, and he was still smiling.

Rufus told Sharasthi, and she felt sick to her stomach, even though she was grateful never to have to see him again.

"Did I...kill him?" she managed to ask.

Rufus chewed on that for a bit. "Who can say? Believe whatever is more bearable."

She chose to blame his fanatic mind. It did not help her feel any better.

Though Rufus saw to it that what happened was kept quiet,

Sharasthi knew rumor of it spread anyway by the number of skeptical and nervous glances she received.

Rufus was not afraid of Sharasthi's talent, but for her and others' comfort they kept their practice sessions outside the camp, in the early morning or late at night.

At first, Sharasthi could not tell the difference between working her Art in the day or at night. As Rufus gradually permitted her to leverage more and more of her power, however, she discovered the difference.

When she conjured shadows out of 'nothing' there was a greater expenditure of aether—because the aether was the stuff of which the shadows were made. An Adept, Rufus told her, was like an instrument turning air into music—the former was aether, the latter being magic's effect. Just as Rufus turned aether into fire, so Sharasthi turned it into shadows.

When fire was present, it took less aether for Rufus to wrest control of what was already there. This same principle applied to Sharasthi's magic.

Her mentor noted this all posed an interesting question, as most Karellan and Lazarran philosophers considered shadow to be merely the gradated absence of light. Zarushan thought, of course, held that the Dark was something real, if intangible.

Sharasthi did not rise to the topic, unwilling to elaborate the finer points of Zaro's metaphysics to Rufus. It reminded her too much of lessons with her grandfather. Though she ached to have something like that again, it seemed a betrayal to enjoy it with a different teacher.

Where Rufus and Sharasthi's Arts diverged the most in all this was in just how available shadows were. As Sharasthi pushed her skills further, she came to realize just how dark the night truly was. Reaching out to touch the shadows that lay as far as the eye could see...it thrilled her as much as it frightened her. She knew as surely as she could flex her fingers that if she reached out to that vast darkness, it would be hers to command, and it would not abide weakness on her part. For a dazzling instant, she would hold a mountain on her shoulders—and then it would crush her into dust.

She said as much to Rufus, and he decided it would be better to restrict her training to the daytime for the foreseeable future.

Not long after that, they reached the port of New Mizkhar and were soon underway on an Imperial ship.

Sharasthi learned something else new: she was dreadfully susceptible to seasickness.

Her lessons with Rufus took on a different shape then, moving to aether channeling—the art of fortifying the body with magic. Rufus had hesitated from teaching her to channel to ward off the possibility of her becoming dependent on it too soon (a recurring theme in her tutelage, she noticed), but seeing her lose the contents of her stomach three times in one day must have moved even his warrior heart to pity.

When she channeled aether, she recalled jumping into the little lake outside Ashmuz in the heat of summer. Cool, refreshing. In an instant, her nausea bled away and she finally recovered her appetite.

To her chagrin, Rufus forced her to restrict her channeling to one hour at a time, and while she channeled he kept a close eye on her with his aetheric sense, chiding her to ease off if she pulled too deeply.

That meant more time clutching the rail of the ship, staring out at the horizon taking slow breaths and praying to heaven as much as she cursed her own constitution.

At least, she noted bitterly, the legionnaires seemed amused. Rufus gave one of his rare smiles when she grumbled about that to him.

"To them, an Adept is superhuman. They're as scared of us as they are reliant. It's a spectacle for them to see you're just a kid yet to earn her sea legs."

"Good for them," she muttered, before groaning and returning her concentration to breathing.

"Should only be another day. Maybe two."

Sharasthi answered with another groan.

It did end up being two days until she acclimated to the waves, and at that point she was able to enjoy sailing. The vastness of the sea, the way it sparkled under the sun and moon.

When she opened herself to touch the darkness, she realized just how *deep* the sea was. It made her previous experience on land seem meager in comparison.

She asked Rufus if they could restrict her training to aether channeling for the rest of the voyage, and he agreed. Besides, now that she had found her stomach, she was expected to do work aboard. That mostly amounted to bailing water out from the rowing deck and (once she had been taught) tying knots. She was no stranger to work, but this work scraped and calloused her hands in ways that temple duties never had—and the ever-present salt water only made her all the more aware of every little cut and scratch. It provided her ample opportunity to practice her aether channeling—until Rufus realized what she was doing and forced her to hold off on healing her work-scrapes until the end of the day.

He wanted her to 'get used to discomfort.'

She obeyed, though it did not take her long to find a loophole—any time a legionnaire took an injury in his work, she offered to heal it for him. That channeling aether to someone else involved channeling it through and healing herself as a consequence was inevitable—but Rufus begrudgingly allowed it as it built goodwill with the troops, something always wise for Adepts.

One day, Sharasthi awoke in the rope hammock that served as her bed and discovered a pervasive excitement humming in everyone's actions. The way they moved and spoke and even breathed spoke of anticipation. Eyes constantly darted up to scan the coastline.

About midday, someone finally called out the first sighting of Lazarra, and a cheer went up from the whole crew.

Rufus released Sharasthi from her responsibilities so she could stand at the bow and appreciate coming into port at the city that ruled half the world.

All her life, Sharasthi had longed to see the City of Lights, the home of the prophet Zaro, the capital of her homeland. She had dreamed of the towers, the gates, the High Temple and the sprawling libraries.

Lazarra, she hated to admit, stole her breath in the same way she had imagined the City of Lights would.

First, she noticed the *sprawl*. Terraced roofs borne up by painted columns dotting hill after hill after hill. And in the heart of it all, a grand wall, inset with at least three gates that Sharasthi could see—Rufus told her there were seven in total.

Further inside the wall, the city's heart rose toward heaven on the tallest hill of all, the Palatine Hill, and even from this distance Sharasthi could see the proud triangular pediment of what must have been the Temple of Arkhon abutting the Imperial Palace.

If any city was to rule the world, Sharasthi thought, it made sense that she would look like this.

Her heart twisted as the thought flitted through her mind. *This is the enemy*, she told herself. *The enemy's home.* Her grandfather's blood was on the hands of the Parthavan Hunters and of the Lazarran Empire.

She would not let this awe steal her loyalty, her conviction.

After docking and unloading the ship, Rufus and Sharasthi appeared before Vantelle to be formally dismissed. With a wry smile, the legate congratulated Sharasthi on surviving the voyage, and bade her prove herself worthy of expectations.

Sharasthi saluted as Rufus had taught her to do and gave her word that she would, which pleased the legate. After some brief words with Rufus about a pending audience with the Emperor to discuss the expedition, the legate dismissed them.

On uncertain feet (apparently she now had to re-earn her land legs), Sharasthi followed Rufus to the Sanctum.

Along the way, Rufus received a good deal of salutes and deferential nods. Sharasthi shrank into his shadow, ducking her head and hoping to avoid the curious eyes of passersby. With a soft-spoken but decisive word, the Adept told her to stop walking like a slave and start walking like an Adept.

Of all the orders he had given, this one she was most loath to obey as she could not see what bearing it had on her ability to perform magic—but this too, she realized, was part of training. If she was going to be an Adept, she had to comport herself like one. This too was a test of what she was willing to do for the Empire—to conform herself to the pattern called an Adept.

Though it put her heart in her throat and made her face flush with embarrassment, she stepped out to walk a pace behind and to the side of Rufus.

"Shoulders, chin," he muttered. She complied, straightening up. It was impossible now to ignore how many gazes she was attracting—but at least she was able to stare straight ahead, fixing her gaze on some point above all the heads. A benefit of so much attention and deference: there was no risk of bumping into anyone.

As they approached the gate to the Sanctum, the soldiers on guard saluted Rufus and after a hearty "*Ave Imperator!*" bade him welcome home. Rufus had told her these were called the Orphan legionnaires, as they had lost their praetor long ago, along with their sister legion. The Adept thanked them both by name and introduced Sharasthi, saying she would be his pupil.

The legionnaires saluted her as well, and she returned the salute in a hasty, if clumsy, motion.

And with that, Sharasthi stepped into what was to be her home for the foreseeable future.

She prayed she would live long enough to leave it behind forever.

PART II

LIGHT AND SHADOW

12

FOLLOW THE LIGHT

One thousand will hear the Truth, one hundred may believe it, and at last one might live in accord with it.

—Zaro's Sayings, verse five hundred and three

"You cannot keep skipping lectures, Sharasthi." Rufus glowered at her from behind his desk.

"Sir," she said in an even tone, "I've already learned the material."

"Information is not the only purpose of the lectures. The other day there was an exhibition of a relic by a Carnifex."

"I know what relics are, I know that it's dangerous for an Adept to use them, and I know"—here she dropped her voice to a murmur—"to be wary of Carnifexes."

Her mentor rubbed his forehead. "Be that as it may, the wedge between you and your cohort is only worsening. One of these days someone might try something."

"They have, sir."

Rufus' glare intensified.

"Some girls stole my clothes while I was in the bath. I cloaked myself in shadows and stole them back."

"And why didn't you report this to me?"

"No harm done. It was like a game, really. I thought this sort of thing is commonplace between Initiates."

"Things happen now and then," he conceded, "but it blows over. I've started to hear from other mentors that their apprentices are growing resentful of you."

Sharasthi bit her tongue to stop saying something that might have qualified as insubordination. "Perhaps the Sanctum should consider putting my score on the rankings, so they can see I'm earning my keep same as they are."

"You're off the ranking board because you're on a different program. And yes, you're surpassing *most* of the expectations placed upon you, but camaraderie is also expected of you, Initiate."

"Yes, sir," she muttered.

Rufus sighed, leaning back in his chair and grabbing a sheaf of documents. "Officer Hannil says you're doing well in language and etiquette training."

Sharasthi nodded. Hannil was her other mentor, overseeing her training with Legion Intelligence. "Have the two of you considered my request to—"

"Denied."

"But sir," she said, frustration bleeding into her voice, "it would solve the 'camaraderie' issue."

"You're on a special track, Sharasthi, but you're still an Initiate. I'm not letting you stay at the Workshop."

The Workshop was the academy for Legion Intelligence agents. Sharasthi went there regularly for training—indeed, even getting there was part of her training, as she was tailed every time she reported. If she did not arrive with sufficient subtlety, as evaluated by her overseers, she was reprimanded. And if they thought she had done an intolerably wretched job, that merited the worst reprimand of them all: a night of 'torture proofing.'

She had no clue who was responsible for putting her through

those sessions, as they wore masks and disguised their voices, but if she ever found out she would add their names to the list of people she planned to get revenge on.

The upside to the Workshop was the private rooms where candidates lodged, as it would be a security risk if too many others—even in Intelligence—knew their faces. There were irksome protocols associated with living in those rooms, but Sharasthi would rather put up with that than go on living with her Initiate Cohort.

She had written up a formal request to transfer to the Workshop and presented it to Rufus and Hannil, but now Rufus had shut her down in a tone that brooked no opportunity for appeal.

"How are your aether exercises going?" he asked.

"Well. In a month or so I think I'll be ready for that test you've been hinting at."

"Good, but we won't rush that. You've made it three years, but let's not get too comfortable and push our luck."

"Of course." Much as she had gotten used to greater feats of magic during her time at the Sanctum, she never voiced displeasure with the rate Rufus was advancing her. Every time she worked her *Ars Tenebrae*, she remembered his words from that night—'like learning to juggle knives with a blindfold.'

"One more thing. Hannil sent this along with your evaluation." He handed her a piece of parchment covered in strange symbols. "He wants you to break this by your next meeting with him."

Sharasthi pursed her lips. She had only worked one cipher so far, and that had been in Lazarran script—she didn't even know if this was a real alphabet. She would need to spend some time in the archive. "Yes, sir."

"Then you're dismissed—on the condition that next week you can tell me with complete honesty you've had a positive interaction with another Initiate."

She clenched her teeth.

"And I mean positive in the way a normal person would think, Sharasthi."

"Understood, sir."

"Good. Dismissed."

SHARASTHI SIGHED, dropping her forehead to the smooth-grained table. Scrolls and tablets lay strewn about, but none of them had what she sought. The cipher was turning out to be even more of a headache than anticipated.

While Hannil had praised her skill in languages and etiquette to Rufus, her Intelligence training was going well in just about every other dimension too. She could keep a cover story straight under intense scrutiny. She could shake a pursuer on the streets and in the countryside alike.

None of that meant much if she couldn't break a cipher though. Intelligence operatives often had to work without immediate oversight or assistance. If she got her hands on a time-sensitive document written in code, there might not be time to get another set of eyes on it before the window of opportunity lapsed.

And of course, she would need to be able to break the code without recourse to a library full of resources. That meant she needed to memorize a whole host of different ciphers, possible variations on them, and not just memorize them but understand the theory behind them so she could recognize novel forms and such.

Turning her head to rest her cheek on her arm, she shut her eyes and thought back to Zarush, to the temple archive and her grandfather's lessons.

He used to say, particularly toward the end of his life, she had a knack for discerning the inner teachings. She had not felt like that was so, but when she first started codebreaking, she hoped whatever her grandfather had seen in her would transfer.

Unfortunately not. It was all so analytical and minute, existing on the scale of letters and words rather than ideas and discourses.

Still, she bet her grandfather could have solved one of these without a problem. She had never reached the point where he could show her the esoteric texts—the mystical scrolls and hermetic interpretations that existed at the fringes of Zaro's doctrines—but she had stolen peeks now and then. They had all been written in code, yet she had seen Vohman reading from them—before he'd lost his sight entirely—with as much ease as she read conventional writings.

If only they had had a few more years...

Her stomach knotted up. After three years, life in Lazarra had kept her busy enough that she rarely had time to recall her grief. It was a strange thing—her grandfather's death drove her onward to the day she might finally have the chance to get revenge, yet it had settled so deeply into her that it did not come to mind much. But always, eventually, it returned.

Then there was Rufus, telling her she needed to build 'camaraderie' with the other Initiates. From a strategic perspective, she knew having allies was useful (though unwitting to her true aims they must be). But it seemed, at best, an uphill battle.

They all saw her as unusual, and that made her a target. She was on a different training regimen. Her performance was not scored on the ranking board. But worst of all, she had arrived already wearing a focus and having manifested her Art—and it did not take long for word to spread that she had managed it after only a month of instruction. From the beginning, she had enemies and rivals just for being what she was. She ignored them as much as she was able. Then there were others who tried to hook themselves to her, hoping to extract some benefit from a relationship with her, but these too Sharasthi had ignored, and they all slunk away when they realized no gain was forthcoming. Such allies could never be trustworthy.

It did not matter much to her; she had her objectives and she could pursue them independently.

But...there was the old grief from losing her grandfather. The scream stuck in her throat that she had stamped down and down and down—so far down she forgot it still echoed in the depths of her soul, until a moment like this came and she recalled the loneliness, the way everything had changed in those horrid final days in Zarush.

She tried to remember the touch of those phantom arms around her shoulders, that mournful squeeze they gave as she sat at the threshold of the temple, her face to the dark and her back to the sun.

That feeling was lost to her, but the feeling of the reverberating cry she had buried deep within, that she still felt. Three years and she still had not managed to weep. That had been lost to her with her grandfather's interment. For three years that scream had whirled deep inside her, and for as much as she threw herself into her mission, eventually it called her attention back to itself, reminding her that she was alone, that she would forever be alone, and it confronted her with the dreadful possibility that if she at last got what she wanted, she would be more alone than ever, because she would have lost the vengeful longing that was her only intimate companion.

Would she finally manage to die, then? Would she then take the final way out, opening her veins in some dark room? Maybe once she killed Claw-face she could let the other Hunters kill her, riddling her with black-feathered arrows.

Thoughts of vengeance and death bloomed in her mind like flowers in the spring. Somehow they soothed and scourged her heart at once.

"Excuse me." The voice was distant.

Sharasthi screwed her eyes shut tighter. She had been on the verge of slipping into a dream.

"*Hey,* you." This time he sounded annoyed. A moment later the sharp *rap* of knuckles on wood sounded beside her head.

Sharasthi jolted upright, eyes wide and scowling. "What?" she snapped, half-realizing she was about to be in trouble if this was an Adept or senior Initiate.

It was the latter—an Initiate with a silver fringe on his red mantle glaring at her with open irritation. That mantle meant he was among the *subordinati,* the final rank an Initiate reached during training, and one step above the *acolyti* to which Sharasthi belonged. He was cleared to go on field missions. More likely than not, he had killed.

Looking pointedly at the silver fringe, she bobbed her head. "Pardon me. Can I help you?"

He snorted, though his expression didn't change. He jabbed a finger toward her right hand, which was lying atop a scroll. "I need that."

Sharasthi pursed her lips. That scroll was a resource on advanced codebreaking, the only one so far with a good lead on breaking this cipher. And there was only one copy of it in the archive. "I...also need it."

"You've been taking a nap for the last half hour," he said in a flat tone.

Well, he had her there. "Wait, have you been watching me?"

He pointed at his own face.

She rubbed her warm cheek, her fingertips brushing the marks from lying down. "Oh."

Really, she should have handed over the scroll right away, that was just the hierarchy. Maybe it would be better to give up for tonight and return to working on this tomorrow...but she was not eager to wander off and sink further into rumination.

The Initiate sighed. "Show me the cipher."

Sharasthi stared for a moment, then slid the parchment over to him.

He loomed over it, his blond eyebrows knitting together in concentration. His eyes were blue, and when he narrowed them he looked almost angry. As his lips moved silently, she realized he had not shaved in a few days, which was against dress regulation. Maybe since his hair was light enough no one had noticed yet.

"First word is *weaver,* in Karellan," he declared, sliding it back to her. "That should be enough to get you started. I'll take that scroll now."

Sharasthi blinked. "How did you figure that out?"

A brief annoyance flashed across his face, then softened as he began explaining. "See this symbol? That's particular to a certain family of ciphers that developed in eastern parts of Karella."

Sharasthi rubbed her temple. "Isn't that a Mizkhari character?"

His finger jabbed the parchment. "It looks like one, but see how there's a tail on the side there?"

"I...assumed that was a scribal error." Her face heated. She *had* noticed, and she had dismissed it.

"Common mistake. Now you won't make it again. It's a *modification* of a Mizkhari character. This cipher developed when there was a particular enthusiasm for Mizkhari culture in eastern Karella. Aristocrats signaled their sensibilities by wearing Mizkhari fashion, reciting their poetry. The character in question is the one for *weaver*."

Sharasthi opened her mouth to ask a question, but he was totally absorbed by the cipher.

"If you try Karellan *weaver* for the first word, it's a possible match, but you need to verify that. If you look at the third word on the second line, it also has a modified Mizkhari character, this time for *daughter.* Try Karellan *daughter,* and it also matches, and you can check the common characters between those words to corroborate."

She was about to try and say something again, but then she saw how engrossed he was—how his eyes lit up with interest, how fast his lips moved—and had to suppress a smirk.

"Next you find all the signal words with tweaked Mizkhari characters, test that method on them, and you should have your key, at least for the first stage. I'm fairly certain this one has a second layer to it. And be careful of the signal word on the second to last line, it might be a trick... What?"

He was looking at her with an arched eyebrow.

Sharasthi realized the smirk had reasserted itself. She covered her mouth and cleared her throat as she rearranged her features. "Nothing, you just seem very enthusiastic about this."

"Is that a surprise from someone trying to get ahold of a manual on advanced codebreaking?"

"I don't think most people get quite so excited about it."

That got her a flat look, as if he couldn't see the point in the remark.

"Also," she added, "I don't think most Initiates could do all that work in their heads, certainly not so quickly. A passion of yours?"

He shrugged, though he did not seem displeased. "We all have our talents."

That sparked something in her mind. She pushed the scroll to him. "Here, you've more than helped me, just promise you'll let me take another look at it before you shelve it."

"I'll probably be here until curfew."

"Perfect." That got her a questioning look, but he took the scroll and headed off.

As soon as he rounded the corner, Sharasthi rushed off to find a Mizkhari dictionary. Then she returned to the table, grabbed her wax tablet and got to work with her stylus. A few minutes later, she frowned, erased it all, began anew.

Time slipped away, and before long the archive had darkened sufficiently that an ordinary person would have had to get some light. But Sharasthi had the *Ars Tenebrae*. One of the most eminent benefits of her Art was that, when she touched the shadows, they opened up to her, letting her see as clear as day. It was handy for working in the archive late at night without having to spend her meager allowance on lamp oil.

After about two hours, she checked and rechecked her work. If she had made a mistake it would be quite embarrassing given what she was about to do.

Cradling her wax tablet, she set out scouring the archives. Most of the tables were barren now. One of the Initiates on duty gave her a stern look as she rounded a corner at speed. "Walk," she chided. "And the library closes to Initiates in half an hour."

Sharasthi made her excuses and asked if she knew where the boy from earlier was working.

As soon as she'd gotten halfway through describing him, the on-duty Initiate said, "Oh, he has a desk on the second level. Just follow the light."

That was a surprise—the desks on the second level were all reserved, and almost entirely for full Adepts. And what did she mean by 'follow the light'?

She slipped up the stairs, grateful again for her ability to see through the gloom given how dark it was, and got an answer to her question.

From a desk in the corner came a brighter glow than any oil lamp could provide. If anything, it was like a torch, but far too even—not to mention that torches were strictly forbidden in this building.

Sharasthi started making her way over. When she caught sight of him, he was bent over the scroll from earlier, one hand raised above his desk and radiating a constant stream of light. *Ars Lumens*—how appropriate for someone who worked late in the stacks. From what she could recall, Adepts of the *Ars Lumens* had a gift of insight and curiosity—sometimes to their detriment. No wonder he loved deciphering so much.

Her next step faltered. Was it dangerous to put herself in the sights of someone born to sniff out secrets? He had not seen her yet. She could leave and nothing more would come of it—at most he would run into her sometime in the future and comment on her rudeness for leaving before he could get the scroll back to her.

She clenched her fingers on the tablet.

Rufus was expecting her to have a report of a positive interaction with another Initiate. If she told him how she had gone out of her way to do this, that would qualify.

She walked forward.

He was so absorbed in his work that she had to poke his shoulder, earning her a scowl. "Hm? Oh, you. Yes, it is almost time. Just give me a few more..."

He trailed off as Sharasthi placed her wax tablet atop the scroll.

"Did you want me to check your wor...what is this?" He frowned, shining his light on the product of her past two hours' efforts. "The same cipher?"

"I was testing whether I understood what you taught me. Hiding things...is easier for me than uncovering them."

"Hm. I suppose," he said in a distracted voice. The code had his attention. He frowned, muttered to himself. Sharasthi suddenly felt abashed. She had been so focused on the work of ciphering her message, she had not reconsidered whether it was a good idea.

Then he snorted, and for the first time he cracked a smile.

"Protocol to introduce yourself. Do not set a bad example for your juniors. How rude."

He leaned back in his chair, appraising Sharasthi with a wry grin. "Actually it's protocol for the lower ranks to introduce themselves first, *acolyta.*"

She blew out a frustrated breath. "This *acolyta* thinks you spend too much time alone in the archive if that's your response." Not that she was one to talk, but he didn't know that.

They looked at one another for a few moments, him maintaining his smirk and raising expectant eyebrows, her trying to look stern.

Thinking of Rufus' annoyed face, she broke first. "Sharasthi," she muttered.

"That's not a protocol-proper introduction"—she opened her mouth to say something inadvisable, but he put up a hand to forestall her—"but I should set a good example for my junior, yes? Initiate Alyat, *Ars Lumens.* Seventh Cohort. Fifth year, *subordinatus.*"

Sharasthi stifled a smile, doing her best to go on looking placid in her satisfaction. "I suppose that will do. Initiate Sharasthi, *Ars Tenebrae.* First Cohort, third year, *acolyta.*"

He nodded. "Well done. Did you actually need the manual back or was that just a front to foist your cipher on me?"

Sharasthi bit her tongue. *Ars Lumens* indeed.

Mercifully, Alyat freed her from the matter. "Doesn't matter, really. It was stimulating. If doing this helps you learn ciphers then bring me more, especially if you come up with any codes of your own. We both benefit."

"Perhaps I will." Halfway through concocting a follow-up, she was betrayed by the growling of her own stomach. Her face flushed as she coughed to cover the sound.

Alyat turned aside, doing a poor job of hiding his amusement. "I skipped dinner as well. There should still be some cold leftovers in the mess if we hurry. We can talk over the rest of that cipher I presume you neglected to work on so you could put this together." He tapped the wax tablet.

Sharasthi cleared her throat again. "If you're so eager to work on more codebreaking tonight."

"I am obvious in my interests, if nothing else."

13

CIRCUMSTANCES LIKE THIS

Despite "issues of fellowship," as the Circle termed them, Initiate Sharasthi's training is proceeding well. In the face of her comparatively late start and unique challenges, she continues to surpass expectations. As the Circle is no doubt aware, her off-book overall ranking is among the top five Initiates in her cohort—and with regard to magic, first. It is clear my tutelage is effective, and therefore, it is in the Empire's best interest that Sharasthi's issues with the other Initiates be overlooked for now. Within six months, things will smooth out. If they do not, I will accept the Circle's *suggestion* that Sharasthi be transferred to another mentor.

—from Adept Rufus' reports to the Circle of Peers regarding Initiate Sharasthi's training

Sharasthi stepped into Rufus' office, where the Adept and Officer Hannil sat awaiting her—the former behind his desk, the latter on the opposite side. She would have to stand.

In contrast to Rufus' muscular bulk, Hannil cut a lithe figure. His lips were thin, his cheeks so smooth Sharasthi doubted he grew facial hair at all. There was something feline about the way he moved, though she had seen with her own eyes how deftly he could alter his mannerisms to play a part.

It was rare to meet with both her mentors at once, so she could not help feeling nervous. She had been scheduled to meet with Hannil at the Workshop, but this morning was told to come to Rufus' office instead. She could not think of anything she had done recently that merited a reprimand—or at least, nothing atypical to the usual.

"Sirs," she said, saluting them both. "*Ave Imperator*."

"*Ave Imperator*, at ease," said Rufus. As the Adept mentor, he had more authority over her, so it was to be expected he would take the lead. "First off, this was initially meant to be Hannil's time, so let's get that settled."

The Legion Intelligence officer bridged his nimble fingers. "You've worked the cipher," he said in a tone that did not anticipate the slightest disagreement from her. It reminded her of how Cassia Vantelle spoke.

"Yes, sir." Sharasthi recited from memory the contents of the assignment.

Hannil nodded once when she was finished. "Perfect. I must admit, I am impressed. I had thought that one would be beyond your abilities."

Sharasthi fought the urge to wipe the sweat from her palms. "Excuse me, but I had some assistance. I'm not sure I could have managed it on my own."

Hannil blinked slowly. "Assistance." He turned toward Rufus, who looked curious as well. The Adept gestured for Sharasthi to explain.

"I met an Initiate in the library who has a penchant for ciphers. He helped me break it. I realize I should have worked it all by myself, but as I was also under orders to build amicable relationships with the other Initiates I thought it a good opportunity."

She had reasoned that excuse after the fact, but it was not *entirely* false. Besides, it sounded like less of an excuse than saying Alyat had plowed ahead and explained the key to her of his own will.

Hannil asked for the Initiate's name.

"Alyat, *Ars Lumens*. Seventh Cohort."

The men exchanged a brief look.

"Alyat," Rufus echoed.

Sharasthi nodded, suddenly worried she had done something wrong. Alyat *was* unique in that he had his own reserved desk as an Initiate—maybe he was working on some important task for the Adept Corps and she was about to be chastised for taking his attention away.

"Well," Hannil said, "under ordinary circumstances I might have chided you for going outside the terms of the assignment, but since you were forthright about it and because this is rather fortuitous, I'll overlook that." One stern finger raised from his bridged hands. "However, bear in mind it is poor form to pit one instructor's expectations against another's. Wise tactic in spycraft, however."

Sharasthi bowed her head. "Yes, sir." The mild reprimand hardly registered. "If I may ask, when you say 'fortuitous'…?"

Hannil tilted his head back. "Alyat, like you, is a bit of a problem. Quite talented in his domain, but quite solitary. He is not on a special course, but he does enjoy some privileges as a result of his analytical skills—which you have seen firsthand, and which the Adept Corps and Legion Intelligence put to great use."

That would explain the reserved desk, she thought.

Rufus said, "Sharasthi, while you haven't been at the Sanctum for as long as others in your Cohort, you are at the age and well past the performance level where you would be expected to make *subordinata*. I was intending to arrange a field mission for you after your next magic evaluation, but given that your constitution remains lackluster by the standards of your peers, it's been difficult to find something that meets Sanctum standards without posing excessive risk to you."

Ever-honest Rufus, Sharasthi thought, keeping her expression neutral.

Her mentor continued, "A few days ago, Legion Intelligence discovered a certain situation that may present an ideal opportunity."

Sharasthi pursed her lips. "You mean I might be able to take an Intelligence operation as my *subordinata* exam?"

"Correct."

Typically an Initiate's first field mission was performed under the watchful eye of their Adept mentor. But if this was an Intelligence-run operation... "Does that mean Officer Hannil will be my supervisor?"

Rufus scratched his chin. "That's where we have to get creative. I can only bend the rules so much when it comes to your tutelage, and frankly the Circle of Peers already thinks you get too much leeway. Not to mention the resistance to ceding any sort of authority to Legion Intelligence. I doubt they'll approve of you getting *subordinata* without Adept oversight. Problem is, the nature of the operation is such that I would blow it by being attached."

"That," said Hannil, "is where the compromise of Alyat comes in. He's earned his silver fringe from the Sanctum, and he is also well regarded in Legion Intelligence."

The pieces clicked into place.

"In other words," Rufus said, "we think the Circle of Peers will approve of you taking an Intelligence mission for your *subordinata* evaluation if Initiate Alyat is on the mission, representing the Adept Corps. And in an ideal world, there's the additional benefit everyone gets of you and Alyat getting better at cooperative work.

"Truth be told, I was skeptical whether you would be interested in that arrangement, but if you've already met Alyat and worked on the cipher with him, then perhaps this is the hand of the gods."

Sharasthi chewed on that. *Subordinati* had far more freedom of movement than the lower ranks since they had to leave the capital for field work. That came with a certain degree of trust from the Sanctum, not to mention the status a silver-fringed mantle carried with those outside the Adept Corps. Conventionally, *subordinati* went on missions under an Adept, but if this arrangement with Legion Intelligence was extended...

Her pulse hastened. This was the next step toward her objective. As a *subordinata*, she could begin building out her web, making more connections...if fortune smiled on her, perhaps she would get a lead to making contact with the Order of the Sleeping Dragon.

"I'll do it. Whatever the mission is, I'll do it."

"Good," Hannil said, "but we also need Alyat's agreement. I am meeting with him tomorrow regarding this operation—if he assents to have you along, then you have the go-ahead and will be briefed. If not, Alyat takes the mission by himself."

Sharasthi nodded, already devising a plan to ensure the former. "Understood."

As soon as they dismissed Sharasthi, she made a beeline for the archive. She was dimly aware she was missing a lecture on Lazarran political history, but what did that matter at this point? Assuring Alyat agreed to the arrangement mattered far more than grasping the finer points of the *de facto* versus *de jure* balance of power between the Emperor and the Senate.

Thankfully she did not have to search hard to find Alyat—he was at his desk, puzzling over yet another cipher. *"Psst."* She poked his shoulder.

Alyat frowned, creeping out of the daze of concentration. "Hm?"

"Can we talk? It's important, I promise."

He arched an eyebrow. "How important? I'm on the verge of something."

Sharasthi bit her tongue. He didn't look *too* annoyed, but she also didn't want to risk that. What if he thought she only saw him as a tool to further her own ends?

She backpedaled. "Right, I'm sorry." Her first thought was to invite him to talk over lunch, since they had eaten dinner together the other day, but if Rufus happened to see her and Alyat speaking in the mess hall, he might suspect her of pulling something. Besides, Hannil had said he was speaking with Alyat tomorrow—there was no need to rush things.

"The olive grove tonight, by the baths. Can we talk there?"

Alyat, for his part, only looked more incredulous as she went on.

"The olive grove. Tonight." He looked around as if to check whether anyone else was listening.

Sharasthi nodded. "Does an hour before curfew work?"

He stared for a long moment. "It should," he said at last, sounding uncertain.

"Perfect—see you then." Before Alyat could get another word out, she slipped away and made her way straight for the Sanctum gate.

In order to leave the Sanctum, Initiates had to identify themselves to the Orphan legionnaires on duty. Most *acolyti* were only permitted to leave on their precious free days. When it came to Sharasthi, the guards had grown accustomed to letting her through more frequently, since she was cleared to go to the Workshop on certain days.

Today was not one of those days, and so if the on-duty guard was a stickler for checking the day's registry, she would not only be forbidden from leaving, but reported to Rufus for trying to do so.

Of course, when she caught sight of the gates, both of the attending Orphans were the sort to do everything by strict protocol.

Sharasthi considered giving up on her idea and just waiting to talk to Alyat tonight, but she wanted to stack the odds in her favor as much as possible—meaning she wanted to get ahold of a bribe.

It was not lost on her that if she had been sociable with the other Initiates as Rufus wished, she might have had the connections to acquire contraband without sneaking out of the Sanctum. Nothing she could do about that now.

What she did have was the Art of Shadows and ample practice sneaking about.

The typical way to get through the Sanctum gates was to go through a door set into the gate proper. On the outside of the gate were several legionnaires on duty, so even if she were to get past the eyes of the Orphans on the inside, she would also need to get away from the outside guards—no mean feat given that the road up to the Sanctum was a straight shot without any side streets or alleys to speak of for at least a hundred yards. In other words, it was designed to foil anyone trying to approach (or leave) unseen. The Lazarran military mind defaulted to open battles, and the architecture of the capital reflected that.

If it was nighttime, she could have used her magic to cloak herself in darkness and—with some deft maneuvering—gotten through. At midday, she would only stand out all the more moving in a shroud of shadows.

It might have been enough to make her give up on the endeavor, but something had fallen into Sharasthi's lap during her training with Legion Intelligence.

Under the streets of Lazarra sprawled the catacombs. There were entrances all over the city, and many of them were well-known since parents warned their children that if they ever wandered in, they would likely never come out.

Legion Intelligence was interested in mapping the catacombs for obvious reasons, and as part of her training, Sharasthi had memorized several such maps and demonstrated her learning by navigating from one entrance to another.

It had really been an accident that she discovered the Sanctum entrance. During one of her wayfinding evaluations, she had found a side tunnel where the map did not indicate one. Anyone else would have missed it entirely, because anyone else would have had to use a torch to see.

The opening to the side tunnel was at waist height and tucked beneath a jutting shelf cut into the rock. The light from a torch would strike the shelf and cast the opening in darkness. With the power of the *Ars Tenebrae*, however, it was plain to see. She had crawled through, eager to earn extra marks on her evaluation for expanding the map—when to her surprise the tunnel had led to the Sanctum.

More specifically, it had led to a false wall in the basement of the bathhouse where the fires were stoked to keep the thermal pools above heated.

Sharasthi imagined some *Ars Terra* Initiates had set up the false wall and the tunnel with their magic, since the tunnel's masonry was far too precise and smooth compared to the rest of the catacombs, not to mention the perfect way the wall was set on a pivot. As to exactly why these hypothetical Earth Adepts of the past had done so, she decided not to speculate.

Though the discovery did inspire her to thoroughly check all the walls in the women's bath for peepholes.

In the end, Sharasthi decided not to report the existence of the secret tunnel from the basement—and today was finally the payoff.

The bathhouse attendants kept a rather sharp watch to ensure no Initiates used the facilities outside their allotted times (all arranged with priority given to the older cohorts of course), but they did not watch the service entrance to the basement as closely. It was child's play for Sharasthi to slip inside. The only light down there came from torches and furnaces, so she wrapped herself in shadows and stuck to the walls.

All the workers occupied with tending fires and hauling water did not have a care in the world for a darker-than-usual spot in the corner of their vision.

Sharasthi took a deep breath and set her hands where she would get the most leverage. Despite a few years of training, her body was still not up to the standards of a typical Initiate. She was almost always channeling aether to fortify herself. Even on her run from Rufus' office to the library, she had used aether to keep herself from running out of breath. She had hoped that with time she would overcome her frailty entirely, but if that day ever came, it seemed to be a long way off.

At an opportune moment, she channeled a burst of aetheric strength and pushed the wall open just enough to slide her narrow frame through, then hastily shoved it back into place. She had admired how quietly the wall moved, but now the muted groan of stone sliding against stone seemed loud as thunder, and all she could do was hope the crackle of fire and chatter of laborers covered it.

In the dark of the catacomb tunnel, she waited with bated breath, sweat beading on her forehead. After a count of twenty, she decided she must have made it through unnoticed, and allowed herself a few deep, relieved breaths as she wiped her brow.

Still, there was no time to waste, so she followed the tunnel to the main network of the catacombs, crawled out under the shelf, and got moving.

A FEW HOURS LATER, Sharasthi was leaning against an olive tree, knocking dust off her sandals. Making her way through the catacombs, finding the right shop, haggling, then making her return and sneaking back in took longer than expected, so she had missed both lunch and dinner. She had emptied her coin purse acquiring the bribe, so she hadn't even been able to buy food outside—but if this panned out well then all would be worth it.

She ran through her line of reasoning for the hundredth time. Well, truth be told it wasn't reasoning so much as an offer, but she was hopeful Alyat would be swayed.

If he ever showed up, that was. Curfew was approaching, and Sharasthi preferred not to take another mark against her record right before a possible mission. It was typical for Initiates to be restrained to the Sanctum's premises until they cleared all disciplinary infractions.

At last, she heard footsteps through the grass and—with her immaculate night vision—caught sight of Alyat walking through the trees. She ghosted over to him. "You're late!" she snapped.

Alyat didn't even look startled; he just turned toward her, briefly illuminated her with his Art as if to check it was really her, and then cleared his throat. "Right. I was debating whether to come."

Sharasthi swallowed, both relieved he had and anxious he had considered otherwise. She decided it was a good thing she'd brought a bribe after all. "Ah, well, you're here anyway," she said, doing her best to sound nonplussed, "so let's—"

Alyat put his hands up. "I came here to say no."

Sharasthi gaped, her stomach dropping into a pit. "I haven't even—"

"I'm sorry, I just thought it would be better if I told you in person rather than leaving you here waiting."

She swallowed. "Hannil already spoke to you then?"

"It's not that—Hannil?" He cocked his head. "What does Officer Hannil have to do with—?"

"The operation!" she blurted out. "Hannil and my mentor worked out an arrangement that the two of us would go on a mission for my *subordinata* exam, but he said you had to agree to it." She pulled out the wineskin she had been hiding behind her back and shoved it into Alyat's hands. "I even snuck out to buy this to bribe you."

Alyat stared at the gift lying in his arms, then looked at Sharasthi and snorted. "*That's* why you called me out here?"

Sharasthi nodded, an angry twinge in her throat.

"You're funny," Alyat said, uncorking the wineskin.

"*Funny*?" Sharasthi scowled. "This is important to me."

"I'm sure it is, but you're still funny. One moment you look serious as the grave, the next you're writing coded messages to tell me I'm rude, then inviting me to the olive grove late at night—to talk field work of all things." He shook his head before taking a drink from the wineskin. "Bit of a devil, aren't you?"

Sharasthi crossed her arms, stamping down the grief-tinged nostalgia that remark stirred. "Is there something wrong with talking in an olive grove?"

Alyat smirked, giving her a sidelong look. Then something dawned on him and he gave a bark of laughter. "Oh. You actually don't know."

Sharasthi looked about. "Don't know what?"

"Nothing. Word of advice though, don't meet anyone else here." Alyat chuckled to himself before taking another drink. "Anyway, this mission. I'll tell Hannil no."

For a moment she thought she'd misheard him. "What?"

"I'm going to tell Hannil I don't want you along. I can't honestly evaluate your performance if you're bribing me."

Sharasthi stared at him. "I was just..." She balled her hands into fists. "Alyat, it's really important to me that I go on this operation. I'm not cut out for a typical field mission."

Alyat frowned. "I heard you're on a special curriculum and you were already an *acolyta* when you got here."

So he had asked about her? Sharasthi shifted on her feet. She had never told another Initiate why she was on a unique course. It would be a vulnerability, but...

She swallowed. "The truth is, I'm weak. My body, that is. I'm on a constant aether draw to meet the physical standards, and when I work my Art...Initiates like me almost all end up dying from aether sickness before earning their commission. It's a constant balancing act to ensure I'm developing my aether tolerance appropriately without outpacing what I can handle."

Alyat took this all in with equanimity. "So if you went on a conventional field mission—clearing out bandits or taking part in some border skirmish—there's a risk you'll overextend your magic, whether to fortify your body or perform your Art, and die."

Sharasthi nodded firmly. "That's the shape of it, and that's why I've been training with Intelligence since I arrived at the Sanctum. I've got better odds if I stick to that sort of work. But the Sanctum will only approve an Intelligence operation for my *subordinata* evaluation if someone from the Corps is also on that mission."

She spread her hands. "I don't know when I'll get another chance like this, Alyat."

The *subordinatus* scratched his cheek. He'd shaved since the day they met, but already new blond stubble was appearing.

"Quite a situation you're in," he said at last.

Sharasthi pursed her lips. He didn't sound moved in the slightest, but now he knew her weak spot. This was why she kept things close to the chest. She knew better than to give someone so much, there was no sense in—

"Take this." He held out the wineskin.

Sharasthi blinked, grabbing it on instinct.

"Now ask me to let you on the mission."

Her mouth worked silently for a bit, but then she found her voice. "Please let me on the mission."

"Well, I can't make any promises, but if I don't see any issues in my meeting with Hannil tomorrow, then all right."

"You—huh? But you said—"

"That wasn't a bribe," Alyat said, straight-faced despite the amusement in his tone. "You brought some wine and shared it while we spoke about your predicament. That's an admissible thing for friends to do in circumstances like this."

Sharasthi knit her brows. "I'm grateful, but what's this about being friends?"

Alyat looked at her with that same flat regard. "Usually people do things on one another's behalf because of friendship. Then the cooperation is its own reward instead of bought and paid for."

"You've known me a few days. We ate dinner once."

Alyat gave her a baffled grin. "*Now* you stand on principle?"

"Hannil said you're like me, so I'm skeptical of this. What do you want?"

"I don't want anything—just to help you out. That's how people do things. I'm not sure what Hannil meant by what he said, but I don't hate people, I just prefer not to be around them all the time."

"I don't hate people either," she protested, "I just..."

Alyat shrugged. "Whatever it is, I stand by my word. Odds are you're coming." He gave her a brief wave and turned to leave. "Thanks for the drink."

He turned to leave her standing there, words rattling around inside. She had trailed off at the end because there was no chance she was about to say aloud that she didn't trust people, that she didn't want to take the chance of getting tied together only for them to be ripped away again.

By the time she got back to her dormitory, curfew had fallen. She had to use her Art of Shadows to slip past a patrolling guard, but even then she was hardly paying attention to what was going on around her. She crawled into her bed, still carrying dust from traversing the catacombs, but she didn't pay mind to that either.

Her thoughts kept turning with the question of whether Alyat was sincere in what he had said, and how she could protect herself if not.

Always, her true objective was paramount. That was her guiding star.

She could not risk anything that might impede her chance of avenging her grandfather. If Alyat thinking of her as a friend was useful toward that end, then good—but it would only ever be from his side.

To Sharasthi, Alyat would only be a tool, an asset, an ally at best. Certainly not a friend. Not anyone close. Not anyone she could not bear to lose.

The image of him snorting and smiling as he decoded her message came to mind. The way he handed back the wineskin and talked her through what was going to happen.

She screwed her eyes tight, bit down on her pillow to smother her frustrated groan. She forced herself to think of her grandfather. Of his burial.

Not a friend. Not anyone close.

Never.

14

A LIFE OF LIES

LET none say Zaro is a renegade! I teach you ought keep the law as though the *ahura* and *daeva* sit upon your very shoulders, each ready to claim you—but I also teach you ought know for what end the law was written.

—Zaro's Sayings, verse five hundred and fifty-seven

SHARASTHI MARVELED at Hannil's ability to manufacture an ingratiating smile. She hoped hers looked at least half as compelling.

"My thanks again," he said, "for your generosity in this matter, Farilus. I can't tell you what a help this will be."

Farilus Escitan returned a pleased grin. "Please, Hannil, you are the one doing me the favor." He turned his eyes onto Sharasthi and Alyat. "How many can say they've had the honor of educating a pair of Adept Initiates."

Alyat bowed his head. "Our thanks for your tutelage and hospital-ity." Sharasthi echoed him.

Farilus accepted the sentiments with a curt nod. "Well, shall I take you about your new home? My wife is quite proud of the flower garden, you know, though I still haven't fixed up that damned shed. But the lilies just bloomed and—"

Hannil cleared his throat. "You will have to excuse me. My itinerary in Ralessa is tight."

Farilus clicked his tongue. "Ah, such a shame. I had hoped to host you for dinner, but such is life in the diplomatic service. Give my regards to old Grasico, eh?"

"Of course, but don't fret—when I collect these two next month I will be honored to share your table." He fixed them with a significant look. "And I look forward to hearing about their performance."

Sharasthi suffered an authentic pang of anxiety. If it showed on her face, all the better.

Farilus chuckled. "Oh, I'm sure they'll meet all your expectations. *Ave Imperator*, Hannil. Safe travels."

"*Ave Imperator*."

Once Hannil was gone, Farilus turned a wry look on the two of them. "I see he hasn't loosened up in the slightest."

Sharasthi allowed herself a small grin. "He is a...demanding teacher."

Farilus gave a bark of laughter. "I can imagine. Ah, no need for the stiff posture, you two. You're guests before you're students. I'm too old to stand on formalities like that." He gave a sly wink. "But keep that between us of course, I do have a reputation to uphold. Come now, let's be on that tour—we should have just enough time to get around the place before dinner is ready."

Sharasthi observed his mannerisms as he pointed out which parts of the villa had been constructed by which ancestor, which legates and praetors had stayed in the guest house—though the greatest honor of course had been when Emperor Dioclete's grandfather Emperor Sulonius stayed on the premises just over fifty years ago, when Farilus had been but a boy.

"Ah, I still remember how the purple fringe of his toga looked in the sun. *That,* I thought to myself, is what the son of a god looks like —praise High Arkhon."

Alyat commented politely as they went about, asking questions at just the moments Farilus seemed to expect them. Sharasthi thought he had a genuine interest in the property's history.

To Sharasthi, Farilus himself was far more intriguing. Because he, like her, was a liar. Unlike Sharasthi, he had accomplices—and that had doomed him.

As the proverb went, *One might keep a secret; two will clink in chains.* Sharasthi thought it a timely lesson.

Farilus Escitan, Legion Intelligence had reason to believe, facilitated a superstitious cult. The current assumption was that he was the leader, but whether or not he was at the top, he was certainly influential.

Farilus himself was quite exacting in his security. Intelligence agents had yet to find concrete evidence of his involvement in the cult, and so the locations and times of their convocations remained a mystery.

Hannil (who was not, in fact, departing the region of Ralessa, but going to take the reins of operations in the town) had briefed Sharasthi and Alyat extensively on what Intelligence knew.

The initial tip-off had come six months ago when one of the cult's members—the brash heir to an aristocratic house—imbibed too much wine in the company of a courtesan on retainer for Legion Intelligence. She had relayed his boasts to her handler, who found them credible. Since then, information-gathering had been underway.

Unfortunately, the young man was not as important a figure in the group as he had alleged. As best as Intelligence could ascertain, he had been to a single convocation where he swore himself to their brotherhood. Hannil suspected Farilus and the true core of the cult were exploiting the lad's ego for his purse, draining his funds to support their operations. Indeed, the only actionable information they had learned since the initial discovery was that Farilus was the youth's superior—which they had learned by intercepting a letter of his to Farilus.

The letters were written in a common code used by the Lazarran aristocracy—something that seemed to irk Farilus, going by his response (ironically also written in the code, as the youth apparently could not manage a more complicated system).

Farilus pulled Sharasthi's attention back when he indicated a bronze sculpture. "And this! An old Karellan work, dredged from a shipwreck lost some hundred years ago. A depiction of the god Doenysos."

Alyat hummed appreciatively. "The reconstruction of the chalice is amazing—it looks original."

"It *is* original," Farilus said with obvious pride. "The only thing that had to be reconstructed was the left hand. Don't ask how much I had to pay for it, but Doenysos is a particular interest of mine. I've become a bit of an amateur scholar of religion in my age. Oh but you don't want to hear about an old man's dalliances—come, if my nose be true, dinner should be just about ready."

Alyat raised his eyebrows. "Religion, you say? I'm surprised—it all seems much the same to me. Lazarra, Karella, the Provinces."

So he was already putting the plan into motion. They had planned to get to this during dinner, but the opportunity had presented itself and Alyat wasted no time in seizing it. Sharasthi nudged him. "*Alyat.*"

He gave her an irritated look. "Just conversation."

Farilus smiled leniently. "I'm sure it must have been quite a shock. Am I right in guessing you a Northlander, lad?"

Alyat's chest puffed out slightly. "Yes, sir."

"*Sir*—just Farilus, please. My next guess would have been Hyrgallian, but you've got the brow of a Northlander, to be sure. And you, Sharasthi, was it? You seem...Talynisti?"

"Close," she said with a polite smile. "Zarushan."

"Zarushan! I should have known. It's a dream of mine to see the City of Lights someday."

"I never saw it myself, but I'm certain Lazarra outshines it." She'd gotten used to telling that particular lie over the years, so she was sure Farilus would take it at face value.

"Mm, yes of course. So you're both from quite distant places with quite different faiths. I suppose it's no surprise you were scouted for the diplomatic service. I would love to hear more about what was most surprising when you came to Lazarra, Alyat. What I hear of Northlander religion is quite stimulating, but it's all secondhand."

He made a conciliatory gesture toward Sharasthi. "Simple intellectual curiosity, of course."

Sharasthi ducked her head, as if abashed, and let herself fall a pace behind. As Alyat and Farilus walked side by side, plunging into Alyat's recounting of the tales and gods he had grown up with, she resisted the urge to allow herself a small grin—you never knew who was watching.

But on the inside, she was quite satisfied to see the plan unfolding.

WHERE SHARASTHI DID NOT MAKE any effort to hide her feelings was on the matter of dinner. Farilus' chef had organized a grand spread to welcome the Initiates, including cuts of beef with so much fat they melted in Sharasthi's mouth. Even as the granddaughter of a Zarushan priest, she had never eaten such a fine meal in her life. For dessert, Farilus astounded them with oranges from Aspagne, which neither of them had ever tasted. The gentleman proudly explained how even if you took their seeds and native soil and planted them here, something about the Aspagnian climate nurtured the particular refreshing tang that just could not be replicated.

Sharasthi found herself wishing Hannil had given them a longer window than one month.

Farilus' wife, Sciapa, was delighted by the praise, assuring them she would pass it on to the chef. She also made no pretense about how she adored having young faces at the table again. Her and Farilus' grandchildren lived several days' journey every which way— "the price of raising ambitious children," she bemoaned, not without a helping of pride—and so she was more than eager to host the two of them in her home. Alyat further earned her favor when he complimented the flower garden, while Sharasthi did not even need to say anything to win her affections. Sciapa had only sons and grandsons (another sorrowful yet proud gripe), and her in-laws had always come to the family as grown women, so she latched onto Sharasthi like the girl she'd never had.

Any conversation about Farilus' hobbies was shelved in favor of the Escitans' questions about the latest gossip in Lazarra and life in the Sanctum. Wine flowed freely, and soon Farilus had shared a couple of stories about what Hannil had been like in their youth.

Sharasthi laughed along, covering her mouth in scandal as Sciapa slapped her husband's arm, chiding him for telling young people such lurid tales. To her surprise, she could not help feeling a certain guilt as Farilus spoke about her Legion Intelligence mentor.

What would it be like to have a friend for decades, to have shared experiences, countless meals—only for the person you knew to be a front, your relationship just another assignment?

Hannil's public-facing persona, since his early years with Intelligence, had been that of an ambassador's aide, now an instructor for up-and-coming members of the diplomatic service. Farilus had worked in the diplomatic service in his youth (a popular vocation for young aristocrats interested in seeing the world), which was how they had met.

When Intelligence discovered Farilus was influential in the cult, Hannil had been tapped because of that prior connection. How delighted had Farilus been to receive that letter from Hannil, asking whether he would host and mentor a pair of young Adept Initiates who showed potential for the diplomatic service?

Sharasthi thought—as she had many times during the preparation and journey here—about what Alyat was to her. They were partners in this mission. Not only did they have to trust one another to execute the plan—they had to trust their *lives* to one another. They had no other allies inside this villa.

She let her gaze drift to the town of Ralessa, lying in the valley over which the villa sat. If Alyat signaled for help with his *Ars Lumens*, it would still take Hannil and his men ten minutes at the fastest to make it on horseback.

When things came to a crisis, it was going to be the two of them. Alyat trusted her. And in a way she trusted Alyat—he was a fellow Initiate, he was here on a mission. It was rational.

But she still thought with scorn of that word: *friends*. He knew a little more about her than the other Initiates. He had done a charitable thing for her. That was it.

She was as false to him as Hannil was to Farilus.

Alyat burst out laughing as their host told a joke—real laughter. Sharasthi's stomach turned as she feigned her own amusement. Even though Alyat was as deceptive as she was toward Farilus, he still had something genuine in him. His deception worked so well because, for the most part, he was simply being himself.

Something deep in her recoiled at that. She loathed that he could be authentic, because she knew she could not. When the mission ended, he would be the true Alyat. She would peel off one falsehood and leave a dozen more wrapped around her.

She had known she would make a life of lies. This was what it took.

The wine cup tempted her, but her part to play was that of the strait-laced junior Initiate. She needed to drink enough to be polite, but to keep a clear head and smooth tongue.

Alyat, on the other hand, was thoroughly enjoying the fruit of the vine. Farilus was more than pleased—especially since it made Alyat so receptive to his jests—so he kept Alyat's cup full. "Enjoy, son, because tomorrow starts the work."

Alyat raised his cup. "I will never be one to refushe—*refuse* hosh-hospitality. And yours is excellent, friend."

Friend.

Farilus chuckled. "I do take some pride in the vineyard. Planted by my great-great-grandfather, you know. He chose this spot to build the family home specifically because of the soil—he was quite the vintner."

"You honor him well," Alyat gushed.

It frayed Sharasthi's nerves seeing him like this. It looked too natural. He was supposed to be serious and leaning over a slew of parchments. "I think you've had enough, Alyat," she said with genuine ire.

Alyat laughed it off. "*One* night. They don't give Initiates wine like this at the Sanctum. You should have some more."

"I'm quite all right. I apologize for his indiscretions," she said with an inclined head to Farilus.

Their host waved it off. "Nothing to apologize for, far as I'm concerned. This is a novel experience, in fact—I can't recall ever seeing an Adept so inebriated."

Alyat twirled his hand this way and that. "I don't like burning it away. In the Northlands, inebriation's ver'important."

"I hear the culture is quite boisterous," Farilus chuckled.

"Oh yes indeed, but you care about religions? It's important for that too."

Something glittered behind Farilus' eyes. Sharasthi felt like she was watching a hunter draw an arrow as a deer lapped from a stream. *Part of the plan*, she told herself.

Alyat took another full draught from the cup. "Like with Densos —*Doenysos*—and his wine. Secret mixes and brews that put you in another place."

"Another place," echoed Farilus.

Alyat shrugged. "Hard to explain. You're still where you are, but..." Another shrug.

"And you've done this?"

Alyat nodded exaggeratedly. "All the men have. Shame really. Without that, I have a much harder time..." He pantomimed swinging a sword. "Wars should be planned sober, but fought otherwise."

Sharasthi grabbed Alyat's wrist as he reached for his cup again. "Really, I think that's enough," she said through gritted teeth. "You shouldn't be talking like that."

His eyes were dull as he stared at her, and she feared he was just as drunk as he was acting. Alyat should never lack bright eyes, she felt. She was nearly about to channel aether into him to burn away the alcohol, but he muttered, "All right, all right," and leaned back in his chair, leaving the cup where it sat.

Sharasthi let out a tight sigh. "I am deeply grateful for your hospitality, Farilus, and I don't mean to impose further, but please keep this to yourself. The Sanctum has us on track for the diplomatic service because neither of us has a particular knack for war."

The man spread his hands. "You don't get to my age without knowing how to seal your lips. And really, it's all in good fun. You certainly would not be the only Adepts—or legionnaires for that matter—without a taste for the blood and mud of the battlefield. I am of course familiar with the Corps' expectations regarding Initiates' cultural integration. Not a word will leave these grounds regarding tonight. Though as a matter of purely academic curiosity, I would be eager to hear more from you about these Northlander practices, Alyat. When you're sober, of course." He shot Sharasthi a placating grin with that last sentence.

"But now," he continued, "the hour is late, and my wife seems to have drifted off." Indeed, the lady Escitan's chin was resting on her chest, she too a victim of the much-lauded vineyard's produce. "What say we retire tonight, and in the morning we will see to the matter of your instruction. The servants have drawn baths for you to wash away the road—just be careful not to drown." He winked at Alyat, who answered with a vigorous but clumsy salute.

THE ESCITAN VILLA'S baths were on par with the Sanctum's, but Sharasthi had not much of a mind to enjoy hers. She kept dwelling on the plan. In an operational sense, she could not complain. If things proceeded as well as they had been, there was no doubt Sharasthi would pass her evaluation and earn her silver. And yet— and yet there was the matter of Alyat.

They had adjacent guest rooms, so it was a simple thing to meet, though even in the apparent privacy they had to be cautious lest someone in the hall overhear.

Alyat's hair was still damp, blond strands sticking to his flushed forehead. The mirth of the dinner had gone out of him, and he unpacked his meager luggage with slow movements.

"Well, I'm glad to see you didn't pass out in there."

He raised his head, eyebrows furrowed. "I burned the wine off before I went in. Would be rude to make the servant fish me out."

"How considerate."

Alyat blinked, shot a look toward the door.

"I didn't see anyone in the hall," she muttered.

"So who is this performance for?"

Sharasthi bit her tongue.

"You're not getting cold feet, are you?"

"*No.*"

"Then explain. I need to be able to count on you."

"You can." Suddenly Sharasthi felt rather foolish, turning over the words that had been rattling in her head since dinner. "I just find it... grotesque."

"I'm not sure what to make of that."

"Never mind," she hissed. Then, in a lower voice, "Just be cautious."

"Right. You as well."

I'm not the one playing the bait. "See you in the morning."

"Mm."

Sharasthi returned to her room, unpacking her own things distractedly. A change of clothes, some writing implements for preparing reports to Hannil.

A gentle knock sounded at her door. Sharasthi answered to find a servant standing there with a familiar red garment folded in her arms. "Pardon the late hour," she said with a bob, "but Master Farilus said we ought to return this laundry to you right away. It's not quite dry yet, but he insisted. Shall I hang it for you?"

Sharasthi shook her head and reached out to take her mantle. "I'll do it, thank you."

"Of course. Good night, my lady."

When Sharasthi went to hang it at her window, she realized the servant had given her Alyat's mantle too. She considered putting it with hers and returning it to him in the morning, but people tended to be particular about their mantles. Only an Adept's focus was more significant a possession.

He's probably still awake.

Taking the silver-fringed mantle into the hall, she opened Alyat's door. "The laundry mixed—"

Sharasthi, having the Art of Shadows, had not noticed the lamp was blown out, the room dark. She only got one step in before Alyat sat bolt upright in bed, his palm blazing with bright light, his eyes wide and harsh in alert.

Sharasthi froze, the garment clutched in her hands.

Alyat, she could not help but realize, had stripped off his tunic before climbing into bed. Having first known him from the archives, she had always categorized him as the scholarly sort—which, having grown up in a Zarushan temple, carried associations of an inert lifestyle that left one doughy.

Alyat, for all his bookish habits though, was still an Adept Initiate—which meant when the arcane radiance cast the room in brightness, the cold gleam highlighted the hard contours of his body.

His arcane focus flashed with reflected light, drawing her eye to his chest where some dark, linear design circled by angular runes was etched over his heart.

Also, he had swung one leg out, as if preparing to jump to his feet and fight, leaving but a corner of the covers guarding what remained of his modesty.

All this struck Sharasthi in a heavy, hurried heartbeat. When Alyat realized the intruder was just her, he let out a taut breath and dimmed his magic. "Knock next time," he sighed in the darkness as he slumped back down into the covers.

"My mistake," she stammered, pulling her unhindered eyes away before tossing his mantle onto the desk and beating a hasty retreat to her room.

After shutting her door and leaning against it, she groaned, putting her flushed face in her hands, desperately hoping he was sleepy enough to forget this all by morning.

Living at the Sanctum, she had not quite followed the other girls' fascination regarding the boys. She had totally devoted herself to her aims, unconcerned with the distraction of the opposite sex.

Now a few years' worth of ignored adolescence crashed in on her all at once.

She paced around in circles, her own need to sleep nowhere to be found. In yet another display of Escitan wealth, her room had a mirror, and every time she caught sight of herself she noted the color had still not left her cheeks.

"This is ridiculous," she told herself, even as images of Alyat kept looping around in her mind. The more she tried to banish them, the more they badgered her.

Eventually she tried crawling into bed and closing her eyes. Darkness invited yet more unwelcome thoughts, so she tried keeping her eyes open and staring at the ceiling.

Her heart would not cease thudding in her chest. *What was that tattoo on Alyat's chest?* It looked nothing like the legionnaire tattoos they would receive on their shoulders at the completion of their tutelage. She wondered if tattooed skin felt different to the touch—

She groaned into her pillow. "This is what fools are like," she mumbled, face down, then tossed left and right before ending up once more on her back.

Doctrines, she decided. *Think of doctrines.*

All is Fire. Earth, air, water, behind it all burns Fire. Flesh is—

She swallowed, screwing her eyes shut before returning to her concentration.

All is Fire. Matter and Spirit are Fire. Life is Fire. Fire burns in the mysterious union of man and wo—

She lifted her head and let it drop against the pillow, blowing out an angry breath.

In the end, what came closest to working was inventing ciphers—though even then she had to be mindful lest Alyat poke his way into her brain and start decoding.

After managing a few fitful hours of sleep, Sharasthi dressed for breakfast.

"Oh dear," Farilus intoned over a plate of fruit. "Was something wrong with the bed, Sharasthi?"

"No," she said with a weary nod. "I just don't sleep well in new places. I'll be all right."

Alyat on the other hand appeared perfectly well-rested. Somehow that gave her a spark of anger that carried her through the day.

And, mercifully, he had either forgotten or chosen not to bring up her nighttime intrusion.

She never forgot to knock from that point forward—though every time she did, something tugged on her heart and stomach.

15

INTO ENDLESS VOID

WHAT IS THE DARK? Where can it be found? It is that which is not, and it cannot abide that which is. Yet it lurks in every place, in every heart.

   —Zaro's Sayings, verse fifty-four

"EITHER WAY," Vedorus drawled, taking another swallow of wine, "much as I adore the ladies of Lazarra, I must vouch for the *hetaerai* of Karella as utterly superb in *every* manner."

Sharasthi forced—another—laugh. "You've had quite the range of experiences on your travels."

He nodded solemnly. "It broadens the mind. Though I must confess I've not had the pleasure of visiting the much-vaunted Silver Lilac."

Most of Sharasthi and Alyat's days with Farilus were, in truth, rather dull. Farilus helped them practice their languages and drilled them on certain foreign customs, but they mostly served as amusement for the gentleman's various guests. This too was meant to be diplomatic training—they were learning to entertain dignitaries, and

Farilus' associates provided ample supply. Retired officers, Senators past and present, even some retired Adepts who lived in the country-side and came to visit now and then.

Evenings were more eventful, as Farilus had a penchant for throwing expansive banquets. Sharasthi and Alyat would dress in their formal attire and work their way about the gardens and dining hall, listening to stories, laughing at jokes, giving word of the latest gossip from the capital. Inevitably, there were young aristocrats of their age at these parties, and they were only too curious to examine the Adept Initiates and, at various turns, seek their favor or attempt to take them down a peg.

Tonight was one such event—and Sharasthi found herself wishing she had taken a conventional field mission. Bloody combat seemed preferable to listening to this lout's prattle. Unfortunately, said lout was Vedorus Tulsche, the nephew of a standing Senator, and so Farilus would doubtless evaluate how she handled this.

She had to admit, she was almost impressed by how earnestly Vedorus undertook the enterprise of ranking courtesans—somehow the same Lazarran stock that produced the most serious soldiers in the world also reared the most devout decadents.

"And you're Zarushan by blood, you said? Remind me of your name, my starling."

"Sarasti."

"*Lovely*. Exquisitely exotic."

It was the Lazarran rendition of her name—which she loathed.

Sharasthi cast a surreptitious glance around the rest of the garden. Farilus was nowhere to be seen at the moment—probably in the dining hall. The same for his wife. Alyat had been around a few moments ago, but now...

"Ah." Vedorus clicked his tongue, taking a step nearer and raising his hand. "You have a speck of dust on your dress, Sarasti. Allow me..."

Sharasthi drew an extra measure of aether to hasten her sidestep, and his fingers passed through empty air where her breast had just been.

He laughed. "I don't bite, dear."

Manufacturing as inoffensive a smile as she could, she replied, "But you did learn seduction from a book."

Vedorus blinked, looking like she'd just thrown her drink in his face, and cleared his throat.

"If you'll pardon me, I'm needed by the lady of the house." She took care to make as gracious a departure as possible, though as soon as her back was turned, she twisted her lips. Sciapa Escitan, as far as Sharasthi knew, had no need of her—but she was always eager to draw Sharasthi into some nonsensical blather. It was as good an excuse as any to make an exit.

Sharasthi found a vacant patch of grass behind a trellis of roses and threw her wine on the ground with a sigh.

She had not been out of line with her retort—an Adept Initiate had enough status in Lazarra that she was entitled to speak frankly to an aristocratic youth—but what etiquette permitted and what was wise were often two different things. Now she might have to deal with the potential fallout of Vedorus bad-mouthing her.

Hopefully he would be too wary of her telling the full story.

By convention, courtship in Lazarran high society had a defined pathway. If a woman wanted to rebuff a man's initial advances (which often happened with the assistance of intermediary associates, though not always), she did so subtly, in a way that let them go their separate ways as if nothing happened between them. Plausible deniability and the dignity of all parties involved were preserved—whatever rumors flew were, of course, but rumors.

But there was courtship, and there was romance. Regarding the latter, there was no ending of ideas, practices, and scandals—all of which were to be found in the *Ars Amatoria.*

The *Art of Love*—which Sharasthi read as part of her Intelligence curriculum—was the work of a brilliant and well-regarded Lazarran poet. So well-regarded, in fact, the Empire had looked the other way on his titling the manual something reminiscent of an Adept's mystical Art. Admittedly, Sharasthi had found his works of narrative verse riveting, and even the *Ars Amatoria*, in *style*, was certainly impressive. In substance…well, it had been beyond her at best, disconcerting at worst. She had been particularly unenthused by the author's instruction a man pretend to brush dust from 'thy lover's fair bosom.'

When she had recognized the gambit, she more or less called into question Vedorus' manhood. One brusque turn deserved another. Sharasthi snorted, imagining how many courtesans had noted his derivative methods but held their tongues for sake of lucre.

Her amusement faded though, as she needed to get back to working the party. Unwilling to go back to the gardens, she decided to stay amongst the bushes and make her way toward the house. Farilus, as a proper host, always ensured the dining hall never ran out of the broad range of foodstuffs he put out, and to Sharasthi's surprise, that had included a Zarushan cheese she hadn't eaten in years. It was a meager comfort in these otherwise dreadful evenings.

She came to a stop, her vision detecting a figure standing in the gloom of an apple tree. A moment later, she realized who it was.

"My, Sharasthi." Farilus raised his eyebrows, then smiled warmly. "You wanted to get away too, eh?"

Her host was absently swirling a wine cup in one hand as he looked toward the gardens. Sharasthi strolled over, picturing a view of this tree from the perspective of the banquet, and realized they would be obscure to all but the keenest observer. "Vedorus Tulsche likened me to a starling."

"Beautiful bird, though I imagine his delivery was heavy-handed."

"Not as heavy-handed as trying to replicate a maneuver from the *Ars Amatoria* on my person."

"…the speck of dust?"

She nodded.

"Gods above," he sighed, taking a drink as he surveyed his guests. With a click of his tongue, he muttered, "Such rabble."

Sharasthi blinked. He was talking about some of the most elevated people in the Empire.

"I have deep affection for them all, of course—even the ones I detest." His head shook gently from side to side. "But sometimes, the noise...the smell... Have you ever smelled Aspagnian perfume mixed with an inebriated glutton's vomit? A touch of filth ruins the loveliest things."

"I'll take your word for it."

Farilus scoffed. "Ah, but now I'm the old man pontificating to the youth. Every station comes with its own pains, Sharasthi. You do a fair job of hiding your displeasure, though."

She cleared her throat. "Clearly not fair enough."

"Well, I'm old hand at this. Hardly anyone has been reading people—and foiling those trying to read me—for so long. Magic is a wondrous thing, but I do have a few decades on you. Not to mention, I'm sure I would be off balance as well if Vedorus Tulsche tried to paw at me."

Sharasthi cleared her throat again, trying to cover the snort that rose unbidden at that image.

Farilus let out an easygoing, tired laugh, then perked up. "Ah, Alyat."

At first, Sharasthi started, thinking he too had somehow joined them in the shadows, but no, he was in the gardens—and with a menagerie of young noblewomen trailing. Sharasthi pursed her lips, then remembered Farilus was observing and tried to put on a mask. Then that too she found herself unsure of—their first day here, he had seen her chiding Alyat for his behavior. Perhaps it was better to keep that up?

"Quite a lad, he is. I'm sure you're both exceptional pupils at the Sanctum."

Sharasthi nodded slowly. "I don't know if I can speak for myself, but Alyat is incredible. His skills earned him special privileges in the library."

"No wonder Hannil got ahold of him. That old fox always had an eye for talent."

Sharasthi subtly examined Farilus' features. What was going on behind those eyes? Was he even now making plans for how to approach Alyat? Could she coax him into taking the bait somehow?

Before she could formulate anything though, Farilus said, "That goes for you as well, Sharasthi."

"Excuse me?"

"You are a remarkable individual, I mean to say. *Ars Tenebrae*, scion of a priestly line, learned beyond your years. You'll do great things, I'm sure." He turned to her, a kind smile on his features. "Great things."

The shadow of her grandfather's face brushed her memory. Fingers of guilt twisted her insides. She knew well how deeply someone could bury a lie, a hidden motive, an agenda—but part of her could not help but hope that Farilus had none. That this was all somehow a grave misunderstanding by Legion Intelligence.

"Well, you've listened to me go on long enough—and you'll have to bear with me yet longer after all this is done with, so take your escape while you can. I'll see if I can disengage Alyat from his harem before that legate's daughter has a swollen belly."

Sharasthi wished she had a drink to soothe the sudden itch in her throat, but at least it was dark enough to hide the flush coming over her.

THERE WAS a routine after the banquets. In the wee hours of the morning, when Sharasthi was bone-tired, Farilus made her and Alyat recite the names of everyone they had spoken with, along with what they had talked about and who else had been present. The gentleman seemed indefatigable, and he expected them to perform as well exhausted as they could otherwise. He made them draw conclusions about who had longstanding rivalries, who had once been friends but now were enemies, who was having an affair and with whom they were having it—somehow Farilus knew all of this, and gradually, Sharasthi and Alyat came to read the signs as well.

Nights with no parties were devoted to their mission. Sharasthi wrote coded letters to Hannil, and when they received their responses, Alyat would decode them. The letters were sent and received at certain dead drop sites in Ralessa, where Sharasthi and Alyat went every other day with the estate's servants on their errands. Soon they had learned the names of the foremost vendors as well as the local officials. Children would wave to them and ask how things were up at the villa, to which Alyat always responded, "Just fine."

Sharasthi dreaded all the mingling and conversing. Every person who came to know her face, she felt all the more exposed. It felt like the exact opposite of what she was supposed to be doing on a mission for Legion Intelligence, yet it was exactly what they had to do.

Their progress in sussing out the cult was slow going, at best. Now and then Farilus hosted certain guests privately, and Sharasthi would use her Art of Shadows to hide in the darkness and skulk near the window to listen in as well she could, but the guests were cautious and hid their faces, so she never got more than a side profile. If she saw one of them on the street, she very well might not recognize them.

Alyat had slightly better luck. He often spoke with Farilus on the matter of religions, particularly Northlander religion. Sharasthi was not present for those conversations, as she was typically keeping the company of the Lady Escitan, but from Alyat's report, he believed Farilus was getting closer to issuing some sort of invitation—or at least dropping his guard around Alyat. If he could lure the man into saying something incriminating, it might at least provide a new lead.

Sharasthi's conversations with Farilus' wife however, she could only endure. The woman was a chatterer, and she expected Sharasthi to keep up with all the details of her and her friends' melodrama. The latest scandal was that her friend's cousin's adopted daughter had broken off her betrothal to a respectable Lazarran officer and run off with a Parthavan horse breeder.

The story caught Sharasthi's interest because of the mention of Parthava, but it soon became apparent there was nothing meaningful regarding the Hunters. If anything, once the initial curiosity wore off, it only frustrated Sharasthi all the more—a reminder of how far she was from answering the wrong done to her grandfather.

The thing she enjoyed most was her nocturnal confabs with

Alyat. Even though they rarely made much progress with regard to their objective, at least he was sane, only concerned with all these parties and gossip insofar as it cohered with their story. Also, after he heard what had happened with Vedorus that one evening, he took care to keep him far away from Sharasthi—not that the Tulsche seemed particularly eager to face her again, but Sharasthi appreciated the concern on Alyat's part.

During those late night meetings, she started to notice little things. How his right eyebrow crooked slightly when he puzzled over a cipher. When he griped about the young aristocrats at the parties, he scratched at his stubble.

There was the unique, half-clipped way he pronounced the *th* in her name—neither a hard Lazarran *t* nor the softer, full *th* of her mother tongue. He got the *r* perfectly right though.

As they worked quietly over their correspondence with Hannil, Sharasthi sometimes felt a little thrill at the knowledge of their shared conspiracy—in the very home of their target—and then as soon as she realized what she was feeling, she shut it away.

She refused to allow herself any sort of deeper connection. They were colleagues. Not friends, no matter what Alyat had said. Certainly not...any of the suggestions that lodged in her mind at night.

One day, Alyat commented that she had gotten quite fast at encoding their letters. Her cheeks warmed. "It helps me fall asleep," she muttered. "I get lots of practice."

"Hm. Practicing ciphers would keep me awake."

"It gives me one thing to focus on. Otherwise my mind runs in circles."

"I suppose I could see that."

Sharasthi narrowed her eyes. "What do you mean by that?"

He shrugged. "You don't talk half as much as you seem to have something going on inside your head."

"Not all things can be spoken of."

He tipped his head. "True enough." He took another look at their latest communiqué from Hannil. Their handler had uncovered a possible indication Farilus' cult was going to gather soon. He wanted them on the lookout—already three weeks of their time at the villa had elapsed. In just a few days, he would be due to collect them and thank Farilus for his assistance, and then this opportunity would be gone.

Sharasthi finished writing their response, which would confirm receipt of Hannil's orders and inquire whether he might be 'delayed' in his return for a week, in case nothing came of this latest lead.

In part though, she hoped nothing happened. It meant she would need to pull off some other feat to earn her silver, but maybe that was preferable to Alyat acting as bait. Even though he seemed to have no fear on the matter, there was always going to be some aspect they could not control if Farilus tried to invite him. So many factors that could go wrong, lead to bloodshed...

Sharasthi sealed the letter and stood, tucking it away. She was always the one to place and retrieve the letters from the dead drops, using her magic to darken the area just enough that even if anyone was looking they would have no clue what she was doing. She'd bring it tomorrow on the usual errand run.

"You're getting to bed early," Alyat observed.

"No, I'm taking my bath late," she sighed, making her way to the door. "The lady always wants to chat in there, so I've started waiting until she's asleep."

"You poor thing," he said by way of farewell.

"Truly." She slipped back to her room, quickly hiding the letter and gathering her things before heading out. The usual servant who helped her with the bath was not there, and the woman there instead said the former had fallen ill. Sharasthi did not particularly care either way, though she noted this servant was more gruff in the way she moved and spoke. It put an image of a sow in her mind.

The water was less warm than usual—the price of going so late— but not outright cold. Even so, Sharasthi couldn't help but wrap her arms around herself as she sat in the pool. The weather had chilled since they first arrived at the villa, so now she had to keep the window shutters closed when she slept.

Maybe I'll ask this girl if she can get me another blanket for tonight.

Her mind then proffered another option for keeping warm, which she fervently dismissed.

Foolish. Just imagine how he'd react if I...

She sank lower in the water, letting it cover her flushed cheeks. She had not asked about the tattoo. Farilus probably knew all about it from their talks about the Northlands. That seemed unfair—Farilus was their target, she was Alyat's partner, why should Farilus know something about him that she...

Foolish. Foolish, ridiculous, nonsensical. Not even worth considering.

She was going to go to bed, wrap herself in blankets, and drift off doing ciphers. She did perfectly well keeping her mind clear during the day, and she would do the same at night. She would not allow herself any imaginings of Alyat, especially not of his arms wrapped around her, warding off the chill...

Her stomach was taut. The water was cold now.

She looked about and called for the servant, but no one came. Sharasthi frowned. Maybe she had been left to fend for herself. There was no towel beside the pool.

Gritting her teeth and channeling an additional measure of aether to fortify herself, Sharasthi climbed out of the water and padded into the antechamber where she'd left her clothes.

"Hello?"

No answer.

Sharasthi shook her head, muttering to herself as she looked for something to dry herself off with. Ordinarily there were a few by the...

"My apologies," said the woman servant, making a reappearance with an armful of towels, along with another girl who likewise had a load in her arms. "They were all at the laundry." She seemed to take longer than was necessary setting down her pile and taking the topmost. "But this one I did warm by the furnace before bringing."

Sharasthi hugged herself, shifting from one foot to the other. "That's nice," she said through clenched teeth. "Today please?"

The piglike woman did not put the towel in her hands though, instead she insisted on drying Sharasthi off herself. That was fine and conventional, but she wasn't nearly as gentle as the usual girl. Instead she was abrasive, practically smothering Sharasthi as she pushed the towel into her face to dry her head.

The forcefulness, the warm, coarse fabric scented with a powerful oil—it stole her attention for an instant, and that was enough.

Something cold touched the back of her neck.

Snick!

Sharasthi's nerves screamed in alert. She threw up her hands, a hairsbreadth from filling her limbs with arcane power—but she could not channel. Could not channel and live, because just as the blade sliced the necklace, a hand pulled it away.

Her focus was gone—and so went her safe connection to her magic. The strength went out of her—the constant strength that kept her firm despite the frailty she was born with.

She didn't have a prayer as they wrestled her down, two-on-one. She tried to scream, but they stuffed the towel into her mouth, then lashed her hands and feet.

When they finally took away the towel, it was only to force some sickeningly sweet liquid down her throat.

A nauseous wave hit her. What mortal strength she had began to fail, her bucking and thrashing fading to numb tremors as her head spun worse and worse. The servants stood up, huffing and puffing, every breath sounding more and more distant.

"That wasn't too much, was it?" asked the pig.

"She'll live," said the other. "Get the robe on her—they're waiting to start."

Someone said something more, but Sharasthi fell through the floor and into endless void, and the world was lost to her.

16

SOMETHING COLD AND GRAND AND HATEFUL

The Karellans adore their mystery rites. Indeed, sometimes I have wondered if there exists even one man or woman among the archipelago who has not been initiated into one esoteric tradition or another. Most of them, truth be told, I find uninteresting after so many years of study. But there are some...I shudder to recall what I witnessed, but shudder more to think of what power was transacted there.

—*The Life and Wisdom of Simeon Binkhok As Told by Himself*

Consciousness returns slowly and in an instant. She tries to move, but her limbs are heavy as stone, and so she can do little more than tremble.

"She's awake."

"Good, we're almost there."

She does not recognize the voices.

Again and again the impulse to channel aether stirs, but numb instinct holds her back.

She tries opening her eyes, but the dark remains. Someone has put a hood over her head. How long has it been since her eyes were veiled by darkness like anyone else's?

Cold—she is cold. There is wind, so she is outdoors. Whatever garment she wears is far too thin, and she shivers so much it hurts.

The constant swaying of the world connected with the ache in her body and a rhythmic sound that could only be hooves—she has been thrown across horseback like a corpse. Her wrists are lashed together, her hands needle-prick numb.

Sharasthi fights for breath. Her thoughts are haphazard. How long has it taken her to realize she is on a horse? Five minutes? An hour?

Then she relaxes, closes her eyes, opens them again. Darkness, still darkness. This is all right, isn't it?

Fool! You need to make a plan!

But can't Alyat make the plan? She needs to sleep a little longer.

Alyat isn't here. You're alone.

Alone? How can she be alone when her kidnappers are right there, taking her off toward...where are they going? She tries asking, but her tongue is slow and her captors ignore her.

Other things float around her skull. Alyat...plan...the plan was for them to approach Alyat. So what are they doing with her? Have they not been briefed properly?

The beast beneath her comes to a halt. Rough hands hoist her off and set her on her feet. Her legs fold and shake like a newborn deer's. Someone pulls the hood off.

People on either side grasp her arms, making her walk as they keep her from falling over.

Trees. There are trees and people hiding amidst the trees. They seem to melt out from the bark and branches. They exchange muttered greetings, bizarre handshakes. Their faces are hidden, but they leer at her with great intensity. She is like an animal at market.

Her heart beats faster, an image of a slaughterhouse rising unbidden in her imagination. The fog of the drug still lies heavy on her, but fear worms its way through, mixing with the pharmakon and working new phantoms. The trees stretch and creak and seem to speak, telling her to get away before the thing under the world swallows her.

What did Hannil tell her about Farilus' cult? Horrid rituals of initiation. What foul things are they going to make her party to?

They're not inducting you—they're using you.

For an instant Sharasthi sees herself lying on a table, knives plunging into her and carving out pieces, clawed hands stuffing her bloody flesh into fang-toothed mouths.

A desperate urge to cry shakes her, but her eyes remain dry and half-lidded, her jaw slack.

They form a procession, Sharasthi and her escorts at the fore, those from among the trees following.

If she had her enhanced sight and full faculty of mind, she might be able to look around and deduce where she is. She has studied maps of the area extensively. Perhaps there will be a clue—some natural formation, or...

But as the thought drifts across her consciousness, they bring her out from the wood, and Sharasthi knows she is utterly lost, because if anything like this was on a map, Intelligence would have scoured it long ago.

It must have been a temple once. Toppled pillars and ruined statues litter the space. Black and white tiles, cracked and smashed for the most part, yet still dizzying to look at, as they dance and trade places whenever her eyes fall upon them.

A marble head stares at her from the ground, a sublime and ecstatic emotion frozen on its immortal features. Dim lamps cast eerie shadows on the sheer and sharp rock face before which the temple sits.

The cloaked forms spread into a semicircle, ringing in Sharasthi. In front of her there is a great darkness. A pit, she realizes, gaping before the rock face.

Someone is standing beside the pit, and as the lamplight flickers, she recognizes the contours of Farilus' face. Gone is the jovial gentleman; he looks as severe as the statues.

Farilus raises his arms. He has a staff topped with a pine cone in one hand, a chalice in the other. He is chanting something—it sounds like Karellan, but not quite. An older dialect. A hymn passed down out of the sun's sight.

Time keeps marching, sometimes running, sometimes walking.

Farilus is coming around the pit, the staff and chalice gone. He has a knife. He cuts a lock of Sharasthi's hair, then pricks her lip and touches the hair to the blood welling up there.

He tosses it into the darkness.

And then something is there, in the pit.

Something cold and grand and hateful.

In an instant, Sharasthi is a girl sitting outside her grandfather's temple, feeling something press in on her soul. She has not felt anything like this since Rufus touched her with the focus.

Everything becomes crisp and sharp. The lamp flames sway like little dancers. The cultists hum to a deep tone. The wind rushes through the grass as though fleeing something.

The thing in the pit presses in on her like a lion cornering prey. Everything in Sharasthi tells her to freeze, to become insignificant, to let its malevolent gaze pass over her—but the thing in the pit will not be dissuaded. She wants to call magic to defend herself, but her focus—

Her focus. Farilus is holding her focus. He is speaking again, the words stabbing into Sharasthi like so many needles.

"Great Oblivion," he says, and the assembly echoes, "*Great Oblivion.*"

"Deep Darkness that *Deep Darkness* Consumes the *that Consumes* Light *the Light.*"

Sharasthi cannot breathe. She cannot even tell if her heart still beats. Maybe the drug has overwhelmed her body and she is already dead.

She wants to murmur some prayer her grandfather taught her, but the weight of that titanic presence's attention crushes her will.

Farilus and his followers go on, the words spinning around her head.

"Thou who art Beneath and *Thou who art Beneath* Beyond All, Thou *and Beyond All* who Brings Cold *Thou who Brings* Nihilum *Cold Nihilum.*"

Her focus, if she could only get her focus—but her captors are still clutching her arms, and she is weak from the drug and the oppressive, unseen eye.

The thing in the darkness is endless. The night itself has never felt so large to her as the malice in the pit—or on the other side of the pit, or coming through the pit. It is not something that should be here, but here it is.

If she could but channel aether for an instant to burn away the poison in her veins, to close the door of perception it has wrenched open, maybe she could fight, could flee, could do something. But the thing almost seems to mock her as the desperate thought trembles within.

"Embrace," intones Farilus, "this offering."

"*Embrace this offering,*" echoes the chorus.

The air changes. The hateful presence burgeons, becomes suffocating.

Farilus beckons for Sharasthi to be brought nearer the pit. She cannot even find the wherewithal to struggle. She is just staring into the black, unable to look away and yet unable to bear it.

The Dark, she thinks. *This is what awaits me in the Dark.*

Now Farilus speaks to her in a low register, almost washed out by the chanting.

"My apologies for our poor manners, Sharasthi, but in this moment you shall become the catalyst for a great work as has never been seen."

Her gaze lists to the side. Her focus—where is her focus? Farilus grabs her chin; his touch is revolting and dissonant, as though slithering snakeskin covers his fingers. When he makes her look him in the eyes, the world shakes. His mouth moves out of time with the sound of his words.

"You must see it, Sharasthi. See the festering city, packed to the brim with the refuse of life. Hear the incessant clamor of the rabble. Smell the noisome reek. See the world as it is."

And she does—in her mind and before her eyes, Farilus' nose becomes a tower, his mouth a gate, his skin the writhing masses dwelling among them, their grating noise filling her ears and their putrid stench invading her nose. Her stomach turns.

"And now see it all reduced to nothing. A boundless, endless peace. Absolute silence. Absolute calm. Would it not be so beautiful? You feel it now."

The air is cleaner in her lungs—the air blowing like a breath, a breath from the pit. The irksome vision fades as her eyes fix on the pure darkness there. Why does her heart now twist in rapture? She trembles. *No, no I do not want that! I must not!*

Farilus smiles—like the heartfelt smile of a father seeing his child take her first steps. "Yes, *yes*—you understand. The One Beyond saw you would understand and elected you, and for that you are very special, Sharasthi—you are rare and worthy beyond aeons of mortals. Now you will stand above the loathsome masses, and at the end of all things you alone will behold that ultimate and lovely stillness, before you too are received into oblivion."

He lets go of her and takes a step back. "Fear still lingers in you, but be assured—soon you shall exult in this great work."

Farilus brandishes the knife. The blade glints in the lamplight, and for but a moment Sharasthi sees a twisted figure reflected in it, a malefic face that is not a face, but some terrible alien thing which her small and stilted mind can only reckon as such to protect itself.

Farilus gives a signal, and the assembly takes up a new chant, harsh and dissonant.

The rock face darkens, the black in the pit rising, joining to the dancing shadows, until the contours of the rock melt into something so black there is no texture, only pure, flat void.

"Let you with faith in silence eternal draw near."

One of the cloaked in the assembly comes forward and kneels at the edge of the pit.

Farilus takes the knife and slashes his throat. With a gurgling spray of dark blood, the man tumbles into the pit, vanishing without a sound. Farilus takes his bloodied fingers and anoints Sharasthi's forehead.

Another comes, and the process is repeated. Farilus smears the blood on her lips. It tastes of copper and vile ecstasy. The chant grows louder, the survivors raising their voices to make up for those offered to the thing in the pit.

With every body that falls in, it looms closer. It is coming through, and it is pulling her in.

There is a place that is not a place that is always and never, and there is a black sun that devours light and radiates cold darkness. When she falls into the pit, it will have her, become one with her. Without words, it tells her this, tells her all the things it will do with her. It shows her mountains of putrefying corpses melting into bones and crumbling into dust, the great cities of the world smoking and broken and buried, every god and king bent and shackled and forgotten. But not all are sundered by force... Before every heap of death, every ruin, every tormented soul, it places little children it has preserved for this purpose: to watch and weep until the only thing they long for is annihilation, until hope and life become anathema to them, until they walk willingly into its maw.

It does all this through *her*, and all the while she screams deep inside herself, because all the while she exacts a horrid pleasure from it all. She delights in the eradication of all things ugly and loud and revolting until absolute peace reigns, until the stars themselves are snuffed out and smothered—until at last everything is *silent*.

She sees herself treading across the vacant stretches of the world, unseen and undisturbed, until she comes to a familiar temple. On the altar, the Eternal Flame smolders, weak and frail. Abandoned and alone. She cups her hand around it and takes a breath—the last breath—and blows it out, and there is only that which is not. There is only Darkness.

Not real, her fragile self whimpers, so quiet she can scarcely hear her own thoughts. *Not real not real nightmares and poisonnotrealnotrealnot—*

Farilus presses a bloody handprint to Sharasthi's white robe. "The vessel!"

"*The vessel!*"

He grabs her hair.

The hands on her arms loosen their grip.

He wrenches her to the edge, pulling her headlong with one hand, his other holding her focus over the abyss. The thing in the pit rejoices.

Those ancient words of Marzud coil in her lungs, creep through her throat, press on the back of her teeth—*Take me now, Ineffable Darkness, that I might know the truth of the lightless Abyss*—and she is a heartbeat from giving them utterance.

And then, without any sign or warning—a spear of blazing, brilliant light bursts through the night, searing into the darkness, uncovering a perfect circle of the rock face.

The instinctive response of a startled mind is to look—and so look on the gleaming circle they do, save Sharasthi, who whirls to seek the light's source.

Alyat bounds forward, leaping far beyond what a normal man could accomplish, a sword flashing in one hand, rays of light beaming from the other.

His blade arcs down on Farilus' wrist, arterial blood spraying in Sharasthi's face, blinding her in one eye as his dead hand tumbles free from her locks.

Crying out in agony, Farilus drops the focus. It falls toward the pit.

Sharasthi's heart *pounds* with more adrenaline than she has ever experienced, a rush so potent her veins and muscles ache as frenzied energy jolts her into motion.

She lunges forward, thrusting her bound hands out as far as she can, fingers splaying desperately.

The pit beneath her yawns endlessly, an insatiable maw eager to swallow her forever.

For a moment that lasts a lifetime, she is certain she's missed it, her fingers closing on air—

Until she feels the bottom two fingers of her left hand catch the focus and press it home to her palm, just as a radiant fist closes around her wrist and heaves her up with superhuman might.

Sharasthi burns aether faster than she's ever dared—and the drug *vanished* from her veins, and with it, the hateful presence looming from the pit.

Alyat set her on her feet as her arms strained against the bindings with aetheric strength, snapping the rope like rotten string.

The dark was no longer an obscure veil to her. She could see all her enemies' faces—see the fright and anger and shock. She commanded the shadows to leap into those faces, smothering them with total darkness. Confusion reigned. Many struck one another with fists or blades.

Those that Sharasthi had not blinded with shadows, Alyat blinded with light, throwing white rays into their eyes before running them through, slashing their arms and legs, skewering their throats.

After casting a glance to the pit, Sharasthi snatched up a sword from one of the cultists Alyat had disemboweled. She was about to wade into the melee, but stopped short, taking another look at the sight before her.

Alyat was not fighting like a legionnaire—he fought in a rage, moving with such unrestrained ferocity that Sharasthi doubted for a moment it was truly the same Alyat she knew. There was something manic in his eyes, something wild. Such speed and power he struck with, she would only get in the way if she tried to fight beside him.

The cultists, by and large not impressive combatants, also seemed to realize the danger their foe presented, as more and more began to turn and run. Sharasthi pounced on these, hemming them in as best she could, forcing them to choose between facing her or Alyat. Alyat cut most of them down before they could even make an attempt, though a few managed a lucky dash into the woods while their comrades fell.

"Farilus!" Alyat snarled, pointing a bloodied hand at the tree line.

Sharasthi whirled, catching sight of a frantic, stumbling form as it slipped into the woods. The message was clear. Sharasthi went rushing after their host, her legs pumping with aetheric speed and stamina.

By the time she reached the tree line however, Farilus had taken off on a horse, galloping at breakneck speed through the branches. Sharasthi grit her teeth and growled, giving chase. It was an easy track to follow, and when Farilus shot a panicked look over his shoulder, he turned pale and snapped at his mount to hasten.

She hunted him through the forest and beyond, into open countryside.

With every second, Sharasthi's fury at the man grew. He had housed them. Welcomed them to his table. Laughed and fêted with them.

And then he did all *this*—and even though she had gone into this mission knowing he was under suspicion, the reality of it infuriated her.

Her head spun as with the fits she suffered as a child. A headache pounded in her temple and jaw.

Aether sickness.

She could not keep up the chase much longer.

So she stopped running. Farilus sped on, rapid hoofbeats sounding as he fled.

Sharasthi took a breath, let it out.

She had always been wary of drawing upon the night, knowing its fullness could overwhelm her in an instant. Rufus had forbidden her from doing so when he was not there to supervise.

But she had to end this—and after feeling the boundlessness of that *thing*, suddenly the night was not so fearsome in comparison.

She opened herself, letting aether flow through her like a surging tide. Seizing on the night, she gathered its darkness into a dome grand enough to rival that of the Imperial Palace in Lazarra, and let it fall on Farilus and his horse, some quarter mile ahead of her.

Mount and rider alike screamed, the beast turning frantically left and right—then went stock still.

Farilus kicked it, shouted abuse, even as he turned about, peering fruitlessly into the darkness enveloping him.

Sharasthi approached, her arm extended to funnel power to the enclosure.

When Farilus could not get his horse to move, he threw himself to the ground and began running.

Sharasthi kept the darkness on him, so that no matter which way he turned, all was sheer empty blackness. The aether sickness built, and she swallowed against a wave of nausea.

Farilus tripped, cursing. He got up only for one foot to slip into a ditch, sending him tumbling and sprawling.

Sharasthi released her magic.

Farilus pushed himself to his feet, groaning and coughing. He seemed much older than he had, hosting those banquets and telling stories at dinner. He clutched the bloody stump at the end of his arm, trying to staunch the flow.

Sharasthi stood at the lip of the ditch, sword in hand.

Farilus blanched even further. "Now, Sharasthi—"

She jumped down, taking the landing easily, and sent a surge of aether into her arm and shoulder as she socked him square in the jaw.

With a startled grunt, he went sprawling on his back, unconsciousness seizing him.

Sharasthi flexed the fingers holding the sword, then bent down and sent a stream of aether into the man, healing his arm.

Saving his life was not a mercy. When he woke up, Hannil would talk to him.

And Hannil had a very particular way of talking to someone whose secrets he wanted to know.

After cutting some fabric to bind Farilus' feet and good arm together, Sharasthi sat down, her head swimming. As adrenaline faded and she eased off her aether channeling, she began to shake. She forced herself to take as even and slow breaths as she could manage.

The same thoughts kept circling through her mind—that she had been about to die tonight. No, to suffer something *worse* than death. Something Alyat had saved her from.

For a moment she feared he had been hurt taking on the cult, but then she recalled the sight of him fighting and decided there was almost no chance of that. The only concern at this point would be reuniting.

Raising her head, she picked out the silhouette of a mountain range to the northwest, its jagged peaks cutting into the starry sky. That more or less gave her an idea of where she was relative to the road and the town. It would take an hour or two to walk back.

Just as she was considering whether she'd need to channel in earnest again to haul her captive away, a bright column of light speared the sky. It glowed for a count of ten, then faded. Soon after, it shone again.

Alyat was signaling their contacts in the town. Hannil and his men would rush to where Alyat had sent up the light.

Sharasthi looked at Farilus, sighed, and braced herself for more aether sickness.

She dragged him to an open stretch of land where she guessed and hoped their reinforcements would pass by on their way to the signal. Now and then, Alyat shot up another light.

To Sharasthi's great relief, she had chosen her spot well. Thundering hoofbeats rolled across the land as Hannil, Intelligence operatives, and legionnaires bore down on her position.

Hannil reined in his horse with a small detachment alongside him, while the rest hurried on to Alyat's signal.

Her handler's cold eyes focused on Farilus, the stump at the end of his arm, then on Sharasthi. "Report," he said in a voice that betrayed no concern despite her obviously miserable demeanor, let alone bloodstained clothes and features.

Hannil's men dismounted and hurried to replace the makeshift bindings on Farilus with strong rope.

"Sir," she groaned, doing her best to avoid sounding completely pathetic, "one mystery rite leader caught in the act of kidnapping an

Adept Initiate and performing an illicit ritual. Alyat is at the site of the ritual with two dozen cultists, most dead."

"I see."

"Sir, permission to sleep off my aether sickness and give a fuller report once recovered?"

Hannil blinked slowly. "Would you prefer an escort back first?"

"It would be much appreciated," she murmured, before succumbing to a sudden wave of nausea and turning aside to vomit what little was in her stomach.

17

SOME DEEPER NEED

Love for all that exists, that is what I see in the Fire: love that warms, love that purifies, love that destroys.

 —Zaro's Sayings, verse six hundred and eighty-nine

Sharasthi woke at noon. After checking her focus was indeed still with her, she let out a long sigh. The aether sickness from the previous day had subsided, but there was work to be done.

After using a basin of cold water to scour away the blood and grime clinging to her face and body, she dressed in her usual attire. Last night she had thrown the bloody robe into the hall before passing out on the bed, and she was glad to see it gone when she emerged.

Legion Intelligence agents were going about the villa, examining rooms and furniture. One directed Sharasthi to wait for Hannil in the dining hall. The table had been set with water, bread, and fruits, so Sharasthi helped herself while she waited. The food revived her, making the prospect of debriefing more bearable.

When he arrived, Sharasthi noted he was drying his hands with a cloth. Not even a speck of blood under the fingernails. She did not ask where he was carrying out his interrogations of the Escitans. There would be guards outside to keep her from stumbling in anyway.

Hannil did not touch the food or drink. He just sat and listened, asking a pointed question now and then.

He did not verbally chastise Sharasthi for letting her guard down—a stern thinning of the lips sufficed. She would gladly take that; Rufus was sure to give her far worse when he heard what had happened.

When she recounted how she had been forced to drink that concoction, Hannil nodded and said they had found more of it in Farilus' hideaway with the 'compelled assistance' of the servants (also currently being held somewhere Sharasthi did not ask) who had taken her focus and administered the drug to her. The ramshackle garden shed the gentleman had always said he was putting off repairing turned out to be a front for an underground storehouse where he kept the implements of his little cult. Sharasthi was embarassed they had not uncovered it themselves, but Hannil said the mechanism hiding the entry was a subtle one.

Among the holdings, they had found a sizable amount of ingredients for a particular blend of mixed wine, as well as the formula for it. That was the substance that had coursed through her veins last night. According to the recipe's description, it was an incredibly powerful pharmakon, capable of inducing trances lasting as long as two days. They had added a powerful soporific root—in fact, the same one Sharasthi had taken to quell her nightmares long ago—to knock her out while they took her from the villa.

As for why they took Sharasthi rather than the bait that was Alyat, Hannil had extracted an explanation from Farilus. Apparently, in his preparatory rituals and divinations, Farilus had determined his god desired 'the little magician dyed in Darkness.' He had not provided a coherent account beyond that—not yet at least.

Sharasthi kept her voice as level as she could when she said, "They used the word *vessel*."

Hannil sniffed. "Perhaps you were to perform an oracular function."

A cold finger traced her spine. "It felt like something more than that."

"On that note..."

Regarding the temple, Hannil suspected it to have once been a shrine to Doenysos Anastaso, a particular manifestation of the god of revelry favored by certain mystery cults. Rituals of that school violated moral taboos and encouraged extreme libertinism, and despite the Senate's ban on the practices nearly two hundred years ago, they persisted throughout the Empire.

But it was not a rite of Doenysos Anastaso that Sharasthi had been dragged into last night. Only the pine cone staff and chalice Farilus had brandished at the beginning of the ceremony fit that profile.

"And *this*," Hannil groused, "is something Legion Intelligence has no reference for." The pine cone atop the staff had come loose when Farilus threw it aside during the ritual. Hannil now showed her what had been concealed beneath: an unnerving lattice of lead crowned the staff. The black metal's form was dizzying to behold; Sharasthi had to focus to realize she was looking at a layered triad of cubes: the innermost, about the size of her thumbnail, sat within the middle, which sat within the outermost, about the size of her fist. The edges of the cubes were not aligned but offset from one another, such that when the staff moved they almost seemed to whirl before the eye, though to the touch they were immobile.

Sharasthi did not test that, instead taking Hannil at his word. The sight of the thing turned her stomach. There was no doubt in her mind that this was a representation of the Thing in the Dark. To touch even its symbol was too much like touching *it*, and...

Her soul stirred with desire for that grand Silence. She crushed the sentiment, her fingernails cutting into her palm.

Focus on the moment. Focus on Hannil.

Her handler was exacting in his questions. He made her describe and re-describe everything that had happened. He did not take notes, but Sharasthi was sure he would write it all down in precise detail later.

To her relief, he was not interested in what she had to say about the pit, and he did not seem to realize or care whether she held back regarding the vision and how she had felt in its grip.

"Alyat didn't see any of that," he said plainly. "Just an effect of the drug and the images Farilus planted in your mind."

Sharasthi was not sure whether that comforted her or not, but she was glad to pass over it. Even to half-recall that nightmare made nausea roil her insides again.

When Hannil was satisfied, he told her to go to Farilus' hidden quarters beneath the garden shed and assist Alyat in deciphering the writings there.

When she asked what Hannil would be doing, he said, without the slightest touch of emotion, that he would resume his *conversations* with the master and mistress of the estate. He took the accursed lead-crowned staff with him.

Sharasthi suppressed a shudder as she took her leave.

Sharasthi found Alyat working alone, stacks and sheaves strewn about what must have been Farilus' desk.

"Hungry?" she asked, proffering a loaf of bread she'd snatched from the dining table.

Alyat accepted it gratefully, gesturing for her to sit. He walked her through some of the materials they had discovered searching the place, as well as the ciphers Farilus had used to encode his most sensitive documents and records. It seemed some of these were quite old, and so likely had come down to Farilus from the previous head.

Sharasthi half-listened, her attention drifting time and again to his even expression as he spoke. It may as well have been just another day in the Sanctum library, going by his demeanor. Memories of what he looked like last night flashed through her mind.

Her fists clenched and unclenched in her lap. She muttered something under her breath.

Alyat turned away from his work. "What was that?"

Sharasthi swallowed, about to fabricate some other line.

Ask, she demanded of herself.

"Why did you wait so long to signal Hannil?"

Alyat shrugged. "If I signaled when I realized you had been taken or while you were still in their hands, they might have reacted rashly and harmed you. It made the most sense to wait until you were safe."

Sharasthi grit her teeth. She'd known he would say that. It didn't make it any easier to hear. "Even though that meant coming for me alone."

"It was the most sensible choice."

"It was more dangerous for you."

"I had my focus and a weapon."

Sharasthi slammed the desk, jumping to her feet. "*Stop* that."

Alyat arched an eyebrow.

"Stop..." Her mouth formed empty shapes before she found the words. "Stop acting like that makes sense."

"We look out for one another in the Corps."

"Within reason."

"It was."

"Then why did I—!" She shut her mouth.

Alyat slowly rose and leaned on the desk, gesturing for her to go on.

She considered whether she could run off. Hannil would scold her for leaving her assignment.

"I thought I was on my own."

"You couldn't have known I realized something was wrong and went after you."

She groaned, then started pacing to and fro.

Alyat snorted, watching her with open amusement. "Didn't I say it back at the Sanctum? We're friends."

"I never agreed to that."

"Would you like a formal retraction?"

Sharasthi came to a stop, fists balled at her sides. "I was surprised. When you came for me. When I realized you were there—*alone*—I was surprised because I didn't expect...I didn't *want* you to rescue me like that."

Alyat gave her a flat look. "You didn't hit your head, did you?"

Sharasthi gave him a weak punch. "No, really, listen to me."

He glanced down at the fist against his chest, then nodded for her to go on.

"Alyat, I...Hannil said we're both problem pupils for the same reason. Too solitary. Maybe I'm wrong, but I get the sense that's just who you are. But for me...for me it's because I lost the person I loved most, the only family I ever had. And ever since then I've felt so alone, but I've never dared try get close to someone else because...I don't know what I'd do if..."

Her hands were shaking now. She pressed them flat against Alyat to still them. He was solid, warm. "And then I thought I could keep you at enough of a distance that I wouldn't...but even as I told myself that, I still..."

Her eyes stung. Her voice was shaking.

Her veins and bones twisted and raged and demanded she turn, run, hide, *get away and stay away*—but some deeper need kept her feet rooted.

"And then you go and..." She bit down on her trembling lip, hard enough she feared she would taste blood. "H-how am I supposed to..."

She was standing at a threshold, scouring herself for the courage to step forward into what lay beyond.

Without a word, Alyat did the worst and best thing he could have. He wrapped his arms around her shoulders and squeezed—and pulled her across the threshold and into himself.

Something deep inside Sharasthi fell to pieces, and the long-buried screams and tears burst out, muffled into Alyat's chest.

She cried, and cried, and cried—three years of smothered sobs and groans and gasps finally given vent.

He didn't say anything, just stroked her hair.

Time disappeared to the back of her mind, and she wished it would stay there even as she knew this was a stolen moment—but at last she had someone's arms around her again. Someone who cared enough to risk himself for her even when he had every excuse to do otherwise.

Her face was hot and wet with tears. She pulled back and sniffed, then murmured an apology when she saw the tear stains. Hesitantly, she looked up.

The bastard was smirking. "Bit late for that."

Sharasthi huffed, burying her face into a still-dry spot on his chest. Her voice was muffled. "No complaints then."

Alyat pressed his hand against her back, pulling her closer still. "Not one."

With her face hidden away, she was not abashed for the small smile taking shape.

The door to the garden shed creaked, footsteps sounded at the top of the stairway. Alyat moved to nudge her away. Time had returned.

Sharasthi decided to banish it once more.

With a burst of aetheric strength, she shoved Alyat to the corner, covering his mouth with one hand and pushing him down against the wall. Her other hand, she waved in the air, conjuring shadows.

A legionnaire came down the stairs. "Initiates, Officer Hannil wants...hm?"

Sharasthi could see inside the darkness and beyond it. The legionnaire looked about, walked to the desk. "Initiates?"

Alyat's breath was hot on her hand. His pale eyes darted to and fro, blind.

Sharasthi pulled her hand away, suddenly self-conscious of the position she had put them in. Alyat seated with his back to the wall, her kneeling against him, her face just inches from his. She craned her neck to watch the legionnaire again. Alyat's breath tickled her ear.

She bit her lip, memories of the night she barged into his room creeping back.

The legionnaire muttered something, turned and left. As his footsteps receded, Sharasthi felt a bizarre disappointment.

She looked at Alyat again. His eyes weren't darting around anymore. His pupils were large enough to almost swallow the blue around them.

The door to the garden shed creaked shut.

Sharasthi knew she should let the shadows fall away.

Alyat smelled of trees and foliage. From when he had snuck up on the ritual last night?

His breath tickled her neck. She swallowed.

She knew she should let the shadows fall away.

But he couldn't see her right now, and she could see him.

His lips parted, a soft whisper coming out. "Sharasthi, is—"

Before she could think better of it, she kissed him. It was more forceful than she intended, knocking his head against the wall with a muted thud.

She broke away, an apology forming, only for Alyat to grab her face and pull her back to him. His fingers tangled in her hair.

Sharasthi felt dizzy. *Breathe*, she reminded herself. It didn't help.

At some point she released her magic and light broke in on them.

Alyat grabbed her chin and pushed her away. His face was flushed. His eyes looked similar to how they had in last night's battle. Something in the pit of her stomach twirled.

"We," he said in a hoarse voice, "are going to need a good cover story for where we've been."

Sharasthi ran her hands along his face. "Haven't you been paying attention?" she breathed. "I'm a very good liar."

"Are you?" Alyat's fingers traced along her jaw, down the side of her neck, sending shivers through her. "Tell me a lie then."

Sharasthi held his gaze, her face growing hotter by the second. "I want you far away from me."

Alyat's face drew closer. Into her ear, he whispered, "I don't believe you."

Sharasthi hoped he didn't notice the mewl that slipped from her lips before he kissed her again.

18

BEYOND REPROACH

WHY DID Zaro seek the mountain and ten years there remain? A man passed before my door. I invited him in and asked from where he had come and to where he was going. Now he told me of his life's transgressions, and I cried, "Surely these are the sins of the most wicked man to walk the earth!" He concurred, and so I asked him of his penance. When he had told me, again I cried out, "Yet surely contrition as this, I have found nowhere beneath the vault of heaven!" He bowed his head and clasped my hand and, without another word, departed. In the astonishment of my spirit, I sought the mountain and ten years there remained.

—Zaro's Sayings, verses one hundred and ten through twelve

AFTER FAST-TALKING their way around the matter of their inexplicable absence, Sharasthi and Alyat returned to their work about the estate.

Or perhaps Alyat did. Sharasthi could not concentrate for the life of her. Thankfully, she was able to lean on the operatives and legionnaires alongside her. They were searching the villa for any more secrets, a search that turned up little by day's end, even with Sharasthi peering into every dark and dim corner they could find.

Once she caught sight of Alyat working with Hannil on cataloguing Farilus' study, and she cursed the blush that crept up her throat.

"Are you all right, Initiate?" asked an Intelligence operative. "You look under the weather."

"Just some lingering effects from last night. I'll be fine."

Thankfully, others were more susceptible to her lies than Alyat.

That evening, there was another debriefing with Hannil over dinner, this time with Alyat and some of Hannil's top aides. There was still a good deal of work to be done unraveling the web of Farilus' work. They had caught some cultists who fled during the battle, but more were in the wind. It would be long and hard work tracking them down and uprooting any vestiges of the organization.

Hannil bemoaned that he had his work cut out for him, while Alyat and Sharasthi would have to return to the Sanctum soon. "Perhaps," he drawled, "I will leave things unfinished until you complete your training and then foist it all upon you."

Sharasthi realized this was Hannil's version of a joke, as well as a compliment. She said she hoped never to have anything to do with this cult again if she could help it, but she would do what had to be done.

Hannil nodded, but then said, "Not as if you have much say in the matter. Tomorrow though I want you to go back to the temple ruins and take another look around. Alyat, you'll continue deciphering as much as you can while I have you here."

With that, the meeting and dinner were adjourned. Sharasthi hurried to the bath, then to her room, where she sat fidgeting on the edge of her bed before she gave up on sitting and started pacing again.

"This all feels rather familiar," she muttered to herself, casting another glance at the door.

He had not *said* he would come see her tonight. But that was the sort of thing that happened, wasn't it? Or was he expecting her to go to him?

Sharasthi caught a glimpse of her flushed features in the mirror.

There are people about, she told herself. *We could be seen.*

She had never considered using her magic to sneak down a hallway to a boy. As soon as she realized she'd had the thought she felt like she had fallen in some sort of ranking, putting her on the same level with all the chattering Initiate girls who ruined her peace in the baths by squawking about boys.

Yet her pride seemed less valuable the more she thought about how just one wall lay between her and Alyat. Just two doors and a few short steps. Or maybe a jump from one window to the other.

In the end, she decided it was between staying in the room and pining like a foolish girl, or sneaking to the other room like a foolish girl. She chose the latter, if only for the relief that came from doing something instead of waiting around.

The hall was empty, but even so she darkened the shadows. She decided not to knock at the door, slipping inside as quietly as she could.

She was about to whisper his name when she saw in the dark that his bed was empty. Coming up short, she peered around. No sign of him.

Sharasthi padded to the bed, hesitating a moment before sitting.

Must be working on more codebreaking.

At first she felt sorry for him, then a moment later she was angry. She hadn't heard Hannil order him to do more work tonight. Was that what he *wanted* to spend his evening on?

With a huff, she planted her face into the pillow. "There's a woman in your bed, fool," she muttered, wrapping herself in the cover. Her face burned. Logic told her she should just go back to her room and sleep, but...

Five minutes. She would wait five minutes.

Sʜᴀʀᴀsᴛʜɪ sᴛɪʀʀᴇᴅ, squinting against the bright light piercing her tired eyes. "Hm?"

The light died. A moment later, a weight settled on the bed. "It's well past midnight," Alyat said in a low voice.

"You're late," she murmured, turning her back to him.

"Am I?" He sounded amused. "Hannil wanted a particular text sorted out tonight, and I lost track of time."

"Mm. That does sound like you."

"You should go back to your room."

"Too tired."

He snorted. "All right." He pressed a kiss to her temple, then snaked an arm around her waist, pulling her in. He radiated warmth into her back.

She smiled in the dark.

"So are you going to keep the pillow?"

"Should've gotten here first," she muttered, already drifting off again.

"A liar and a thief," he murmured, kissing the back of her head before settling down. "What next?"

Wʜᴇɴ Sʜᴀʀᴀsᴛʜɪ ᴀᴡᴏᴋᴇ, she nudged him and kissed his cheek before saying she was going to be on her way.

Alyat muttered for her to take care. She stroked his head. *Poor thing, up all night working codes.* Then again, he enjoyed it.

After slipping back into her room and changing, she set out for the site of the temple.

The temple ruins were vacant. Sharasthi had expected to find more Intelligence operatives and legionnaires combing the area. Perhaps they had fanned out to search the broader area? But still, there should have at least been...

As she stepped across the ruined threshold, she realized someone *was* here—standing right over the pit where that horrible presence lurked. He was wearing foreign attire, his hair much longer than the Lazarran fashion, yet his face smooth.

"Halt!" Sharasthi cried, loud enough to summon anyone nearby as she drew her blade. "Who are you, and why are you here?"

The man seemed unperturbed by her weapon. His attention was fixed on the rent in the earth where she had felt that terrible, dark power.

Sharasthi reached out with her aetheric sense.

Nothing.

The man clicked his tongue. "Here of all places." He sounded bitter.

There was something in his tone that startled Sharasthi. An authority she had never heard before. An anger not like that of a man, but like a storm's—beyond reproach.

Sharasthi swallowed, gathering her will. "Who are you?"

"We will get to that someday, I expect." His brow was furrowed, and he still had not looked up from the pit. There was something odd about his features, but Sharasthi couldn't quite discern what it was.

"I must apologize," he said, his countenance dark. "This aperture escaped my notice."

The point of her sword dipped. It suddenly seemed superfluous in her grasp. "I...don't understand."

He waved it aside. "You have no need. I've sealed it, and I will ensure no others remain. Take heart that what sought you that night is a foe you will not have to face. Your enemy remains who it has always been."

"My enemy?" The Hunter with the claw mark on his face flashed through her mind. The banner of the Lazarran Empire. Sharasthi's hands were sweating. "How do you know who my enemy is?"

He looked up at last, his gaze on her heavy as a mountain. "For that matter, a veil over your fate will do you well. Ordinarily that would be out of bounds, but I shall consider it justified amends for my oversight here."

His gaze flitted to her side for a moment, as if he were examining the columns behind her. He dipped his head in an almost imperceptible nod, a grave sentiment on his features, then returned his crushing attention to her. "I shall seal your memory until next we meet, lest this distract you from your immediate purpose."

Sharasthi stumbled back a half-step. "Who are you?" she asked again, voice trembling. She channeled her aether, but it felt as reassuring as wearing a bedsheet to battle. "What do you mean a veil? Sealing memories? At least tell me—"

In an instant, he was in front of her, his fingers brushing her forehead, his strange and striking eyes locked on hers.

Sharasthi blinked, words dying in her throat. She looked around.

Right, she was standing in the ruined temple grounds where Farilus and his followers had tried to use her for their twisted ritual.

Sharasthi frowned. Something was off about this, and not just because of her recollection of that horrid night.

She cautiously approached the pit. When she worked up the courage to peer over the edge, she found it was only three feet deep. She did not step in.

When the Intelligence operatives made their reappearance, Sharasthi upbraided them (as well as she could, given her unease) for abandoning the site.

Confusion reigned, as everyone testified they had been ordered to patrol the area for a short while.

No one could recall who had given the order.

At the end of her search, Sharasthi left the place with a shudder, her eagerness to never see it again dampened only by the persistent sense someone was watching her as she departed.

19

TO DIE OR GO MAD

> Lᴏɴᴇsᴏᴍᴇ ᴇʏᴇs ᴅʀᴀᴡ ʟᴀɴɢᴜɪᴅ sɪɢʜs,
>   I am drunk on a girl I cannot coax to smile.
>   —Fragment of Kleisaph's poetry

Wʜᴇɴ ᴛʜᴇ ᴅᴀʏ came for Sharasthi and Alyat to leave, Hannil met with them one last time early in the morning.

"Would that I could keep you both on hand for longer, but the Sanctum is tight-fisted with its charges. Even so, Alyat, take these files with you and continue working on them, write if you find anything noteworthy.

"Sharasthi, by the time you return to Lazarra, Adept Rufus will have received my report via messenger hawk. I should be back in the capital within the month. Don't relax too much now that you'll be out of my sight."

Finally, he gave them orders and permission to take a boat down the river. Initiates did not have the right to use Adept Corps authority to commandeer transit except in emergencies, so this was a rare privilege. They would be back in Lazarra within three or four days if they made good time; it had taken more than a week coming up overland.

Sharasthi and Alyat said their farewells and were off, riding horses appropriated from Farilus' stable. The steeds did not seem particularly bothered by their master's absence as of late. They would be treated well by the legions. It was unlikely Farilus' children would try to claim them, or anything else that belonged to their father—not when the ire of the state was so strong against him. Eventually, some Senator (acting under advisement from Intelligence) would bring up the legal matter of what to do with the storied Escitan villa and grounds, and it would be apportioned to whichever claimant would best serve the interests of the Empire.

All of that was beyond Sharasthi's care though. What really mattered to her, at the moment, was what Hannil's report to Rufus contained.

It did not take long for Alyat to notice her angst and guess the cause. "You'll get your silver."

"And if I don't?"

"Trust me, your performance was satisfactory. Moreover, the Corps would rather you have *subordinata* status and start pulling your weight in the field."

That made sense, and it eased her nerves. Still, it was hard to feel confident when she pictured Hannil's dour face writing the letter, so she forced herself to think on something else. "Thank you again, then."

"Hm?"

"I owe you for letting me come on this mission."

"What's all this about?" he scoffed. "We cleared that slate a month ago."

"Yes, well...I'm grateful still."

Alyat shrugged. "As it turned out, you were in far more danger than I was, so let's call it even."

"Even though you risked yourself to—"

"Sharasthi," he sighed, "you don't need to keep score."

She pressed her lips together. "I don't want to seem callous."

He snorted, which earned him a narrow look. "How about just acting normal?"

"What if normal me isn't particularly charming?"

"Being uncharming can be charming in its own way. Besides, the difference is endearing."

"Difference."

"Between how you act in public and in private. If you make too much of an effort to be likable then soon other people might find out. Can't have that—I might need to start competing for your time."

"That sounds exhausting, so you need not worry, but either way..." She turned her head aside, her cheeks warming. "You'll be the only one to see what I'm like in private."

"See, that's what I mean."

Sharasthi sniffed. "I don't know what you're talking about."

"How easily you blush, for one."

"Zarushans are a hot-blooded people."

"I have every reason to believe that."

"And you?" Sharasthi turned back to him, her curiosity taking hold. "Tell me something about Northlanders."

He looked up to the sky as he thought, blond eyebrows furrowing. Eventually he said, "Contradictory. Generous in their gift-giving but greedy in their piracy. Loud and profuse in mead-halls and on battle-fields, yet prone to isolation and quiet at home or in nature. Reverent before the gods, vulgar beyond belief otherwise."

Sharasthi listened, trying to imagine Alyat fitting in amongst a rowdy bunch of revelers. Maybe it did make some sense how well he played the part of a lush at Farilus' table. "And is it truly always cold?"

"Cold is relative. Compared to Lazarra, absolutely. But spring still comes up there, flowers bloom. There is a legend that in the utter-most northern reaches of the land lies a hidden country sheltered by mountains, untouched by the harsh wind, rain, and snow. Frejeim, a place blessed by the gods to enjoy eternal summer."

"That sounds nice."

"It's also supposedly inhabited by giants who eat the flesh of unworthy visitors."

"And what qualifies as unworthy?"

"No clue. But once in a while you do hear of some men going off in search. Most never return."

"Were you ever tempted?"

"Oh, every boy is sure he'll be the one to find it. We used to spend afternoons playing in the woods, drawing up names for our warbands and longships, arguing over what would sound the best in the songs to be composed in our honor. Then you grow up, your worries become more practical and immediate." His eyes seemed to be on something far away. "Hah, if any of them could see me now…"

Sharasthi's heartstrings twisted. Alyat was somewhere else for a moment, some place she did not know and could not share with him. She wanted to close that distance. She wanted to open herself to him so he could know the places she contained within herself, the places and emotions no one else knew.

Then he snorted, shook his head. "Well, such is life."

Sharasthi smiled thinly, masking the ache. "So it is."

THEY TRAVELED WEST, following a tributary of the Mother River. Anytime they encountered someone on the road, they received bowed heads, sometimes salutes from retired legionnaires. They stopped to speak with a road patrol who confirmed the area was clear of trouble. They were likely to make good time.

The destination was a small town that served as a shipping hub for the region. And not only did Alyat and Sharasthi indeed make good time, they reached it but a few hours after sundown the same day they had left—a privilege of being able to channel aether into their horses to keep them strong and tireless at speed.

In part, Sharasthi loathed the haste they rode with. The sooner they returned, the sooner the rhythms of Sanctum life would swallow her up again. This time alone with Alyat, she wanted to stretch it out as long as possible—but she did not say as much, of course. And

Alyat was a dutiful Initiate; there was no question of him slacking on his own volition.

When they got into the town, he said he would go to the harbor and arrange for their passage on the first boat downriver in the morning. Sharasthi went to a nearby inn to find lodgings for the night.

Given the late hour, she had to knock loudly, earning a grumbling answer of "Yes, yes! A moment!"

Sharasthi adjusted her mantle as she waited.

The lock clicked, the door opened just enough to reveal a baleful eye. "We're all—!"

The innkeeper choked on her own words, the lone eye going wide. "My deepest apologies, Adept," she gasped, opening the door and bobbing her head like a chicken.

"Only an Initiate," Sharasthi clarified, as regulation required. "I don't suppose you were about to say you are all full?"

"Still! A great honor! Please, come in, no we're not all full—well, almost full, but of course there is space to be made for yourself. We know enough to keep an extra room if needed!"

Sharasthi realized the woman must be even more agitated than she appeared, as she kept waving for her to enter despite the fact that she was holding her horse's reins. "I think," she said slowly, "I will need a stable first."

The innkeeper stared. Then, at last, comprehension. "Oh! Yes, of course. I'll have the boy do it."

"My colleague is coming from the harbor; he has a horse as well."

"Ah, of course, of course. There'll be room for the two horses. Room for two...oh." She swallowed, dabbing at her forehead, muttering to herself and keeping her eyes anywhere but on Sharasthi. "We do only have the one room, I'm afraid, Adept— *Initiate*. I could send the boy to check at the other inn up the road, but, well, their food, you see. And the—"

Sharasthi cast a subtle glance over her shoulder. Alyat wasn't in sight yet. "We are soldiers, ma'am. A roof and bed at all is more than enough."

"Yes, yes, quite good. And with my husband's cooking in you, you'll sleep the sleep of the dead. *Haha!*"

Sharasthi ground her teeth, suppressing a grimace at the woman's needling laugh. Among the things she hated most about the Adept Corps was the way it made people look at her, grovel to her. She would have preferred to be nobody, but of course she could not do that. The Corps required she wear her mantle, bear her power publicly. Such was the way of the Lazarran Empire.

Still, something of her irritation must have finally gotten through to the woman, because she bobbed her head a few more times, muttered something about her husband and the boy, and bustled off.

Sharasthi stood outside, rubbing the horse's muzzle. *One room.* Her mind started going places that made her glad for the dark masking her features.

Alyat returned as the boy was taking away Sharasthi's horse. He passed the reins to the lad, who gave a deep, if clumsy, bow and asked whether Alyat had ever killed anyone.

"A few," he said humorlessly.

Well, the boy loved that, and held the reins with reverence.

"So," Alyat said, coming over to Sharasthi, "they did have room?"

"Enough."

Alyat arched an eyebrow. Sharasthi shrugged, inspecting the otherwise empty street.

"Hm. Well, I smell food. Shall we?"

After a hasty meal consisting of the evening's warmed-up stew and dregs of wine (the food was indeed tasty, though somewhat dampened by the proprietors' constant hovering about and self-abasement), Sharasthi and Alyat retired to their room.

"It *is* tight, my apologies," said the innkeeper, "but it stays warm. The water is cold, I'm afraid."

"That's fine," Alyat said. "We're used to it."

"*Haha!* Yes, soldiers of the Empire. Well, just leave the basins in the hall. Will you need waking?"

"Dawn."

"I won't be a minute late for you." She hovered, patting her apron as if searching for more words.

"We've had a long day's journey," Sharasthi said.

"Yes, of course, sleep well," she chimed before shutting the door a bit too loudly and muttering an apology through it.

Sharasthi and Alyat shared an exasperated glance. He cracked the first smile, which broke her, and then they were both snickering.

"Always something," she sighed.

"Indeed." He eyed the washbasins in the corner. "Well, your feet look dirtier than mine, so."

Sharasthi kicked at his shins; he sidestepped easily. "Well," she drawled, "I'll get to that."

Alyat rifled through his pack and pulled out one of those texts Hannil wanted decoded. The beds were really two cots on the floor, so Alyat sat on his and put his back against the wall. He began reading by the light of his Art.

Sharasthi turned away from him and took the stool beside the washbasins. The water was chilly, but at least they had soap and a separate vessel for washing feet. As she rinsed her hands though, she fought the urge to look over her shoulder. Her mouth was dry.

Are you really just going to sit there and work?

She bit her tongue. The room *was* warm, as the woman had said. Warmer than was comfortable. She was glad for the cold on her hands.

She swallowed. "It's hot."

Alyat grunted.

She gave in and peeked. He was totally engrossed in the text.

"Could you...give me some light?"

He gave her a puzzled look.

"I'm feeling a bit strained," she half-lied. She was still drawing on the aether; she could see just fine. He would have been able to sense that.

He didn't push back though. He set aside his work and came over, shining a beam into the water. The bronze reflected back the light, sending luminescent dapples all over the room. *Pretty*, she thought.

In the glow, she saw sweat glistening on Alyat's neck and forehead.

"Lean forward," she murmured.

He gave her a short glance, then complied. She took her washcloth and sponged his ears, face, throat.

"Nice, isn't it?"

He made a low sound that she wasn't sure how to interpret. Her face was warm. From the room. From him.

There was a reflection like fish scales moving across his chest.

"You smell like horse sweat."

"So do you."

"That's no way to speak to a woman."

His eyes were startlingly bright as they caught the glow of his magic. "Are you asking for an apology?"

She looked away, dabbing the cold cloth at her neck. "Not an apology."

His hand closed over hers. "You said you're tired."

"Mm."

Cold water trickled down her face and neck as he pressed the washcloth to her temple, her forehead. The collar of her tunic was wet. "Alyat?" she said, her throat tight.

"Hm?"

"No more light."

Everywhere she kissed him, his skin seemed to burn, and everywhere he kissed her it seared like a smoldering brand. They fumbled together to pull his tunic over his head, and when it was finally gone she smeared cold water over the tattoo on his chest, then pressed her lips to it, cold and hot melding against her face.

There was a string inside her, drawing tighter and tighter. Every kiss, every caress, every shed piece of clothing, every breath at her ear and against her throat tugged it further. She bit at his jaw, then whispered at his ear, "I'm either about to die or go mad."

He kissed her cheek, her forehead. "We should be going to sleep."

"I can't sleep like this," she sighed.

He rolled onto his cot, pulling her to lie atop him. Her head leaned on his chest, thrumming with his pounding heartbeat. "Just breathe with me."

She followed him. At first her own pulse rattled too strong to relax, but the bellows of his lungs were strong and even and hypnotic.

"Still hot," she murmured. Alyat blew down her back, his breath cooling the water and sweat on her skin. She shivered and nuzzled deeper into his embrace. Her eyes blinked lazily. She almost felt as though she had taken the pharmakon again and was floating in some place outside of time.

Eventually she realized she could see her cot a few inches away. She could roll over to it and sleep.

Alyat's fingers were absently tracing circles on her lower back, skirting the edges of her underclothes. Sharasthi looked up at him. His eyes were closed, his head back. His fingers were slowing. He was drifting off.

Greed for the moment seized her, and she bit down on his shoulder.

"Hm?" His eyes opened lazily as he raised his head.

"What is this?" Sharasthi brushed her fingers against the tattoo.

Alyat grunted, his head falling back down. "Proof of passage. When a youth in the Northlands comes of age, he's sent into the woods with a hatchet and the clothes on his back. 'Come back a man, or not at all.'" He shrugged. "I came back, so they gave me this mark."

"Is it a wolf?"

"A bear. I killed one and brought back its pelt."

She recalled how he had looked tearing through foes, whirling with his sword and burning with light. She wondered if something of that bear dwelled in him.

She traced the symbols ringing the animal. "And what does this say?"

She felt the words lodge in his throat for a moment, then come forward. "Aelyath Arynson. That if I fall in battle where none living know my name, it might pass into songs as that of a worthy warrior, friend or foe."

That stirred yet more questions in her, but before she could choose one to ask, she looked and saw the droop of his eyelids, the heaviness of his rising and falling chest.

"Aelyath," she whispered, so soft he couldn't hear her. She tucked that sound away like a treasure in the vaults of her heart.

She kissed the bear etched into his skin, letting her lips linger there to feel the steady beat of his heart. Then she traced her way to his throat, kissing again his beating pulse, his jaw and cheeks, hair prickling against her face.

"Only men get the tattoos," Alyat murmured.

"Really?" She went on kissing his face.

"Mm. Yours would go here though." Sharasthi yelped as he squeezed her breast.

She nipped at his ear and hissed, "I thought you were falling asleep."

"I was," he grumbled, before hooking a leg around hers and pulling a grappling move that left her pinned beneath him. "Not so much anymore." A calm glow blossomed in his hand, casting light over her. "And it's not quite fair how you can see in the dark."

Sharasthi's face flushed, and she called the shadows to cover her.

Alyat gave her a dry look. "Really?"

Something in that look made her stomach flip. Words failing, she settled for sticking her tongue out. She wasn't expecting him to lurch forward and take it in his mouth.

"*Mmph!*" Her heart leaped into her head. As their mouths meshed together, she felt dizzy—dizzy in a way that made her want to leap off a cliff into the ocean, dizzy in a way that worked the world up into a buzzing foam.

When they broke apart to breathe, Alyat pressed hungry kisses into her neck, her ear. In a hoarse voice he said, "You can't hide anymore, not from me."

She nodded, still catching shaky breaths. "Prove it to me," she whispered, pouring her magic into the dark, wrapping shroud after shroud around herself. "*Please.*"

Alyat's hands traced down her stomach, caressing her chest, the hollows of her hips, thrills and shocks pulsing through her. His hands burst ablaze with radiance, burning through the shadows.

Sharasthi pushed against the brightness, smothering the light, keeping herself and the room plunged in darkness—even as she silently begged Alyat to overwhelm her, to show he had the strength to look on her as she was.

For a moment, a flicker of Alyat's magic broke through, like a bolt of lightning in the night, and she saw his face cast in stark illumination—full of wry humor and delight, delight in her and this moment, and she felt her heart go to pieces and a trickle of tears slip free from her eyes.

Suddenly the light burst through in its full intensity, and the air coursed with swirling and blending currents of white luminance and curling smoky shadows, and Sharasthi saw him over her, and she saw the startled look on his face as he caught sight of the tears glistening on her cheeks.

And she let herself smile—smile so wide and honest it hurt. Her first tears for him had been of sorrow, but these were of joy.

"I'm not hiding," she whispered, as if she couldn't believe it herself.

Alyat shook his head, his features settling into a warm, assuring look. "Took some work," he chuckled, taking hold of her face before pressing two kisses to the corners of her eyes.

She giggled, her head spinning again as Alyat pressed another kiss to her lips. His chest against hers, she felt his heart hammering, and she longed to let that rhythm become the whole of her being. As their kisses deepened and their hearts and bodies melted into one another, Sharasthi yielded herself to the rhythm and light and embrace of the one she loved—*she loved!*—and in the interplay of light and shadow and magic and flesh, she lost herself in Alyat's arms and thrall and consuming passion.

20

WE NEVER WILL

WHY DO I laugh even amidst so much lamentation? Because this too is but a flickering of the Flame.

—Zaro's Sayings, verse nine hundred and fifty-one

SHARASTHI WAS NOT ALONE. Not anymore.

She was lonely, from time to time. When she was away on field missions, or when Alyat was away. But there always came another time when they were together, and his touch melted away all the frost that had taken hold.

While such a relationship between Initiates was not forbidden, they kept it discreet as best they could. It was a vulnerability, one that could be used against them. More than ever, Sharasthi was wary of hostile forces.

Rufus, of course, caught on before long. And while he outwardly groused about how she could have applied herself better if she were not distracted by Alyat, she could tell it was bluster. He no longer pestered her about needing to build bridges with the other Initiates.

Even so, this time too had to come to an end. When Alyat

completed his training and earned his commission, he was suddenly gone for much greater stretches of time. Sharasthi became far more attentive to dispatches regarding the work of the Empire and legions, always alert for any news Alyat might be in danger, or worse.

The stars aligned in their favor, however, on the day she earned her commission. In the morning she received the tattoo on her shoulder, then went with the other graduating Initiates and their mentors to the Palatine Hill.

Emperor Dioclete himself bestowed their gold-fringed mantles on them. Ordinarily the order was the inverse of the graduates' rankings, with the highest honors bestowed on the last. Sharasthi had never been formally ranked, and so she received her mantle first. She was twenty years old, which made her the eldest of the graduates, but it had taken her just six years.

When Dioclete draped the mantle around her shoulders and bid her rise, their eyes met.

She recited the proper formula: "My life and blood for you, my Emperor."

Something shifted in the Emperor's expression. Something slight, so slight Sharasthi doubted anyone but her could notice it—a twitch of bemusement.

In the back of her mind, there was a flash of insight, but it was like a flash behind a curtain. She *knew* why the Emperor looked at her like that, and yet she did not.

And as soon as she realized that, it was gone from her, and the Emperor had stepped back and moved on to the next. After all had received their mantles, he returned to his throne to complete bestowing their commissions. The ceremony finished when all saluted and declared, "*Ave Imperator!*"

There was a procession through the streets. Sharasthi was grateful she was not in the position of honor. She wished it could go faster, thought about slinking away using her magic, but Rufus had his eye on her. It would be best not to act out in any way today.

All she had to do was make it to the evening.

The Corps held a banquet to celebrate the ascension of the newest

Adepts, but somehow Sharasthi managed to keep away from all the well-wishers and congratulations. Her eyes kept flitting to the entryway.

Of course, it was her luck that she was looking away when he arrived. Not until she felt a presence at her side and heard him say, "Excuse me, wine for a weary soul?" did she know he had returned.

She stifled what she was sure would have been an embarrassingly wide smile. "You would make me pour wine on my day of celebration?"

Alyat's expression was perfectly neutral. "Oh, this is all for you?"

"So I hear."

He raised salt-encrusted eyebrows, the white flecks almost invisible amid the blond. "Then perhaps I should leave you to it."

Sharasthi sucked in a breath. He smelled like the sea. "Now that I think again, I don't care so much for all this."

Alyat smiled, leaned close enough to whisper. "So...you'll get me that wine after all?"

Sharasthi bit her tongue, but he was already out of reach, making his way to a table laden with cups full of sparkling violet.

Rufus appeared. "He made it."

Sharasthi nodded.

Her mentor gave her an appraising look. "I think you've made enough of a showing tonight." Then he grunted. "You're a little too obvious when it comes to that boy."

She hastily scrubbed the joy from her features. "Just the wine," she muttered, knowing full well that Rufus knew she couldn't get drunk. Nowadays she kept herself on a constant draw of aether.

"Of course. Well, enjoy your youth." He gave her a severe look, clapped a hand on her shoulder. "Well done, Sharasthi. You surpassed expectations."

Adepthood had only ever been a means to an end for Sharasthi. She had no love for the Sanctum or Lazarra or the Corps. But Rufus had cared for her.

She bowed slightly. "I would have died in the throes of aether sickness a long time ago if not for your watchful eye and careful training, Rufus. You deserve more credit for my being here today than I do."

Her mentor was never one for feigned modesty, so he did not belabor the point. He only gave her a nudge on her back. "All right, now get out of here before some other grayhead makes me introduce you. You're good at skulking."

"I try."

With the festivities still in full swing, it was not complicated to hook her arm through Alyat's and tug him along the edges of the room while he drained his cup. Right before they slipped into the open night air, he deposited the empty vessel on a startled-looking Initiate's tray. The girl looked at the pair of them as they were leaving, went bright red, and pointedly turned away.

"You're normally more subtle," Alyat said.

Sharasthi shrugged. "It's been a long day." As they walked along the path, she caught sight of the olive grove down the hill. A nostalgic grin crept onto her face. "Remember when I asked you to meet me down there?"

Alyat laughed. "You had no idea."

One of their more memorable exchanges was when, after returning from that mission to Farilus' villa years ago, Alyat had finally explained to her the significance of the olive grove. She had asked why, when he had met her there, he was already declining when he hadn't yet known she wanted to ask for his help.

And so she had blushed to her ears in embarrassment when he explained the olive grove was notorious for Initiates seeking a private place for a tryst.

"At least," she said, "you were a gentleman in your denial."

"Well, you were covered in dirt and cobwebs so it wasn't too difficult."

A claw of guilt squeezed her heart. She had never told him she knew of the secret way into the catacombs. Did she *need* to tell him about that?

He squeezed her hand, pulling her back to the present. "Well either way, you certainly had my attention from then on. More than you already did."

She squeezed back, using her magic to veil them in shadows as she leaned close to press a kiss beneath his ear. "And we did get back to the grove eventually," she murmured.

"Once or twice."

She shook him off. "Oh," she said with a pout, "so it was that unmemorable." Even as she said it, she was already darkening the area further.

Alyat grabbed her and spun her around, locking their lips together. "More like," he said between kisses, "I lost the faculty—to count properly when I was with you."

"That—*mm*—is acceptable."

He pulled away first. "Now let us be out of here before one of the dozens of Adepts in this place senses your cloud of gloom and comes to investigate." She opened her mouth to retort, but all that came out was a stifled yelp as he smacked her backside and sent her stumbling forward.

"You didn't have to put aether into it," she drawled.

"Since when are you so brittle?"

Sharasthi bit her tongue, fighting to keep the smile off her lips. She took in his dry smirk. The amused glint in his eyes. His stern, then sardonic mien.

Every night for months she had missed this.

"Thank you," she said.

"Hm?" Alyat cocked his head.

"For coming back in time."

Alyat shrugged, looking off in the distance. "Just worked out that way."

Now she allowed herself the smile. No, he had pulled some strings to make it back. Even if he wouldn't admit it.

That was a funny habit of his, always trying to hide anything he did for her sake. She thought it was because he feared she would make an obligation out of it. Debts were anathema to Northlanders, from what she garnered. He had groused to her now and then about how everyone in this part of the world kept a tally of what they owed and were owed. As far as he was concerned, things should be done for the sake of them. A gift given in recompense for something was just a duty.

She locked both her arms around one of his, leaning into his side. "Well, coincidence or not, tonight the gate's open to us. And there's a place overlooking the harbor I wanted to show you."

SHARASTHI SIGHED, pulling the cover up to block the chilly sea breeze blowing through the window. Her head was pillowed by Alyat's arm. The lapping of the waves against the dock beat a steady rhythm. Harbor establishments were generally on the seedier side, given the penchants of sailors, but she had found an inn straddling the harbor area and the edge of the aristocratic regions. The upper crust had to get their fill of the sea as well, of course.

That it had cost her most of that year's allowance to rent the room and buy the wine didn't matter in the slightest. She was a full Adept now—she'd have more than enough of a stipend.

And now that she was an Adept...who was to say how many more times they would be together?

"Do you think," she mused, "Rufus and Hannil could pull some strings and get us assignments together?"

"It would be imprudent," he said. "Besides, I can't work as well when you're there. Always keeping an eye out, ready to raise hell if someone raises a hand against you."

She stretched up to kiss his cheek. She had even missed how his stubble pricked her face. "You're sweet, but I *am* an Adept as well, you know."

"Adepts die."

She pressed her face into his neck, breathing in the sea and sweat on him. "I like to think we never will."

ALYAT'S DEEP BREATHING, his steady heartbeat, the rolling of the waves —everything around Sharasthi was calm. Everything within her was tumultuous.

She did not want to sleep. Sleep meant waking up. Sleep meant goodbye.

Alyat was here, and it would be months—it could be *years*—until he held her again. His scent, his warmth. It was a cruelty of the highest order that this was all she got of him before they parted ways.

In a way, the best moments were the worst. When she was missing him—it hurt, but it was something she could look forward to the end of. When he *was* here though, that was when she had to dread the next moment that became the next moment that became the next moment. Every heartbeat was one moment closer to the end.

And it wasn't just the loneliness—she could bear loneliness. What was harder and harder to bear was herself. Or rather, what possibilities lay within herself.

She suppressed it as much as she could, but in these moments beside Alyat, when she let her guard down because she felt safest, that was when she was most vulnerable. The memories of the thing in the pit. How she had almost gone into the Dark forever. How she had, in those last moments, been ready, like Marzud, to embrace it. To betray the faith handed down to her from her grandfather and her lineage. To betray *herself*.

She had the capacity to do such a thing. She had nearly tipped into the abyss.

And if she could go so close to the edge once, who was to say she would not do so again?

It was only thanks to Alyat that she had not been lost. He had saved her in a way he might never truly understand.

For years now, she had feared what would happen when she was in the wild on her own. No Alyat. No supervising mentors.

If such unimaginable power beckoned again, could she say no to it? Did she *want* to say no to it—to deny the strength to bring about everything she had sworn herself to: vengeance on the Hunters and retribution against Lazarra.

What did she desire?

Sharasthi burrowed deeper into Alyat's side. In his sleep, he muttered something, his arm unconsciously pulling her closer.

Him. She wanted him.

He would be her anchor.

He would be her salvation.

THEY HAD to wake before dawn. Pulling herself away from his warmth was a torture, one Sharasthi only got through by keeping her mind off what came next. She focused on dressing—a drawn-out process when Alyat was there—and putting her hair in order.

They said their farewells in the room, where they could be assured of privacy. Alyat kissed her hard. She realized she had kissed him the same way before he'd departed on his first assignment. A desperate, forceful gesture. *Don't die,* it pleaded, words too fateful to risk giving utterance.

"Let's come back here someday," she said, wrapped tight in his arms, standing on her toes and pressing her tearful face into his shoulder. She hadn't meant to cry, but at some point it had just happened.

He rubbed her back. "Someday." He kissed her forehead. "Be careful, Shara."

Drawing a shaky breath that rattled the knives stabbing her insides, she let him pull away. She wouldn't hear him call her that again for a long, long time. He left first, and she hugged herself and dried her tears with the inside of her mantle. A part of her longed to go to the window and see him again, but she knew the tears would return if she did.

So she waited, took more tremulous breaths until at last they evened out, and stepped outside.

The sky was gray, the sun hiding behind low clouds in the east. Sharasthi hastened to the Sanctum and gathered her already packed things. She had her own room now—a place to call hers any time she returned to the capital. She could not think of it as home though. Her home was on a ship sailing west, and within the hour she was to board a ship due south.

The one thing in the room she cared for was a gift Alyat had sprung on her last night. A bronze mirror he had liberated from the holdings of a traitorous aristocrat. It was small, only about the size of her palm, but she had never seen such beautifully polished bronze.

She set the mirror on the desk beside her bed, then a moment later picked it up again and looked at herself. Her eyes were dry. Her hair was in place.

Turning her head, she traced her fingers where Alyat had kissed her last night. Now her skin was unmarked, but...

She sighed, the memory somehow already seeming to come from a lifetime ago.

Last night, while they had lain in each other's arms, she stopped channeling aether. She had wanted this for a long time, but when the time came she had still feared dropping her strength. With Alyat though, she could be frail. She could be weak—and who could guess when they would be together again?

Now, of course, there were no lingering memories of his affection. With her ever-present need for aether, she couldn't carry Alyat's kisses on her body, even in secret. They would always be elided from her skin. A little curse she'd never imagined. It almost made her laugh to imagine the horror her younger self would have felt to know such thoughts troubled her now.

She set the mirror down, another sigh rushing unbidden from her aching chest.

She took up her bag and left the room behind, sparing one more glance for the mirror. Whenever she returned, whether or not Alyat was here, at least this trace of him would be.

Sharasthi returned to where her morning had begun—the harbor —and found her ship. A marine legion vessel named the *Boreas*. The north wind.

As she boarded and the ship set out for Caroshai under oar, she could not help thinking the name was some sort of cruel jest.

PART III

NIGHT-CLOAKED WITCH

21

DREADFUL FAMILIARITY

Sharasthi slashed the man's throat, pulled her blade back, and
drove it through his heart.

With a gurgle and a startled look on his face, he sank to the
ground, staring at his own life spouting onto the streets of Caroshai.
His hand limply pawed at a knife sheathed on his hip, then went still.

In the dark of a moonless night, the blood was nearly black.

Sharasthi's heart pounded, loud enough she feared her targets
would hear through the walls.

Five months. Five months she had stalked the streets of Caroshai,
hunting leads and working contacts with Legion Intelligence,
scouring for the slightest hint as to where this group of dissidents was
operating out of.

She had nearly caught them two months ago, missing them by

less than an hour. They had an uncanny knack for evacuating their bases and safe houses before she and Intelligence could raid them. It was so impressive she suspected there was a mole inside either her operation or Caroshai's magistracy, but if there was, they too were exceptional in eluding detection.

Tonight though, tonight she finally had them.

And she had not dared wait for Legion Intelligence to mobilize a team.

With the new moon leaving the city under a thick darkness, there was no better time to strike.

The hideout lay within the slums—a hard enough area to operate in even with the cooperation of Caroshai's government. The city was an ancient friend and ally to the Empire, but was not under Imperial rule, which restricted what was feasible.

That was another reason Sharasthi had chosen to act so swiftly. If there was a mole inside Caroshai's magistracy, as she suspected, then by the time Intelligence got permission to send a force into the slums, the plan would be leaked. That was what had happened two months ago, she was certain.

She was not making that mistake again.

Even if it meant she had to slit every throat in this place herself.

A voice came from inside the door. "Oy, Baram, what's taking—"

Sharasthi sprang on the man as he stepped outside, wrapping him with shadows to blind him, smothering his mouth with a thickly gloved hand as she dispatched him.

After checking he could not scream out, she moved inward. She had no clue as to the layout of the place, but she had the shadows.

The aim of this group, as best as Intelligence had garnered, was to turn Caroshai against Lazarra. It had seemed an impossibility at first, but even just over the last few months Sharasthi had seen anti-Imperial sentiment grow. If Caroshai turned, the Empire would lose its only major ally in the Southlands, which would put the colonies at risk of invasion.

All in all, a serious assignment for Sharasthi's first mission as a full Adept. She was to bring the leaders of the conspiracy in under arrest, or put them to death if that proved the more prudent option.

Sharasthi ghosted into a room, the hinges creaking. Total darkness engulfed those sleeping on the floor within. She went to work.

It turned her stomach. The smell of blood. The way they would bat at her arm as she covered their mouths before opening their throats and puncturing their lungs.

She had drilled on mannequins countless times at the Workshop. She could kill silently with her eyes closed. These people had friends. Families. Lovers. But what was she to do?

Killing them was the only mercy she could afford. She had no love for the Empire; she did not care if it was to Lazarra's disadvantage if she killed all these men instead of bringing a few in to be tortured. She would lie and say she didn't have an opportunity, or she would say bloodlust got ahold of her, or even just fear.

A lad scarcely younger than her writhed under her grip.

Don't think about it don't think about it don't think about—

The mission would be complete.

She drove the knife into his lung. Again. Into his throat.

Her gloves were soaked, every twitch of her fingers squeezing blood from the fabric.

Maybe she could return to the capital after this was over, get a different assignment.

The sound a man made when stabbed in the lungs—it was a hollow rattle, less than a choke or even a gasp. She kept her hand over the mouth, hearing nothing but the rush of blood in her ears.

Her own breathing was even. That was part of the training as well. Lose your breath and you were liable to pass out during your work.

Work. She had never fully appreciated the way Intelligence called it that. As if it were as simple as running errands, picking grain, slaughtering livestock.

Work.

The last one sleeping in the room had more struggle in him than most. He tried to bite Sharasthi's hand. His compatriots' blood oozed from the glove into his mouth, trickling down either side in sickening rivulets.

Sharasthi stabbed the lung—and missed as he wrenched his body sideways. She cut a gash along his side. He threw a punch into her gut; he may as well have been striking a wall, for all the strength aether granted her.

Sharasthi grimaced. Someone's blood had sprayed her face. She tasted it at the corner of her mouth.

Die! Die! Die!

She brought the knife down again and again. His muffled cries drove her mad. *Silent! Just be silent!*

His foot lashed out, striking a metal bowl and sending it crashing into the wall, loud as thunder.

Sharasthi cursed under her breath, wrenching the knife upward and shattering ribs with aetheric strength. The fight finally went out of the man.

She stumbled back a half-step. Blood. She was soaked in blood and sweat.

The hinges creaked.

A cry of alarm.

A man stared into the blackness, trying to thrust his lamp into the gloom yet finding no purchase. Her presence in the city was more or less known by now, and certainly known by the conspirators if they indeed had that mole.

Sharasthi wondered if he smelled the blood. The reek of it stained the inside of her nose.

The man turned and ran, screaming for help, screaming murder. Sharasthi gave chase.

His lamp cast frantic shadows on the walls—Sharasthi sent forth her magic, letting those shadows burgeon and fill the hallway.

The man screamed all the louder, but only for a moment. Then Sharasthi was upon him. Three stabs in the back as she brought him down. One empowered strike with the pommel at the base of the skull, shattering the spinal column.

Others were shouting now.

"Out! Out!"

"Barricade the door and run!"

Sharasthi hissed. She wanted to be away from this damned city.

She wanted to be done with hunting and scouring.

She couldn't let them get away. If they got away then her mission stretched onward.

Tonight. She was ending it tonight.

Sharasthi threw her shoulder against a door. It broke inward about a foot, stopped by some sort of brace. She wormed through the gap. Someone threw a spear at her, but everything around her for ten feet was choked with shadows. They hardly knew what they were fighting, lurking in the obscure plume. The weapon struck the wall beside her harmlessly.

The room she had forced her way into was much bigger—she guessed the biggest in the place. Shelves upon shelves, which the inhabitants were scrambling to empty of their contents and escape with.

Even in the dark, they knew their territory, scampering through the door on the far side of the room, sliding down a ladder into the underground. Sharasthi moved among them like a phantom, her knife slicing and darting out like a tongue of steel.

Those she struck cried out, clutching their wounds.

She saw Hannil's disapproving glower. '*Not clean,*' he chided. *Not clean.* Strike to kill or strike to incapacitate—but never strike thoughtlessly.

Someone was scrambling around by her feet, clutching a scroll ruined by his blood.

I'm sorry, she thought. He shouldn't have been in unnecessary pain like that. She struck to kill.

Her targets were getting away. With a shock of aether to her legs, she flew across the room and brought one down. His arm stretched out after a fleeing compatriot. "*Go-achk!*" Sharasthi opened his throat and drowned his dying word. The other man did not even look back to watch his friend's final moments. That was good; that was how she had been trained as well. The mission came before everything else.

Sharasthi leapt up from the corpse and chased after the running man. He grabbed at something on a table, fumbling desperately for it —risking his life for a metal plate. What such thing could merit that?

In the dark, he tripped—a twist of fate that saved him from Sharasthi's blade as it passed through the empty air where his neck had just been. She pounced on his prone form, driving her knee into his back with enough force to knock the breath from his lungs.

The metal in his hands fell out of his grasp, struck the ground with a rattle.

Sharasthi drew the knife back, ready to drive it through his heart.

And then she saw it.

For an instant, she was a little girl, huffing in the dusty gloom of the temple archive, keeping her feet through a dizzy spell.

The gods laugh.

The man beneath her groaned, gasped. Sharasthi forced him onto his back, pressed the blade's edge to his throat. She released the shadows. The man gaped as her face appeared from the dark.

She snatched the bronze disc from the ground and held it before his face. "Why do you have this?" she hissed.

His features hardened. "Just kill me," he coughed.

Sharasthi sucked in a breath. "*Ordo Draconis Laevisomnis.*" And though she had not called to mind those old words in years, they rose to her lips with a dreadful familiarity: "*The Republic of Lazarra is going to fall. Dark days are coming. My children, do not trust yourselves to the smooth words of the thousand-eyed spirit who makes himself out to be lord of all. Verily I tell you, his words are but vain seduction, and he will free you only to make you his slave.*"

His eyes widened and widened further. His lips parted.

Sharasthi ground her teeth.

Just kill him!

She saw her grandfather on the altar. Heard his cries.

From long-buried memories, her youthful vow arose.

Scrambling to her feet, she backed away, then threw the seal of the Order of the Sleeping Dragon onto his chest.

"*Go,*" she snapped. "If I see you again, I'll kill you like the rest."

Clutching the seal as he got up, he looked at her with a mystified expression. He did not thank her or say another word, just ran.

Sharasthi's fingers ached around the hilt.

Silence.

An agonized scream broke out from her lips. She grabbed an oil lamp and threw it on a pile of documents left behind. The fire took and grew. She made her way back through the carnage, stepping over bodies. The blaze kept growing.

When she got outside, she raised the alarm. Startled faces appeared, gaped at the woman dripping blood shouting about fire— but smoke was in the air.

By the time her colleagues in Intelligence arrived with a force of legionnaires, they had nothing to do but join the bucket brigade.

As the sun rose red over Caroshai, Sharasthi washed her hands in a jar of water left behind when the blaze was finally subdued, telling truths and lies about what had happened.

22

PEOPLE LIKE HERSELF

Can the murderer, the fornicator, the blasphemer be redeemed? Only by giving himself wholly to the Fire and trusting its Judgment is righteous.

—Zaro's Sayings, verse one hundred and fifteen

Music and song filled the air of the Palatine Hill. So too did the aroma of sizzling meats—beef, chicken, pork, fresh-caught fish. Slaves dressed finer than all but the most wealthy of merchants made their ways about with food-laden platters, wine from the best vineyards and best vintages, delicacies from across and beyond the Empire. There was more than one person could hope to sample, even if he arrived on an empty stomach.

An Emperor's firstborn son, after all, was only born once, and the entire city was glutting itself at the expense of the Imperial coffers.

Sharasthi wondered how many others were contemplating the fate of Dioclete's eldest. After all, it was not uncommon for Lazarran Emperors to adopt heirs they found more worthy than their natural children.

A number of praetors were in attendance on the Palatine Hill this evening; no doubt some of them were scheming how they might earn that very honor from their lord. The cause of tonight's festivities was but an obstacle on the road to glory.

Cassia Vantelle was not in attendance, as she was putting down an armed uprising in Karella. Rufus was there as well, once again useful to the woman—though she was no longer a legate as when they had come to Zarush, but a praetor, having been raised to the office before she turned thirty, an unprecedented feat. Sharasthi was glad for the woman's absence. The thought of her always set Sharasthi's nerves on edge, reminded her of how this all came to be.

Her grandfather's death. Her leaving Zarush and becoming an Initiate.

The only bright spot in all of it was Alyat, but he wasn't here either. He was probably toasting to the Imperial household's health with the Lazarran provincial governor in Aspagne right now.

It had just been bad luck that she was in the capital when this celebration unfolded.

Ordinarily, she would have lingered by the edge of things (there were ample places to lurk out of sight on the Hill), but as she learned rapidly, most of those places had been claimed by intoxicated and amorous revelers. Yet another reminder of how far Alyat was and how long it had been since they saw each other.

Sharasthi did the mental calculations yet again, as if somehow this time it would provide a secret to when they would be reunited. Fourteen months. Fourteen months since they had been in each other's arms.

They exchanged letters of course, but even that could grow more painful than it was worth. At some point, reading his words only became yet another reminder of how he was not there. It was almost preferable to hear nothing from him, if only so she could try to forget and let the time pass easier. A day anticipated always came slower.

"Pardon me, Adept," said a man she did not know.

Sharasthi frowned. Plenty of people had tried to speak with her tonight, eager to curry favor with an Adept, but usually she at least had a vague idea of who they were. Senators wore distinctive garb. Merchants you could recognize from the desperate stench of striving to belong among the aristocracy. The aristocracy itself was known by their inviolable air of pomp.

The man's clothes were not overly fine, though they were kempt. His build put her in mind of a leopard. Lithe, capable of violence in a burst.

She did not know his face, yet something in his eyes told her he was quite familiar with her.

"I believe you have me at a disadvantage."

His lips formed a smile. "Zageth."

Ah, she knew that name. "Praetor Vantelle's latest optio. You must have made great haste in coming here to represent her."

"Yes, she wished she could have been here, but the Myrmidons are quite a thorn."

"You don't seem worried."

Zageth inclined his head. "You, like me, owe a certain debt to Cassia Vantelle. You know what she is like. What she desires, she will have."

Sharasthi cast a glance toward the pavilion where Dioclete was still receiving well wishes and congratulations. "I'm sure she will. So the praetor told you of me."

"Indeed, and she wished me to convey her congratulations on your commission. A few years late, for which she apologizes. I believe she wanted to tell you in person, but the work of Empire has kept her busy. At some point even she must acknowledge some things will not go her way." That thin smile. "Even she can be foiled, now and then."

Sharasthi did not like this man. He was wearing a mask, of that she was certain, and beneath that mask was the sort of person who would do anything to achieve his ends. She preferred not to linger in the company of people like herself.

"Well, my thanks to Vantelle and to you for relaying her words to me. I will be sure to write her as much. Now, if you'll excuse me, I believe I see an old friend by the fruits table." She manufactured a smile. "A pleasure meeting you."

Zageth extended his hand. "The pleasure is all mine. And I owe you my thanks."

Sharasthi clasped his hand. Calloused, firm—a killer's grip. "I can't imagine what for, given we've just met."

He took a half-step forward, close enough that Sharasthi had to stamp down an impulse to strike him. His mouth came near her ear, and his voice was hardly perceptible under the din of conversation and music. "True, but two years ago you met a friend of mine, in Caroshai, under the most unusual of circumstances."

Sharasthi's blood went cold. She kept her smile, forced a laugh—she always managed her most compelling laughs when she was unnerved. *He can't mean that.* "That was quite some time ago. I can't remember."

Zageth pulled back, his smile unchanged as he folded his hands behind his back. "He had quite a story to tell."

"It was a long and tiresome few months. Perhaps if I met him it would jog my memory."

"He's across the sea at the moment. Besides, he said it would be best if that encounter remained the only one."

"I hope it wasn't something I said."

"I'm afraid it may have been."

Sharasthi searched his eyes. Her impression of him was unchanged, but now she had no choice but to entangle herself. "What a pity. Even so, I'm glad I was able to meet you, at least, before you must return to the praetor's side."

"I leave for Karella the day after tomorrow. There's a performance of my favorite play on tomorrow night at the Grand, so I'll get to savor a bit more of the capital's delights before returning to the field. Have you ever seen *Ixia Patria*?"

"I can't say I'm one for the theater."

"Well, this one may convert you—and I've got the best seats in the house, one of the suites in the upper section."

Sharasthi knew perfectly well that was one of the worst places to watch from—but it was ideal if you wanted to talk away from prying ears. "I may have to take you up on that."

23

FATED TO BURN

CHIEFTAIN: This rabble is come from the sea, dripping with salt and stinking of fish, and say they dream of a city! I would not trust them to dig a latrine. Take your gods and hie to the hills, strangers, for never will the people of Ixia bow to your ilk.

SEER: Be careful in your speech, my lord, for beneath the weariness of travel I glimpse some noble bearing in them. Goodly strength and piety cannot be hidden by rags and reek—indeed, it flows in the blood.

—*Ixia Patria*, Act One

SHARASTHI HAD NEVER BEEN to the Grand. In all her life, the closest she had come to watching a play was during the annual New Year ceremonies in Zarush, when there had been reenactments of the oldest stories of the gods, the sorts of stories that predated Zaro's revelations about the nature of the Eternal Flame.

The production on tonight was a historical play based on the Founders of Lazarra, specifically their exploits once they landed here in the Ixian Reach after their long sojourns across the waves of the *Mare Magnum*.

Zageth watched with interest, seated beside her. There were two more people in the room with them, but they were seated by the door and Sharasthi could not see their faces—not because of the dark but because they stayed with their backs to her.

The scene unfolding on the stage depicted the Founders approaching the first town of native Ixians on the coast and making an offer of vassalhood. If the Ixians would kneel to them and worship their gods, then they would receive the honor of joining in the life and inheritance of the city that would stand on this ground—a city to rule all the world.

The townsfolk laughed at the sorry state of the Founders, having just made landfall after such long voyaging, and they said they would never give their daughters to men of such pathetic stature, nor would they have anything to do with a city that was sure to fall into ruin.

And so the Founders killed half of them and drove the other half into the hills.

As the story went, other towns and tribes of Ixians drew near and joined themselves in marriage and subjugation to the Founders, but never did that first tribe ever receive forgiveness for slighting the Founders and their dream of Lazarra. Some said that to this day the brigands living in the mountainous regions were the descendants of those Ixians.

Sharasthi did not know how much of it was historical, nor did she care. All cultures were founded on grand stories. Whether there was a kernel or heap of truth in the stories, whether they were spun entirely from the imagination, the reality that rested upon those tales could not be denied, and so neither could the tales themselves.

Her grandfather had believed in the story of Zaro. He had also believed in the story of the Order of the Sleeping Dragon, passed down to him on a bronze seal.

Zageth was a still man. He did not tap his foot, did not cross and uncross his legs. He just observed. Sharasthi waited for him to make a move; after all, it had been he who organized this.

When he at last broached the matter, he did so in a low voice. "You did a great thing for the Order, and at great risk to yourself if you had been found out."

"I knew I would not be."

"You did not fear as much when we spoke yesterday?"

"If I had been found out, I would not have been confronted like that. A Carnifex would have come for me in the night, and now I either would be dead or enchained in some dark oubliette."

"Such things happen to those in this life. I've lost many compatriots."

"Yet you still live."

"It is always the worst who survive, don't you think? The Order has nearly been wiped out before—we cannot afford much intradependence. If you betrayed me tonight, no matter what tortures I may be put to, perhaps three, four others would be at risk."

"Out of how many?"

Zageth shrugged. She did not press.

"And so when I learned what you did in Caroshai, I assumed you were already part of things. Then, despite some probing, I found no indication." His eyes shone in the night, reflecting the torchlight ringing the stage below. "Rare indeed is one who knows the words of the Last Consul yet is not counted among us."

Sharasthi remembered hiding the seal in the temple archive in her little spot, the spot not even her grandfather had known. "Something from a past life."

"Reticence is good. It has been slow going to reconstitute ourselves since the last purge. Some of this generation are like you, coming from outside Lazarran stock. A sorry thing, and yet necessary after what happened. Ciell Aenan placed seeds of his hope for the restoration of the old Lazarra all across the world, hoping they might one day bear allies."

"I assume the head is Lazarran."

"One assumes."

"Have you met him?"

"I suspect I have."

"You'll forgive me if I'm not particularly inspired by this conversation."

Zageth's mouth crooked into an almost sadistic smile. "Were you hoping to be? This is not a venture for those who require such things. The gods filled us all with more than a fair measure of madness. I desire the restoration of the Republic, but I did not swear myself to the Order because of that desire. I do not do *this* out of a want for something. I do it out of myself, because I must."

Sharasthi looked ahead, over the opposite edge of the amphitheater, into the darkness of the sky. Had not she sworn her vow in exactly the same manner?

Yes, she longed to avenge her grandfather, but it was not that longing alone that had spurred her. Longing waned. Emotions cooled. She had not sworn her vow out of anger alone, but because it was something that had to be done. Just as matter had to fall to earth. Just as fire had to rise to heaven. Just as life formed and perpetuated across countless generations—it did so *out of itself*.

"That," she murmured, "is something I understand. I do not care for the Last Consul's vision. Lazarra gave me power, but it cannot return what I lost, no matter what I do for the Empire that is or the Republic that might be.

"When I was a child, I had a sense of what my life would be. Now, instead, I lie and kill, because when a wrong was done, I had no choice but to do as I did. What I have done since. And if I were given the chance to change anything I have done since that day...I could not."

Her head tilted back, her eyes closed. "When I was an Initiate, I had to read the dialogue between...now I do not recall the names. Minor philosophers in the scheme of things, their one lasting contribution an argument over freedom and fate. One said man is free, the other that the gods have fixed all things. I thought it was so foolish...

"All is Fire. It wills to burn. It is fated to burn." She opened her eyes. "Yes, I understand."

She held out her hand, and Zageth took it.

24

A GRIM WEIGHT

A MAN CAME to me in tears, saying, "Prophet, my wife and children call your words folly. Will they suffer in the Judgment?" Understand this: not all can bear the Truth, and this is no sin, in the same way it is no sin for a dog to eat vomit. But for those who can bear the Truth and still reject it, the Judgment will be harshest. A warrior must swing a sword, a farmer must sow crops, and the strong must bear the world.

—Zaro's Sayings, verse five hundred and twelve

THE SOUND of waves gently crashing on the shore haunted the predawn air. A chill breeze whisked in through the window, rousing Sharasthi from her sleep and driving her to nestle further into Alyat's side.

He never seemed to grow cold; if anything, the colder it got, the warmer he seemed. Idle fantasies of fleeing the Empire and hiding in the Northlands drifted through her half-slumbering mind. She would like to lie in his arms while a snowstorm raged outside, if only to prove to the storm she was invincible with him.

In the past year, Alyat had taken a scar along his side, etched from under his right arm down to his hip. She kissed it, then traced her fingers along it. He had not told her how severe the injury was in any of his letters—not until she saw it in person last night did she know. It had not even been a battle, just a madman with a carving knife, screaming about ghosts and spirits. Alyat had put him down and flooded the wound with aether, but it had been an ugly gash, and it healed as a grim scar.

Sharasthi tried not to think about what would have happened if the bastard had struck with better intent. If he had pierced Alyat's heart, or brain, or spine.

She knew how fast men died when a blade skewered just the right spot. Would he have reacted quickly enough to save himself? He was strong, intelligent—but even Adepts died.

The thought was strangling her heart, so she looked up at his face. He was still sleeping. His beard was thicker now. That might have been her influence. He had always toed the edge of dress regulations with his facial hair, but now he hardly bothered. On the whole though, he still followed all the rules and protocols.

Except when it came to Sharasthi. For her, he found the wherewithal to step around things. Another one of those gifts he gave without expectation.

Right now, he should have been a few miles up the road in Ouranopolis, the capital of Karella. There were ongoing negotiations with the Krypteian Five Families regarding their relationship to the Empire. Dioclete found their neutrality during the Myrmidon Resurgence—which Vantelle had crushed—a despicable thing. Alyat found it all tiring. He had made much of his career in work with Legion Intelligence and the diplomatic service, and yet he despised working with men who trafficked in lies and secrecy.

Sharasthi's heart twinged.

Yet he cares for me.

Over the years, they had a few precious chances to work together under the banner of Legion Intelligence, but this was not one of those times. As far as Alyat knew, her only business in Karella was as a supervising Adept for a field mission. She had a pupil of her own now, a lad named Jan whose first mentor had died partway through his tutelage. Jan did not have much of a heart for war, but he loved animals—as befitted a practitioner of the *Ars Theron*, the Art of Beasts —and like Sharasthi, he had no love for the Empire.

She cultivated that carefully. While Jan did not yet know about the Order, he knew enough about Sharasthi's true disposition toward Lazarra. She hoped to place him with the Imperial Post. His Art would be a worthy justification, as it would enable him to put the messenger hawks to better use.

And having a man inside the Post would be a great asset for Sharasthi and the Order.

Alyat too, had no idea about the Order. He had no clue that two years ago Sharasthi had met with Zageth and struck hands in conspiracy. He had no idea that yesterday Sharasthi had slipped away from supervising Jan and the other Initiates to meet with a Krypteian who was a longstanding friend of the Order.

Her task had been to ascertain whether any among the Five Families might be sympathetic to their cause. Unfortunately, after Vantelle finally crushed the Myrmidon Resurgence, Karella as a whole was reticent to take action against Lazarra. With the right hand broken, the left was not eager to enter the fray.

The sea breeze blew again, and Sharasthi sighed, full with nostalgia for the night she earned her commission, the night before she left for Caroshai. They had been by the water then. This place was quieter. She liked the quiet, by herself and with Alyat. He was someone who understood the delights of silence.

But soon the sun would be up. She had gotten away from the Initiates twice now—two times more than she should have. They wouldn't know of her absence, if she got back before they woke.

But getting back required leaving the bed, and leaving the bed meant leaving Alyat.

The longer they worked in this life, the less and less they saw each other. Now even when she did get to be with him, there was guilt. She did not write letters as often as she once had, because every time she felt all the more acutely what she was leaving out. She had to watch what she said around him on account of the cunning, keen mind she so loved.

Yet still she lay in his arms, whispered her love to him—was that just using him for her own comfort, to balm a wound she had been carrying since she was small?

He could tell she hid things. She knew he could tell. They knew one another too well for him not to realize. He paid too much attention. Yet he did not press her on it.

The thought that one day he would demand to know it all terrified her. She was terrified to lose him, but also terrified of hurting him, not just by her own deeds but by mere association.

If the Empire found her out, they would put the screws to him as well.

Running away to the Northlands, or to anywhere else far away... was it really just a fantasy? Might there be a chance there? A shred of hope for something else?

A knock sounded at the door. Sharasthi sat bolt upright. Her presence could not be known here. Whoever it was must have been seeking Alyat. He finally woke, groaning slightly as he got up, tugging on clothes. Sharasthi sank back down to the bed, using her magic to darken the room.

Whoever it was, he handed something to Alyat and left in haste. A runner, most likely.

Alyat shut the door and turned, already reading the dispatch in his hands.

"Are they upset," she asked, "that you're all the way out here?"

He grunted, his expression hardening. "Doesn't matter if they are."

She propped herself up, searching his face. "What's wrong?"

"Kars died. Killed in action."

He had been one of Alyat's pupils.

"I'm sorry."

He sighed, sitting down on the bed. She started rubbing his back.

He never wept. She could not think of one time she had seen him do so. But she could see he was in pain.

Moving to wrap her arms around him from behind, she murmured, "It's not your fault."

"Hm."

"Really, Alyat. No one could have prepared him better."

"I hope he agrees, down there in the hells."

She went on stroking his chest. His heartbeat was solid and strong as ever, faster though. That was a strange thing. Grief, brought on by the opposite of life, hastened the blood. Yet no one else looking at Alyat would have guessed the turmoil within him.

In an odd way, she was grateful the news came while they were together. Otherwise what could she have done for him? Sent a letter? No one else could hold him like this.

"Also," he muttered, "I'm due to return to the Sanctum for a while. They want me to train another."

"They've got someone for you?"

"Not yet, but they're anticipating one or two more additions to Seventh Cohort."

"You'll do well by them."

His sigh was heavy.

"I know."

"Odds were against Kars from the start anyway. They sent him to Parthava, even after the last two were killed."

Sharasthi's arms tightened around Alyat. "Parthava," she echoed. Right—Alyat's pupil was the third Adept to be assigned to the Parthavan campaign, and now the third to die in it.

And she was at the conclusion of an assignment.

Before she realized what she was saying, she murmured, "The Hunters."

"Dead in a hail of arrows."

She swallowed. "Do you have," she muttered, "something to write with?"

Alyat half-turned, looking at her from the corner of his eye. Blue, sharp. "*Sharasthi.*"

Not his sweet name for her, not *Shara*—her whole name. How much he could say just like that...

He knew, of course. She had told him, on one of their stolen nights, how her grandfather had died. How she'd sworn to pay that back. How that vow had fueled her labor as an Initiate.

Almost a decade since she had earned her commission. Almost fifteen years since she had watched her grandfather's bones go into the ground.

She had tried to hide from that too. From her own oath. The oath that had been her whole world, the only thing she cared about for years.

But it had found her. It had found her in Caroshai. It had found her on the Palatine Hill. It had found her here in Karella.

Always, she had to hide. First she had hidden her heart from the pain of loss, brought on by Vohman's death. Then Alyat had drawn her out of that.

But the specter of the past had only given her a reprieve. Always, it returned. And now it forced her to hide her heart again, this time from the one she should have never hidden from.

"I must," she whispered.

Alyat pulled away from her touch, pivoting to face her straight on. "They'll kill you too." Never one to mince words.

She reached out to touch the bear mark over his heart. "Death visits often. We've both always slipped away."

"I know what you're like, Sharasthi. You're not born for violence. I see how it revolts you. How you scrub under your nails even when you're a horizon away from murder. Someone else should bring the Parthavans down. Go there once the campaign is won. Search for your grandfather's killer then."

"You're hoping he'll be already dead."

"He may be dead now. What if you go only to learn that, and then you're stuck there, a volunteer for a war you've no heart to fight."

She shook her head, though she could not explain how she was so certain. "He's probably the one who killed Kars. Or at least had a hand in it."

His voice was cold. "You don't know that."

Memories. The memory of the Hunter with that strange and beautiful bow in hand. The memory of Claw-face striking her grandfather, casting him atop the altar.

The way her grandfather had groaned as he burned, and how the Hunters had been frightened and ended him with an arrow.

"You have no love for the Empire, Sharasthi. I can tell that much."

Her fingernails dug into her thighs, the pain a distant reality. "It doesn't matter if it's for Lazarra or anyone else. My *grandfather*, Alyat. The only family I ever knew."

His calloused hands took hers, enfolded them in their rough warmth. The red crescent gouges in her skin healed, leaving just flecks of blood. "And me?"

A grim weight struck her chest and sank into her stomach.

Fire burned—it could do nothing else.

"I have to."

In that instant, she felt the doors shut again, leaving her in the dark.

Alyat looked at her, then stood. "I'll get you that stylus and parchment."

As he rifled through his things, she drew her knees up to her chest, hugged her legs.

She was cold and naked and alone, and Alyat seemed miles away across the room.

25

WHEN THE EARTH KNEW NO COLD

YES, the Hunters of Parthava are frustratingly reclusive, but by custom show great hospitality to guests who approach with sufficient deference. I spent some months living among a tribe known as the Rysta. I never was permitted to glimpse their cultic rites or hear the legends that lay behind them, but they claim to have received them unchanged and uninterrupted from thousands upon thousands of years in the past.

—The Life and Wisdom of Simeon Binkhok As Told by Himself

"ADEPT SHARASTHI," said Legate Taric of the Seventh Imperial Legion, "give me some good news."

She stabbed her finger at the map of Parthava spread across the table. "We were making gains in the north, but then a Hunter force came up and reinforced the Coalition troops."

The legate grimaced. "Same story."

The political arrangement of Parthava was unusual. The oldest in the land were the Hunter tribes. They ranged through their ancestral territories in the south of the country, obeying their own laws and abiding by their own customs.

The Hunters did not rule Parthava in the same way the Emperor ruled Lazarra. They preferred to keep to themselves, leaving the cities in the north and center to the rule of kings. Historically, there had been violence between the cities and tribes, but for the most part the urbanite Parthavans regarded the tribes with a blend of respect and fear. The Hunters represented the fount of Parthavan culture and blood, and it was believed the favor of the gods toward the entire land hinged on whether the Hunters upheld their strange, rarely witnessed rites.

In order to resist the Lazarrans, the cities of Parthava had unified as the Coalition. Kings and councils forged a pact to stand together against the Empire, contributing as many men as they could. That said, most cities could only field citizen militias, with some of the more powerful ones contributing a standing army. Against the professional soldiery of the Lazarran Legions, they gave an admirable effort. In battles on the wide, open steppe, the maneuverability and range of their cavalry archers made for formidable engagements against the legion, which was constituted predominantly of heavy infantry augmented by light infantry and cavalry auxiliaries.

But the Coalition troops could only do so much against the Lazarran war machine. Gradually, the legionnaires—marching in armor-studded lockstep—would drive through the showers of arrows right to the city gates. And the Parthavans, being by constitution given to love of open spaces and abhorring constraint, all too often had easily breached walls. Their gates were meant to repel bandits, not the greatest army the world had ever known.

Just one year ago, the Seventh Legion had controlled half the country, and it was thought Parthavan capitulation would come soon given the arrival of Lazarra's most formidable asset: an Imperial Adept.

That Adept's arrival turned the tide of the war—in Parthava's favor.

Not two weeks after he joined a siege effort, the Hunter tribes broke from their disinterested neutrality. Their legendary black-feathered arrows rattled in the quiver as they stormed the unawares legion, sweeping through their ranks and placing impossible shots through the gaps between shields, under the iron brims of helmets.

As soon as they struck, they vanished—leaving in their wake chaos and confusion and a bloody, bolt-riddled corpse wearing the red and gold mantle.

In Sharasthi's advanced briefing and throughout the hectic weeks since her arrival, she had learned it was still the Hunters giving the legion the most trouble. The militias of the Coalition cities fought admirably, but not mightily enough to withstand the Seventh Legion on their own.

In comparison, the Hunters were a nightmare. They did not fight pitched battles. Instead they struck in lightning-quick raids at all hours. After a week of hounding the legion through the night, they would switch to attacks at noon. They would begin raids only to pull back before bloodshed could happen, then another warband would strike somewhere else.

And any time they did end up in a conventional engagement, the Hunters would turn tail and ride off on those god-blooded horses of theirs. Giving chase was suicide for one simple reason—the legendary Parthavan shot. Their mounted archers trained from youth to turn and fire backwards from the saddle—and the Hunters made the best of the Coalition riders look like amateurs. This made for one of the most ridiculous sights Sharasthi had encountered in her military career: when Hunters retreated, legionnaires took cover.

Any time the legion came close to a strategic victory against the Coalition—be it taking a city or capturing a key natural formation—the Hunters appeared, riding like phantoms on the wind.

Legate Taric cursed. "If this doesn't turn around soon, I've half a mind to start burning forests."

The legate's optio cleared his throat. "That would be unwise, sir. Assuming we intend to maintain a presence in Parthava after—"

"*I am aware*. I am also aware that we've been playing out the same losing strategy for months on end. And"—he tipped his head toward Sharasthi—"Dioclete will have my head if we lose another Adept."

Sharasthi had come to take the legate's brusque manner of speech in stride. Some of his subordinates skirted about him, but that only worsened his demeanor. The best way to handle him was head-on—though she looked forward to it as much as plunging into cold water.

"On the matter of my death," she began, "I've reviewed the Hunters' raids since my arrival. The plan to keep my location obscured seems to be working."

Taric grunted. "For now."

The Hunters had made great sport of the Adepts on the Parthavan campaign. In fact, the most frequent cause for the Hunters' abandoning their hit-and-run tactics was an Adept taking to the field. They could not resist the opportunity to kill one of the Lazarran mages. It seemed to whip them into a nigh religious fervor.

Sharasthi was again reminded of what Claw-face had said to her grandfather. *'We hunted Marzud.'*

Alyat's pupil, Adept Kars, despite his youth, had in fact survived the longest of the three Adepts who'd come to Parthava. He had realized that challenging the Hunters openly was a death sentence for an Adept, and so he had adopted an irregular schedule. He did not remain with any given company for more than a day or two. He would travel halfway to a certain front, then turn and go to a different one. He had moved in disguise, sometimes with decoys wearing replicas of his mantle.

Even so, it had only worked for so long. The Hunters had a knack for sniffing out the Adept. It put some of the men on edge.

When Kars had died, there were five legionnaires disguised as decoys within arm's reach of him.

A Parthavan warband had set upon the company. Not a full-heated battle, but a skirmish. Kars had been moving into position to make the best use of his *Ars Terra*.

Then, as one of the decoys told it, an arrow took him in the throat, another in the eye, and he was gone.

The pair of Hunters who had fired the shots had been hanging back from the fray, surveying the engagement. They had picked Kars out and killed him. Not one decoy had been touched. It lended credence to what informants inside the Parthavan Coalition had suggested: there were Hunters who could perceive magic.

At first a mere rumor, now assumed to be fact—there were certain Hunters whose single aim was to track and slaughter Adepts. So far they had brought down three, and doubtless they were eager to make Sharasthi the fourth corpse.

Before she arrived, Intelligence had been ambivalent on a more fantastical piece of information: that these Adept-killers had golden eyes and were the most revered of the tribal riders, inspiring awe in their kinsmen and frightening the city-dwellers. When Sharasthi heard the reports, she readily confirmed it. All those years ago in Zarush, she had seen their wondrous eyes herself. These Hunter golds, as they came to be known, were of the same ilk as Claw-face and his compatriot.

Claw-face had called her something then. *Varmakis*. He had said he would not harm her because she was one, and she had not known what it meant. The term did not exist in the Parthavan dialects of the cities, but her intuition told her that Claw-face, by some sort of mystical power—the same mystical power that enabled the golds to hunt Adepts so ruthlessly—had known she had the potential to become an Adept.

But whatever rule or principle had bound him that day to stay his hand from harming her, it did not bind the Hunters who had killed Kars and his predecessors. If anything, it seemed the opposite was the case: the Hunters *relished* the opportunity to slay them.

Sharasthi would not become their latest prey. Not until she had killed the Hunter with the claw mark on his face. If she happened to die then, so be it, but she would not accept such a fate until her grandfather's murderer was dead.

One of the first things she had asked when she arrived was whether any Hunters fitting Claw-face's description had been seen. Some legionnaires testified as much, but there was not enough consistency. The Hunters moved too unpredictably to establish reliable reports on particular warbands.

What she did know for certain was that the other man who had been there when Claw-face killed her grandfather was alive and active in Parthava.

There were far more holes in Legion Intelligence's knowledge of the tribes compared to the cities, but some things were credible. The most famed Hunter was the so-called Son of Thunder, Tobron of the Ochita. He was considered the divine child of the Parthavan goddess Kashakran, as testified by his sacred bow strung with a strand of her hair.

No matter how many years had elapsed, Sharasthi still remembered every detail of her grandfather's murder. She remembered the beautiful, bizarre bow that rider had held. She remembered how Claw-face had called out to him: '*Tobron!*'

Tobron was in his forties and famed for having taken up Kashakran's bow at just fifteen. Legion Intelligence suspected he sent the warband that killed the first Adept.

Assassinating Tobron was one of the foremost priorities for winning the war, but it seemed nigh impossible as his tribe dwelled deep within the Bildani Wood.

Parthava was a land of two terrains: the steppe and the forest. The former constituted perhaps three-quarters of the land, with the remaining portion taken up by one great sprawl of dense woodland in the southern reaches. The Bildani Wood was impenetrable, even to the best Scouts, who came back disoriented and dazed if they came back at all. City-born Parthavan informants were no help, and those from small villages even less so—they feared malicious ghosts and terrible curses if they dared set foot in the Bildani without a Hunter guide. It was the provenance of the tribes and the tribes alone.

Tobron's tribe, the Ochita, was not the largest, but from what Intelligence had garnered, it was among the most revered, tracing its lineage uninterrupted back to—as local superstition put it—'the days when the earth knew no cold.' Within the Bildani, they were untouchable, and no one had seen Tobron outside the Wood since the Seventh Legion arrived.

As such, the legate and his advisors more or less held no hope they could win this war by killing him. It was a chief goal that would take a miracle—so they prayed and offered sacrifices and made plans for what they *could* perhaps achieve.

Legate Taric's scowl only worsened as he asked, "Has anything changed with the Triumvirate?"

The Triumvirate—as the legionnaires had mockingly dubbed them—were the three most powerful Coalition generals. Most of the professional soldiers in the Parthavan ranks were under their command. One of them was also king over the largest city in the land, and so he was de facto head of the Coalition.

Before the Hunters entered the fray, getting at the Triumvirate had presented a great challenge, but one theoretically possible if the legate deemed it necessary. Now, every member of the Triumvirate had a Hunter warband for bodyguards, not to mention the numerous additional riding parties attached to their armies. Intelligence furthermore had reason to believe these warbands were training the Coalition armies. The war's prospects only grew dimmer by the week for the legion.

The legate's optio shook his head as he perused reports. "No movement from the Triumvirate. King Santruch is still holding against our northernmost forces, Pachur controls the center near the Bildani, and we have no good information regarding the third. Intelligence's best guess is that he's in position to reinforce whichever front most needs his attention."

Taric had an extensive repertoire of vulgar oaths, which he creatively deployed in that moment.

Sharasthi examined the map in the command tent, a map she had pored over countless hours by now.

The north and center, owned by the Coalition and reinforced by Hunters. The south, the impenetrable domain of the tribes.

"Legate!" A Scout came into the tent, fire in his eyes. "I've got something."

Taric's eyes narrowed. "It had better be good."

The Scout nodded firmly. "You recall the Warda tribe?"

He grunted. Before Sharasthi's arrival, the legion had negotiated a peace with a tribe calling themselves the Warda. They were small and uninterested in war, and so all they had asked was a promise the legion would not touch the flora and fauna of their territory.

The Scout continued. "The Ochita wronged them, violated an old treaty."

Sharasthi perked up. "How grave is this treaty violation?"

"It's superstitious nonsense—an Ochita rider crossed through Warda territory with an empty quiver—but the Warda are incensed. They're willing to ally with us if it means they get first crack at Tobron's territory after the war."

The legate traced the area on the map with his finger. "Some steppe land and a deep pocket of the Bildani? Too good to be true."

Sharasthi crossed her arms. "Well, the Warda are not particularly useful themselves. They only have about a dozen war-capable riders, maybe twenty if the old came along. They could never hope to beat the Ochita under their own power."

"Even so, I'd think they would ask for something more."

Sharasthi eyed the map. "The Ochita are small, but they're revered enough that the Coalition-allied Hunters are willing to let Tobron be their figurehead. Perhaps their land is sacred in some way. If the Warda will take our side over something as minor as an empty quiver..."

The Scout raised his hand. "If I may, there is something more."

The legate scowled. "Out with it then."

"While it's not a necessary term to the agreement, the Warda have asked that, if we accept, we make defeating the Ochita a priority—"

"If I could so easily—!"

"—*and* they've offered a prime opportunity for just that. There is an old and difficult path blazed by the Warda forebears, but no longer used much. They think the other tribes may have even forgotten it. If you follow it, it can take you all the way from here"—

the Scout stabbed the legion camp nearest the Bildani Wood, and he took a moment to look at all present—"to the Ochita."

All were silent.

Sharasthi spoke first. "If we can get at Tobron..."

The legate shook his head. "If something goes wrong, that force is lost."

"But Legate," Sharasthi said, her tone rising, "if this trail *is* real, then our much longed-for miracle is possible."

"Such a meager possibility does not justify a suicide mission."

Sharasthi clenched her jaw, then turned to the Scout. "Have you seen the trail yourself?"

"No, Adept, I came here as soon as the Warda made the offer."

She fought the urge to grind her foot into the ground. Her intuition told her to take this opportunity, but the legate was right, it would be absurd to send a force so far into the Bildani on the word of some Parthavan tribesmen motivated by a grudge.

Then, she saw it. She tapped a section of central Parthava, steppeland north of the forest. "This is Pachur's battalion." Pachur of the Triumvirate.

The legate made a disgusted sound. "The bastard. Even before the Hunters got involved, his cavalry archers were a magnificent pain in the ass. Now?" He spat.

Sharasthi spread her hands. "Forget the Ochita then. Let's test the Warda. If they can take an ambush force from the camp to Pachur's army, through the Bildani, we can hamstring the enemy there. Our Scouts are harried at every turn on the steppe because they can't stay hidden from Parthavan patrols, and the Bildani is impossible for us to navigate.

"Pachur would never expect us to attack from the forest. It might as well be a wall protecting his flank. For once, we would have the advantage of surprise and superior positioning. A confident foe is more vulnerable to ambushes than a wary one. Gods willing, we get a chance to kill him and cut the Triumvirate down by one."

A prefect knuckled the table. "I'd pledge two companies to that effort. Doubtless the Scouts will be eager to finally penetrate the Bildani as well."

More voices joined in, assenting to the viability of the plan.

It is the role of a leader to maintain a cool head when enthusiasm takes others in. Legate Taric played the part well, weeding out less suitable companies from signing on. Bit by bit, a plan took shape and was refined.

A vanguard of Scouts and four elite *triarii* squads would travel through the Bildani with the Warda. Following about a day behind them, also with Warda guides, would come a larger force composed of two full companies with auxiliary cavalry units.

Meanwhile, the legate would lead the main force to meet Pachur's battalion head-on in three days. By the morning of the third day, the ambush force would be in position and prepare to strike his flank with a focus on eliminating any enemy Hunters and—if possible— assassinating the Triumvirate general.

There was the obvious matter of whether the Warda would double-cross them, but the legions had a standard remedy for that possibility, summed up with an adage attributed to a legendary Scout officer: 'Even the most treasonous of men can't wrong you if you've got a knife to their balls.' They would take hostages from the Warda until the mission was successfully completed.

The only matter unsettled was whether Sharasthi would be there.

"I go with the vanguard," she declared. "There's no better use of my abilities."

The legate shook his head. "You've lingered here one day too long already. The Hunter golds will sniff you out—and the ambush force with you."

Sharasthi had adopted Kars' pattern of irregular movement about the legion, but she had taken it to even further extremes. If only Hannil could see her now—even he might be impressed by the extent to which she was implementing her Intelligence tradecraft. She had nothing to fear from ordinary Parthavans, and even most Hunters she was confident she could evade.

The prime threat was the Adept-killers, the gold-eyed Hunters who could perceive magic.

She should have moved to another location already, but it had been necessary to meet with the legate and senior officers. Immediately after this meeting, she was supposed to be double-timing out of here.

The legate's concern was legitimate. If the Hunter golds found her in the Bildani, that was it for her and the legionnaires with her.

The legate rapped the table. "The force will go without Adept Sharasthi. We can't take that kind of risk."

"I appreciate the concern, legate," Sharasthi retorted, "but I fear the greater risk is if I don't go. Without my magic, they run too great a risk of detection. The Hunters' eyes are keen, and this is the enemy's territory. As you said, we cannot trust our soldiers' lives entirely to the Warda. I'll cloak the vanguard."

The legate's fingers drummed on his arm.

Something occurred to Sharasthi, and she chose to press with all she had. She would take a page from Kars' playbook—but with a twist. "Send decoys. Give some Scouts my mantle and send them, subtly but not subtly enough, in the opposite direction. Make it look like I'm getting into place for an operation to retake the territory we lost in the north."

"Draw the golds away," mused Taric. Sharasthi could see he was nearly ready to bite.

"If it turns out the Warda really can guide us through the Bildani, and if this trail of theirs really is viable for transporting an ambush force..." She touched the blade on her hip. "If this opens a road to killing Pachur and Tobron and breaking apart the Hunters, it would be foolish not to try."

The legate let out a heavy sigh and leaned his palms on the table. "All right. The plan is as follows. Adept Sharasthi's vanguard will clear the way and verify its integrity, and while she gets into position, I'll approach from the west. Then, we launch a pincer attack on Pachur's battalion. A conventional engagement in the west that he's expecting, with a surprise attack on his camp from the southeast. If he's hemmed in on two sides, then he'll either have to fight in an enclosed environ disfavorable to ranged cavalry, or he'll retreat to the north—my money's on the latter.

"If possible, we take Pachur's head, but the situation is precarious enough that I don't want any acts of extreme valor on an outside chance. Give him a chance to flee.

"Once we've claimed that territory, we'll have a wedge into the center of Parthava. We'll push forward and break the country in two, separating the Hunter-controlled south from the Coalition in the north. Then we turn our attention to shattering the Coalition, and feeling out whether the Hunters are open to a truce—preferably once we have the Adept sequestered deep inside some city walls."

There were exchanged glances and mutters, quiet at first, then louder, more eager.

"If you are not in place, Adept Sharasthi, I'll be forced to fight a far more precarious battle, or to back down. Neither of those bode well for morale or mortality rates. You want to take a risk? Here you have it. Guarantee that you can execute your part, and we have a road into the next phase of this war."

His eyes narrowed. "Well?"

Sharasthi lifted her head. "I'll need your subtlest Scouts and finest *triarii*."

The legate scoffed. "*Adepts*. I'll give you the pick of the litter."

"Then what are we waiting for? Let's meet with the Warda and discuss the plan."

26

ADEPT-KILLERS

I ONCE STAYED with a certain prince who cultivated an interest in arcane matters. A man of good repute and education, he confessed a boyish longing to experience the ecstatic journeys of which he read. I assured him it was a desire whose unfulfillment he would have to come to terms with, for he was far too sane, and such men never advance beyond abstract study. Those who tread the hidden paths—they sense the call in their bones, in their blood.

—*The Life and Wisdom of Simeon Binkhok As Told by Himself*

THE WARDA HAD GIVEN Sharasthi three men. Two of them did not share their names, so she only knew what to call the leader—a young rider named Hamma with uneven stubble on his face. She had picked up some of the Parthavan language since arriving, and thankfully the Warda's dialect was not that different from what she knew. Even so, they had to speak slowly to understand one another.

He had been chosen for this task by the leaders of his tribe, and it was apparently an honor he could not have refused, even though Sharasthi guessed he had wanted to. He did not explain why the

Hunters were so interested in killing Adepts, but he did say that it was unusual.

When Sharasthi asked what *varmakis* meant, he frowned and asked where she had learned the word. She said she'd heard it from a Hunter long ago, but mentioned nothing about Tobron or Claw-face. Hamma scratched his stubble, muttering something she couldn't understand and walked off to scout ahead. That was his typical manner when she asked a question he did not want to answer.

Sharasthi glanced over her shoulder. The vanguard with her numbered about thirty legionnaires and fifteen Scouts. The legionnaires were sweating horribly in their armor, and some of the Scouts had offered to share the burden of equipment. The Lazarran heavy infantry were not given to traipsing through the forest, as a rule, but they were nothing if not adaptable. The mission plan required them to be in position within three days. They would do it, Sharasthi had no doubt. She also had no doubt the larger force following them would make it as well.

One of the pleasures of being an Adept was working with the legionnaires. Whatever her feelings toward the Empire, Sharasthi still had an affection for the soldiers. They were hardy folk of good humor—or appropriately miserable humor when the situation called for it. And they rose to the expectations placed upon them.

The men of the Seventh in particular were admirable. The legion's motto was "By Vigilance and Preparation." Not a single soldier was missing equipment or out of line. They had drilled to such perfection that sergeants hardly needed to give directions when the time came to make or break camp—everyone knew his part and played it well.

Hamma came back from his scouting. "We are going to be near other paths soon. You...hide your men."

Sharasthi nodded. "And you?"

Hamma shook his head, taking a half-step back. His eyes darted to the focus around Sharasthi's neck. "I know how to be hidden."

Well, she could hardly blame him for his trepidation. Even within the legions, ample soldiers were fearful of Adepts. Men of war could be a superstitious lot. It was common to hear that anyone who spent too much time around Adepts started to go a little sideways in the brain. She could only imagine how unwilling a Hunter would be to move under her magic, given how seriously they took the supernatural. One of Hamma's two companions spent an hour every morning praying to a small effigy of a goddess. When she had asked Hamma about it, he said, "Once, he prayed to Kashakran that if she would grant him a perfect bowshot, he would offer such devotion to her. She granted his petition. If he broke faith, she would punish him, for the Huntress of the Heavens is a strict divine."

Sharasthi had frowned. "And what was the bowshot for?"

"Betrothal trial."

She had not pursued the matter further.

Sharasthi passed word to the sergeants that they were to bunch up. It was time to move under shadow.

The soldiers packed together, forming up into something like a tortoise formation, but longer and narrower. There would be enough light for each man to see the one to his front and at his sides. They would need to step surely.

Sharasthi took a breath and stretched out her hand.

In the fifteen-odd years since she first manifested the *Ars Tenebrae*, Sharasthi had not only expanded her reach—she had obliterated her mentor's expectations. Her aether tolerance, Rufus suspected, was among the best in the Corps, matching some of the greatest veterans. When Sharasthi called the shadows and bid them move, a veil of darkness billowed out across the soldiers. To their credit, there were no mutterings or curses—just some grim faces.

She nodded to Hamma. "Onward."

The Hunter surveyed the display of magic before him. He did not look startled, but he did take it in for some time.

"Hamma?"

He grunted. "We go. Quiet. If we hear anything, we stop and be still. People can pass very close on the ways of the Bildani without knowing one another. Trust the forest."

THE REST of the day passed without incident. They did not even encounter the sounds of other parties using different paths through the Bildani. Sharasthi was tempted to take that as a favorable omen.

At night, they bedded down to the side of the trail. Hamma and the other two walked the perimeter and impressed upon Sharasthi, who passed the message to the men, that under no circumstances was anyone to leave the vicinity. If they got out of sight of the group, they would be lost. The Scouts took some offense at this, but acquiesced.

"I will go to check on the larger force," Hamma said. "If anything goes wrong, the other two will know what to do. Listen to them."

Sharasthi asked their names. Hamma shook his head. "Their names are not good for speaking in this part of the Bildani. Call them *Warda*, if you need." And with that, he departed. Sharasthi watched him vanish around the bend. She stamped down a vague feeling of being stranded. The other two Hunters were still with them.

There was nothing more for her to do tonight except sleep. In such a precarious position as this, they would all be sleeping in their armor, which was a pain but one they were accustomed to. The arcane exertion had left Sharasthi with a mild headache, but the fact that she was only in the earliest stage of aether sickness after doing so much work kindled satisfaction. Again she was grateful for Rufus' tutelage. While she would have preferred more comfortable conditions so she might rest deeply to clear the strain she was carrying, she could bear this.

Wrapping her cloak tight around her, she stuck her arm under her head and closed her eyes.

In an instant, she found herself in a dream. She was walking through the Bildani, someone at her side. When she turned her head to see who it was though, only the trees and the slope of the earth met her eyes.

"Hello?"

No answer came. She went onward.

Still, she was certain someone was there. She could almost hear their footsteps.

The longer she walked, the more the Bildani changed. The trees and the earth and the wind and the animals—they all seemed suffused with some indescribable potency.

The sound of clinking metal beside her.

Jerking to a halt, Sharasthi turned about in a circle. "Where are you?"

'*—up.*'

It was a voice so faint, it might as well have been the rustling of a blade of grass. "Up?"

Sharasthi craned her head, looking at the sky, which somehow appeared through the thick-woven canopy. And then, in an instant, she realized the trees and branches and wind all seemed to flow—to flow from the east. Despite no sign of the sun or stars overhead, she knew it was the east.

All of a sudden, there was a hill, then it was a mountain, and she stood right at the foot of it.

'*—up.*'

Sharasthi stared, unable to see the crown of the peak. It stretched up and up into an endless expanse.

'*—up. —ke up. Wake up.*'

Beyond her sight yet known by her spirit, a great and luminous power dwelled atop the mountain, thundering in some ancient tongue.

"Wake up!"

Sharasthi gasped, sitting bolt upright, her hand closing around the hilt of her sword.

"Wake up!"

"Ambush!"

"From the north! North!"

"Get up, fools!"

"Heads down! Bowshot!"

"Wake up!"

"Stay low!"

Clanking armor, rattling swords, whistling arrows. Screams of pain and death.

Sharasthi scrambled to her feet, drawing her weapon. Where was the enemy?

Sharasthi threw waves of darkness into the trees, her magic choking the air with gloom. The arrows slowed for a moment.

A moment.

Legionnaires were on the ground, black-feathered arrows sticking from their bodies in a macabre display. Many still on their feet likewise bore the telltale missiles of the Hunters in their flesh.

Were their sentries dead? Where were Hamma and the other two?

Sharasthi still couldn't see the enemy. She had to assume they were all around.

Only one hope then.

"Form on the trail," she bellowed, "and break for the main force!"

What legionnaires were able to obey, did. Their training asserted itself, and they pulled Sharasthi into their center. A sergeant had his hand on the back of her head, keeping it low as they ran. "Shields high!" he shouted. "Move your fee-*urkh!*"

An arrow sprouted from his throat. Sharasthi swore as he went down. The man after him tripped over his body and fell behind. Before he could catch up, he was pierced from a half-dozen directions.

Sharasthi had darkened the air, but it did little good. Too many arrows from too many directions. Men took wounds, fell and died.

Like a flaming needle, an arrow stuck into her shoulder. She groaned and snapped the shaft, already cursing what came next: aether healed the wound, her flesh closed over the buried broadhead, which tore and twisted with every jolt of movement. An instant later, another arrow slashed across her calf, and she counted it a small blessing that it had not lodged inside.

More legionnaires were dropping, leaving larger gaps for the Hunters' arrows to slip through and reach her.

Sharasthi healed herself, and when a legionnaire or Scout took an injury but kept pace, she healed him too—she had to drop her sword to keep both hands free, so fast the injuries were coming in—but she could not give them speed. She could only channel for those she touched. What was she to do, pick the two closest and run off with them, leaving the others behind?

A legionnaire stumbled, saved only by his comrade's quick grasp. "It's too dark!" one of them cried. "We need more light, Adept!"

"Any more and they'll home in on us!" But even as she said it, she knew it was a fool's errand.

The main force was too far off. They were dying too quickly.

"Adept!" hissed a Scout. "Leave us and get away! The legate must know to abandon the plan!"

Sharasthi did not respond, save to bark that they had to keep moving.

Another man fell. Two more.

Hardly a dozen remained.

The rain of arrows was too thick. The distance too great.

She took an arrow to the back of her thigh, stumbled. A legionnaire stood over her, sprouting a cluster of arrows in the half-second it took her to pull the arrow and close the wound.

I'm wasting their lives.

Her heart wrenched in her chest.

She had always abhorred the salute. But these men deserved it from her now.

"*Emperor and Eagle*," she snarled, her mouth bitter.

"Emperor and Eagle!" chorused too few voices, shot through with bravado and pain.

Sharasthi plunged the world into total night.

There was a break in the bowshot.

Pouring as much power into her legs as she dared, she bounded forward, leaving her men behind in moments.

The terrible whistling returned, as did the shouts of dying legionnaires.

Arrows flew after Sharasthi, but all went wide. They could see the dark, but they could not see where in it she was.

The Hunters began shouting to each other—and then they stopped. She heard horses neighing, hoofbeats.

The Hunters entered her darkness.

Sharasthi went stone still.

Some were on horses, others on foot. Some had arrows fitted to strings, while others had drawn blades and hatchets. They made their way slowly, heads cocked, listening, sniffing the air.

Sharasthi's hand floated to the knives at her belt. She folded her fingers around one's handle, and slow as she could, drew.

The steel *hissed* against the leather.

Two Hunters whirled on her, drawing and loosing arrows.

Sharasthi threw herself into a roll. One missed, the other grazed her arm. The Hunters were shouting, then fell silent again. They were moving in on her.

Sharasthi swallowed.

Just run, she told herself.

But she needed to get some measure of vengeance first.

She applied her tradecraft. Step lightly, extend the toe. Watch with the corner of the eye. Breathe no more or less than necessary.

A Hunter with an arrow on the string passed by. Sharasthi girded herself, then made her move.

It took a great deal of force to slash a throat, particularly when striking from a bad angle. Sharasthi did not hold back, channeling enough aether to hack clean through bone.

He made a gasping, gurgling sound. On either side of his face, blue earrings swung with the violent motion of his death throes, and for just an instant his wide, fearful eyes fixed on her in the dark.

Sharasthi threw herself to the side. An arrow glanced off her armor. Two struck the dying Hunter.

Lucky.

More Hunters were closing in. They were calling to each other again—Sharasthi guessed they were sharing positions. She did not wait for them to return to silence.

She drew her second knife and lashed out. One Hunter, she

stabbed through the back, into the lungs, another she drove a blade up into his chin.

Arrows—all missed. She kept her momentum, running up on another cluster of them.

One struck out blindly with a curved sword. Sharasthi ducked it and disemboweled him.

The arrows stopped. They must have been too fearful of hurting their fellows. Sharasthi pressed her advantage.

Slash, cut, stab. She did not give war cries or bloodthirsty howls. She fought silently as she could, leaving as the only sign of her passing the half-choked wails of her prey.

She eviscerated another Hunter, leaping over his body as it fell to the forest floor.

Arrows flew again, though they went wide. Still, Sharasthi knew she had to go while the balance of things was in her favor, lest she die to some lucky shot or swing.

She sprinted down the trail, leaving the Hunters behind. As her canopy of shadows left with her, she heard them raising shouts of alarm and firing after her. She fluxed the darkness, expanding it to her left, then to her right. Sometimes she let it lag, so that she was nearly at the front of it. The Hunters had no clue where to cluster their shots.

Sharasthi ran and ran. Her head was pounding from aether sickness. By the time she made it back to the main force, she'd be in the next stage. Well, she could bear it for the price of survi—

Instinct more than thought saved her. Something shifted up ahead. She threw herself to the ground. An arrow whizzed through her hair.

She rolled to the side, got to her feet.

A Hunter on a stark black horse broke from the trees, blocking the trail. He had another arrow on his string already.

Sharasthi grit her teeth. She would cut a wide berth, then go back to the—

The Hunter drew and aimed for her.

Her stomach dropped into the depths of the earth, because just as his eyes narrowed at full draw, she saw it.

She threw herself as far as she could, tumbling through mud and moss as the arrow hissed far too close.

He was one of *them*. One of the golden-eyed, one of the Adept-killers.

She turned and ran, zigzagging like a madwoman.

His sight must have been imperfect in piercing her shadows, but it was powerful enough.

She took an arrow in her shoulder, just an inch off where she had been shot before. She didn't dare drop a knife to pull it—so she let the wound heal as it was. As she ran, the arrowhead tore and tugged at the muscle, opening it ever so slightly again and again.

She kept moving, moving as fast as she dared, moving in the wrong direction. It didn't matter—once she was clear, she could find her way back.

But the Hunter kept after her, his horse thundering through the trees. She poured yet more aether into her legs, running so fast one of her sandals snapped and flew off. A rock gashed open the sole of her foot. She kept running.

Another arrow, this time lancing the side of her neck. Blood spurted, then staunched.

The world was spinning. She was hearing things—lions roaring, children crying, voices speaking languages she'd never heard.

'*Run.*'

The voice from her dream had come to haunt her in consciousness.

'*Flee.*'

She was running deeper into enemy territory, deeper into the Bildani. How far had she gone?

The Hunter's pursuit slackened, his shots became less frequent. Sharasthi kept running. At some point her other sandal had broken off. She dropped her canopy of shadows, focusing on putting all her power into keeping her body moving.

'*Hide.*'

Through gritted teeth, she hissed, "*Where*?"

'*Hollow.*'

Sharasthi tossed her head about. The trees were waving and weaving before her eyes. "I'm listening to a hallucination."

But then she saw it—a hollow in a fallen tree.

On her stomach she burrowed backwards into it, clutching her knife in a white-knuckled grip, eyes fixed on the patch of forest floor where any moment she expected to see her pursuers appear.

Lying in the dark, she felt the world whirl about her as incense filled her lungs and singed her tongue with aromatic smoke. "Grand-father," she moaned, covering her mouth. "It's back."

Vohman's face came through the wall of the tree, half the flesh burned away. "Easy, child. It will pass."

Sharasthi tasted sour bile. She forced it down, shut her eyes. Channeling. She needed to stop channeling. It would only get worse if she kept the flow of power running through her.

As soon as she stopped, she began to shiver. Her feet ached. Healed wounds began to itch. She still had part of an arrow stuck in her shoulder. She reached back with a trembling hand and yanked on it, stuffing her cloak in her mouth to stifle the groan. A trickle of blood rolled down, pooling at her armpit.

Vohman nodded, one blank eye rolling in its socket as he said in Rufus' voice, "That's a broadhead, Sharasthi. It has to be cut free."

She tasted sour again. "Hallucination. Acute aether sickness. Can't vomit. Being tracked. Quiet quiet quiet."

"Yes, child," said Vohman, "Be—"

'*Quiet,*' said the dream voice.

Hoofbeats. Real, or just another symptom?

Parthavan voices, half-understood.

"—*ermakte* came this way—hurt—close."

"You did not—tell—go back."

Sharasthi stuffed her cloak between her teeth again to keep them from chattering. The Hunters went on. There were at least three of them, but their voices blended together. They seemed to be arguing.

"Tobron—see—quickly."

"—steppe—army—."

"Others—search."

Their horses whinnied, hoofbeats sounded.

Sharasthi stayed still as long as she could. Her muscles burned and ached. Slowly, she inched forward, moving her head closer to the hollow's opening.

Her grandfather was sitting on a rock. He leaned down to peer into her hiding place. Had it been the left side of his face that was burned earlier? It was the right side now.

"Rest, child."

Sharasthi started to nod, but the motion continued until her forehead struck wood.

27

WHAT WAS ABOVE AND BELOW

You say I have come down from the mountain to blaspheme our gods—never! What was revealed to me there, I now pass on to you, that you too might know their nature, so you might honor them all the better.

—Zaro's Sayings, verse one hundred and eighty-seven

Sharasthi fell through an endless sky. Stars whirled past, each singing in its own language, each language beyond the faculties of the human mind to comprehend.

She floated in the sea—or rather, something like the sea. Something was buoying her up, but it was not water. It was not cold or briny. Neither was it warm or fresh. She was far beneath the surface, but there was no crushing pressure. White sparks and golden smoke danced overhead, burning bright against a pure black. She turned her head, and still more lights moved there. She rolled onto her stomach, and there were still more.

A great luminescent sphere rolled past, catching her in its wake, pulling her along. She did not fight the tow. A dim hope the dream would last a long while curled through her consciousness. She did not want to wake up.

Someone else was there, floating with her. 'Wake up.' The words pricked at her soul. The same voice that had tried to warn her of the ambush and guided her to the hollow.

"Leave me alone," she murmured. "Leave me to die."

There was a sound like clinking chains.

Sharasthi turned her head. The voice was there, among the black and the brightness. "Where are you?"

'Wake up and make haste, Sharasthi, or lie here forever.'

Sharasthi slipped out of the great sphere's pull and went on drifting. "I choose the latter."

Quiet. Then, 'And Alyat?'

A heaviness formed in her chest, and she began to sink.

'And your grandfather's vengeance?'

Heavier and heavier, sinking faster and faster. She rolled to face the depths. She could see the surface now—she was falling toward it, falling toward a surface on the bottom of a waterless, light-filled sea. Strange flickers and flashes of light played on that surface like floating oil.

"Who are you?"

Again, the sound of clinking chains.

'There is a way out of the forest.'

If she was in time, she could abort the battle. But then what? Go on struggling in this doomed contest against an enemy they could not hope to trounce? How long would she last before the Hunter golds caught her? The Empire could not afford to keep spending Adepts on this war.

Watching ethereal lights play on the surface below, she murmured, "I dreamed of a mountain whose roots were broad as the Bildani, whose crown was power unfathomable."

The voice was silent.

She remembered the pit in the ruined temple. An ordinary pit where dying men had vanished into the maw of a fathomless horror.

An unknowable power had tried to come through, to draw her in. Yet in the day it had only been dirt.

The worse her aether sickness had gotten in the Bildani, the stranger things had become. The more she had felt. Were they mere hallucinations? Or, like that awful night, was she seeing some hidden but astonishingly real power?

Words of the prophet came to her lips: "'In the astonishment of my spirit, I sought the mountain.' There's a way to reach it, isn't there? What lies atop the peak?"

'*It is forbidden for you.*'

"Why?"

'*I may not say.*'

"Take me there."

Clinking metal. Silence. The sensation of a distant struggle, as of wind battering stone.

Sharasthi drifted nearer the surface. By leveraging her will, she arrested her descent. She was not letting this opportunity slip away.

'*Get up and flee!*'

"I will die in Parthava as I am." Sharasthi remembered the visions the thing in the Dark had shown her. The might she had possessed. She did not understand the power of the mountain, but it was not alien like that of the thing in the pit. It was something like the magic she already possessed. It was bright and roaring.

All is Fire, she thought.

'*You must trust me! You contemplate a grave sin, Sharasthi, the depths of which you cannot comprehend.*'

An obscure line from the prophet half-emerged from the recesses of recollection. "'Bless the wicked...' Is that what I am to be? Is that what it means?" She stared into coruscations of light but a few inches away.

"I will seek the mountain," she said, "whatever the consequences."

The voice was silent. Chains clinked. Then it spoke, solemn and resolute: '*Follow the path. Follow the dead. Follow the rite.*'

No longer able to hold herself in unconsciousness, Sharasthi fell through the luminescent film and opened her eyes to yet more blackness. Rough, damp wood grated her forehead. The air was cold. Branches shook in the wind. Her body was heavy. She took a long breath, the wet smell of the log filling her nostrils, and she crawled out of her hideaway.

Night lay upon the forest. The apparition of her grandfather was thankfully long gone, but the ache in her head told her the aether sickness had not cleared.

Even though I must have slept through the entire day.

Her stomach clenched. They had set out with three days to get into position. That left her about thirty-six hours to get back to the legate and warn him not to commit to the battle.

First things first, she had to get her bearings. Fortifying her limbs with aether, gritting her teeth against the way it exacerbated her sickness, she clambered up the nearest tree to peer through the arboreal canopy. She sought the stars, only to find a heavy cloud cover lying overhead. She shut her eyes, let out a sigh. "The gods are against me." Scouring her memory, she tried to piece together the cardinal directions, but her flight had been too frantic and her mind too warped by aether sickness. She was as likely to find north by casting a die as using logic.

The only guidance she had was from the dream voice. Had it yielded to her will, in the end? Was it even really an intelligence, or had it simply been some fancy spun out of an aether-sick mind in a strange domain?

Follow the path. Follow the dead. Follow the rite. What the last two meant, she had no idea—but she knew how she could find the path.

First though—she wiped her knife clean and stuffed a mouthful of her cloak between her teeth.

"Mmph!" With suppressed moans and heavy breaths, she cut into her shoulder. Fingers slick with her own blood, she probed between hot muscle and sinew until she finally had a grip on the arrowhead. It sliced open the pads of her index finger and thumb, grating against

the bone. When she finally had it out, she threw it to the earth and stomped on it, muttering vile oaths into her gag.

After channeling to heal her impromptu surgery—sharpening the pounding of aether sickness in her skull—she bit down yet again, screwed her eyes shut, opened them, and closed herself off to the aether before setting to work on the broadhead in her thigh. Then there was the one in the back of her other shoulder—which she could only barely reach by stretching to her utmost, making the endeavor of cutting through even more harrowing and painful.

When she had finally extracted them all, she stared at them, then tucked them away, resolving that if she survived this, she'd have them made into a necklace.

Horrible as operating on herself had been—it was only preparatory for the true work that now began. Sharasthi drew upon the *Ars Tenebrae*. The dark of night became to her like the day, and in moments she had found the hoofprints of the Hunters' horses.

She pieced together where they had ridden from and where they had gone. Her headache worsened, but the pain was bearable. The greater problem was that so long as she was wielding the Art—even as meagerly as to pierce the darkness—the sickness would not subside. Her recovery would be stalled at least until dawn, in the best-case scenario. If she used her magic in any substantive way, she would risk worse sickness.

Yet the voice had said she needed to hurry, and on that point she agreed. Sharasthi forced her feet to move. Left, right, until she built to a jog. She kept her draw on the aether light to avoid exacerbating the sickness, though her constitution strained.

As she neared the path, she dropped to a crouch and sidled closer, taking shelter behind a ridge of moss-covered stone.

Though it would be tricky without a Hunter guide, she could go back the way she had come and return to the Seventh Legion, west of the Bildani. It was the only route she knew with any degree of certainty. It would be the obvious choice—and that was exactly why she hesitated.

The Warda had betrayed her and her men. It was almost certain they would have patrols on the route in case Sharasthi or any other survivors tried to backtrack.

The other option was to go east, where the mountain had loomed in her first dream in the Bildani.

Perhaps I've already gone mad and I'm just chasing my own tail.

Hoofbeats rolled through the air. Arrows rattled in quivers.

Sharasthi pressed herself flat into the earth. Blades of grass trembled under her shallow breath.

Parthavan voices—three at least. She struggled to make out words, but their tone was grim. The horses' gaits struck a purposeful but unhurried beat.

After they had passed, she waited a five count then peered over the ridge.

The Hunters had their bows in hand, but no arrows on the strings.

Lain across the horses' backs: the bodies of their slain comrades.

They were bringing back the corpses Sharasthi had made.

Follow the dead.

Sharasthi waited until they were nearly out of sight, then began her pursuit.

FOLLOWING THE HUNTERS, Sharasthi slipped further into the clutches of aether sickness. She dared not trust her body to keep pace or to react in time should the situation change. So her head throbbed, her fingers twitched. Further and further into the forest she went, and further and further into the spinning, swirling madness she had hardly escaped the day before.

All the while she told herself this was what the voice impelled. And she would respond that perhaps the voice was merely her own death wish masking itself in plausible rationality—*go to the heart of the enemy's camp and die like a proper soldier.*

She dared not let the Hunters out of sight, lest she find herself lost in the Bildani, but she also dared not chance one of them throwing a glance over the shoulder and spying her—so she lingered as far back as she could, cloaking herself in shadow.

Less than an hour prior, she had cursed that the gods were against her; now, at least, they threw her a meager consolation, that the Hunters did not have one of their golds in company. Even so, Sharasthi's nerves wound and screeched with every rustling leaf, for fear one would any second arrive and scent her magic. Perhaps they were all stalking the trail back to the west, expecting Sharasthi would flee.

Why hadn't she fled? Because of things half-glimpsed through the aether-sick haze of her dreams? Whatever this mountain was, could she truly reach it? Could she grasp the power there without losing herself?

All is Fire. I will remain what I am.

Now and then, a flood of nausea too horrible to bear ravaged her, and she had to hasten off the path quick and quiet to expel whatever bile remained in her stomach. Sour filled her mouth. She threw fistfuls of dirt over the yellow spew before rushing back to the chase. The fourth time it happened, she caught herself wishing the Hunters would hear or smell it, just so they could turn around and skewer her. Then they would stand over her corpse and jest how her stomach was so empty there was nothing left to leak through the arrow-holes.

Just keep moving.

Her head. Her pounding head. Her brain must have rotted half-away. If someone cracked her skull open and looked inside, he would see a shriveled, blackened mess. Soon she would collapse and the Hunters would find her in a puddle of her own drool and vomit. Then they would take her home and tie her up like a dog, teach her tricks, feed her scraps.

Keep chasing.

Thirsty. Gods was she thirsty. Her mouth was a rancid desert. Her swollen tongue disgusted her, as if it were a foreign object threatening to tip back into her throat and choke her. Maybe if she bit it off she could drink or drown in her own blood. Just as the Marzudi Gormish had.

All illusion. All Fire. Burn. Keep burning. Nothing to do but burn.

Her delirium tempted her more and more to either charge her foes or lie down in the dirt—anything but go on enduring. She made deals with herself: ten more steps, then she would stop—but just another twenty, another fifty, another hundred, and then...

At some point the Hunters had left the trail. Sharasthi could not remember when or where. If she lost sight of them now, she would have no hope of finding her way again. She bought another five hundred steps from herself, then another thousand—and then, they were at the village.

Calling it a *village* seemed wrong though; by Lazarran standards it was more like a camp. The only thing that looked permanent was a smooth, glassy menhir erect in the center. Engravings littered the surface, but she could make none of it out, neither words nor images.

Radiating out from the standing stone like spokes on a wheel were bright-dyed, fur-adorned yurts. In and out of these moved Hunters—men, women, children. Even in the dark of night, they were up and about with a frantic energy. Sharasthi guessed there had to be hundreds of them. She hoped it was just the aether sickness making her see triple, but it was a frail hope.

Flattening herself in the cover of the tree line, Sharasthi watched with aching eyes as her quarry rode toward the village. People had realized they were here, had raised notice. Faces were grim. They wanted to see the dead.

The Hunters dismounted their horses and laid out their moribund cargo. Even from afar, Sharasthi heard the gasps. There was one body in particular—Sharasthi recognized the blue earrings of a Hunter whose throat she had slit—that was garnering attention.

A teenage girl forced her way through the throng, breaking through the arms of those trying to keep her back. She looked at the dead man with the blue earrings and started crying. The Hunter who had brought the body put his arm around her. There was a resemblance. Sharasthi could not remember what the corpse's face looked like—a blank shape in her mind with earrings swinging on either side.

Revulsion bubbled up inside Sharasthi, threatening to turn her stomach inside out yet again. She crushed it.

The Hunter patted the girl's back. From the glimpse of his face that Sharasthi could see, he was as stern as the stiffs on the ground. It was the face carved on men who had seen too much. Eventually all soldiers—save the truly mad—reached that tipping point. Men like that either lay down forever or they committed to the fight with the stone-faced certainty of those who have already consigned themselves to death.

Sharasthi would prefer to kill him in his sleep if possible. Not out of pity—pity had left her. It was all pragmatic.

Another Hunter appeared from the village, from the direction of the stone. A tall man with long hair, some of it in braids, most in wild shocks. Sharasthi recognized him at once by what he held in his hand —a bow unlike any other.

Tobron.

A marrow-deep fear moved Sharasthi's hand to tear the focus from her neck and drop it in the dirt. Closed off from the aether, her body panged with a grim ague, and she almost heaved her vacant stomach out her throat—but she held silence. Even as a cold sweat soaked her clothes and her bones shuddered, she held silence.

If any Hunter had the mystical sight, Tobron did. What had he seen when Claw-face came for her grandfather and threw him on the holy pyre?

Tobron looked on the bodies. The weeping girl moved to clutch at his legs. He muttered something, put a large hand on her head. In his face and gesture, Sharasthi saw the clear lineage of the first Hunter who had comforted the girl. That revulsion churned again, and Sharasthi throttled it with cold determination.

A father, a son, a daughter—a dead...what? Another brother? A cousin? A betrothed? Families always died piecemeal, the survivors left to reckon with what cruel misfortune had visited them.

At least Sharasthi could do them the favor of putting them all down at once, so they did not have to go on as she had. That girl would not have to grow up bent on vengeance.

The son said something to Tobron—loudly, firmly. People went quiet.

Tobron's face turned more severe. He shook his head.

The youth said it again.

Tobron barked a harsh recrimination.

Some understanding came upon the daughter, and she wailed a short and pitiful phrase at her brother, her trembling hands gesturing madly at the body before them.

The youth repeated his declaration yet again—Tobron gnashed his teeth, the girl covered her face, a worse wave of sobs racking her.

Tobron's lips moved—either silently or with sound too soft for Sharasthi to hear—and he turned his back, walking with as much joy as a man going to his execution.

The girl went to her brother and struck him across the face, then fell upon him, crying into his neck. He did not react.

The crowd was stepping back, getting down on their knees, backs erect. A circle formed around the siblings and the dead.

Sharasthi watched with grim fascination and whirling consciousness as Tobron returned, his features hidden behind some sort of animal mask. Only his mouth showed, and from it came strange and sonorous words. Though she understood not a whit, her heart pounded against her ribcage and for a moment she feared she'd faint.

All those kneeling bowed their heads twice to the ground. He walked around the circle, calling out in their tongue, and when he paused people called back with no rhyme or reason Sharasthi could discern. He waved his strange bow about his head, yet his other hand, steady before his chest, held a red lacquer bowl.

After four ambulations of the circle—each time drawing nearer the center—he at last stood over the two youths. The girl was clutching the lad tighter. Tobron said something to that blood-stirring tune.

The son tried to push her off, but she stayed rooted in place. A disturbance rippled through the scene.

Tobron repeated his part, and when his daughter remained as she was, he said in an unmistakably paternal tone, both stern and sympathetic, "*Charas. Ven dyar chitel.*"

The girl trembled for a moment, then relaxed. She kissed the lad on the cheek she had struck, then the other, and stepped back. The strife had gone from her, replaced by a resigned, mechanistic mien.

Her face still wet with tears, she knelt beside the corpse and removed the blue earrings. As she stood, Tobron resumed his chant. He lifted high the red bowl, lowered it. He touched the sacred bow to his son's forehead, then proffered it for the lad to kiss.

At a word from Tobron, the girl took the earrings and pierced them through her brother's lobes.

A ruby droplet flecked his shoulder. He got down on his knees, bowed his head to his father, and then lay on his back.

Tobron lifted the bowl to his own lips and filled his mouth with whatever substance lay within.

The circle covered their eyes, as did the girl, now on her knees as well.

Tobron spat frothing indigo back into the bowl and held it to the youth's lips.

He drank it down, then let his head rest against the grass.

Something changed. Something in the air. Sharasthi shuddered as she recognized the sensation of aether. Even without her focus, she could sense aether rushing through the place. It took all her ragged will not to open herself to it.

All were still and quiet. Tobron stood tall over the scene. Even the wind hushed.

All waiting...

Sharasthi flinched when it happened, when the lad's back arched and his eyes rolled back to the whites and his throat made a gasping, sucking sound and the girl wailed again and the circle let out a heavy sigh and Tobron looked up at the sky and groaned, his knuckles white on the bow—and the boy's body went limp and dead like that of his kinsman so near on the ground.

Sharasthi watched as the girl cried out and fled into the Bildani. She watched as Tobron oversaw the regathering of all the corpses and their carrying away. She watched as the blue earrings were given to Tobron, who at last withdrew.

And when all had gone to mourn or fulfill whatever duties they had, Sharasthi moved again, scooping up her focus from the dirt and clutching it in her fist, opening herself once again to the power of the aether.

And as she did, she heard that voice—so soft she almost missed it—whisper, *"Tobron."*

She stalked after him. It was not a difficult guess where he had gone. Nearest the standing stone in the center of the village was a large yurt, unlike the others. Sharasthi slipped through the fur curtains.

Her focus was in one hand, her blade in the other.

She hardly even noticed what was around her, she just knew her quarry was not there. There were more curtains sectioning off other rooms. Left or right?

A current of aether whisked by, and she followed it to the left.

In this room too, Tobron was not to be found. Herbs hung from the roof in bundled sheaves. The air was thick and aromatic, smelling...Sharasthi stopped in a moment of bewilderment, realizing she could only name the scent as *aether*. Or rather, the confluence of all the scents summed up in a way that she had only known as the sensation of that unseen energy.

Follow the rite.

Furs and herbs and...the red lacquer bowl. The bowl was set atop a low table, with a carafe of water and a mortar and pestle beside. Inside the mortar was a fine ground powder.

Aether curled around it, swirling and rising, rising, rising into some place Sharasthi's senses could not reckon, but which nevertheless she knew to be there. Like the peak of a mountain, hidden in clouds.

The dream voice was murmuring now, giving utterance in some unknown tongue.

Sharasthi found herself kneeling before the table. Something was close—so close she could almost touch it, but ever out of reach. A distance that halved and halved and halved again, and so the gap forever remained, however imperceptible.

Here was the means to close the distance. Here was the mountain that pierced the heavens, joining what was above and below.

She set down her weapon. With the focus still digging into her palm, she poured the dark contents of the mortar into the bowl. Then from the carafe, a pristine stream of water.

She dragged her finger through the mixture, no longer questioning if she was mad or sane or in control at all. The concoction was like the last gasp of twilight before the day finally dies into night.

A sound from nearby. A voice—a human voice, half-muffled by a thick curtain—asking a question in Parthavan tongue, coming nearer.

Sharasthi downed the mixture, and the voice and the room and the world vanished into a blind and deaf darkness.

28

GODSPEECH

THE RYSTA HUNTERS found my Talynisti lineage a curiosity. In particular they wished to know if I have any ties to the Mithallkiym. When I shared certain mementos of my time traveling with the desert tribes, they were delighted. They said that, of the Four on High, they have the greatest reverence for ha'Mithalleik, the Wandering God. At first I suspected this affinity arose from the Hunters' love for roaming wide swathes of territory, but near the end of my stay with the Rysta, one of their seers told me the Parthavan name for ha'Mithalleik—*He Who Walks Between the Stars*—was first pronounced by their goddess of the Hunt, Kashakran.

—*The Life and Wisdom of Simeon Binkhok As Told by Himself*

THE ELIXIR FILLED her mouth with fire and lightning and honey and blood.

Something *pulled* Sharasthi, pulled her up and up and up, and she screamed as she soared through the empty black and into a blinding realm.

She was atop the mountain, the mountain from her dream.

The same *something* that had pulled her up now forced her down to her knees.

"What transgression is this?" thundered a voice.

All around, figures appeared in cascading blooms of iridescent light, their forms like those of men and women. Their hair blew around their heads like wildfires in a gale. Under the weight of their unblinking eyes, Sharasthi felt more than naked; she felt in her soul how they saw down to the absolute depths of her being.

"By pharmakon, an intruder dares the heights and here finds herself."

"How to redress such a sin? How to reward such folly?"

"One of the Far-seer's slave-warriors!"

Sharasthi could not keep up. Every voice of the chorus was too alike one another and too dissimilar from her.

"And a night-daughter. Speak if you can, child in chains."

When the sound of clinking metal reached her, Sharasthi's insides churned like the sea in storm.

She turned her head—and there beside her was something like a human. Her body was not like any mortal flesh but instead like the night sky folded into feminine form. Stars dappled her torso, glinted along her shoulders, burned in her eyes—yet it was not any sky Sharasthi had seen.

The woman raised her head, setting the chains around her neck clinking again. She looked at Sharasthi. The stars in her eyes shuddered, like they might snuff out, and Sharasthi read absolute compassion in those lights.

The woman's arms stretched toward Sharasthi, a mere few inches until her bonds arrested them.

Sharasthi's heart ached so violently she thought it would rupture. "It was your arms," she croaked, lurching forward—fighting the crushing weight of the mountain spirits' attention—to throw herself around the woman, to clasp her hands.

The night-daughter gave a mournful squeeze—it was the same touch Sharasthi had felt all those years ago at the threshold of the temple. It had felt like a goodbye then. Tears coursed down

Sharasthi's face, wrenched forth by a reunion she had not even known to desire.

Speech flew between the spirits, incomprehensible to Sharasthi, when at last one said, "So, though this mortal already knew your touch, you subjugated yourself to the Far-seer's shackle."

Sharasthi tried to speak, but a harsh gaze from the spirit forced her jaw shut.

"Sin upon sin—compassion repaid with carceral bonds!"

Sharasthi had never been so lost in all her life. If she could only ask a question, only plead for a moment's grace—but in every awful face she read the same portent: doom.

"She will be thrown to That One."

A chill ran through the assembly, then words of assent.

The expanse above the mountain stretched, stars flew past—and then a great yawning black lay open above—or was it below, for with a sudden *lurch* Sharasthi felt herself pulled toward the darkness.

The darkness—it was *that same* Darkness from so many years ago, the horrid void that had hungered for her in that pit in the ruins of an occult god's temple. It would devour her at last.

Sharasthi clutched the night-daughter tighter. Her lips were sealed, her tongue twitched dumbly inside her mouth. A stifled groan choked her throat.

What a fool she was, indeed. She had come seeking a new power —and instead they would hand her over to that first power, the power that had horrified her, the power she had narrowly escaped. She had come here of her own will. She had demanded it of the night-daughter, who had warned her to turn away and begged her to trust her. Yet Sharasthi had not been satisfied. Now here she was.

But then, the night-daughter spoke.

"You cannot!"

The spirits' attention settled on her frail, spangled form. "Still, you find strength—but to deny justice to your tormentor?"

"Sharasthi is not my enemy, nor is she yours."

The spirits conferred on this in a flash, then one said, "Such folly from a child so wretched as yourself may be excused. Only the sighted Hunters of Parthava may ascend this mountain by the quatern elixir. The mortal transgresses, and she slaves for the Far-seer! If we should discard her to That One, it is meet and right."

The night-daughter's fingers clutched Sharasthi's. "Behold, noble ones—see the touch of the Wanderer upon her."

The spirits loomed nearer. "There is no mark," one declared.

"Is the night-daughter frayed too thin?"

"Perhaps she must be rethought."

"Look closer, all of you," sounded a voice Sharasthi had not yet heard. Feminine and regal, dangerous and wild.

The chorus made obeisance, and Sharasthi's very soul trembled as the speaker approached, censing the air with all those attributes her voice carried. The goddess—for she was surely a goddess—had the likeness of a woman with flowing white hair that twisted at her temples in vinelike braids and rushed down her back in waterfalls. She was garbed in furs belted at the waist, furs whose first-wearers were like no living beast Sharasthi knew, and two great timber wolves padded at her heels, their coats coruscant with silver moonlight. On her hip was a quiver full of lightning, in her hand a bow—a bow Sharasthi had seen moments before.

The bow the Hunter Tobron carried—or rather, she was now certain, the one on which Tobron's had been patterned.

The goddess looked on Sharasthi with such overwhelming authority she thought her bones would break.

"He has hidden it well—no doubt to conceal it from the Far-seer's gaze—but here it is." And with that, the archer reached *into* Sharasthi's head. A half-born scream died in her throat. It was not a fleshly pain, but it was *searing*.

Her touch pierced skin and bone and brain—and then it reached something and *shattered* it.

Sharasthi's eyes rolled back, this time the scream bursting out with enough force to prise apart her lips. Memory rushed upon her —memory of the man she met at the pit where the Darkness had desired her.

A striking and strange countenance. Words of enigma. *'I shall seal your memory...'*

A crushing presence. A fingertip brushing her forehead. *'...until next we meet.'*

That presence manifested, crushing Sharasthi further into the rock, and a moment later appeared its source. Fluttering robes, flashing eyes.

"Lady Kashakran," he said. "Had I not taken care, I might have come to you with violence. What right do you have to break a seal of my making?"

"The right of territory—for this mortal has come to my lands and ascended the mountain without cause."

"To be sure, there is a cause."

"There are wrongful causes and rightful. The former is nothing I am bound to honor."

The man—the one the night-daughter had called *the Wanderer*—spread his hands. "Before all others under the moon, you received me, O Huntress of the Heavens. We have a bond of friendship, do we not?"

"It is that bond that bids me tolerate for a moment this one's sin—but were it not for the night-daughter's warning, I might have acted unwittingly against that friendship. Your touch is subtle, Wanderer."

The other spirits had withdrawn, gathering behind Kashakran.

The Wanderer looked at Sharasthi, and something in that look made her want to hide in the deepest cavern. "You have left the veil intact, and for that I thank you. I might not have been able to draw another."

"This mortal has had a brush with That One."

"Yes, and I assured her she would never have to fear it again. You would have made a liar of me, Kashakran." He cast a cold glance upward, and for an instant Sharasthi thought she glimpsed the form of Hate itself in his features.

The wolves began to growl, but fell silent at a gesture from their mistress. "I will not cast her to the Dark, but her crime shall have consequences."

His expression smoothed as he turned his attention to the goddess. "Living will be consequence enough. By your authority in this land, free the night spirit and spare the Adept."

Something turned inside Sharasthi. *Free the night spirit?*

Kashakran scowled. "Sin is sin. Law is law."

The Wanderer held for a moment, then in a tone somehow both grave and light of heart: "Did the Zarushan prophet speak wrongly when he said even the murderer, the blasphemer, the fornicator might be redeemed?"

Kashakran's eyes filled with winter.

"And in a bygone age, at the telluric threshold—"

The goddess rattled the lightning in her quiver, and booming thunder echoed through the heavens. Her gaze was fixed on some distant point, and remained there until all was quiet again. When she spoke again, some of the harshness had left her. "Do not speak of such things before lesser ears."

The assembly of spirits was bristling, anxious, withdrawing further. Sharasthi felt the weight of their attention on her diminish. Her tongue began to loosen.

"What then is your counsel?" asked the goddess.

"If you will not use the power of the land to liberate the night-daughter, then merely return the Adept to the terrestrial as she is."

"And so let her and her Empire ravage Parthava? Let a night-daughter remain in chains? The Hunters have ranged these lands since man first heard godspeech."

Sharasthi strained her will further, further than she ever had working magic. A soft murmur shuddered in the base of her throat.

"I remember, Kashakran—I was there when the first Son of Thunder strung the bow."

"Then you know my answer. The Adept must—"

"*Wait*," Sharasthi groaned.

Tidal waves crashed on her, forcing her face into the brutal rock. A moment later, a hand rested on her head, and the crushing power broke over her like rain on a roof. For the first time atop the mountain, Sharasthi took a full breath, trembling. When she finally lifted her gaze, she saw the Wanderer's face. His eyes were mismatched, she realized. One blue as brightest sky, one brown as richest earth. Somehow it did not seem strange to see the god kneeling as he held protection over her.

"I would advise silence, Sharasthi."

But he left his hand there, a bulwark against the divine storm. Sharasthi swallowed and looked at the night-daughter. This unseen presence that, in some strange way, had always been with her, always cared for her.

"I confess," she said slowly, "that much of what I have heard is beyond me. I confess that I came here seeking power. I confess that this spirit warned me against my transgression. But...this spirit sacrificed for me. She brought me here because I demanded it of her. She warned me against it."

The night-daughter's shoulders sagged, the stars in her eyes burning softer.

Kashakran's wolves snarled as the goddess spoke. "She chose to subject herself to those damnable shackles, and so she could not resist your will, however wretched."

"But you can set her free? My sin should not be cause to waste her—"

"Wanderer," said Kashakran, the contempt in her voice striking Sharasthi dumb, "you plead mercy on this one's behalf, but now her pride asserts itself. The pride of all who transgress upon the heights. She came seeking power, and now she would twist compassion toward that desire."

Sharasthi shook like a leaf in a gale, regathering her wits. "They are the same thing in this place, are they not?"

The chorus of spirits whispered among themselves, and Kashakran looked on her with a slim measure of respect. "I should not be surprised that He Who Walks Between the Stars would find such a cunning sorcerer. The breaking of the night-daughter's chains is indeed the power you seek—but your death would also accomplish her liberation." Her wolves cackled.

The night-daughter cried out. "I will endure the chains!"

"Folly," Kashakran hissed. "The folly of young thoughts. Even if you would abide your state, I shall not. Those bonds are the implements of the enemy. The Adept shall perish by the Son of Thunder's hand."

Sharasthi despaired. "I cannot die until my vow is fulfilled, but if—"

"If you offer your life once your vengeance is satisfied? A foolish spirit seeks a foolish human. Your soul will not survive the judgment, for what brought you here is profane obsession. Even now, in the presence of divinity, you cling to it, for *vengeance is your god*, Adept, the principle to which you would subject all others."

"*Justice*," Sharasthi implored.

"The stars wrote justice in your soul, but it has been twisted. I do not fault righteous hate, but you have not the temperance to master it. Pride and anger! I should let the land stain her fingers judging such a black soul?"

Despondent, Sharasthi tried to find purchase somewhere, *anywhere*. Then, in fear and trembling, she flew to the old Truth her grandfather had given her: "All is Fire."

Something changed in the Wanderer's touch—and Sharasthi's heart seized upon it, for somehow she knew she had found the footing she so desperately needed. Now her words came almost without thought, flowing from some deep and distant place. She looked into the god's strange countenance, into heaven and earth. "Before vengeance, before hatred—there is Fire. What is it to me what shape the Fire takes, for it is All."

Kashakran raised her chin, looking on Sharasthi with half-lidded eyes. "Even the tongues of mortal magicians can utter profound secrets. Take heed, Wanderer, she is close to discerning—"

"*Quiet*," declared the Wanderer, and silence reigned. "Now it is my time to stay your voice on matters lesser ears ought not receive."

The absolute stillness pervaded for what seemed an era.

Kashakran spoke again, and there was a careful edge in her tone. "Permit me to slay her. Before she grasps the fullness of it."

The Wanderer turned to Sharasthi. "Speak."

Sharasthi dared to look Kashakran in her awesome visage. "You are wrong, Huntress of the Heavens. Vengeance is not my god. The one thing I believe in is that which I have always believed—that Truth placed in my mouth from birth. Subject me to the judgment, and the land will take not a single stain, for what I am, so is the land, *and so are—*"

The goddess rattled her quiver three times, drumming up such an awful roar as Sharasthi feared would deafen her forever.

One divine finger rested on a lightning bolt, ready to snatch it and set it to the string. "She would use the First Mystery as a catalyst for magic. You know where such a thing leads. Destroy her. Or this comes to theomachy between us."

Hopelessness once again seized Sharasthi, her last chance fading like a slit artery's pulse.

But then the Wanderer spoke. He raised a finger at the Thing in the Darkness. "Sharasthi, years ago you saw *its* will for you, did you not? When you comprehend what you call the principle of Fire, the truth will shatter and remake you. It is knowledge mortal minds are not meant to contain in full. You will be forever changed by it, and if you falter, if you take the wrong path, you will open yourself up to the Darkness. You escaped that fate once. You should not chance such a thing again." His strange eyes spoke of grief and warning.

But Sharasthi had meant what she said: the only thing she truly believed now was the Truth of Fire. All happened as it ought. How the Fire burns is a mystery, yet it burns the only way it can: rightly. "*Please,*" she begged, "whatever it takes."

"So be it." The Wanderer removed his hand from her and rose to his full height as Sharasthi crumpled with a gasp under the awesome weight of divine presence. "I will pull aside the veil over her fate for a moment. Regard the path she seeks."

Kashakran looked at her with cold, brilliant eyes. A deep shudder rolled through her. "Hm."

"Are you still so resolute she must be slain?"

"Striking possibilities, but possibilities only."

"All is possibility until the moment of collapse."

"Then why should I trust you to bring about the proper collapse? Your name is old, but you are bound by laws as deep. What if you should err in your preparations?"

"If she turns to the right or to the left, I will end her myself."

Kashakran's grip tightened on her bow. She raised a finger—not to the Darkness, but just askew of it. "Swear upon the Vanguard Sun's blade, may it never fail."

There was a baleful edge in his voice. "That is what it will take?" The Wanderer stood, still and solemn. "I swear upon it."

Like a nova bursting in the night, a blinding vision of eight flashing wings around a flaming sword seared Sharasthi's soul—and vanished quick as it had appeared. The Darkness seemed to stir with malice.

Kashakran eased a measure, but only a measure. "And what of the Convergence? You would allow the Far-seer to destroy yet another?"

Still mordant, he looked at the assembly and raised an open hand. "When last did a spirit of Parthava forge the proper soulbond?"

There was silence from the gods of the land.

"To lose a Convergence grieves me, but it can be rebuilt. The Hunters do not need the Convergence so long as they have the elixir. Let the cities fall. Direct the Son of Thunder to withdraw the Hunter tribes from the fray. Parthava will survive—and the Hunters, if they are clever, will remain free until the time comes to settle it all."

Kashakran listened with a severe mien. "Thousands of years I have known you, Wanderer, yet never have you baffled me more." She turned her head, looking out into the roiling mists. Then she turned back to him.

"For such an awful request, you must vow recompense."

"What would you have?"

"I asked a great thing of you," she declared, "now I ask another. The position of honor when you wage your war."

"The war against Arkhon is not mine to command—I only give aid where I may."

The Huntress raised her bow to the yawning, black expanse of the Darkness. "I speak of *that* war."

The Wanderer once again stood in stillness. "Indeed, Kashakran, you demand great things."

"You demand great sacrifices of us."

"And if it should take ten thousand years until you are repaid?"

"A blink before everlasting glory. So be it."

The Wanderer took a long breath—a moment that would always haunt Sharasthi for some reason she could never articulate—and clasped hands with the Huntress. "So be it."

The night-daughter's chains shattered.

Sharasthi began to fall—fall from the mountain, down to the earth—and as she fell she saw the awesome gazes of the Wanderer and the Huntress upon her, and she heard the latter say, "A measure of the moon's madness, to protect her from what she is to know, and to guard her from grasping the absolute depth."

The goddess' eyes flared *white*. Sharasthi heard the two wolves howl an ethereal song that echoed down to the root of her being.

The Wanderer's eyes, too, became a pair of distinct and divine suns. His mouth moved, but Sharasthi heard none of his words. Rather, she *felt* in every shred of her being the significance of that terrible truth: *All is Fire.*

29

THE MERCY OF MADNESS

Bless the wicked, who have taught us to hate sin. Woe to the righteous, who have taught us to loathe virtue.

—Zaro's Sayings, verse one thousand and sixty-six

Sharasthi woke to the world with a deep gasp. The lacquer bowl slipped from her hand, clattered on the table. Her clothes were soaked through with sweat.

Everything was shot through with light and aether and spidersilk strings of emotion and thought. The ground was dirt and Solidity and rock and Belowness and the air was vapors and Lightness and Fluidity and her body was flesh and Vitality and bone and blood and Transience—

The night-daughter appeared, her body dark and aflame, and cried out, "Sharasthi, narrow your sight!"

She could not—her mind was a window without shutters. Wolves howled and laughed.

Sharasthi thrashed. She knocked over a table that was wood and Bearing and stained with something that was here and There.

The night-daughter's eyes spun and flashed like iron wheels on chariots under the moon. "Lady Huntress!" The wolves laughed all the louder.

A hand of flesh and Power and—

Eyes. Eyes full of gold and Seeing and anger and Knowing.

Tobron's eyes.

The howling of the wolves became a distant thing. The gleaming lights faded as Tobron's mystagogic gaze arrested her. He did not blink.

"Look away for a moment," he said, "and the madness will return, and I will hand you over to it. The goddess of my land and bow tells me you are the little *varmakis* girl from Zarush, whose kin my own put to death so many years past. Now you come, no longer mere *varmakis* but *ermakte*, to return that violence. You rob my people of our sacred secret, and our own goddess pardons you and bars me from retribution. *Speak*."

She was walking on the edge of a cliff; every word she pronounced quietly and carefully, lest it tilt her mind over and into the yawning void. "Retribution...is mine."

"A glutton for blood. You have taken it already."

"No...the murderer...a claw on his cheek."

Tobron's iron grip tightened on her face. "My brother is long dead, and today you slaughtered his only child. Or does not my own nephew lie dead by your hand, from which cause my own son perished by the elixir your unworthy body and soul have blasphemed."

Her entrails turned to ash. "You lie to...protect him."

Tobron's eyes were brilliant and hateful and sincere. "Brechaer was his name. His eyes were second only to mine. He passed through the fourfold ascent in the time it takes the amber moon to turn to white. A seer and Hunter worthy to string the bow of Kashakran. Nine years ago, in fighting over territory between our people and another, a friendly arrow took him through the throat, and his body was given to the wild.

"Your vengeance was robbed by chance and an unsteady hand, *ermakte*. Even so, you ended his bloodline. You robbed us all of lives and kin, in the name of the Thousand-eyed Spirit."

"I did what I did...because I swore a vow."

Tobron's breaths were steady and forceful. "Such was your right. And it is my vow to the Lady of the Hunt that spares you the vengeance that is *my right*. But hear me, *ermakte* of the Night, for the Son of Thunder sees a dreadful fate upon you. For twelve settings of the moon, you will ravage without sleep or sense. The lunar law will rule your blood and the howling of the Huntress' companions will not leave your ears. And when your task is done, Parthava will kneel, and my people will withdraw to our hidden ranges to lick our wounds and mourn our lost until the time comes to Hunt again. But you will survive, bearing the weight of your sins against my blood, witnessing all the dark and hidden horrors that in pride you have opened your eyes to, until at last you see that most awful of wonders, and at your end you will think your life a string of treacheries. So says the Son of Thunder who bears the bow divine."

Tobron picked her up and threw her across the room, through the curtain into the vestibule. She tumbled across furs and Glory and cushions and Welcoming. The burning gleam returned to it all.

The night-daughter was at her side. "Sharasthi, you must narrow your sight!"

"*Cannot...how,*" she gasped, gritting her teeth and fighting to keep reality in place. Everything was burning and melting into Everything. The walls of the yurt and the flesh on her bones and the air in her lungs—all of it was...*Fire.*

The wolves howled and laughed.

Tobron was standing over her, again wearing his mask and holding his bow in hand, the string glowing with reflected Divinity and bristling Potential. He too was dissolving into the All-Pervasive Ever-Lasting Fire.

The night-daughter cried, "Control it as you control your magic! Close the conduit!"

Tobron spoke, "She sees the First Mystery, which the Hunters of old learned from He Who Walks Between the Stars. A mind unprepared for such truth splits under the weight of its hubris."

He set his fingers to the bright bowstring. "This," he said, "is the mercy of madness redoubled—punishment shall be your salvation!" And he plucked the bowstring and an eight-faced note echoed that had been echoing all her life and before her life and after her life, and her soul shuddered and and and—

And the wolves are howling and running beside her and laughing at how she moves, and she laughs with them, and she finds a mare and asks the mare to let her on, and the mare calls her a madwoman, but she is already riding, and the wings of the night spread out from her shoulders, and she grasps a dead man's blade in her hand, and the hilt is like sweat and fear and pain, and the tall trees of the Bildani look on her with sympathy and let her pass as she rides at bleak pace under the guidance of the woman who is the night—

And the woman tells her where to ride and thus she rides, and the wolves vanish into shadows but appear in the sky watching and laughing, and when she breaks from the woods and into the unawares throng of her enemies they howl, and the song in her blood whirls faster, and the heady rush of the aether is an unfaltering flood in her arms and legs, and there is no ending to the darkness she creates and casts upon her foes, and so there is no ending of blood flowing under her touch—

And she crashes through them like thunder through mist while the dead man's blade in her hand sings a giddy song as it unstitches mortal flesh and drinks grim crimson rivers, and among those many enemies is a man with authority and he tries to flee, so she fills her horse with yet more aetheric torrents and rides down her prey and hacks through his neck and then she holds his head by the hair and rides on as it dribbles warm-then-cold blood down her arm and spatters her face and tastes in her mouth like metal as it dries on her skin—

And she is riding on, throwing torches on tents and thickets and riding through and past plumes of smoke, and there are men under the Eagle crying out her name and telling her to turn back, but she keeps riding and filling herself and her mount with the power unseen and she rides through the brightness and the darkness, and she speaks to the woman of the night and to men of flesh about to die and she learns where to go and who to kill and on and on she goes through the brightness and into the darkness—

And in the great darkness she sits among laughing and whispering trees and she sets the first man with authority's head on a mound of earth, and down from the stars come the wolves of the goddess and they cackle and bring a deer whose broken neck flops between their lightning fangs, and she sets upon the deer with her own teeth and tears at its skin and flesh and fills her stomach with its red and raw body and slakes her thirst with blood that tastes not so different from blood of men, and the wolves howl their approval as they dine alongside her, and the moon rings with a crystal harmony that shudders her bones and drives her to her feet again—

And the mare flees from the wolves and the blood, so she ties the dead man's head by its hair to her belt and begins to run and she does not tire because her stomach is full of a hunted beast's life and there is no ending to the aether rushing through her and the sun races to die and bursts to life again in the span of a breath and in turnings of the brightness and the darkness she catches a wild stallion by his mane and tells him to bear her in the names of the Lady of the Hunt and He Who Walks Between the Stars and the horse snorts and hums a vindictive hymn as he charges across the endless green under stars and sun—

And he bears her far and fast without tiring, and he tells her the lineage of his bloodstock to the days when the earth knew no cold, and when they come upon yet more foes he does not falter in step or speed but carries on like a vibrant wave, and so great is his haste that even arrowheads fall aside when they strike his coat—

And when she finds the next man of authority, she blinds him and all his army with a great blanket of night in the day, and she takes his head too and ties it beside the first, and she turns to ride for the great city where the final such man waits for her to come and kill him, and she stops under the moon so the wolves might bring her another deer, and the horse looks on with disgust and disputes with the wolves throughout the night as she chews on the flesh and drinks of the blood, and the two heads of the dead men look on in dumb silence, when in the heart of night comes a naked dwarf with butterfly wings riding atop a pony and blowing a horn and pointing and snorting and pronouncing horrible woes upon her, and both the wolves and the horse laugh to hear what will befall her, and she laughs too as the blood runs down her chin and the flesh catches between her teeth—

And when she rides upon the city, her steed leaps the wall in a single bound and his hooves throw sparks in the night, and there are men with bows and golden eyes full of loathing but they do not draw their bows because the wolves are laughing and the moon is singing and the dead man's sword in her hand and the magic in her soul and her fist and her gaze cannot be turned aside and she finds the man of authority and kills his defenders and kills him too and he is saying pleading things when she kills him but she cannot hear them for she only knows the language of stars over mountains and wind among trees and rivers in earth, and so she ties the third head to her belt and goes out into the endless expanse of grass under the glittering black-iron night—

And the stallion leaves her with a grim word and the wolves bring a hare instead of a deer and they leave snickering and the mocking dwarf does not make himself known and the grass and flowers are silent like the three heads set on mounds of earth she shapes with her hands, and so she speaks to the men she has killed and tells them of everything she can recall, tells them of a little lake and a man on fire and a mountain piercing the heavens, and she speaks every secret and every regret and every curse and everything she will never tell a living soul, and the moon shines down and sings its song, and the face of the moon is iridescent and lovely and accusatory and conspiratorial and startling and full of pale fire, but it is only a particular fire and not the Fire itself, so she can bear it as she sits and speaks and sates herself with the little hare, until at last the moon's song leaves her ears and flies out of her soul that it might play on in some other place or mind—

And then Sharasthi dropped into the black.

PART IV

THE FIRE BEHIND ALL THINGS

30

THE GIRL WHO HID IN THE NIGHT

ALL IS FIRE. Some days I do not think much of it, some days I do not live as though it is true, but true it remains: All is Fire.

—Zaro's Sayings, verse five hundred and one

SHARASTHI TUGGED AT HER MANTLE. "STRAIGHT?" she muttered.

Lylah's ephemeral locks of nocturne hair flowed about as she turned her head to look at the nearby legionnaires, all in formal kit. "They can hear you, Sharasthi."

"They don't speak Zarushan, and half of them already saw me when I was like *that*."

"Yes, it is straight."

"Thank you."

Lylah's body looked vaporous in the sunlight. Her voice thinned in the daytime as well. Sharasthi had once asked, a day or two after she woke from her nights of madness, how it felt. Lylah had struggled to put it into words, saying it was like asking why the wind blows. It was simply the way of things. Then she had paused, asked if

Sharasthi remembered what she had seen *that night*. What Tobron had called the First Mystery.

Bits and pieces. She remembered Tobron's golden eyes. His dreadful oracle. She remembered the goddess Kashakran and a chorus of spirits and the strange Wanderer.

She remembered what Tobron said happened to Claw-face—to Brechaer, that was. How she had killed Brechaer's son—the Hunter wearing blue earrings—and how that had led to Tobron's own son dying by the same elixir Sharasthi survived.

But so much of the rest was like torn strips of parchment, faded and stained. A word here, a few letters there. She had a memory of so many things burning, herself included. Sometimes when she sat still and her mind wandered, for a moment in the corner of her eye loomed the Tree behind every tree, the Blade of Grass beneath all blades of grass, and her eyes would water and her heart quiver and then everything would be as it was.

Lylah had tried to guide her into better controlling that perception, but it was like a key had broken off in the lock. Sharasthi could not open or close it any further, it was stuck there. All she could do was keep herself steady, focused on the immediate instead of the Beyond. It felt not so unlike her fits as a child.

"Adept Sharasthi." Legate Taric was approaching. They clasped forearms. "We've made it home. Just one more endeavor."

Sharasthi cast a glance toward the walls of Lazarra. "Would you prefer another battlefield?"

"That is where I'm most at home, but *that*"—he inclined his head to the city—"is what I do it for."

"Emperor and Eagle," she said flatly. One advantage of spending so many days behind enemy lines was that people did not read her lack of enthusiasm for the Imperial cause as suspect—they saw it as just another scar taken in the line of duty.

"Just a few hours, Adept, and then you can slip off to whatever dark corner you inhabit."

"If the Emperor truly wanted to honor my service, he would let me skip this business."

The legate chuckled. "But what would the men think?"

Sharasthi hesitantly reached up to touch the golden laurel atop her head. "Yes, well, I'm sure I don't know why they would grant me such an honor after I lost their brothers in the Bildani."

"You were betrayed and ambushed, but by your actions you prevented many more casualties. Many of them will tell their children about how you rode by, the general's head in hand as you rode past, plumes of darkness billowing high. 'We told her to come back, but she had the fire of vengeance in her eyes, and she would not turn from her task until it was well and finished, the enemy trounced.'"

"And then I was found in a field sleeping like the dead and hauled back on a cart—what a hero." Sharasthi could not actually remember, but she had pieced as much together from what reports she'd heard.

"Glory in your deeds, Adept. That's an order. You never know who will be watching you."

"Aye, sir."

When they mounted up, a shudder went through Sharasthi. She smelled Parthava. Blood and horseflesh and grass and aether. Lylah tilted her head. "Sharasthi," she prodded. "Attend."

She nodded, muttering that she would. The legate's eyes flitted to her for a moment, then fixed ahead again. Sharasthi straightened herself in the saddle, brushing back a coiffed lock that had fallen into her face. She had woken from her tear across Parthava to find much of her hair gray. Compared to the constant risk of glimpsing the conceptual essence of everything in the world, she found it a light consequence for transgressing the spiritual domain.

She wondered what Alyat would think of it.

Alyat. She had not sent him a single letter. She had sat down to try and write, but not known what to say. Now she wished she had at least said *something.* 'I'm coming back' would have sufficed.

Too late now. Life spiraled onward. *'You will survive,'* said Tobron, the Son of Thunder, and he had spoken it like a curse.

Yes, she had survived. She remained.

A trumpet was blown. The legate gave an order, which became an answering trumpet call.

The gates of Lazarra were wide open.

The Seventh Legion, following the golden *Aquila* and the banner "By Vigilance and Preparation," made their triumphal entry into the city.

Sharasthi and the legate were a ways back, so she heard the deafening cheers from afar as they shuddered against and rolled over the walls and through the gate. They were entering through the First Gate, the same she had entered through as Rufus' apprentice when she came to Lazarra fifteen years ago.

She had come with a vow of vengeance in her heart, and now, all these years later, she had fulfilled half of it. Or rather, she had discovered it was already satisfied. Her grandfather's killer was dead.

Her mind flew back to the first moments she had awoken in Parthava. No fatigue, no aches, not even aether sickness. Alone in a spacious tent, she had pushed herself up in bed, marveling at how...*normal* she felt. She had been bathed and dressed in clean clothes. But something was off— something had been off since she first stirred, something besides how she was feeling, besides the cleanliness and strength.

Her focus was missing. And then she realized, she had dropped her focus in Tobron's dwelling.

"Am I dead?" she had finally murmured. She was certain she had been wielding her Art of Shadows—or had that all just been a dream?

The answer to her question came from the space beside her. "You live yet, Sharasthi."

Where only a moment prior there had been empty air, the spirit called the night-daughter was there. And yet, it was not so much that she appeared as Sharasthi perceived that she had already been there.

She looked at the spirit for a long while, taking in the everflowing locks of hair, the stars burning and twinkling across her form. "How long...?"

"You have been asleep for three days."

Sharasthi shook her head. "I mean, how long...have you been with me?"

She made a sound like tinkling bells. "You were two thousand and two hundred nights old. You were curled up in your hiding place among the reeds by the lake. You were coughing and crying. I had noticed you before—the girl who hid in the night. I thought you were interesting."

"Interesting," Sharasthi echoed. Six years old. Her sickness had rooted into her. She had begun to grasp she would never be free of her frailty. The cool evenings and nights were easier on her than the hot and bright daytime. Six years old. That was also when...

"My fits started then."

"You were always sensitive to the unseen, but growing up in a temple, hearing your grandfather's teaching on the hidden truths... you became more and more attuned to our side. I tried to give you an anchor, something to steady you against the currents and winds, but I could not give you a true soulbond."

"A soulbond."

"The unifying of human and spirit wills. A rare thing in these days. Most begin as ours did—when Rufus touched you with the arcane focus, a foul technology, but one to which I submitted."

"I...felt you then. You were holding me. I thought...it was like you were saying goodbye."

Another sound like tinkling bells. "Yes, what a tenderhearted child you were that you could discern so much. But it was not a true goodbye—I stayed with you all throughout. I was chained."

"*Why?*" Sharasthi spat out. "Why do that?"

The night-daughter looked off to the side, though Sharasthi had the sense she was looking Somewhere Else. "Once, you were speaking to the man Zageth. You were in the dark. You said you can only do what you will do, just as the...just as what you call the Eternal Flame can only burn. It is like that for us, even more so. When humans understand what it is like to act perfectly according to their nature and will, that is when you and us are most alike. To be spirit is to exist according to a pattern. That is the best I can explain my choice."

Sharasthi did not understand, and yet she did. She hung her head for a while, listening to herself breathe. "Do you have a name?" she asked eventually.

"I am Lylah."

"We usually begin with that."

Lylah made a startlingly human gesture: waving her hand to-and-fro in front of her. "I cannot take offense over mortal customs."

"Hm."

They talked more—about what it meant that they had forged a full soulbond when Kashakran shattered Lylah's chains; about how Sharasthi had slain countless Parthavans, including the Triumvirate, during her nights of madness; about how powerful her magic was now that she could safely work aether without a focus.

Then, someone begged pardon and entered. A physician. "Adept Sharasthi," she said, "Thank the gods you are awake and well." She was beaming.

Seeking to confirm Lylah's account—and Tobron's grim oracle—she asked, "How fares the offensive?"

The answer: "The Parthavan cities surrendered this morning and the Hunter tribes have already withdrawn from the theater of war."

Sharasthi nodded slowly. "Good," was the only word she could find.

Then, something else came to her. Something that turned her stomach. "And the Warda tribe?"

The physician's face turned sour. "The Warda hostages got away the morning Legate Taric was to fight Pachur. As for how they did it... the legionnaires guarding them could not explain it. It was a bloodless and silent escape. The whole tribe is in the wind now."

Sharasthi sighed. For an instant, a dull longing for yet more vengeance ached in her chest—but that would be suicide at this point. The deal with Kashakran had been struck. Besides, it was hard to muster the will to go after Hunters again. No doubt the Empire would get around to retaliating against the Warda. That was one of the grand things about Lazarra—her memory could be long indeed, her justice inevitable on a scale of decades.

The physician had one more thing to report. "The legate waived the death penalty for losing prisoners given the extraordinary circumstances. It will not even go on the guards' records."

"Good. It wasn't their fault." She would not have been able to explain beyond that, but she had seen enough of the Hunters to know they were a people beyond the pale of conventional humanity. And Legate Taric, she assumed, had been just as eager to rid himself and his men of Parthava as she was.

In the now, the First Gate of Lazarra—the Gate of Piety—loomed wide before Sharasthi. The cheers built in magnitude. Sharasthi straightened herself, raised her chin. This was what victory earned: pomp and spectacle.

Legate Taric raised his arm before passing through the portal. Sharasthi simply kept her eyes forward. The golden laurel atop her head seemed leaden.

"*Ave Imperator!*"

"Glory to the victors!"

The adulation smote her eardrums. The road to the Palatine Hill seemed to stretch, delaying the moment she both dreaded and desired—the Emperor's reception. If she survived that, it would be over, and then in private she could wallow in her pride. For now, she just had to endure—

"*Salute!*" barked a voice she knew like a raven knows the skies.

In the corner of her eye, she saw red. The same red around her shoulders.

Steady, she commanded herself. She did not clench her teeth or swallow. She did not furrow her brow or frown. She did not smile or nod. She did not jump off her horse and run to him.

She turned her head and observed—the representatives of the Sanctum. Adepts and *subordinati* and *acoylti* and *probatii*, all of which she disregarded because standing over the latter...

Alyat. His face was inscrutable. She hated that, even as she was certain hers was much the same.

Then his lips thinned—so subtly no one else would notice it, but for her it meant: '*Took you long enough.*'

Her heart tried to force its way through her throat, so she tore her eyes away, passing over the awestruck face of a tan, dark-haired girl standing in front of him, and then her gaze was riveted forward once more.

Lylah hummed by Sharasthi's ear. "That child is bound to a fire spirit, like Rufus. A rare thing—as is her potential."

Fire.

"You can see such things?"

Lylah began to talk, but Sharasthi's attention was already elsewhere. She was thinking again of the Fire about which her grandfather taught her. She was certain Tobron had spoken of it too, though her recollection was fragmentary.

There was Something beyond and betwixt the world. It could be glimpsed at great hazard. Whispers of it had been passed down.

There were questions Lylah refused to answer. The nature of the Eternal Flame was one of them. There were things she left out when she recounted the meeting with Kashakran and the spirits of the unseen mountain. The Wanderer. Lylah would not say anything about him, only that for him to show himself to a mortal and put a seal of protection and concealment upon her was *a rare thing*. Lylah said that often, which made Sharasthi question just how rare these things could be.

Most disquieting of all, she would not tell Sharasthi what had happened in those moments her grandfather burned atop the pyre—when he began to wail and the Hunters became afraid of him. She said Vohman had *grabbed hold of something*, but what that was or how he had done it, she would not say.

Alyat. She could not speak to Alyat about any of it. She would say she could not remember anything, that she had been in some sort of fugue.

How could she keep lying? The Order of the Sleeping Dragon was bad enough. Now...?

Sharasthi observed the parade route at a remove. Winding through the streets, passing thousands, tens of thousands of faces.

She remembered the Parthavan girl, Tobron's daughter, crying over her cousin and brother. Two deaths of many Sharasthi was implicated in. All these Lazarran faces—what were they to her? Who would she weep for? Alyat. Rufus. Her lover and her teacher. Two souls out of innumerable multitudes.

Her vow was half-discharged—but so many years of labor had not mattered a whit for that. All that remained for her to do was fulfill the other half: Cassia Vantelle, the Emperor, the god Arkhon.

Sharasthi had been elevated to the Circle of Peers—a high honor for an Adept of her age. She would have ample opportunity to leverage that office for the cause of the Order.

Would she ever tell Alyat? If it was the night before a coup, could she take him into her confidence, or...

"Alone in the dark," she murmured.

Lylah said nothing. The crowd roared, drowning her whisper out.

Ever since she decided to go to Parthava, she had been alone. This was all just the outworking of that. She had made her vows and she was living by them—whatever that demanded.

Zaro said, 'One vow steers a life, two mold it, three crush it.'

She had her sum of two. Vengeance and the Order. She had made her choices—if indeed she had ever been able to do otherwise.

At the terminus of the triumphal parade, Sharasthi and the legate climbed the steps of the Palatine Hill and presented themselves before Emperor Dioclete.

Lylah shuddered, hiding her face. "At all costs, keep your sight shut, Sharasthi." She began whispering to herself in some language alien to the human mind.

Sharasthi kept herself composed as she knelt and saluted. Dioclete declared and bestowed honors.

When she looked into his eyes, her spirit felt a cold wind blow— but break against something. Like taking shelter in the lee of a rock amidst a storm. The Emperor narrowed his eyes so slightly, it might have been a trick of the light. "I am sure," he said in a low voice, "your future holds yet more brilliance for Lazarra, Adept."

Sharasthi inclined her head. "May it be so. My life to serve you, my Emperor."

Then she rose and turned to look down upon the masses. Legionnaires, officers, Senators, commoners, aristocrats, Adepts, dignitaries.

Under the blazing sun, for a moment she thought the whole city was aflame.

'*There is Fire*,' said Zaro.

Sharasthi had seen it. *What an awful weight to carry.*

31

GUILT AND HATRED

Fɪʀsᴛ ʏᴏᴜ ᴀsᴋ why I laugh, now you ask why I weep. Is not Zaro, too,
but a man?

 —Zaro's Sayings, verse nine hundred and sixty

Sʜᴀʀᴀsᴛʜɪ ᴅʀᴏᴘᴘᴇᴅ the golden laurel to the floor. The metallic clatter
echoed off the walls of her room. She threw her mantle on her bed,
peeled off the rest of her formal kit and left it in a heap. She had
bathed that morning, but after spending the day parading under the
searing sun and then mingling with oh-so-many faces at the banquet,
she felt filthy. Exhausted as she was, she dragged herself to the
Sanctum baths.

Her footfalls were slow. Even though almost no one was about
except the night guards, she still wrapped herself in shadows and
kept to the darkness. It wouldn't do for the Adept of the day to be
seen trudging about the grounds in an oversized tunic and lacking
her mantle. She did keep her replacement focus around her neck. It
made Lylah uncomfortable, but Sharasthi could not risk anyone real-

izing she could perform magic without it. She still feared someone on the Circle would pry into the matter of when she had lost her first. She could only hope the 'impossibility' of working magic without a focus would protect her from such inquiries...though Lylah said Carnifexes knew the truth of the matter there. Another indeterminate worry to shoulder.

Taking a longer way to the baths, off the regular path, she ignored the accusatory voice in the back of her mind. She ignored it as she convinced the bleary-eyed attendant to let her in despite the odd hour (sometimes it was good to be well known), and she ignored it as she scrubbed her skin raw in the frigid water.

"Sharasthi," Lylah ventured, "why not get in the hot pool?"

Teeth chattering, she shook her head. Lylah was a keen intellect, but some human behaviors defied her comprehension. She was not about to try and explain how she longed to distract herself and also to punish herself for wanting that and to distract herself from that too and...

Lylah tilted her head.

"Just want the cold," she muttered.

Refusing the attendant's help, she scoured herself dry with a towel and made her way back. A prickling headache burrowed into her skull through still-damp hair.

When she got back to her room, the door was ajar. The sight put an icy knife into her heart.

She reached out with her aetheric sense, so much sharper since Parthava, and brushed against his—it was so distinctly *his*—presence.

The urge to flee flickered in her consciousness, but she knew the time had come. A pang of guilt lurched through her chest. Even now, he was the one stepping toward her. He was the one who had come to her, and not the other way. He had always played that part—seeking her, drawing her out in spite of herself.

Nudging the door further open, she stood in the frame with its unseen air of Boundary and looked at Alyat.

He was inspecting the bronze mirror he gave her years ago when she earned her commission. His face tilted up.

Their eyes locked. Neither said a word.

Sharasthi's tongue worked inside her mouth, faltering on unborn words: *I'm back. I missed you. I'm sorry for a hundred things.*

He spoke first. "You look cold."

She nodded.

"Come here."

The distance between them collapsed. His strong arms wrapped around her, and she healed and broke in the same instant. He smelled of pine and oil and home.

His calloused hands folded over her frigid ears, his warmth stinging her skin. He kissed them, kissed her cheeks. Their lips fit together. She was going to lie to him with these lips.

Stop.

She pressed her hands under his shirt. His muscles contracted against her icicle fingertips. She remembered him killing for her. She remembered crying and smiling under him in that cramped room in the inn.

Stop.

His fingers clasped her chin as he pulled away for a moment. She wanted to keep her eyes closed. She needed to open them.

In his eyes: concern and desire and questions and love and all of it bare and honest. Eyes like blue lamps burning into her with searing Insight.

She filled herself with dark fog.

He searched her features. He stroked her hair. "What happened?" he finally asked.

"Whatever was in the reports." She despised herself.

"Before that. What happened...I don't even know when. What happened to make the letters stop? What happened to make you so careful with your words? What happened? Something was wrong before. Something is even more wrong now."

Sharasthi felt Lylah's presence so near. Alyat was holding her, yet he felt so far.

"I don't know what you mean."

"Don't lie."

Her eyes stung. She couldn't bear his gaze anymore. When she shut them, burning tears squeezed out. "I can't tell you."

"Look at me." His voice was cold. Not cold with anger. Cold with hurt.

"I can't."

"Look at me."

She did.

"Did you ever trust me?"

Knives in her stomach.

"More than anyone on this earth."

Meetings with Zageth by torchlight. Words uttered by divine personages.

"You're lying again."

Even her truths were deceptions now. She needed to hide. From Alyat, Alyat who had drawn her out from years of hiding. Alyat who had made her no longer alone. She needed to hide from him.

Her heart hammered. Her breath quickened.

I'm losing him now.

She could have prepared for this moment a hundred years and not been any stronger.

"Please, have me," she hissed, guilt and hatred splitting open her chest.

Stop.

"*Please*, Alyat." She smashed her mouth against his, forced her tongue between his lips.

I need to keep him.

She tried to pull him to her bed. He stayed rooted, broke the kiss. "*Shara.*" His voice was gravel, his eyes like frozen pools reflecting starlight.

She grabbed his hands and forced them onto her. "Just—just take me," she stammered. When he pulled away and tried to speak, she started tearing at her clothes. "*What*—am I not enough? Do you have someone else, is that it?!" Her voice had gone shrill.

Alyat stepped back and leaned against the wall. "What are you doing?"

She had accidentally rent her garments with aetheric strength. Her knuckles were white, her fists full of fabric. Her breath was coming fast and shallow. Her head spun.

Sharasthi sank to the floor.

It's me. I'm begging him to accept me and reject me. Because I cannot do it of my own will.

The prophet said, 'Be faithful in wounding those you love.'

Her head hung, then crept upward.

"I'm sorry, Alyat. I can't do this anymore."

He was still, then he knelt down. "Can't do what?"

Lie to you. Hide the truth from you.

"I can't keep wronging you like this."

"Then stop."

She shook her head. "I don't think I can stop until the day I die."

"What is it? Do *you* have someone else?"

"I never wanted anyone else for a moment." A breath of honesty that scoured her deceitful insides.

"Then what is it? Tell me, and we'll fix things."

Her lips trembled. It took all she had not to spill every last secret.

She shook her head. "Don't ask me to do that."

Please! Save me!

He heaved a sigh. "All right."

She covered her face with her hands, trying to muffle her sobs as best she could. He stayed there for a while, then got up, took the blanket from her bed, and draped its worthless Comfort over her shoulders.

Once he was gone, Lylah sat beside her on the Belowness of the floor, silent. The spirit did not try to comfort her or chastise her. She just was there.

"Why," Sharasthi groaned, "is my life one where both you and he came into it?"

Lylah considered this. "I do not think the answers would help, Sharasthi." She put an ethereal hand on her shoulder, then pulled closer to hug her. It was the same phantom touch as that day before the temple. Just as faint. Just as sorrowful.

She remembered, not for the last time, Tobron's words.
'You will survive and suffer.'

32

LIKE DREAMS

FOR EXCEPTIONAL VALOR in the line of duty, for giving of blood and body, for manifest virtue and piety befitting the best of Lazarrans, and for distinguished leadership both in the field of battle and the halls of the Sanctum, Adept Rufus shall receive from my own hand the highest honor.

—from an Imperial Proclamation issued by Emperor Dioclete

THE DOOR TO RUFUS' office was open. Dust particles floated outward, disturbed from their many months of peace. The Adept of Fire had not been here for some time.

As Sharasthi stepped inside, she frowned. "I suppose I shouldn't be surprised."

Her old mentor didn't even glance up from what he was doing—he just grunted, which for him was a way of asking her to explain.

Sharasthi sighed, looking at the stump where his right forearm used to be. "Retiring and you still don't ask for help."

She looked about. Documents piled high, many yellowed and

crumpled. Various effects—a Karellan helmet claimed as a trophy of battle, the back-half of a snapped arrow, most of the feathers long since fallen off. It was still Rufus' office, to be sure.

She had not set foot in this room in ages. During her time serving in the field, their communication had been limited to occasional letters. In the time that had passed since her return from Parthava, she had only seen him twice: first at her installment to the Circle of Peers six years ago, then a few days ago at the ceremony. He had made it a point to come back from his field work for the former, saying it was 'proper for a mentor.' Rufus himself had been a Peer for some time, but hated how much it kept him from the field and so had stepped down. He said it was an appointment that suited Sharasthi better than him. After so many years in the Sanctum keeping a close eye on her training, he had been eager to get back to action.

Action, though, had brought him back to his office—presumably for the last time.

Rufus' thin smile tugged at the scars on his face. Most were old and faded, but two of them—the worst of the lot—were fresher. The sight of him was not a surprise to her now, though there had been some shock when she first saw him at the ceremony where Emperor Dioclete honored him and released him from service. If he had not undergone *Viva* surgery, those scars would have looked even more gruesome. "I would think as a Peer you'd have more important tasks than to help an old man move out."

"I'm sure if anyone thinks there's something more important, they'll come and find me. Besides, it was only thanks to my place on the Circle that I knew about this, since you're so damn reclusive."

He shot her an amused glance that said, *'Rich coming from you.'*

Sharasthi returned a brittle smile. "I'm glad you're alive."

Now he scoffed. "So the rumors are true, you have cracked."

"Cracked enough to help an old man *with one arm* move out."

He fixed his stump with a skeptical leer. "One and a half-arms, I'd reckon."

"One hand. Just tell me what needs doing. I'm sure you can still manage that."

"The question is whether you can obey."

"I wonder."

As she helped him sort through his belongings—most of it would be thrown out or sent to the archives, but a few things he would keep —they made idle conversation about Rufus' final assignment. Sharasthi had gotten most of the details from the official report, so it was mostly just a way of killing time. He told her what *Viva* surgery felt like. The Adept of Life who treated him had dug fragments of bone out of what remained of his arm—while it didn't do anything in terms of function, it did reduce some ongoing nerve pain he had experienced since the amputation.

The ambush had begun when enemy combatants dropped boulders on top of Rufus and his legionnaires. He'd been quick enough to get himself out of the way, but he had shoved a legionnaire clear— and the boulder that would have crushed the man ended up pinning Rufus' right arm. As enemy combatants swarmed on either side of the narrow mountain pass, Rufus had not hesitated—he fortified his left arm with aetheric strength, drew his sword, and hacked through in one move.

As he told her of the fighting, he fished in a pocket and drew out the necklace strung with the Parthavan broadheads Sharasthi had been shot with. She had given it to him at her elevation to the Circle of Peers. "One of the more macabre things a pupil ever gifted me— yet call me a superstitious old codger, I dare say it gave me some luck in the thick of things. My final battle."

Sharasthi felt a bittersweet smile curling her lips. "I hope it did."

It had been a bloody fight with heavy legion casualties. Rufus earned yet another commendation for valor and honor. *The* commendation, in fact. Sharasthi did not know where Rufus had stowed his Imperial Purple-fringed toga, but that did not surprise her. He had never been one to show off his accolades.

As a Peer, Sharasthi knew Rufus had been offered the chance to continue serving despite his impairment. An Adept of the *Ars Vulcana* was a rare thing, after all—he would still have been a plenty valuable asset.

But she also knew, without asking, why he had turned it down. It was the same reason he had been willing to take years off field work for her sake. When Rufus was responsible for someone, he took that more seriously than his own self. He would never risk the lives of legionnaires on him being anything less than fully capable.

"I have to say," she said, "I can't help but wonder if it's my fault you're not staying on at the Sanctum as an instructor."

"Hah. You were a headache now and then, but not so horrible I'd give up teaching entirely. I'm just tired of the city. So much haste and noise. The battlefield's the only place for those in my life."

"You're not going too far though."

"No, no, just up the coast. I'll have the sea and a little dock. Some orange trees. Come visit when you get sick of those grayheads on the Circle."

"You know they groused to me about getting you to stay on. They can't bear the thought of losing our Adept of Fire."

"I'm sure, but they'll have another. Alyat's apprentice is nearly due to earn her commission, isn't she?"

Sharasthi sighed. "She is. That's on my plate as well."

He raised a bushy eyebrow.

"Her final field exam went wrong. The attending Adept and the other Initiates—gone. Two dead and one missing, according to what she sent in via messenger hawk."

"Hm."

"Her ship is due in tomorrow. The Circle is launching an inquest."

"You think she'll handle it well?"

A nod. "She's Alyat's."

Rufus grunted.

He had never been one to pry about the two of them, which she was grateful for. Even so many years after that horrible night, her chest still panged when she thought of him. But life went on.

Life went on.

"Rufus..."

Something in her tone must have changed, because he stopped what he was doing and turned his attention fully to her.

"That conversation we had, when you told me what it means to be free. Do you still think that way?"

"You mean do I still live because I choose to?"

She nodded.

"Not a force in this world could keep me breathing another day against my will."

"And do you think you'll stay that way until age takes you?"

"I expect so, but freedom is freedom—even from one's own expectations."

She digested that.

"And what about you, Sharasthi? Are you still free to live and die?"

Was I ever, truly?

That day, decades ago, Rufus had told her that any warrior who survived the brush with death became taken with philosophy. In a way it was true, but now experience had shown Sharasthi just how many 'philosophies' there were in this life. Some men became somber, staring death in the eye and awaiting his cold advent with an unflinching eye. Others took up the cause of hedonism, seeking merriment today for tomorrow was uncertain. Only fine wines and finer women and all other forms of ephemeral delights justified this doomed life. Was that freedom, or just another sort of slavery?

Are any *of us ever truly free?*

"It's hard to know, sometimes. I just keep putting one foot in front of the other, and that's taken me places I would never wish another to tread... It's funny, I can so plainly see you dying, old and recumbent in a chair facing the waves. Some servant will find you there and think you're just sleeping at first. I'll get a letter and go to your funeral."

"I've set in my will that you have the first right to ignite the pyre."

A bittersweet warmth rumbled in her chest. "That is a heavy honor. Thank you. I can see that too—my hand putting the torch to the pitch. But...I cannot see anything else of my own fate. There are things I long for or imagine, but they are like dreams. Banks of fog I cannot pierce."

"What a troublesome apprentice you are, asking your mentor to contemplate your death."

Sharasthi put together a melancholic grin.

Rufus searched her features. "Curious though I was, I didn't press you on what happened in Parthava the last time we met, and I won't now. Whatever it is though, I can see it changed you, Sharasthi. You're older than you should be—not your hair, I mean, but your spirit. You were always an old soul, I suppose, but I remember watching when they raised you to the Circle and thinking how I saw you as a girl, then a young woman—and suddenly you could fit in with the rest of us antiques.

"But even so...I'd like to think that sometime, long after I'm ash in the wind, you will die in a time of peace, and you will think to your-self that you are glad you chose to live so long."

Is that possible? Is it even something I want?

"I wonder...well, you had better not make your exit anytime soon, so I can come visit and pester you over this again."

Her old mentor chuckled. "I suppose I'll never be free of you."

Sharasthi imagined the designs of the Order coming to pass. A palace coup, a civil war, violence in the streets, armies marching, assassins' blades—so many shapes the future could take. What might Rufus say to her, if it came to pass and the Empire ended? Would he be ashamed, proud, or would he be indifferent—just another day to say *yes* or *no* to the burden of being.

A part of her hoped he would die before then. That his remaining days might be those of peace, undisturbed in his quiet place by the sea with a little dock and an orange grove.

As for her own fate, no, she did not think the peace Rufus wished for her would dawn. But that was a burden for her to carry, not him.

"Well," she sighed, surveying the sorted piles and crates. "I think that's everything. Do you have someone to carry these or should I conscript some Initiates for you?"

Rufus waved her off. "Taken care of. Now, do you have time for a drink before I leave this city behind, or do you need to prepare for that inquest?"

The latter was true, but she'd be damned if she said so. "Just try not to lighten my purse too much, old man."

33

SHE WILL BE MINE

BY THE TIME I met Sharasthi, she already seemed a figure born for the histories. People spoke of Parthava as the forge that had made her so, and they said so reverently. But as I catch whispers of her youth—the gloomy girl distant from her fellow Initiates and seized by tides of sentiment—I wonder if she saw it otherwise. I wonder if she would have chosen a quiet life in the shade. History will remember Adept Sharasthi the Night-cloaked Witch, the taker of Parthava, the mentor of the Lion; but I wish I could have known the woman underneath the titles and legends. Into the annals of time, she will go on hiding her true face.

—The Memoirs of Flavia Iscator

WEARY WAS Sharasthi's first impression of Reiva. She had glimpsed her from afar before, but this was their first time meeting formally. Her first chance to truly scrutinize Alyat's apprentice.

Some soldiers came back from war with their eyes too wide, scouring every corner for the enemy. Reiva's were alert, but calm. She had undergone a horrible trial, but it had not broken her. That was something the Adept Corps and the legions could only hope to prepare their charges for. It could not be taught in the same way one learned to swing a sword or raise a shield. If the spirit broke in the mill of war, then it broke. The strength to transcend came only from within the warrior.

Sharasthi had the unique privilege of discerning that strength when she opened her awareness. Compared to now, her aetheric sense before her awakening in Parthava was a cracked and fogged glass. A conventional Adept would labor many decades to even come to such keen perception.

Reiva's presence was a steadily burning torch. The spirit bound to her was quite a force too—though Sharasthi felt more than saw him. The arcane focus around Reiva's neck interfered with that somehow.

Six years ago during the triumphal parade, Lylah had told Sharasthi Reiva had incredible potential. Now it was plain to see how true that was. The girl's magic was formidable. Her soul blistered with passion and ferocity.

Yes, Sharasthi thought, *she would lie for a comrade.*

Of the four members of the Adept Corps on the mission, only Reiva had returned. Such a catastrophe demanded an investigation by the Circle of Peers.

Adept Brefon had died at sea.

Initiate Luo had been killed by pirates on the island, his body recovered.

Initiate Tolm had vanished, along with a small watercraft in the pirates' lair.

Reiva gave her full account multiple times. It was checked against the written account she had submitted before the hearing, as well as witness reports gathered from the marine legionnaires.

Under questioning, Reiva never changed her story, no matter the manner they pressed her. Though her fatigue was evident, she maintained her posture and spoke with a clear and even voice. Her emotions were under firm control in a way Sharasthi found reminiscent of Alyat.

The first time Reiva wavered was in describing Initiate Luo's death. Her jaw clenched. It was subtle enough that Sharasthi knew she was either trying to mask it, or she was such a good actor as to know how to fake that under intense suspicion.

Either way, Sharasthi had to give her professional respect—but she knew it was the former. The girl was too forthright.

The second time she showed emotion was not so subtle. It was when Sharasthi brusquely said, "It must be noted you stood to gain from Tolm's disappearance."

The girl's eyes flashed. Her voice was chiseled stone. "Tolm deserved first more than any of us. Doing anything to steal that from him would make it a worthless title."

"Of course, merely an observation." No one on the Circle seriously thought Reiva had killed Tolm, but it was better for Sharasthi to nullify that line of inquiry than risk someone else pursuing it. Sharasthi approved of the anger in her response. She had learned to recognize that sort of indignance in interrogations: it was the reflex of an honest soul accused.

Reiva was telling the truth.

And so, she was lying. Unlike Sharasthi, she had too much honesty in her. No matter how careful she was about her words, the anxiety of deceit still fomented behind her features. In that moment, her anger had let Sharasthi glimpse with absolute certainty the truth behind her words. Tolm deserved to graduate first.

Tolm escaped, leaving her with the guilt of lying to cover for him as well as the guilt of bearing a title she feels is, at least in part, unearned.

Poor thing.

As for whether the other members of the inquest could see what Sharasthi saw—she doubted it. She also did not care for the Empire to catch Tolm or catch Reiva in her lie for his sake. If anything, she hoped they got away with it.

By now, at thirty-five, Sharasthi had gotten a sense for when to lie on another's behalf. She had also seen all too often (among enemies and allies alike) how that could leave a clue, tying you to the anchor that would drag them down to the depths.

It was possible, if unlikely, that if she twisted things in Reiva's favor here, it would somehow come back around to her—at minimum in the form of alleged incompetence. Tolm could reappear, or perhaps Reiva would let her guard down, get drunk, and spill her guts. It could happen next week. It could happen in five years. That was the problem with conspiracy—the chance of getting found out *never* disappeared. It hung over your head like a sword swinging by a string. Sharasthi had a bouquet of blades over her head by now. She was not eager to throw another into the mix.

But the girl was Alyat's pupil. She had received good instruction.

More questions flew at Reiva regarding Tolm's disappearance. Adept Dorban—one of the oldest Adepts still serving—asked if she thought Tolm had taken the missing pleasure craft out to open sea. Reiva said she had heard the vessel was unworthy of such use. Adept Surille prodded at whether that was reliable information, seeing as Reiva had gotten it from an enemy combatant.

Sharasthi decided she would give the girl the chance to state it plainly. It would be a risk, but if she got through this, all would be well. "Initiate Reiva. Did Initiate Tolm give you any indication that he *would* have taken the craft out if he thought he could sail it successfully?"

A moment's pause. Reiva shook her head. "No ma'am. Initiate Tolm gave no such indication."

Good girl. "Or, put it this way. If Initiate Tolm could have left the Corps, do you think he would have?"

Something flickered in Reiva's eyes. "Tolm was worthy of his place as first Initiate, ma'am. He spoke to me of his intent to earn his commission and use the fruits of his labor to the greatest extent he could."

Sharasthi did not read a single lie in her words—the finest sort of deception. She nodded and held her silence from that moment on.

After Reiva had been dismissed, the Circle conferred in privacy. Sharasthi spread her hands. "She doesn't know anything."

Dorban scratched an old scar running from the corner of his eye to his gray temples. "So certain, Sharasthi?"

"You could throw her in an Intelligence interrogation cell and they would unearth nothing more than what we heard today."

Dorban's lips twisted in a sour grimace. "Let's not get them involved. You're as close to Intelligence as I care to get."

Sharasthi smiled flatly. "Why thank you."

Floating overhead, Lylah laughed with a sound like ringing bells.

A FEW MONTHS after the Circle of Peers resolved their inquest into the loss of Adepts Brefon, Tolm, and Luo (the latter two having received their commissions *in absentia* and posthumously), Sharasthi found herself summoned to another meeting regarding Reiva.

She was not looking forward to it, but she knew it had to be done.

Lylah appeared at her side. "Is this not a risky engagement?"

"It is," she murmured. "But I need to see."

"To see...?"

Her footsteps struck the stones of the road; she could almost hear echoes of Waymaking and Connection. "To see if my hatred is still enough."

Lylah was silent a moment. "Hatred is a dangerous thing, Sharasthi."

"So is a sword, but only a fool wages war without one."

By the Fifth Gate, the Gate of Courage, Sharasthi found the headquarters of the Ninth and Tenth Legions. She was able to walk in without announcing herself to the guards, and immediately an aide greeted her and escorted her to her destination.

Every step through the halls, Sharasthi felt her soul shrinking down, down to the size of a fourteen-year-old girl.

When they came to the door, the aide knocked.

Zageth answered it. "Adept Sharasthi, welcome. Thank you for your time."

"My pleasure. We have met, haven't we? Optio..."

"Zageth." He bowed his head and waved her inside. "It was at the celebration of the Imperial Heir's birth."

There, seated behind a majestic desk, was the woman herself. Cassia Vantelle.

"*Zageth*, of course. Praetor Vantelle. *Ave Imperator*."

Vantelle rose from her desk, the wood pregnant with Authority, as a nostalgic smile worked onto her features. "*Ave Imperator*, Sharasthi. *Adept* Sharasthi. So many years since you've earned your commission yet only now am I able to congratulate you in person."

"Yes, my hair's gone gray."

Vantelle laughed. "How we suffer for the Empire."

"Indeed."

"Leave us, Zageth."

The two of them sat down. The door shut.

Vantelle appraised her. "I recall saying to a little girl in Zarush that Lazarra held great opportunity for her. I have an eye for talent, Sharasthi, but...you are something else."

"You do me too great an honor, Praetor."

"Hm. I recall you saying something like that back then too."

"People never really change."

"You don't think so?"

"If I could be a different person than I was...twenty-odd years ago, was it? I would. When I was born, my grandfather drew my astrological chart. He had me marked then."

Vantelle clicked her tongue. "Your grandfather was certainly a sagacious man, but part of why the Empire forbids divination is precisely because it inculcates such attitudes."

"There's wisdom in that."

"In the proscription, or in resignation to fate?"

Sharasthi inclined her head. "Regarding proscriptions and fate—you summoned me to discuss the matter of Adept Reiva. You want me to approve her for active duty."

Vantelle drew her lips into a line.

"Your eye for talent?"

A curt nod. "Just so."

Sharasthi touched her hair. "I mean no offense, Praetor, but your hair was not this gray when you were my age. You said I am 'something else,' and in that you are more right than you realize. I think it would be negligent of me to let Reiva return to the field so soon."

Vantelle bridged her fingers. Her eyes scrutinized Sharasthi, and Sharasthi waited. Lylah whispered encouragement in her ear.

"Pardon me if I am off the mark, but do you bear me some ill will?"

You and everything you stand for. "Not at all, but I must beg your pardon. Today is not a good day for me. Ever since Parthava, now and then my fits come back."

Vantelle narrowed her eyes, searching her memory. "From before you became Rufus' apprentice?"

"They are more bearable, and they've changed in some ways, but yes."

"I was not aware."

"It's not something I speak of. But I'm sure you are aware of the rumors."

"Rumors. You mean how you talk to yourself, how you labor under a woeful cloud."

Sharasthi nodded.

Vantelle scanned her head-to-toe. "I again find myself suspecting some antipathy from you, Sharasthi."

"This has nothing to do with you or my coming to Lazarra. Even if I did bear some *antipathy*, as you put it, only a fool would hold on to such a thing for so many years. Lazarra is my home now. My identity is that of an Adept in service to the Emperor. I am also responsible for my juniors. I will not clear Reiva for your aims or for the sake of the campaign on Talynis."

Sharasthi stood up. "If she is going to serve, she will have to convince me herself that she is strong enough. Flattery and appeals to the glory of Empire are but words. I do not doubt your eye, Praetor Vantelle, but I know firsthand what can come of living up to your expectations."

Cassia Vantelle rose. "That little Zarushan girl has become a Lazarran after all—that much is clear. Indulge me a question before you leave, Adept. If you had already made up your mind, why heed my summons when a message could have sufficed?"

Sharasthi smiled thinly. "Old times' sake?"

The praetor raised her chin, eyes glinting. "Is that it?"

SHARASTHI ENJOYED the temple of Somnus. The priests let her spend as much time as she wished in the rear garden. Lylah said Somnus himself was kin to her, in the strange fashion spirits drew their ancestries, which Sharasthi had only tried to ask about once.

Ever since her awakening in Parthava, Sharasthi had felt them. Gods.

If she opened her aetheric sense, she could perceive them lurking everywhere. She could not see or hear them—not usually. Lylah said they preferred to conceal themselves in this era, even from those like Sharasthi. But Sharasthi had a hunch they *especially* did not want humans like her to be aware of them. Lylah had said it was a complicated matter.

There were some spirits, like Somnus, whom humans recognized as gods, usually because of their tremendous power, or because they had formed in bygone days some covenant with mortals. Sharasthi had asked if Lylah could become a god. Lylah had said it was not a matter she wanted to consider. "Gods," she said, "are subject to certain...*constraints*." Sharasthi got the sense there was much more to that last word than Lylah was willing to let on. The night spirit was evasive on many particulars of the unseen world, calling them *unimportant* or *irrelevant* to Sharasthi.

Once though, Sharasthi had been insistent in her questioning, and Lylah had exclaimed, "It is *dangerous* for you to know too much. You've seen one of the deep mysteries, and you can still glimpse the essences of things. Too much understanding could unravel you in a way that would make your experience in Parthava like a bad dream in comparison. Or it could draw the sort of *attention* neither of us desire. Ignorance can be a shield, Sharasthi."

She had taken the lesson to heart and scaled back her inquisitions.

Today, as she approached the temple of Somnus, she opened her awareness.

From within the painted marble halls, the soporific presence of the god radiated. The longer she attended to it, the heavier her eyelids weighed. Stifling a yawn, she stretched her sense to the garden behind the temple.

Reiva and her spirit both blazed in her awareness, the spirit more so, but the Adept was astonishingly potent—far more than at the inquest a mere few months ago.

Sharasthi murmured, "You're certain she hasn't awoken yet?"

"Her bound spirit is still enchained. But you might say her eye is opening. And her soul...if she stepped into a Convergence today, she would not be prepared for the judgment."

"I thought you said my path was abnormal?"

"Judgment is typical—divine disputes and bargaining are not."

"Hm." Sharasthi nodded in greeting to the priests of Somnus as she passed through the halls of the temple. "She's in the garden already."

They looked startled she knew as much. If only they realized she could nigh hear their god's ruminations.

The sun fell through boughs of olive trees onto Reiva, seated with her back to Sharasthi. The set of her shoulders was heavy. The poor girl had been transported across leagues and leagues while in the throes of aether sickness. She had undergone *Viva* surgery. The dread responsibility of dozens of deaths lay on her.

Sharasthi, in her heart, wanted to convince the girl to give up on going to Talynis—especially now that she was primed to awaken. If she settled for less glorious work for a few years, she would certainly distinguish herself in some other way.

But Sharasthi felt the zeal radiating from Reiva's soul. And she knew what it was like to have great talent and the opportunity to leverage it fully. Anything less would be sheer agony.

And so she also wanted Reiva to convince her to give clearance.

"Adept Reiva."

The girl sprang to her feet, whirling about with a salute. "*Ave Imperator*, Adept Sharasthi."

Her eyes too had changed since the inquest. Then, Sharasthi had thought she looked weary. Now she looked haunted and haggard. But somehow, still vigorous. Still full of vitality.

"It is my honor to speak with you. I...was inspired by your triumphal parade after the Parthavan campaign seven years ago."

Inspired? She tried to remember Reiva's face during the parade. Wide eyes, perhaps? Her own attention had been all for Alyat then. Sharasthi found herself wondering if he and Reiva had spoken about her. She put such considerations out of mind.

"Is that so?" she mused. She tilted her head as she examined Reiva anew. "Did you desire the same glory I received?"

She looked stricken. "I did." Sharasthi imagined Reiva lying awake, night after night, re-imagining her decision to pursue the relic-bearing enemies in Hyrgallia.

Sharasthi remembered what had happened the night of her own return in glory, when she and Alyat had finally torn apart. "Hm. Perhaps you should not have. One of the greatest cruelties the gods send is the granting of wishes." She remembered Tobron pronouncing Brechaer's death, and then pronouncing the misery that would haunt her steps the rest of her life.

Reiva's fists clenched. "Perhaps."

"There is no *perhaps* about that. What is still in question, though, is whether what you suffered will have a long-term effect on your career within the Corps. The praetor is quite insistent you be cleared, but I would be remiss in my duties if I were to simply roll over—even for one so illustrious as Cassia Vantelle."

Reiva needed to realize that, for all Vantelle's power, the Sanctum only bowed to the Emperor. If she tried to lean on the praetor's will to get her own desires, it would betray a confusion of priorities, a desperate grasping.

"I've recovered almost completely from my physical injuries, and I haven't suffered any symptoms of aether sickness since Adept Gylos operated on me."

"Good signs," Sharasthi acknowledged, "but that sort of thing passes quickly by the time one is a fully commissioned Adept. Tell me, have you suffered nightmares?"

The look on Reiva's face said it all—and this was where Sharasthi was most interested. "Some. Recollections of the battle. I see the faces of my allies and enemies. I see death."

Visions of the mountaintop flickered through her mind. "Death as in people dying, or *Death* as in..." She waved toward the roiling spiritual presence in the temple. "The brother of Somnus." The temple of Mors lay not far away, but Sharasthi preferred to keep away from it as much as possible. *That* god always looked back at her.

"Dying. I do not dream of gods."

The stars across Lylah's body glinted. From her perch in the air, she tilted her head, peering closer at Reiva.

"Never?" Sharasthi pressed.

A war of minute strains and tics rolled across her face. The mist of recollection hazed her eyes.

Sharasthi opened wider her perception. The blaze in Reiva's spirit died low, then flared frantically. For an instant, Sharasthi thought she smelled dust on the air, heard a distant, nigh-recognizable voice on the wind.

"Not for a very long time. Before I was brought to Lazarra."

Lylah leaned back with a "Hm." Sharasthi echoed the sound.

At the very least, I'll have to keep an eye on her from now on.

Sharasthi proceeded in questioning Reiva on her recovery. When she suggested Reiva had suffered extreme aether sickness, the young Adept retaliated with a lengthy and well-articulated counterargument. Sharasthi had to smile and praise her, seeing her express her mentor's sort of analytical thinking in such an impassioned, *Ars Vulcana* way. If Alyat had a daughter, she would have grown up to be just like this.

Her smile wilted.

"However, I have testimony from the legionnaires who transported you from Hyrgallia to Lazarra that you often muttered in your sleep—and some say while you were awake—in nonsensical babbling. Other times you frantically whispered to yourself about fire. Not to mention your eyes wheeled about as though you saw things that were not there."

Reiva stiffened. "I...I don't remember any of that."

A stab of sympathy went through Sharasthi's heart. *I say none of it with condescension, child. I know it all too well. Even so...* She held up a finger. "Exactly. Memory loss, delusions—maybe even a psychotic episode. I know it's uncomfortable to consider, Reiva, but you were almost certainly suffering the third stage of aether sickness. It's a miracle you even survived the transit."

Her face fell. It might have been a trick of the light—or her eyes were glistening. "Fire—but it makes sense I would talk about fire. Gods' sakes, it's my Art!"

Lylah shot Sharasthi an accusatory glance. Sharasthi fought the urge to sigh. She had been almost a decade older than Reiva when she faced her trial. She also had the fortune of coming out of it with a *war* won for the Empire. People saw her dead allies as the noble fallen—a tragic footnote to an otherwise majestic achievement.

Reiva had gone on her first mission wearing the gilded mantle and come back with ample losses and but one battle scarcely won. She had plundered from the enemy those strange Beast Relics—an incredible trophy to be sure—but she had come back herself in a litter, leaving the Fourth Legion without an Adept.

But she had come back. Set aside all strategic considerations and notions of glory—she had come back. Had she despaired of that? Had she resigned herself to death at one point, even longed for it?

Reiva looked up again. Something she saw in Sharasthi face's startled her.

Lylah brushed Sharasthi's shoulder with the back of an incorporeal hand.

"It's a hard thing," she said, before she realized what words were flowing out of her mouth. "Coming back when you've been so far gone. It's an experience that changes you forever. Never try to hide that truth from yourself, Reiva. It will only hurt you worse when you can't run from it anymore."

Reiva blurted out, "But I can't show weakness. An Adept is the blade that does not break."

Arms around her shoulders—Lylah's arms, Alyat's arms.

"Forged for the Emperor's hand, yes, so we are told." *A hand I'd crush if I had the might.* "A flaw in the indoctrination procedures, if I am to be honest. Blades shatter, but you can reforge them, and then they are blades again. But if the blade was convinced it would never shatter in the first place, it might start to question whether it was ever *really* a blade. It might start to think things are better as a pile of steel splinters—for it and for the world."

As the substance of what she had just said registered, Sharasthi frowned at herself.

"So sentimental," Lylah mused.

And arguably subversive. "You are not to repeat that bit about the flaw in the Corps' indoctrination curriculum. That's a project of mine and I'd rather not preemptively spoil the attitudes of my Peers by rumors fluttering through the Sanctum."

Calling it a *project* was a stretch, but at least by framing it that way she could plausibly explain herself if Reiva loosened her lips around the wrong ears. She certainly did not want any scrutiny falling on Jan as a subject of her independent ideas about training Adepts. As Imperial Postmaster, he was too well-placed to chance anyone asking whether her pupil had been improperly formed.

"I understand. And thank you, Adept Sharasthi."

She nodded, eager to set the matter aside. At least the girl's admiration likely sealed her compliance. "Now, you mentioned fire. Tell me about the burning tree. Based on your report, you were unconscious when the blaze started. You have no memory of how it may have been set aflame."

"My will was shattered; the slightest draw of aether threatened to drive me into the darkness. I passed out expecting to die in the cold."

"You were the only surviving human there, so far as we know. So the possibilities are scant. Either the gods intervened for your sake, or you did it yourself in a fugue state. What you thought was loss of consciousness may have been an *alteration* of consciousness."

Reiva scowled, incredulity writ plain on her features. "Impossible if I could not draw aether, though. This was an evergreen in Hyrgallian winter—the amount of power needed to turn that thing into a torch would have undone me."

Sharasthi looked toward the temple of Somnus.

Her personal theory was that something similar to her own experience in Parthava had occurred—that Reiva had broken her limits and, in a moment of delirium, wielded aether beyond what she had thought possible.

However, Lylah had formed a different suspicion in response to Reiva's account. The spirit said it was possible her bound spirit of flames had ignited the tree, though the conditions for such a thing were rare beyond imagining—at least, in these days.

Sharasthi and Lylah were in agreement that, most likely, Reiva had dimly perceived her spirit in the throes of her condition, sensing his fiery essence as her mind drifted beyond its normal bounds—but saying anything of that was beyond the current moment.

But there was still enough that she *could* tell Reiva. "I admit, it is a difficult theory to swallow, but not without precedent. Even allowing for the inflation of rumors and the way soldiers tell their tales, the reports of what I accomplished in Parthava seven years ago...I would have called it impossible as well, and yet if there's even some accuracy to the stories, I must assume that it is possible for an Adept to draw upon a greater well of power under certain conditions related to the lowest hells of aether sickness."

The distress in Reiva's soul quelled, which Sharasthi was glad for. She wished she could have said more, but Reiva was still firmly in the psychic grasp of the Empire. Some secrets would have to stay hidden —for now at least. Already the vague contours of Sharasthi's next moves were taking shape.

Vantelle wanted to use Reiva. That was fine—Vantelle had wanted to use Sharasthi, and the Empire had gotten more than a fair return from that, but playing out the long game always brought surprises.

Sharasthi still did not perfectly understand how the Wanderer's veil over her fate guarded her from Arkhon and the Emperor's clairvoyant magic, but she had not died yet. It was time to push things further.

She turned back to Reiva. "I've decided."

The girl's back went rigid, her eyes widening.

"I will clear you for active duty on two conditions. One, you must refrain from using your Art for another two weeks, so your soul may rest and cleanse itself."

As expected, Reiva blurted out her affirmation at once. Some life seemed to return to her, and even her bound spirit's presence swelled with exultation.

"Temper yourself," Sharasthi warned, "the second condition is harder, since it is out of your control. After your rest is complete, you will be in one of three states. You can guess two of them."

Reiva nodded. "Either a full recovery, or...or I'm a cripple effectively."

"A dreadful fate for one who has tasted the arcane Arts. Possibly the end of your career with the Adept Corps, unless you could finagle some other way to be useful. It goes without saying that if magic deserts you, you will not be cleared to serve as an Adept."

Lylah shook her head. "Why such cruelty, Sharasthi? She's begun to awaken, that much is clear."

"But there is a third possibility—one I do not inform many Adepts of for fear of...hazardous behavior. This third possibility is what I experienced in the wake of my time in Parthava."

Reiva leaned in, rapt.

"You may develop a new awareness of your powers. If that happens, write to me immediately. I will see that one of my personal ciphers is delivered to your quarters—use it for any letters you send me."

Lylah sighed with a sound like ringing bells. "Ah, I see. Playing off her admiration for you, drawing her into your confidence."

My apologies, Alyat, but your pupil has too much potential for me to stick to my own fields here.

Reiva's tone was awestruck. "I'm honored, but also confused. What do you mean new awareness? Expanded aetheric sense?"

Sharasthi cocked her head. *Who knows—you could end up talking to the manfiest intelligence from and through whom your magic emanates.* "That might be part of it. I cannot say for certain. You would be able to manipulate aether in ways that previously seemed impossible. Imagine waking up one day with a third arm—all of a sudden, all the limits of your reality have shifted. I have no records of a Fire Adept experiencing this before, so I cannot predict anything specific—*if* this happens, mind you."

A tension had worked up in her jaw since she realized she was encroaching on Alyat's territory. She needed to say this, for her sake as well as Reiva's. It brought back her own guilt about hiding the truth from Alyat, but necessity was necessity.

"One more thing, Adept Reiva. The reason you need to use the cipher. This is one of the deeper mysteries of the Adept Corps. You are not at liberty to tell *anyone* about this—not even Alyat. Even some of my colleagues in the Circle are ignorant of this."

Reiva looked startled. "But why?"

Something gnawed at Sharasthi's insides. *If only I could tell you the whole truth of it—though even this taste is gruesome enough.* "Think back to how it felt, Reiva. The dread, the certainty of doom. The pain, like rusted nails pushed through your veins. Your nerves scoured by a brush of shark's teeth. Now imagine what would happen to the Adept Corps if it were known that surviving extreme aether sickness could awaken deeper powers in an Adept."

Reiva swallowed. "I understand."

"Good. I will see that the cipher is delivered by tomorrow—well before you are due to leave." She stood, Reiva following suit.

The young Adept's arm twitched like she was about to raise it in salute, so Sharasthi headed her off with a proffered hand. "Good luck, Adept. May you find strength and wisdom on your way." An old Zarushan blessing.

After a moment's pause, Reiva clasped Sharasthi's hand. "Thank you. Thank you, I...I hope I do. But what if I fail again? What if this is just a painful extension of something that should have ended in the north?"

Sharasthi looked toward the bed of violets. She loved those flowers, loved how at this time of year, just before the spring, they seemed to muster their will for life. "I have an intuition for these things, Reiva. I do not expect failure from you. You may think I'm wrong—you may even have evidence in the coming months to show me I *am* wrong—but life winds and weaves in strange ways. Today's failure is tomorrow's door to opportunity. Never forget that. And don't die, would you? I did enjoy this meeting."

Reiva stood straighter. Her soul was awhirl with Fire, so strong Sharasthi almost felt physically warmer. "Thank you for this honor, Adept Sharasthi. I will give Praetor Vantelle the good news."

Sharasthi suppressed whatever twisted smile threatened to sneak onto her features. "See to it that you do."

Use her as you see fit, Vantelle. In the end, she will be mine.

34

A SERPENT WAITING TO STRIKE

When I am gone, you will mourn me and malign the time, but I tell you now: all happens exactly as it ought. This is the Truth of Fire.

    —Zaro's Sayings, verse one thousand two hundred and eighty-nine

Seated in her office in the Sanctum, Sharasthi was drafting her formal request to take Reiva's place with the Fourth Legion in Hyrgallia. Such a posting ordinarily would have gone to a lower-ranked Adept—certainly not someone on the Circle—but Sharasthi was certain she could convince her Peers to sign off on it.

This was one of those times when Sharasthi's stated intent and the truth were well in alignment: she wanted to go to Hyrgallia to study more closely what had happened to Reiva. She suspected, having read the reports and now spoken to Reiva in person, there were yet clues to be found. Her own interest in the matter was obvious, given her experience with aether sickness. Knowing what she knew, she could also state with what was sure to appear as brazen confidence that Reiva was going to manifest novel talents soon.

Lylah suspected that if they could examine the area where Reiva had fought the relic-bearers and (perhaps) lit the tree on fire, then they would find support for one of their theories as to what had happened out there. Sharasthi's latest conjecture was that area had a weak Convergence, while Lylah suspected the Wanderer had done something.

"Why can't you just ask him yourself?" Sharasthi muttered. "I would think spirits can communicate across great distance."

"I would think by now you realize that things of our side are not so simple as mortals suppose, Sharasthi." Lylah bristled. "Though yes, I admit it is possible. It is just that he...is atypical."

Sharasthi's quill slowed. "You always get evasive on this matter."

"There are things that cannot be uttered. Not even you, knowing as much as you do, are worthy of some secrets."

"More precautions 'for my well-being'?"

The night-daughter seemed tense. "Not so deep as those matters...just..."

Sharasthi sighed. "Very well. I've gotten used to it by now."

Lylah seemed mollified by this.

But then another question popped into her mind that she could not resist asking. "Is he...really just one of the Four Gods of Talynis?"

And then Lylah was uneasy again. "He is abnormal."

Sharasthi clicked her tongue.

A knock sounded at the door. She glanced up. "Enter."

She opened her aetheric sense just in time to realize who it was before the door swung open.

Alyat stepped into the room, his every fiber speaking fury.

Training kicked in—Sharasthi assumed a mask. She arched an eyebrow as she looked at him. "Alyat. This is about your protégée?"

"It is."

Sharasthi further attuned herself to the aether. Alyat's soul was blistering as he strode to her desk and leaned on his knuckles.

Of course she had known something like this would happen—she just had not thought it would come so soon. Seeing him loom over her like this stirred old memories, fluttering her heart.

She closed those emotions off. This was a bout.

"Reiva nearly died half a dozen different ways in the past month. She's under a mountain of pressure—from herself and from the Corps. And you think it's a good idea to send her to *Talynis*."

Sharasthi waited. She could see it irked him, but she preferred to draw him out further.

After a moment, he said in a forthright tone, "I respect you, Sharasthi." It pleased her to hear it, but she kept her expression neutral. "You're clever and strong. But this is my apprentice we're talking about, and I'm not going to roll over and accept your usual brand of secrecy and half-truths."

That sent a pang through her chest. In spite of it, she constructed a wan smile. "*Lumens contra Tenebrae.*"

He responded as expected. "Don't reduce this to our Arts."

"I'm not reducing anything. The longer a person practices their Art, the more they align to its essence—whether it be virtue or vice. You need to shed light on things; I need to keep things close to the chest. We couldn't live any other way, and neither could the Empire. If it were otherwise, there would be no need for the two of us to exist."

Alyat pinched the bridge of his nose. "You're evading."

"Such is my way." She shrugged. She had meant what she said to Zageth when he brought her into the Order years ago—that a person could only be what she was born to be. The longer she lived, she only resigned herself more and more to that truth. "But no, I'm trying to get you to think about Reiva. *Ars Vulcana,* Alyat. Fire. She needs to burn bright—if she does not live up to the ideal that her Art creates within her, then she will fizzle into smoke. Or worse, she'll descend into the vices of her Art. Unbridled hatred and resentment. She would want to burn the world into which she could not fit."

He sighed. "I never said, nor would I ever say, that she should be caged in Lazarra. But Sharasthi—*Talynis!*" He slammed a fist down on the wood.

She saw his protective...almost paternal concern. Reiva had nearly died, and now Sharasthi approved of sending her into yet another crucible. It twisted her heart. For all his cold and gruff exterior, this man had one of the most caring souls she had ever known. "Alyat. You're worried about her."

His eyes glinted. "Plainly."

"And you are letting that worry overcome your better judgment. You come from the Northlands."

He sighed, but Sharasthi pressed on.

"Isn't it true that they send boys out into the woods in the dead of winter with nothing but a hatchet and the clothes on their back and tell them, 'Come back a man, or not at all'?"

"*I* told you about all that."

"And yet you've forgotten it." Sharasthi almost regretted the words as she said them. The night Alyat had told her of such things—that had been their night together in the little room at the inn. Not a moment of that night could she ever forget, and for a moment she feared Alyat would take her to accuse him of just that.

But there was no recrimination or anger in his eyes. As his fists clenched atop her desk, she saw uneasy acknowledgment.

She couldn't know whether he was remembering that night at the inn. In fact, she would have bet against it. He was too single-minded for that, like a horse who sees a spot on the horizon and charges for it, all the world to the left and right falling away into nothingness.

But she was remembering, and she chose to steal herself a small pleasure in the name of rhetorical pathos. Her hand slid forward, folding over his. His hands were still bigger than hers—of course they were—but it struck her like a revelation.

"*Our* mentors took a chance on us, Alyat. They took the chance we would die, or come back maimed for life, or shattered in body and soul. Your protégée went out into the world, and it nearly killed her. And now she needs to go back, because if she does not, then she will never truly live again. You know this."

She could not tell Alyat the other reason Talynis was the right place for Reiva—Flavia Iscator. The Legate of the Ninth Legion was a stalwart member of the Order of the Sleeping Dragon, her family being one of the few—perhaps the only—surviving generational legacies in the organization. It was a secret that might have assuaged him, if only she could have said it, if only he could have known for what reason it was good news.

Alyat looked at her hand. For a moment, nostalgia flickered in his eyes. "Shara"—her chest seized up—"she left as a slave. Now she's going back there, and she's going to have to kill people who speak the same language put in her mouth at birth, people whose veins flow with the same blood that flows in hers, people who worship gods she was made to turn away from. There is a *reason* for our codes. And if someone is to overstep one of our most fundamental, then it cannot be Reiva. Not now, not so soon after what happened in Hyrgallia."

His words were so quintessentially him, a surge of affection shot through her. Her thumb, seemingly of its own accord, brushed across his knuckles. She should have pulled back by now—but greed for the moment stayed her.

"Or maybe facing the demons in her native land is exactly what she needs to do, in order to heal from every wound she has carried since she left."

"That's a monumental *maybe*."

As soon as that last word left his mouth, Sharasthi realized where she was again. Who she was to him. She pulled her hand back. Their faces were masks to one another. There was something absurd in that. But on the masks stayed. This was about Reiva, his apprentice. Not them. Their days were past—now there were only half-full moments like this.

"I wouldn't have cleared her if I hadn't thought she has the potential to become one of the greatest Adepts of our time. If I hadn't thought she could do what would be required of her."

He scoffed. "Because it is always best that we do what is required of us."

That chipped her mask.

She had thought they were clear of the past, but then he went and threw her back in, back to that day in a ramshackle bungalow in Karella when she had chosen revenge, when the gap between them first began to stretch into the chasm that now lay there.

Words stirred in the root of her throat. Apologies. Explanations. Outbursts. Curses. Confessions.

But by now she had smothered them all too many times. They had not a prayer of escaping her lips. She waited them out, let them die again. It was too late. It had been too late for years.

Alyat too was waiting, perhaps caught in his own inner war. He too quelled it, and when he spoke, did so in that cold professional tone. "I also came here because I need to consult you on a matter of intelligence. I've caught wind of some sort of organization—criminal perhaps, though I haven't heard anything specific about them. The Order of the Sleeping Dragon, they call themselves. Do you know them?"

A cold sweat slicked her neck and back. The world tilted, and for a moment Sharasthi saw the hidden Fire within and the Forms behind it all. By a formidable *wrenching* of her will, she forced her perception back into order.

Alyat—by virtue of his Art, his personality, and years of experience with Legion Intelligence—was difficult to deceive. For Sharasthi in particular, that was almost impossible. She had always, when possible, relied on lies of omission. She had written letters sparsely. When they were together she had avoided talking about any risky subjects to the greatest extent possible. All that had, over years, driven them further and further apart until at last she collapsed under the weight of her falsehoods and secrets.

But here and now, there was no way out. Their eyes were locked. His question was direct—the kind of question where weaseling out was more of a tell than any other response.

So when she said "No," she said it with full resignation to the fact that he would know she was lying to his face. And while she could tell he was not telling her the whole story, she could hardly fault him for it given her position.

They looked at one another, their gazes the closest they could come to acknowledging the falsehood between them.

He spoke first. "You will tell me if you recall anything, or come across anything new?"

"Of course."

He straighetened in one crisp motion. "Thank you, Adept Sharasthi."

She nodded, dropping her eyes to the papers strewn across her desk. "You are welcome, Adept Alyat."

As he left, she cast a glance at his back. Unbowed. Uncompromising. Untouchable.

The door shut. Alyat's footsteps receded. Sharasthi maintained her even breathing and flat demeanor until she could no longer sense his aetheric presence.

Her heart was hammering out of her chest. Her stomach had fallen to the center of the earth.

Lylah reached out a hesitant hand. "Sharasthi?"

She crumpled, her face burrowing into the hollow of her arms as she uttered a muffled stream of the most vile oaths she knew.

Lylah was silent.

When Sharasthi finally gathered herself and raised her head from her desk, she sighed, clutched her heart, then pressed her hand to her forehead. Strands of hair hung in her face. She swore again.

"Who's after him?" she finally mumbled.

"...after him?" echoed Lylah.

"Someone's trying to bring him in."

"Or perhaps he's simply caught on to the Order."

"If it was just that, he wouldn't have asked me. It has to be something unusual. Someone contacted him, I'm sure of it."

"Or, perhaps, he..." Lylah trailed off.

Sharasthi narrowed her eyes. She turned to the spirit. "You never go quiet like that."

"Speaking with a human for so many years has left impressions."

"What were you about to say?"

Lylah turned aside. "What if he is on the trail of the Order and realized you are involved. Maybe he is trying to warn you."

Sharasthi's head drooped. "I wish you had stayed quiet."

"It is possible, is it not?"

A limp nod.

"So what next?"

Sharasthi closed her eyes, considering. "I'll proceed as planned. Go to Hyrgallia, investigate Reiva's awakening and the source of those aberrant Beast Relics. If Alyat *is* after the Order, I'll be far enough away that I'll have ample warning if I need to disappear. If a Carnifex comes after me…"

"You are strong enough now that, at night, you could match one… most likely. But Sharasthi, if your intuition is right and someone in the Order is trying to recruit Alyat?"

Sharasthi's hands tightened into fists. "He'll be fine," she whispered.

He's going to shine a light into the wrong hole and find a serpent waiting to strike.

"You're anxious."

"I can't warn him to forget whatever he's heard. The risk is too great."

He would warn me though. Of course he would.

"Sharasthi…"

"Vows are vows, Lylah. Secrets are secrets."

But…

She held her own hand, stroking the fingers that had caressed Alyat's just minutes ago.

"After Hyrgallia…" she muttered.

"After Hyrgallia—what?"

"After I finish this business in Hyrgallia, after I have a better sense of whether Reiva could join us…if Alyat was to also…"

It was a vague and improbable hope. But perhaps…

If she were to tell him everything, bring him into her darkness once again—could things be like they were at the beginning?

35

THE OTHER MAGIC

There are always traditions 'of the left hand,' as those of us who make a study of wisdom and mystic lore refer to them. And they are always difficult to find, but they can be found. Certain Endric gurus are notorious for it, but on this side of the Spine, the Karellans have made the greatest practice of them, even to the point of outnumbering conventional religious forms. That does not bode well for Karella, as such an imbalance cannot long be maintained.

—*The Life and Wisdom of Simeon Binkhok As Told by Himself*

The charred bark of the tree crumbled under Sharasthi's touch. She rubbed ash between her fingers, grimacing.

It did not look much like the site of a massacre. The blood was long gone, the bodies burned or, in the case of the enemies', left as carrion. Yet here and there, clues lay. A fallen buckle peeking through melting snow. A scrap of iron from a shield rent by bestial claws.

Lylah floated at Sharasthi's side. "Such a stench."

"I'm hesitant to find out." She glanced at Captain Scanlon and his legionnaires. The remnants of Ironback Company kept guard at an appreciable distance. This was the spot where so many of their comrades had perished; it was no wonder they were not eager to come nearer. Not only that, but they seemed wary around Sharasthi, for which she could not begrudge them. It had been convenient, in fact, since they complied without fuss when she ordered them to give her space for her investigation.

The night spirit traced an ethereal finger through the air, as though following some contour. "It is jarring, but you would do well to sense it for yourself."

Sharasthi took a breath. Nothing for it then.

She let out a hiss as she opened her aetheric perception. The burned tree and the snow-dusted stone pillars burst into brilliant and unnamable colors. Shadowy figures bent and wove in and amongst the flows of energy.

"What is all this?" she murmured.

Lylah let out a low hum, which sounded to Sharasthi the same way the colors looked. "It is like a weak Convergence. The veil was never fully breached here, but thinned by many rites and sacrifices. Here the realms lie closer together than anywhere else for many leagues."

"What a fine coincidence that Reiva should have fought the relic-bearers here." As if there was such a thing as coincidence in this world.

"And there is much to tell of it. Look at the burns."

Sharasthi peered at the tree. If she concentrated, she could see not only the physical reality of the burned wood, but also the lingering memory of the tree that had once been there.

Trees, living for so long in one spot, tended to leave distinct impressions in the aether. If she opened her perception further, she would have seen the Evergreen Tree, but looking so deep rarely afforded her benefits, not to mention that even at this level of sight, the stimuli were overwhelming.

"Can you see what happened?" asked Lylah.

Sharasthi reached out to touch the bark again. Her fingers passed through layers of unseen reality wrapped around the matter, and she detected yet more lying within. Distinct among the energies was the smoldering residue of arcane fire. Magic always left a jarring mark, as it was an act that merged a mind's will with natural power. A wildfire would have made a mark, but it would not have seemed out of place the way these burns were. An act of arson would have burned the tree, but it would not have reflected so starkly in the aether.

"It was burned by magic."

"Indeed."

"Can you tell if this vindicates one of our hypotheses?"

Lylah let out a hesitant hum, the stars on her body twinkling in harmony. "I cannot say. It may have been Reiva, or it may have been another agent, such as her bound spirit."

"You said there were very particular circumstances in which that could happen."

Lylah made another hum, this one uneasy. The flow near her trembled.

"What is it?"

"How well can you differentiate the powers here?"

Sharasthi sharpened her perception. The cold wind chilled the sweat beading on her forehead. "It's all old, I can tell that much. It feels like magic."

"Imagine you are trying to distinguish a group of Adepts from one another."

Sharasthi closed her eyes. The currents of power still glowed and scintillated in her mind. It was more diffuse than an individual, but the presence of the place radiated in more or less consistent patterns. "Two?"

"Three, in fact, but one is so faint and similar to another that even I struggled to discern it."

"Three," she echoed, opening her eyes. "One must be the original power of the place. Born from the presence of the gods and the religious practices performed here."

"That is the most distinct." Lylah reached out with a star-dusted hand and teased a luminous ribbon free from the greater current. "You might call it ambient. It is what seeps through from the other side. Usually benign, though certain astrological and spiritual phenomena can stir up storms that are hazardous to sensitive humans nearby."

Sharasthi glanced over her shoulder at Captain Scanlon.

Lylah made an appreciative sound. "You noticed his disposition?"

"His emotions affect the aether more than most."

"If he had attracted a spirit, he doubtless would have been caught by the Empire's screenings for magical aptitude."

"Lucky him."

Lylah raised her chin. "I will ignore the implication."

"You play at humanity so well." Sharasthi turned her attention back to the site. "So that's the first power. For the second...there is something familiar here. Like catching a whiff of food you haven't smelled since you were small."

"Human memory is a curious thing—so tied to your bodies, so liable to decay."

"Next time I'll ask the gods for perfect recollection."

"For humans, the inability to forget is an ancient curse."

"I will be more grateful."

"Yes, but even so you should be able to recognize this power. Search by the tree."

Sharasthi furrowed her brow as she complied. She pushed her perception further—beginning to see Stone and Snow and wisps of the All-Pervasive Fire. As she neared the blackened remains of the tree, burning footprints resolved in the snow, and in their shape she saw the one who had stood there.

"The Wanderer," she breathed. A chill ran down her spine as she dulled her aetheric sense. "Lylah, when I spoke with Reiva, I asked her if she'd ever dreamed of a god. She denied it but...I felt something nostalgic then, and you seemed very interested in her answer as I recall."

"Reiva was—whether she knew it or not—lying."

"And you did not think to bring this up until I prompted you?"

"*He* is..." Lylah sighed—or rather, imitated the sound of a sigh—and said, "As I've warned you, there are some things you are better off not thinking on too much. I hoped, against my rational faculty, that the intersection of the Wanderer and Reiva's life would not be relevant for a while yet."

"Yet you knew it was possible, because his presence here has something to do with your hypothesis that Reiva's bound spirit set the tree on fire while she was unconscious."

"Correct."

"What's the connection?"

"He can...*act*...in ways that others cannot. He can cross boundaries."

"Like that between the spiritual and the material."

"Just so."

"Quite a talent for the fourth god of a small desert land. Why does he have his hands in so much of this?"

"He is opposed to the Far-seer."

"So are other gods, you've told me." She rubbed her forehead. "Damnation but I'm sure he and Kashakran said something on the mountaintop that was..."

Lylah exuded malaise.

"You won't remind me, I presume."

"His touch in all of this is foreboding. There are laws that constrain his influence, so the fact that you have come across him so often..."

Sharasthi frowned, peering at the night-daughter. "Laws set by *whom*?"

Lylah fell silent. "Even if I wished, I cannot speak further on this matter."

With a slow exhale, Sharasthi turned toward the stone structure.

"Some principles bind our speech in the same way gravity binds mortals."

"Gravity..." She'd heard that word in a lesson, years ago.

"The principle that causes weight."

"Mm, the lost *Ars Gravitas*. But that was rare even long ago, I think."

"Some spirits are more hesitant to form bonds than others, even in the best of times. With the Far-seer's reign...on that matter, the third power present here. Have you picked it out yet?"

Sharasthi stretched her perception yet again. Lylah had said two of the powers were much alike. It was more likely this one would be similar to the first Sharasthi had sensed—the original power of the place. The Wanderer was too alien in comparison.

But though she pushed herself almost to the point of seeing the Ideas, she could not separate it out.

Rubbing her eyes, she muttered, "It's indistinct."

Lylah hesitated a moment. "When the Many-eyed Spirit took dominion, the balance of power in the spiritual realm shifted, just as it did in the mortal realm. Forces realigned, or dissolved, or vanished. But now...this is a different sort of contender against the Far-seer."

The night-daughter reached out and plucked something from the air. She held it before Sharasthi's eyes, cupping her other hand around it, as though protecting a candle from wind. "Can you sense this?"

An ache lanced between her temples, but she could just barely detect what Lylah had grasped. "It's like..." She checked again. Her intuition only allowed one possibility. "It blends well with the ambient power of the place, but...like someone I passed on the road in a dream..."

Lylah gave a significant look, the stars in her eyes flaring to novas. "It is the *other magic*. The older magic."

Sharasthi thought she must have misheard. "The other magic. You say that as if I should know there is such a thing."

"Forgive me, but..."

"Another secret?" Sharasthi narrowed her eyes. "No...no, there's something more here."

Lylah's form shuddered. "Forgive me," she said again, "but I did not tell you before because I never thought you would encounter it again."

"*Again*? You mean..." Her stomach knotted. "When my grandfather was on the pyre?"

"He grasped this power, for a moment. The Hunters saw as much and killed him before he could complete the work taking shape."

Sharasthi forced herself to take a breath. The frigid air knifed her lungs. For a moment she saw Snow on Fire and screwed her eyes shut. "Go on."

"I should have considered this possibility after the report of the relic-bearers that attacked Ironback Company."

Still controlling her breathing, Sharasthi cracked open her eyes. The world was merely the world. She sighed. "You're saying that's why those Hyrgallians were able to use the Beast Relics to turn themselves into wolf-men? This *other magic*?"

"Just so. Those relics were made or altered with old sorcery."

"And that shouldn't be possible."

"Not at such magnitude—not since Zaro's day, certainly not since the Far-seer's ascent—but...there have always been some, like your grandfather, who remember the hidden ways...and when one channel is blocked for too long, the pressure may drive open others. Widen those that were narrow, or even force new ones into being. Centuries of the Thousand-eyed Spirit's rule have had consequences we did not anticipate. What happened in the temple of Ashmuz was like a trickle of water through a cracking dam. Now..."

"I'm sure the Far-seer anticipated this."

Lylah nodded. "If he manages to add the dark paths to his arsenal, the lands beyond the Spine would be hard-pressed to hold against Lazarra."

Sharasthi glanced northward, toward the rumored locale of Duke Faydn's hideout—the heart of the Hyrgallian insurgency.

There were so few still free from the Empire's grasp. A smattering of Hyrgallians. The Hunter tribes. Rumors circulated among the Peers that Dioclete aimed to subjugate Caroshai within a few years. The Northlands and the Southlands would not take long; there were already colonies among the latter.

Those were all minor inconveniences, though, in the grand scheme of things. The rule of the Empire was near total, from the western Ocean to the Spine in the east. With the exception of Talynis, guarding the way through the mountains. For however long the Talynisti held out, they were the choke point. But once Talynis fell: Endra, and the rest of the world, would be in Dioclete's sight.

Endra had their own Adepts. The rest of the world had Adepts, Adepts like Sharasthi, not restrained by the arcane focus but with the full power of a conscious soulbond.

Lazarran Adepts, unmatched in these lands, would be hard-pressed against forces of awakened mages.

"That's why he took so long," Sharasthi muttered. "The Thousand-eyed Spirit. That's the one piece that always eluded me since I learned the truth. If the Emperor has foresight, why would it take so long to expand? Lazarra could have taken everything in a few decades. The First Emperor could have lived to see it."

Lylah made a distressed hum. "But he took his time. For this."

"This sorcery—what else can it do?"

Lylah's stars dimmed. "Anything—so long as the practitioner can pay the price."

"Lovely."

"Dioclete has almost certainly realized what the recovery of the aberrant Beast Relics means. He anticipates that crushing the Hyrgallian insurgency will also yield what he needs for the next era of conquest."

Sharasthi's mind raced. "He'll send a Carnifex before the end—he won't trust me with something so significant and unknown. As we get closer to pinning down the rebels, a few months, perhaps. I'll need to get the praetor on my side."

"Marcus Gallius is an honest man. I cannot fathom the Order's designs upon him."

"The Order needs someone respectable as an alternative to Dioclete. I wasn't expecting such a short time frame though. I thought this campaign would be the beginning of bringing him in—now it must happen far sooner."

"Tread carefully, Sharasthi. You walk the edge."

"Too late to retreat now." She turned on her heel and walked away from the site of the massacre.

Captain Scanlon watched as she approached. He did not hide his unease well.

Better to start currying favor with the legionnaires before making a play for the head.

"Success, Adept?"

After one last quick survey, she said, "Indeed."

Scanlon did not ask for any particulars, instead sticking to a practical, "Shall we begin the return journey?"

Sharasthi was already walking toward the horses, but she gave a perfunctory nod. He hustled after her. It was just cold enough for their boots to crunch the snow. Soon the creeping warmth would soften the powder to a slurry.

He came level with her, which she respected. As her subordinate, he could have slunk along at her heels. Most in his position likely would have taken that option. However, he was still keeping a bit of a distance.

She purloined the question Vantelle had asked her not so long ago. "Do you bear ill will toward me, Captain Scanlon?"

"Excuse me, Adept?"

She hummed. "I did not want you to attend me, but your praetor insisted. Understandably. This area is close to the reported location of Duke Faydn's castle, and you know better than I its horrid significance."

Scanlon shrugged. "We're legionnaires. We do what is required of us."

How dutiful. She suppressed the urge to grin. "Even if that means babysitting a madwoman?"

He coughed. "Adept—"

"I am familiar with the stories, Captain. Some of them are even true." *And some of the truth is even further beyond the rumors' horizons.*

"I don't know any stories about you, Adept."

She glanced at him, noting the wary look in his eye. "Truly? I am not sure if I ought to encourage you to seek them out. But enough of that. What matters more to me is what you think of Adept Reiva."

His composure more or less remained intact, but her practiced eye marked the subtle ripple of tension through his body. He was uneasy—maybe even afraid.

Well, Sharasthi did not want to terrify him, but to build a bridge. She pressed forward. "Do you resent her?"

His silence said enough, but eventually he did give voice to his thoughts. "Yes."

Sharasthi always appreciated honesty, for all she did to peer through lies and weave them herself. Scanlon, she sensed, was not the sort of person to whom falsehood came naturally. Whether by conscious choice or simple nature, he was a man who preferred to keep things forthright.

Relieved she did not have to cut through any dissembling, she mulled over her next move. She had it by the time they mounted their horses.

"I do not blame you for it, but I would counsel you against indulging such feelings." She inclined her head toward the site. "What happened there—what brought an end to more than twenty of our comrades-in-arms—has happened before and shall happen again. It is enough to drive a soul to madness."

At least, that was how she kept from loathing herself for all those deaths in the Bildani under the hail of black-feathered arrows.

Scanlon looked at her, unspeaking yet still taut as a bowstring.

"Would you lead the way, Captain?"

He nodded and nudged his horse into motion.

That was enough for now. She had sown some seeds that, with fortune, would bear fruit by the time she required. She would have to praise him and his troops to Praetor Marcus Gallius when she gave her report. That would be a step toward inculcating some favor with Gallius as well—every commander liked to hear his subordinates reflected well upon the character of the legion. That might even get her Scanlon and Ironback Company as her regular liaison.

Lylah floated nearer to Scanlon, staring keenly at his features. "He would have an affinity for...a spirit of stone, perhaps?"

The captain suppressed a shudder and rubbed the back of his neck.

36

DOWN TO THE DARKLING ROOTS OF THE WORLD

I WAS on the way to a certain town when word came they had put an innocent man to death. Nevertheless, I went to stay there and supped with the people for a night before moving on. Scandalized, my friends asked why I did not go around the place.

Understand that every good act the wicked perform will add this charge in the Judgment: "If you knew well to do thus, why did you also sin like so?" It does not afflict my conscience to break bread with a murderer—every morsel he feeds me will add to the pile of his torment.

—Zaro's Sayings, verses one thousand and seventy through seventy-one

As THINGS WENT, Sharasthi did not even have to request the praetor make Ironback Company her ongoing liaison; Marcus Gallius made that call himself. The other change was that the company was no longer a company, but was now Ironback Strike Force. The roster would remain tight, so they could act with precision and fluidity. In Sharasthi's eyes, this all validated Gallius' reputation as a discerning leader. On their first meeting, she got the impression he was a bit shocked by her demeanor and operational style—there would always be friction there—but it spoke well of him that he could make space for Sharasthi to work as she did within his domain.

Regarding her mission on behalf of the Empire, she had reported the massacre site had lingering aetheric resonances. By now, writing a report that gave enough information to satisfy the Sanctum's (and the Emperor's) expectations of her, while also concealing as much sensitive material as she could get away with, was old hat. One of the greatest benefits of having climbed to the Circle of Peers was that status and respect tended to stick. It was difficult to earn admiration, but once it was in place, people did their best to maintain that perception. Humans always invested a piece of themselves into their judgments of others. If anyone thought Sharasthi's work was unimpressive or unfaithful, they would look the other way for a while, assuming or hoping she would turn things around. Everyone had their lower periods—that was easier to stomach than the possibility a Peer was incompetent or shirking excellence. On the other hand, there were always those willing to tear others down for their own gain at the slightest hint of vulnerability. She would only have so much leeway.

She had told the truth in her report that her priority was investigating the source of the abnormal Beast Relics, but of course she left out the lead Lylah gave her; namely, that the Hyrgallians insurrectionists had at least one practitioner of the 'other magic' in their ranks. Tracking him or her down presented a challenge, but that animated Sharasthi. Leading a hunt through the forests suited her better than taking part in pitched battles.

After all, such work was how she had made her name.

Soon she would have the Fourth Legion's Intelligence attaché disseminate word the Night-cloaked Witch had come to Hyrgallia. The ostensible purpose was demoralizing the enemy, but Sharasthi hoped it would also serve to bait the relic-maker into some sort of confrontation. She would have to stay on her toes.

All told, her mind buzzed all hours of the day. Now as evening deepened into night, she was going through her correspondence. Soon she would go out on a three-week reconnaissance mission with Ironback, so she wanted to ensure nothing urgent was left waiting. There was always *something* that needed her attention as a Peer, but one of the payoffs of being back in the field was that she could shuffle less important work to her colleagues at the Sanctum.

Reiva's last letter had come a few days ago. She reported that her Art had grown further in the novel ways Sharasthi had suggested. In particular, the ability to ignite fire magic from a distance was manifesting. Sharasthi had replied with a letter describing how the talent would only grow stronger as she practiced it and meditated on the nature of aether. With time, she would come to understand in a profound sense how aether here and aether there were all part of the same flow—the only limits on an Adept's influence were strength of will and constitution.

No doubt Talynis was testing Reiva, but she would come through the other side refined, Sharasthi was certain. With good fortune, Flavia Iscator would have opportunity to nudge Reiva toward the Order. The girl believed in the Empire, to be sure, but with care she could be brought around to believe in the Republic. The fact she had lied to protect Tolm gave Sharasthi hope that, when forced to choose, Reiva would prioritize personal loyalty.

Sharasthi grimaced. On the other hand, that same character could lead to ample complications in Talynis specifically. Well, there was nothing to do about it now. She would just have to trust that Iscator would keep a good handle on the situation. She did not know the legate well, but Zageth held her in high regard. The two of them also shared the precarious position of being members of the Order while being two of Cassia Vantelle's closest subordinates. It took a sharp mind and cool head to manage that year after year after year.

Sharasthi tossed the rest of the letters on the table. Yes, a cool head—and immense deception. The willingness to lie without hesitation every day to those beside you.

Even now, Sharasthi still had to lie.

Zaro said, 'A falsehood can walk many miles for many years, but the truth need only walk one day longer to overtake it.'

Time, it all came down to time. How long would it take to find the Hyrgallian sorcerer? How fast could Sharasthi ascertain whether Marcus Gallius was a viable prospect for the Order's aims? How long until Alyat sniffed out the truth?

So much up in the air. It left her tense. Waiting was no stranger—everything she had accomplished took many years to come to fruition. Still, she preferred to minimize reliance on outcomes beyond her control.

Spurred on by that, she drafted a missive to Jan in one of their more impenetrable codes. The message was brief and simple—she wanted him to make a plan to steal the Beast Relics.

She stressed that it was *just* a plan; there was no deadline for action. In fact, if they needed those things anytime soon it would mean a worst-case scenario. Jan was a great asset as Imperial Postmaster, and stealing from the Reliquary would likely come at the expense of his cover. But that was why having the plan ready mattered. If the need arose, the situation would be so dire that rapid execution would be of utmost importance.

For security's sake, she would wait until Jan sent a messenger hawk directly to her, then she would send the letter back with it. It was always preferable to minimize the number of hands communiqués passed through. And since Jan used his Art of Beasts to impress upon the birds the mission to seek Sharasthi herself out, whether she was in Camp Mandelus or miles away on a mission, she could—

A keening shriek pierced the air.

Sharasthi blinked, looking up as she pressed the wax seal. A second cry confirmed her initial thought.

"Well, bless the gods."

She stepped outside her quarters, looking up to the sky. By her Art, she picked out the circling form of the messenger hawk in the dark above. The beast gave another cry and swooped down.

After scratching the bird atop the head, Sharasthi retrieved the package tucked in the harness and replaced it with her letter to Jan. The hawk alighted and rose into the sky, a lost feather floating down to the snow in its wake.

Now that she took a closer look, she realized she had received two things—one that had the look of an official dispatch and another that seemed like a mundane letter.

Just as she was going back inside her quarters to read them, another hawk's cry cut through the chill air.

Sharasthi glanced up to see it winging for the camp's postal station. She pictured Jan hastily packing and sending two hawks to the Hyrgallian campaign's headquarters—one for her and one for the praetor.

She frowned. *It's nothing. Just news.*

Even so, the dispatch felt heavier in her hand.

She broke the Corps seal, unfurled the scroll. It was a motion she had performed thousands of times, but this instance seared into her memory, because then appeared the words jumping up from the parchment—

Adept Alyat has passed on

—and Sharasthi could not read them. Her eyes saw. Her mind could not comprehend how such familiar shapes had become arranged in such an impossible fashion.

His name. Death. Those things did not belong together. Reality stopped, rejecting the notion.

But the words remained there, testifying that this impossible thing had happened. People died. Her grandfather had died. Soldiers died. Enemies died.

Alyat did not die—he fixed her with wry looks, he hunched over scrolls, he slept with a frown on his face.

Her body shook. Her mouth tasted sour. She was on her hands and knees. She needed to vomit. Something unbearable had worked its way into her, and her being was desperate to expel it. Sweating, shaking, she forced herself to breathe. Her head spun.

Lylah was saying something, but it was lost under the ringing.

Sharasthi stared at the spirit. She still heard nothing but the ringing and her heartbeat.

Her mind was splitting open with a screech.

Sharasthi looked at the Ill News lying on the Belowness. She could not remember when she had dropped it. How long ago had she read it?

I lied to him.

A knife. Her hand held a knife gleaming with Division-unto-Death. In its surface, she could see a face that must have been hers.

When she turned it, she could see the mirror image of her wrist pulsing with Life. Something inside her head told her the jugular vein would be better. She would pass out before she could channel healing aether.

I killed him.

Ringing. Sound of her own muffled breathing.

Lylah screaming.

Fire. Endless immortal undying Fire in my veins. I cannot die. I am everything that is and ever was and will be and I will spurt out in blazing red across the snow and melt and mingle with it down to the darkling roots of the world.

Lylah trying to hold her, to put her spangled arms around her shoulders but a spirit is a spirit and thought is only thought and Sharasthi does not think she is mad enough to believe that illusion right now because she can see everything as it is down to the last detail.

I lied to him.

I killed him.

A knock at the door.

"Ah," she mutters, "he is here." Hauling herself to her feet, she goes to receive Death, to fall into his arms, into the frost, into Alyat's cold arms, there she will slip the bonds of Enfleshment.

Scanlon blinked when he saw her. "Adept. Are you...?"

Sharasthi heard Lylah crying out—finally heard her.

"Sharasthi! Come to yourself! Think of your aims, of your plans—will you give your enemy the victory now?"

"What are you doing here?"

The captain shifted his weight. "I thought I heard…" He did not seem sure himself.

Sharasthi looked at her bound spirit, still uttering a stream of sharp words from her mouthless form. "She can be loud sometimes."

"Excuse me?"

"Can you do something for me, Captain?"

"You do outrank me."

She handed him the knife. "Hold on to this."

After a moment's hesitation, he took it and stuck it through his belt. The Division-unto-Death faded from its edge as her intent left it.

"Give it back to me in the morning."

Scanlon waited. "Are you…unwell, Adept?"

She stood in the door's Boundary, staring past him at the torchlight haloes throughout the camp. Stars of uncaring Fortune and Destiny wheeled overhead.

"Adept?"

"Yes, Captain?"

"You have not dismissed me."

"So I haven't."

Her mind still racing, she slunk back from the Boundary, dimly aware Scanlon was still present. The captain must have closed the door at some point and was now seated on one of the rickety chairs. He did not try to talk further, or if he did, Sharasthi did not notice.

Alyat was dead. The thought hammered her again, no less horrible than its first assault.

"Information," she muttered, staring at the dropped letter like it was a coiled snake.

Lylah interposed herself. "Perhaps you should rest first, Sharasthi." Her tone was concerned, frightened. "You are… disturbed."

"I don't see your point." She walked through Lylah and reached down. Her fingers twitched at the air. She grabbed the Ill News, parchment crinkling in her grip.

Like forcing herself to look into the sun, she turned her eyes on it.

A terse yet sympathetic note of condolence floated above the cold, official text. She recognized the Sympathy in Jan's hand. In an instant she saw him receiving the heap of dispatches due for dissemination. He grabbed the first one, scrawled his missive in such haste he did not even take time to sign it, and sent it to her. He had never known the precise extent of her and Alyat's relationship, but he knew enough.

"Good kid," she said to the word *sorry*. "Will I cause your end too?"

Scanlon made a questioning sound. She ignored him.

Closing her heart off as far as she could, she read the dispatch twice over.

She already knew he had been killed. The words confirmed it. He had died of an 'aneurysm.' A Carnifex. Anyone with a measure of insight who read it would understand. A deafeningly quiet message: be faithful to the Empire, or perish.

"But how did Alyat err?" He had known about the Order, but in what capacity? Was he being recruited, or had he been hunting?

Lylah watched in silence as she paced to and fro, murmuring her thoughts.

She needed to get in touch with Zageth and Flavia Iscator—one of them was bound to know. That sort of direct communication, especially now, was risky. She would make use of Jan's position with the Post...

Reiva. Reiva had just lost her mentor. Cassia Vantelle would leverage that to pin Reiva under her thumb. And did Reiva already know Alyat had been investigating the Order? Would she risk picking up that trail, or would the threats of a Carnifex and her already precarious position be enough to ward her off?

On and on spun Sharasthi's thoughts. Her spiritual perception eased bit by bit as she bound her animal humanity, making it acquiesce to the levers and gears of cold, callous reason. It was the gift of reason that ennobled the human above all other creatures; why then did the exercise of reason enslave the faculties which sentiment pleaded were most human? Was it human to be enslaved? Was there such a thing as freedom in this world?

Her feet ached. Her eyes burned. She was prowling to and fro like a caged beast. How long had she been in motion?

Scanlon's eyes were closed, his chin on his chest.

Her mouth was dry. She was talking. She had been talking to Lylah, but Lylah had not spoken back in…how many hours had it been?

The dull gray light of a breaking Hyrgallian dawn filtered through the shut window.

Someone knocked. "Adept," called a man. "Praetor Gallius requests your attention at once."

Scanlon was awake, standing up as he rubbed his face. He looked at Sharasthi expectantly.

"Not now," she answered the runner.

She could feel the incredulity through the door. "Pardon me, Adept?"

Scanlon looked agog, but she was not about to budge. "I'm staying here for now. If the praetor wants to speak, he can find me here."

She had no time. She was dead-tired, but if she lay down, she knew she would not fall asleep until the next nightfall at least.

Scanlon eyed her like she was a starved panther. He was not, she noted, returning her knife.

"I don't know," he eventually said, "where to begin with my questions. So unless there's something you would prefer I know before you stand before the praetor…"

In truth, there was not much she could say that would be of benefit in speaking to Gallius. Or at least, nothing she could explain in what little time she had. If she had started last night…but it was too late for that.

What she did manage to say was: "I received a casualty notice last night."

Scanlon made a gruff sound in his throat. "My condolences."

Another knock sounded, this one louder than the first and markedly indignant.

"Adept, this is your praetor."

Scanlon glanced at Sharasthi, then stood and went to open the door.

"Have you been fraternizing with the Adept, Captain?"

Yes, it would look like that, wouldn't it? It did not particularly matter to Sharasthi what Gallius believed in that regard. All that mattered was whether she could win him to her purpose.

When the praetor stepped inside, Sharasthi already knew what she was going to do.

"I'll tell them."

Lylah looked wary.

"Sharasthi, if this—"

"It's not some disguised attempt at self-annihilation, Lylah. We've no more time for preparatory schemes anymore. The Order must make its play."

Gallius looked about the scene of strewn papers and equipment with a cold eye. Then he appraised Sharasthi.

She knew she did not cut an impressive figure. No doubt she looked haggard from her restless night of grief and strain. Her hair had worked into wild tangles through the hours of finger-raking and head shaking. Her eyes stung. The ache in her back and neck told her she was hunched. And her arms, in spite of herself, would not go down to rest at her side, but rather stayed fastened together across her body, like gates guarding against the invasion of yet more woes from without while also sealing any further expression of bereavement from within.

"This is how you appear before your praetor, Adept?"

"You appear before me, technically."

Lylah gave Sharasthi an incisive look. "You are frightened."

The praetor set his jaw. "At least Scanlon had the dignity to dress himself properly."

"Dignity or shame, but let's not get into the weeds of that."

The nonsense coming out of her mouth was an attempt to keep herself from turning to what she needed to say. Maybe if she just spun along with the praetor's misperception, she would have a way out of this confrontation.

She knew now was the time, but this was the kind of step from which she could not retreat.

She muttered, "Tell me to do it, Lylah."

Gallius asked something, to which she retorted, "I am not speaking to you."

Lylah's head tilted back, as though she were looking through the roof into the endless sky beyond, seeking some inscrutable message.

"My condolences, given the loss of your colleague, Adept."

Sharasthi's fingers dug into her arm. She forced them to ease, though the tension inside her remained. "Accepted." Maintaining a standard vocal register in dire circumstances was a foundational piece of training. That did not make her any less monstrous in her own eyes for managing it.

Condolences. One of the most common words in their way of life. Scanlon had said it just minutes ago. Coming from the praetor though... there was something grimmer about that. Alyat's death was a piece of news circulating. All across the Empire people would read it, discuss it.

Gallius had wanted to speak to her when he heard of it because he, like so many others, was keen enough to discern what was unwritten. That he knew Alyat had been murdered was obvious. No man came to stand among the Emperor's precious chosen without the good sense to discern conspiracy.

What did he want from Sharasthi now? Was it mere curiosity? Was it self-preservation?

Scanlon must have read the hesitance in the air, because he cleared his throat. "Praetor, should I take my leave?"

Sharasthi intercepted the question. "You stay. I'm working something out, but once I do, you're both going to know."

Gallius looked bemused and glanced at the door. "I know you're used to being the sharpest mind in the room, but even a simpleton such as myself can tell that Alyat's death is suspicious."

Had any joy remained in her, she might have chuckled. If only he knew how carefully the Order had observed and vetted him. If she had not known better, she would have thought his modesty was false, but his spirit was candid through and through.

"If you were a simpleton, Praetor, I would have lied and sent you off."

"You're hiding something."

"I have been, and now I will bring it into the light. Or perhaps I am bringing you into the dark with me."

Lylah's stars pulsed in manic symphony. "So you've made your choice."

Under her breath, she said, "Once again, I found myself faced with the sense that the greatest choices are hardly choices at all. Or at least, if I wanted something else, I needed to decide that long ago."

"I cannot say if what you do is wise, Sharasthi, but every day I see lines of sorrow carved deeper into your soul. It pains me."

"You've always been a sentimental spirit, haven't you?"

Lylah turned her head aside. "Do as you intend—I have nothing more to say."

Sharasthi straightened. The night-daughter's words loosed a final chain, and with it fell away whatever trepidation had lingered.

In the corner of the room lay her storage trunk. The men's eyes followed her as she went to it. The contents were simple—some clothing, equipment. The bronze mirror Alyat had given her the night of her commissioning. She had stopped leaving it in plain sight a long time ago, but never dreamed of discarding it. Now the touch of cold metal accused her as she set it aside.

Her hands closed around a bundle at the bottom. An iron lockbox wrapped in a spare cloak.

She unwrapped it, cradled it in her arms. It seemed heavier than its proper weight. From a pocket inside her clothes, she withdrew the key.

The *click* of the lock slashed loose some impossible knot in her nerves, a knot decades old.

On top, a handful of Alyat's most precious letters. Words written in their own code, devised piecemeal on stolen nights between frantic embraces. Words no other eyes would ever see, words cherished in her heart deeper than anything else in the world—anything else in the world, save one thing.

In the end, every soul has one loyalty that supersedes all others.

Her fingers stung as she lifted the letters, revealing the bronze seal.

As a child, her grandfather had shown her a seal just like this. That night was the start of it all—the beginning before the beginning of her life as it had come to be. With that seal, her grandfather had initiated her into a grand secret, a pact spanning centuries and leagues. So many years later, she had received another from Zageth, just like the one her grandfather had shown her. Across so much time and so much distance, the same vow bound her, the same vision.

Ordo Draconis Laevisomnis.

Now she stood in her grandfather's place. She thought of his body burning in the Eternal Flame. Burning. Burning.

She offered the seal to Praetor Marcus Gallius. He scrutinized the design. His eyes widened, color draining from his face.

"What do you know," Sharasthi said, "of the Order of the Sleeping Dragon?"

EPILOGUE

I DO NOT DECLARE FAMINE a curse or prosperity a blessing. What know I, whether the woes of today work the joys of tomorrow, or still further whether those delights may bring yet more weeping? Only on the Last Day can such things be reckoned.

—Zaro's Sayings, verses four hundred and nine through eleven

PRAETOR MARCUS GALLIUS mused on war. He had done so almost every day of his life, but today those musings were different. Today his thoughts were on civil war.

There would be such a war, of that he was convinced. The question was on which side he would find himself. Not so long ago, it would not have been a choice—he would have served his Emperor however demanded.

Marcus' faith in Lazarra was not blind. To build and maintain this thing called Empire, many dark things were necessary—in the past, present...in the future, to be sure. He knew that, and he had swallowed his displeasure, because he had truly believed in what his forebears had handed down to him.

The Gallius family had only been named as such in living memory, an honor Dioclete bestowed for Marcus' grand achievement of conquering Gallia for the Empire—a deed that soon brought in Hyrgallia as well. For so many generations, the cousin peoples of these lands had stood proud, their old warrior blood fierce enough to rebuff the legions. The blood of the mountains, they called it, the blood that flowed down in two rivers—the south to Gallia, the north to Hyrgallia.

Then, fifteen years ago, Marcus had broken the Gallians. Not long after, the Hyrgallian king had knelt, wishing to spare his land such bloodshed as their southern kin suffered. One Duke Faydn had been aghast and, after a few years of silent preparation, launched his insurgency with a curse upon his king's 'shameful cowardice, unknown to the blood of the mountains.' Many of the people—noble and common alike—stood behind Faydn, and that was the war Marcus Gallius waged now, his life ever-tied to these lands by decree of the Emperor.

But Marcus' family was old, even if the name was young. Before, they had been the Sacchi. It was a long-standing tradition that they were of Founding stock. Not one of the glorious Founders—not warriors or priests or princes. Shepherds and stonemasons. The Sacchi name had not been one of renown, but they were Lazarran through and through. Generation by generation, they had built the city and then the Republic. They had raised the walls and mixed the mortar. They had tilled the fields and tended the flocks. Through plague and fire and mayhem, the Sacchi endured, faithful and proud. When the Republic fell and the Empire rose, they answered the First Emperor's call and became soldiers. Engineer auxiliaries at first, then legionnaires. Marcus' great-grandfather Caius, a mere sergeant, had won the fabled *corona muralis* for being the first man over the wall in the taking of the Aspagnian capital Ispalis. As a child, Marcus had polished the gilt parapets and ramparts of his family's second-most treasured heirloom, Caius Sacchi's Crown of the Wall.

Second-most treasured. Most documents from the time of the Republic were lost during the Dark Days, but Marcus' family had preserved one thing through all the havoc: a certificate of citizenship. The name of that bygone Sacchi patriarch had long since faded, but the seal of the consul's authority—that of *the Last Consul*, his name Ciell Aenan so rarely remembered in these days—still clung there.

Marcus believed in Lazarra. He believed in it because Lazarra, in many ways, was the work of his family. His family *was* Lazarra. What dark things she did, he saw as done for the survival and flourishing of his own blood. Distasteful, but justified in such a grim and cruel world as this.

But Adept Alyat had been an honorable man. The sort of man Marcus thought typified what was righteous about Lazarra, even though a Northlander by birth. What could have justified the clandestine murder of someone like *him*? A murder no doubt meant as a warning to others.

And then Adept Sharasthi had shown him that seal.

Ordo Draconis Laevisomnis.

He had heard of the Order, of course. Long had they been a thorn in the sides of Emperors and praetors. One of Marcus' own uncles had taken part in a military action that apprehended and executed over two dozen conspirators of the Sleeping Dragon.

Marcus believed in Lazarra. So, it seemed, did the Order. On its own, that was nothing surprising, but what had surprised him was the name on that seal. Ciell Aenan. The Last Consul of Lazarra.

Adept Sharasthi had told him how her grandfather came to know of the Order, how he had inducted her into that knowledge. How Alyat was murdered because someone had been trying to bring him into the Order, and Alyat, honest man that he was, had turned over some stone and shined a light into some serpent's hole—and caught the loathsome eye of a Carnifex.

Sharasthi was sure she would soon receive a similar visit. Marcus too, she warned, would face such an end, depending on what choice he was to make. Not what he chose—what choice he *was to make.* If the Emperor exercised his Art of Foreknowledge, he would not even have to wait for Marcus to make a move. He would simply know whether or not Marcus would remain loyal to him.

And given what Sharasthi had discovered here in Hyrgallia regarding the site of the Beast Relic massacre, she suspected the Emperor would peer into that future any day now, if he had not already.

To call it much to consider would be the understatement of the era. And the chaos unfurling in the east only added to it.

In Talynis, the Ninth Legion had retreated from the capital of Dav-maiir. Praetor Cassia Vantelle was missing. Flavia Iscator had reassumed command of the legion, but she had taken them into the desert. Their current location was unknown, and there were rumblings among the praetors that she was going rogue.

Alyat's notorious apprentice Reiva—who just a few months ago had been under Marcus' command here in Hyrgallia—was also missing. There were reports she had turned traitor and sided with her ancestral land of Talynis. Legion Intelligence was still hesitant as to the veracity of that, or whether it was just a confused rumor born of reports the Talynisti had Adepts of their own, the so-called *Desert Sages.*

What a mess. He was not built for such games of intrigue. He had worked in the day, leaving it to others to do what work was needed in the night. Others like Adept Sharasthi.

And still, there was one more damned thing.

A letter on his desk, delivered through a subtle channel just yesterday. What timing, to come the day before Sharasthi's deadline.

The letter had come from Duke Faydn. It was the first direct communication Marcus had received from the man in months, and it was but a few words:

Among the giants' bones, let us and our witches meet.

Surely Sharasthi was implicated, and he hazarded a guess that Faydn's 'witch' had something to do with some aberrant Beast Relics.

Just then, Marcus' optio, Viro, stepped in to let him know the woman herself had arrived. Marcus said she could enter.

She had given him time to make his decision. That was a very risky move on her part, he appreciated. She desperately wanted him on her side, but that courtesy could only go so far. If he did not decide today, then she would take her leave.

Even as she stepped in, he could not believe he was considering this. Until he said the words, he would not believe his own choice.

In a sense, he had already made his choice. That he did not arrest Sharasthi as soon as she showed him that bronze seal, that was tantamount to throwing in his lot with her. To cover it up now would be a bloody affair. And still, Marcus was not one for that sort of skullduggery.

Adept Sharasthi no longer looked like a woman bereaved. Her eyes were clear, her face set, her attire in order. "Praetor."

Marcus held the letter out. "What do you think of this?"

She read it, then tilted her head to the side and murmured something, then seemed to listen.

He wondered if Faydn's witch did this sort of thing too.

"We should accept the meeting. That is what I would counsel."

"Assuming I choose to join in your conspiracy."

She inclined her head. "If you'll indulge me a moment, Praetor, I doubt you have any more choosing to make. I'm not sure any of us make choices, really. I think, like falling snow and beating hearts, we are things that happen as the outworking of some inscrutable and invisible...what you might call a Will."

"So you think that Will has already chosen what part I am to play. And you think it is in your favor."

"Something like that."

"And would it follow, then, that all which opposes us also does so as an outworking of that Will? The Emperor who will declare us traitors. Our comrades-turned-enemies who will kill us and whom we will kill. The Carnifex by whose hand Adept Alyat was murdered. All that is of the same Will, in your philosophy?"

Sharasthi stood there. Her eyes tightened, but her voice was even. "All is Fire"—she breathed—"and the Fire burns."

Marcus' finger tapped a steady beat on Faydn's missive. "Perhaps you are right. Perhaps not. In truth, it matters not to me. What I care for is Lazarra. And somehow, even if it be by some contagious madness that leaped from your mind to mine, I have come to think that the will *of Lazarra*, at least, is with your cause."

The praetor leaned back in his chair, letting out a long sigh. "Yes, Adept Sharasthi, you have dragged me into the dark with you. As for me, I only pray that what we do here will be judged well by those who remain in the light. So there is but one question: shall we declare war first, or wait for the Emperor?"

THE END

ACKNOWLEDGMENTS

This novel was the most challenging and fun to write yet, and it would have been a poorer work if not for some people who deserve more recompense than a few words in the back of the book—nevertheless:

My parents and brother are my foremost believers and far more certain of my writing's merit than I am. Not all writers are so fortunate to have so supportive a family. My dad, once again, was first to finish reading the draft, and told me (as expected) that it was too short. I don't think I'll ever write enough to satisfy him, but from the author's side of the equation that's a good thing. My mom pushed me to develop a deeper understanding of Sharasthi's character, and her feedback on Part Three in particular was essential in the revision. My brother Noah still thinks it's "pretty cool" that I'm an author, which is pretty great.

As always, immense appreciation for Cade and Daniel who understand the deeper reality and with whom I can discuss anything.

Cade, after so many dinners and calls, sees inside my brain and keenly maps all the threads woven through my work, even some I am not aware of. I also did him a disservice in the Acknowledgments for *The Empire's Lion* when I forgot to thank him for graciously allowing me to steal his idea of two characters meeting by beating each other up in a fight club.

Daniel is an inexhaustible source of encouragement at all hours, and he always keeps me from taking things (myself included) too seriously. C.S. Lewis said friendship begins with "What! You too? I thought I was the only one," and somehow we manage to keep discovering the truth of that.

Graham deserves special appreciation for applying his horror expertise and helping me raise the cult ritual scene to the next level. He pushed me to think far more thoroughly about what That One is and what it wants out there in the Dark.

Matt, once again, gave the most extensive feedback, generous with his time and ideas. Even when we do not see eye-to-eye on things, Matt's thoughtful analysis of themes and character pushed me to deeper understanding of not just the story I was trying to tell in this book, but future stories I intend to tell as well.

Michael McClellan continues to be a wonderful friend and mentor in the domains of writing, life, and more. I'm perennially grateful for the opportunity to talk shop, discuss ideas, and swap reading recommendations with another man in the arena.

Meadow Holt, fellow author and friend, filled a longstanding lack in *The Imperial Adept* series by illustrating the wonderful map which adorns this volume.

My gratitude goes out to my beta readers—my family, Cade, Daniel, Graham, Matt, Sarah H. Soren, Jeremy & Sarah S.—and anyone else I may be forgetting whose support and input helped make this book what it is.

Hail Ovid, ancient expert of elegy and epic! May your memory receive in good humor Sharasthi's evaluation of your amorous advisings.

Lastly, my thanks to you, the reader, for giving your time and attention to this book. We only get so many hours in this life, and I receive it as a high honor that you would spend some of yours with my stories.

ABOUT THE AUTHOR

Nathan Tudor has researched ancient religion at Oxford, traveled the seven continents, and mastered the art of speaking in the third person. His debut novel *The Empire's Lion* tells an epic story filled with action, identity, and the struggle to do what is right in an upside-down world.

When he's not writing or reading, Nathan can be found debating matters of no particular consequence with his friends, falling down research rabbit holes, and trying to craft the perfect vodka martini.

Allegations that he hired an alchemist to give him the tread of a cat and the ears of a fox are categorically false.

ALSO BY NATHAN TUDOR

The Imperial Adept

Adept Initiate

The Empire's Lion

The most-up-to-date version of this bibliography can be found at nathantudor.com